T0146627

Also by C. William Giles:
......Of Tortured Faustian Slumbers
The Darkness of Strangers

C. WILLIAM GILES

BLACK

SIX Tales of Darkness and Nightmare

authorHOUSE®

AuthorHouse™ UK
1663 Liberty Drive
Bloomington, IN 47403 USA
www.authorhouse.co.uk
Phone: 0800.197.4150

Published by AuthorHouse 11/05/2018

ISBN: 978-1-5462-9905-9 (sc)
ISBN: 978-1-5462-9906-6 (hc)
ISBN: 978-1-5462-9904-2 (e)

Print information available on the last page.

This book is printed on acid-free paper.

To Chell
For more love & support than I could ever have hoped for.

Special Thanks:
Chop, Pop & Max (for everything)
Debby Janikiewicz (for her time)

Contacts:
cwgimmortal@gmail.com
Facebook: C William Giles
Twitter: @CWilliamGiles

About The Author

Author of two previous novels, this is his first collection of short stories. Please, enter his dark world and leave a little of the happiness you bring. But don't let the door hit you on the ass on the way out.

C. William Giles lives with his girlfriend in Liverpool, England

P.S. Hope this is what you had in mind, Dad.

contents

BLUE

Monday, 5th January 2015

Right, I suppose I should start at the beginning. My name is Jacob Blaine. I'm 38 years old and this is the first time I've ever even considered writing anything close to a diary or journal, or whatever the fuck this is!

I'm sitting alone at home as I write this on my laptop. I'm a single male; my girlfriend of four years broke up with me about three months ago, which I was devastated about, I must admit, but, that's life I suppose.

As I said, I've never done anything like this before. To me, diaries are written by teenage girls and journals by melancholy poets or people trying to 'find themselves' by getting in touch with their inner emotions on a journey of discovery and analysis. Seriously? Who does that shit? I always thought, fuck that! Yet here I am, writing my own piece; I never would have believed it and maybe this will all end up being deleted, so, whatever I write may never be seen!

You're no doubt thinking why am I writing at all?

Well, to be honest, I've recently had an overwhelming urge, or need, to start documenting things. Whether this becomes something of a chore and I get bored of it (I'm prone to do that), or, if it becomes something that I can actually look back on and smile at the absurdity, we will see. I damn well hope it's the latter. It might be something that becomes useful and means that I can rationalise events that have taken place. You never know, future generations might use it as something to remember me by! Ha, that's a fucking laugh!!!

In all seriousness, I think that my mind is slipping. Yes, it was traumatic losing Caroline last October, but I've lost or left girlfriends before and sometimes it's been awful; certainly this loss was greater than any other, but that doesn't explain how I am coping (or not) and the state of my mental stability now.

3

Anyway, I'm pretty sure I'll get to all that in future entries, so if you're reading this and I start to get pathetic over her, feel free to skip a page or two. Either way, I'm sitting here, as I said, with my laptop. This is all very new to me so please bear with me; I will try to explain and document everything that I can.

I've been having strange dreams recently. Yes, I know that lots of people have strange or unexplained dreams, so nothing too unusual about that. But I think of myself as a very level-headed and rational kind of guy and, if I'm honest, I'm starting to get scared. I'm scaring myself.

I'm feeling drawn to hurt somebody - not anyone in particular - just the act itself and I don't know why. I don't feel myself at all. But that's because......I think there's somebody else in my head with me...

This is getting me nowhere, so I think that the best thing to do would probably start at the beginning.

I work in IT management. Yes, it's a boring fucking job, but there's a possibility that you may be in the same job or a similar field; if so, I apologise, but let's be honest, it truly is a dull job, isn't it? Anyway, my day was always a tedious nine-to-five existence but I won't bore you with details. If you know the job, you'll understand and if you don't, I'll avoid putting you to sleep. At first, I would want to go out after work and socialise with my colleagues, have a drink and unwind, but that became such a chore trying to persuade them to come out even for just a quiet drink. The occasional times I did get a couple of them to come with me, they turned out to be incredibly dull people who just talked about work or their kids that I found myself making excuses to leave early even though it had been my idea to go out! Eventually I stopped trying and gave up, even if somebody else brought up the idea.

Anyway, about a month ago, I left work and made my way home. It was early December and the Christmas lights were all over the city; it wasn't actually snowing but there was an icy drizzle falling, making the streets slick, wet and slippery and it was really fuckin' cold. My office was in the heart of the city and though I have a car, I didn't use it to go to work as it was a nightmare to park and it would cost a small fortune. So, like a lot of other people, a small army it seemed, I used either trains or buses to get into town and then walked the short distance to my work. I'd gotten used to it over the past nine years or so of working there and I enjoyed reading on the train - when I could get a seat that is.

I was walking to the train station, freezing cold, slippery under foot, tired and irritable and I just wanted to get home. It was 5:30 or so and the streets were dark and wintery but crammed with people doing their Christmas shopping, which, believe me, didn't improve my mood getting pushed and bumped by carrier bag laden citizens, or idiots wielding umbrellas on the crowded pavements.

It was only six or seven weeks since Caroline had dumped me and that made me feel very low and bitter, and seeing all that Christmas tat and plastic cheeriness only served to sour me on the whole idea of joy to all men. I'd actually gotten her a beautiful antique ring for Christmas, kind of an engagement ring, but I'd been holding off on asking her officially. I suppose you could say that I was playing it by ear for the time being. I had been rather pleased with myself because I hadn't left it until the last minute to think about Christmas presents this year; I was feeling quite positive for the first time in years. Then, in the middle of October, the end! She had met somebody else apparently - I was no longer what she wanted. She was moving on with her life and career and I no longer figured in her plans. Charming.

Sorry. I don't want to talk about that for now; it's still too raw, so I'll get back to my tale.

I eventually reached the station; I was miserable but irritated too, partly by my new found loneliness, but also by the people surrounding me. As I said, I was cold and wet and achingly tired, and my eyes were stinging due to the fact that I'd spent the entire day staring at a computer screen. I just wanted to get home. I waited in line politely, unlike some, and presented my return ticket to the dull eyed rail staff at the gate who said nothing as I passed by, while still being prodded by the excessive bags of shopping held by someone behind me. I didn't look round. I just sighed and focused on getting home, much like the rest of the cattle being herded down to the platform.

We all stood on the platform waiting patiently, or not so, in some cases. There were people with large amounts of the aforementioned shopping; some parents with screaming kids; business people in suits; teenagers with headphones, ignoring everyone else; a collage of differing people who all wanted the same thing - a train. Then the announcement came that the train, due in five minutes, would be delayed by a further five. My heart sank and a collective groan rose up from the assembled mass. Mutterings, sighs and swearing could all be heard - I swore under my breath myself, being too tired to even speak the words out loud.

I turned to my left for no apparent reason, other than there was nothing to take my interest directly in front of me, just the backs of people's heads. As I turned, I saw a man, an office worker by the look of him, in a suit and overcoat, leather gloves, holding a take away cup of coffee in his right hand. He looked just like me, other than he seemed in his early fifties and had the coffee; I could've done with a hot coffee just at that moment. Momentarily, it struck me that I didn't want to still be doing the same job when I'm that age. It was bad enough approaching my first completed decade!

The guy was about twenty feet away. A natural pathway had developed between the commuters, which seems to be the natural way of things in such circumstances. People line up, almost like zombies, in rows on platforms (or so it seems to me). As he approached, his left hand reached inside his jacket pocket and he produced a phone, answering it with a grunt. All the while he continued to approach, I stepped back half a step - the crowd ensured that that was all that was possible. Etiquette seemed to dictate that as he approached, I look the other way; it would be creepy if I was looking at him as he walked up to and past me. I turned and looked to the right instead, but was almost knocked down as he barged straight into me, spilling his latte, or whatever the fuck it was, all over me!

I stood in surprise and disbelief. The people behind me, whom I had, in turn, stumbled into, pushed me forward and off them. I wasn't hurt in any way, but I was certainly annoyed and bemused as to just what a fucking idiot this guy was. I looked up and frowned at him, my hands out in a gesture of "What the fuck mate?" but he kept moving down the platform. I looked down at myself and saw the coffee spilled all down my overcoat and dripping onto my shoe. I couldn't believe it, and then, to make matters worse, I heard him on his phone say to whomever that he'd just been bumped by "some prick" that spilled his coffee! I'm sure it wasn't my imagination but I'm positive that he raised his voice so that I could hear him over the platform chatter. He moved off into the distance and crowd, no doubt pleased with himself, while I stood there incredulous.

It was at that point that I heard 'it' for the first time. A voice in my head spoke.

"And you're just going to let him walk away?" it said. "He's laughing at you."

Initially, I turned to my left and right, but the commuters either side had already forgotten about the incident with the suit and were now awaiting the imminent arrival of the train. I turned around in my cramped space to see who was behind me, waiting to have somebody to complain to. I wanted somebody, anybody, who would agree that the other guy was at fault and should have apologised. Those behind me merely looked back with blank expressions; I knew then that it wasn't any of those people who had spoken, and definitely not with the kind of acidic voice that I had heard.

Now I know that people say things about their 'inner voice' or such things, when really it's just that they think of what they should have said or done, their mind giving them alternatives, hindsight, or maybe sometimes it's just their conscience creeping out. But this seemed to me to be an actual voice; not my own voice either, but one with its own personality and mind. It even had an accent for fuck's sake, but I couldn't place it.

Thankfully, a welcome distraction came in the form of the train's arrival – finally! The noise of the train was quickly greeted with the activity of the rabble, who now readied themselves to board, pushing and shoving each other to get to the front of the doors, which opened, allowing a large throng of people to disembark. Arguments started as eager passengers tried to board before others got off, but I was distracted as my mind searched for the 'other' and my eyes still looked for the suit with the coffee.

Suddenly, I was brought back to the situation at hand as I was pushed aside by a woman with yet more shopping. My mood had turned sour and I pushed her back in retaliation. In turn, she glared at me as if I was the initial offender, but I wasn't having any of it. It struck me as I looked around that we weren't all going to get on this train; it was close to capacity as it was and a lot more people were getting on than off and I thought 'Fuck this' and pushed myself to the front. I didn't care who was in my way, I was getting on regardless.

There weren't any seats left (big surprise) but I found space to stand as the doors closed and some people were left behind to wait for the next one. Suckers. I found myself smirking at them, which was not like me at all really - I would normally have been more sympathetic, but not on that day. The train set off and I looked down, as most people do on trains it seems, with the unspoken rule that no eye contact shall be made. Then I saw again my stained coat and shoe, which pissed me off all over again and I looked up and down the carriage, where I noticed at the far end, the suit with the coffee still on his phone.

"There he is, the fucker. Why don't you do something?" came the voice again.

Again, I looked around even less certain that someone was speaking to me this time. Besides, the noise of the train rolling along blocked out any conversations people were struggling to have. No. This time I knew for sure that the voice came from inside my head and I didn't know what to do. I ignored the voice, though somehow I could almost sense displeasure; 'it' was disappointed in me. It was more than that, though; it seemed annoyed or angry! It was almost like a silent atmosphere between a couple after an argument. With that uncomfortable silence within, I travelled home.

Eventually, the train pulled in to my station and I struggled and pushed my way to the doors, apologising for brushing past, but getting no apology in return from those standing in my way. The doors opened and I stepped down and naturally looked up the platform as I walked to the steps to exit the station. Only a couple of other people had gotten off at my stop and they were walking in front of me, when I heard a voice I knew - though this time it was definitely not in my head. It was the suit still talking on his phone, though now quite loudly over the noise from the departing train.

As the train eventually left, everything suddenly seemed very quiet and serene. Mine is a small station in the suburbs, very peaceful most of the time, but not now. The tranquillity was rudely punctuated by the loud mouth on the phone, still talking loudly, and seemingly loving the sound of his own voice. He walked past me as he had been further along the carriage, obviously still in a hurry, because he moved at speed though he was no longer carrying his coffee. No doubt he just left it on the train for somebody else to clean up.

"Aren't you going to at least have a word with him?" came the voice in my head again.

This time I replied, though under my breath and not quite sure how or why I was replying to myself.

"What am I supposed to say?"

"Well, how about, 'Hey motherfucker - what the fuck was that back there?' Maybe you could start with that," was 'its' response.

"I wish I could, but..." I mumbled.

"But what? You're a pussy," 'it' snapped.

I didn't know what to say. It was bizarre enough that I was literally talking to myself (or was I?). As I walked through the open doors of the station, I felt dog-tired and cold. The crisp and clear evening air numbed my nose, causing me to sniff as my breath plumed out into the night. I tried to ignore the voice as I left the station behind. The suit was now off his phone and hailing a passing cab; I wondered where that prick lived. I'd never seen him in this area or at that station before. I wondered, too, if he had just moved into the district. I hoped not. I didn't like the idea of bumping into him again. At that point, it seemed my inner voice knew what I was thinking and despaired of me.

"Are you fucking serious?" It said in a voice even colder than the night. "You couldn't even confront him! If it was up to me..."

"What?" I asked of it.

"Let's just say, for now, there would be consequences."

It said nothing more. That day was my first encounter with the 'other' – oh, how I wish it had been my first and last, but at least now you have some idea of my tale - and there is much more to come! You will, I hope, also understand why I had to start getting it all down here. I don't know about my other entries in future, but I will explain about other things that have already happened as much as I can and hopefully, future entries will decline as my situation improves. I can only live in hope.

Thursday, 8th January 2015

It's been a few days since my last entry. Monday I think. Well, when I went to bed that night, 'it' came to me as I slept. It scared the shit out of me to be honest; it was still just a voice in my head and I couldn't see anything but it felt...........malevolent - that's the only way I can really describe it. It's the best way I can even attempt to sum it up at the moment.

It felt like a dream, which quickly turned into a nightmare, yet I couldn't relate any scene to you. I just felt as though there was a thick piece of black velvet between me and 'it' and there was this voice - my God what a voice. It was hideous. Icy, black and dripping with pain and torment: vile yet seductive, with so much rage and darkness.

By the way, I've decided from now on to refer to 'it' by a name, so I'm just going to call it 'Blue'. You may wonder why Blue but there is no real reason, other than I was having blueberries at breakfast today and thought it would be a simple name to use. Also, I consider it a male. It sounds male and I don't think any female could have such a voice as this - I would hope not anyway! Giving it a name and identity of sorts makes it more tangible to me. Whether it is something real or I am actually going insane, I couldn't say at this point, but giving it a name comforts me a little, convincing me that my sanity isn't in jeopardy.........yet. Plus, I've seen in horror movies that 'others' tend to be given names by kids: Captain Howdy, Mr Boogie and so on. So, for the purposes of this journal, Blue is my 'other'.

Anyway, as I was saying, Blue came to me in my sleep the other night. He said that he knew what I'd been doing, writing this journal, explaining my first experience of him. He said I must not continue, so I asked why, and he said that he liked to be in the shadows, away from the light. He didn't say too much but I get the feeling that he likes his anonymity. I don't really expect anyone to be reading this anyway so I don't know why he seemed so agitated but he was. When I questioned him he got very angry.

You are probably wondering why I write as though he is a friend of mine. Well, I definitely wouldn't say that, but over the last few weeks I've learned to live with him, like a host to a parasite you might say. Don't get me wrong, I don't want him here inside me, but I don't have a lot of choice in the matter. He disgusts me; I have barely scratched the surface of my experiences and as I mentioned at the beginning, I'm scared to death of him or what he could do. More to the point, I'm scared of what he could make ME do!

In the last few weeks, there have been images in my head, images that he has put there. I know that for a fact because he told me so and sometimes I've woken from horrific nightmares in a cold sweat and actual tears, whilst hearing his sick laughter at my distress, then he'll ask me if I enjoyed it. At other times, he will make conversation with me, just banal chat about my day, but at the same time he will comment on something that's happened at work, for instance, giving his opinion as to how he saw it because he was actually there.

I've come back onto here because, despite Blue's 'annoyance' shall we say, I wanted to put down another specific event that happened. It was just before Christmas - the 19th I think. Anyway, it was the Friday before Christmas and our office was closing for the holidays. I decided to go out after work for a drink by myself; I hadn't been out for a while and felt like I needed to unwind a little. Other people were going out, too, but I declined and went my own way. I knew where they were going but I wanted a quiet drink alone. Yeah, I know that doesn't sound very sociable but it's just what I felt I needed at the time.

Anyway, I went out to a little pub I know down a side street and thankfully it was pretty empty. I bought a drink and found a quiet spot towards the back of the room. I sat by the window and watched the snow fall, feeling calm and relaxed for the first time in quite a while. As it was only a side street pub, there was little in the way of footfall or traffic, allowing the snow to lay largely undisturbed on the ground. A surprisingly tranquil feeling passed over me in that moment. Blue was still there though - I could sense him, if not actually feel him. He was thankfully quiet.

Unfortunately for me, my peaceful evening was shattered by a group of office workers who had no doubt all just finished work for the holidays too, judging by the loud and raucous entrance they had made. Five men and four women came barrelling in, singing awful Christmas songs and stumbling into each other. It seemed that their party had started at the office a lot earlier because I could see that a couple of them were already smashed out of their heads. Surprisingly, they managed to get served with drinks, so no doubt the bar would increase its takings for the evening considerably.

It felt to me as though Blue had just woken up from a nap, or, more likely, he had been disturbed and woken by the noise. That's the only way I can describe the sensation of him suddenly coming into my mind. But awaken he did. His anger seemed to build and his nasty voice boomed around my head like a cacophony of gongs. My heart sank and my shoulders and head must've visibly drooped at his 'arrival'. He began to scream obscenities at the revellers (all 'in my mind' of course) but it was difficult to suppress the words, such was his building influence upon me.

I could feel words forming in my throat, but I had to make sure they stayed there; the last thing I wanted was to get into a fight - especially where I would be heavily outnumbered. His vitriol was building and I could feel my resistance to him waning, so I quickly finished my drink and headed for the door. I had no choice but to brush past the group, trying to ease past as best I could, but one of the men stepped back into me, his drink spilling on the floor. I suddenly had a flashback to the train station incident and the suit with the coffee. Thankfully, though, the man in question quickly turned around and apologised for getting in my way. I was expecting a barrage of venom from Blue but all seemed averted.

I smiled and said it was alright and continued to the door. My guard was down now, however, and just as I stepped out into the night, an awful violent scream came out of me. It was Blue trying to vocalize his anger; even though it had been a trivial matter and it was over, his rage seemed to boil over. Luckily, the door closed behind me and I don't think the other patrons heard me (him). If they had, they would probably have thought I was throwing up, which gives you an idea of the sort of noise 'we' made.

Outside, I didn't want to talk to him, but I could feel him gnawing away at my mind. He was snarling and spitting but I refused to be drawn into his aggression. I was pleased with myself because it seemed to do the trick; he settled back, as if skulking back into the shadows of the deeper recesses of my subconscious.

I smiled to myself for the first time in a while as I wondered whether, just maybe, I'd learned to tame the beast. I continued down the side street, slipping slightly in the snow even though I tried to tread carefully. I watched the winter continuing to fall gently against the blackness of the night sky. It was beautiful. The hustle and bustle of the streets, with its traffic and partying revellers, was now fading away behind me as I took the long way around to the train station, and for the first time in a while, I wasn't in any particular hurry.

I continued on my way until I heard a noise just ahead. I paused and stared into the darkness and shadows, stepping closer and startling an old man scavenging through the bins behind a local cafe. He looked at me as I stood looking at him still keeping my distance. Satisfied that I wasn't a threat to him, he continued to forage for scraps. I continued to stare, I gasped at the realisation that this wasn't an old man at all - the guy was probably younger than me! I was caught with a lump in my throat and an overwhelming sense of pity for him drenched my senses. The fact that he looked younger than me sharply resonated with me as I wondered what the hell life had dealt that poor man.

I stepped closer and my foot crunched in the snow beneath me, causing him to spin around quickly, slipping on the icy ground and falling down in a heap. I moved closer still, putting my hand inside my jacket to retrieve my wallet - it was the very least I could do. Perhaps wary of strangers and concerned for his own safety, the man mumbled,

"What do you want, what are you doing?"

"Relax, mate. I was just..."

But I was cut short. A sudden scream in my head, a violent and hysterical scream like nails down a chalkboard, halted me in my actions of kindness. I had started to stoop down to the man to give him some money, but I bolted upright in agony, my hands clamped on the sides of my head as if trying to hold my brain inside my skull.

The man was clearly stunned at my actions, confused as well, no doubt. The horrendous sound subsided and I composed myself, taking deep breaths, a wave of calm returning. I looked down in front of me to see the homeless man staring at me, bemused. Only then did I fully realise where I was and what I was about to do. I reached back inside my coat and produced my wallet, opening it and proceeding to take out some cash, but then,

"Don't you fucking dare," snarled Blue.

"What?" I asked, confused.

"He is filth; he doesn't deserve it."

"Fuck you," I replied, angry at his suggestions, the argument continuing between Blue and myself, with him becoming increasingly vile in his condemnation of the man. I defended the guy, though I had no knowledge of him aside from his appearance and apparent situation. I even tried to reason on his behalf that he wasn't begging for money, but was away from the crowds and looking for food. That wasn't good enough for Blue and his tirade continued. Eventually, I told him that he may be in my mind but I control my body and with that I checked my cash and was about to pass it to the man when he said,

"No thanks mate… You need it more than I do." He looked wild eyed and terrified

I hadn't thought, but clearly he had seen (and heard!) a well-dressed man, alone, arguing with himself about giving him money. The guy had been shivering in the cold before I arrived, but now that Blue had made an appearance of sorts, he looked absolutely petrified and was actually shaking with fear. Sadly, that was the point at which Blue took more control over me and the situation, now using me to vocalise for him.

"What the fuck? His money not good enough for you?" He snarled into the man's face.

"Leave him alone; the guy's terrified," I replied, my voice slightly trembling in trepidation.

"Look, please man, just go. I don't need your money that bad." He started to sob, unsure whether he was having an argument with one or two people. For that matter, neither did I.

What followed shocked me to my core. I wasn't sure who did it. Technically, I suppose I did it, but in actuality, it was obviously Blue.

"Scum!" screamed Blue as he rained a vicious punch down onto the man now sprawled in the snow. The blow caught him on the left cheek bone and I could hear it crack and echo in the darkness, though the echo was dulled somewhat with the snow. The man yelped and sobbed more as his hands and arms instinctively came up to cover his head. In response, Blue kicked him hard between the legs, naturally causing the man to double up in agony, giving Blue his chance to unleash further punches onto the helpless man.

Our roles were reversed now as I screamed in my own head at him to stop, much like he'd been doing to me. Blue was in control, such was his rage and hatred, though of what I couldn't say. The only respite came for the man and myself when my own body gave out with the physical exhaustion and could no longer inflict pain upon him. Still Blue cursed me for my weakness as I came to my feet. I breathed hard and looked around but there was nobody there. I could still hear the distant revellers partying, their night of fun carrying on for them, but not for the poor wretch lying at my feet.

I was the one shaking then and not from the cold. I was in shock at what he (I?) had done, I was panicking yet all I could hear in my head was Blue mocking my frailty and weakness, he laughed to himself and at me. I sickened him apparently and I was unworthy of his presence. I tried somehow to calm myself before resolving to get away from the scene because there was surely no way I could rationally explain any of this to anyone. I felt I had no choice but to leave so I straightened my clothes and picked up a couple of handfuls of snow to wash the blood from my hands. I walked away, too ashamed to look back, and surprisingly, my calm mood started to ripple back over me and I partially smiled, in my way I suppose I was trying not to draw attention to myself by just being another happy person out at Christmas. As I walked to the station, I didn't look back. I didn't want to see the smashed and broken man I had left in my wake. The sickening thought of all that blood staining the snow was enough for me to keep walking.

The next morning, I awoke with agony in my hands, my knuckles raw and blood stained. It took me a few days to be able to use my hands properly and I had to go to the hospital to get myself checked out, where they found that I had a couple of broken bones, too. I'd told them that I'd been jumped by a couple of guys, which obviously this led to the police (stationed in the emergency room) asking questions. But a smart guy in a suit is always only going to be a victim rather than a perpetrator, right? I told them I'd been robbed and they believed me - they even congratulated me on my 'bravery' for fighting them off, but said I should've reported it at the time. I told them that I didn't want to cause more work for an already over stretched police force and they lapped that up too. I gave a basic description of the phantom muggers and they even offered to drive me home! I thanked them, but declined, and left after my treatment.

I stepped outside and vomited on the pavement, nauseous at my own lies and the appalling thing that I had done, or rather that Blue had done. For his part, Blue just laughed endlessly in my head all the way home. I thought later that I should at least have called an ambulance, anonymously, for the man but I was scared for myself. It's humiliating to think about and to my complete and utter shame that I did nothing. I trawled the internet for information about the homeless man, but there was nothing - clearly he wasn't news worthy. I just hope he survived.

Even though it's been a few weeks since 'that' night, my hands are aching as I type, my guilt tormenting me almost as much as Blue torments me. I need to sleep.

Wednesday, 21st January 2015

It's been a couple of weeks since my last entry. Blue is getting increasingly angry with me for writing all this down but I feel I need to keep a track of everything. I've realised that he does seem to sleep - or something like it at least. There seems to be quieter times and if I try not to disturb him, I can actually write. I'm still figuring out what disturbs him to be honest, which is why my entries are few and far between and not at regular intervals. I'm doing my best and I hope you understand.

He torments me day and night. Sometimes it's little things gnawing away at me, other times he seems to be going berserk, as if he's decided to smash up all the furniture in a room in my head, so to speak. Therefore, when he's at rest, I will try to get as much documented as possible. He will punish me later but this journal has, in a brief time, become my only refuge. What else can I do? Who else can I turn to?

My colleagues have started to comment on my appearance. At first it was sympathy because they assumed I was just looking tired and depressed after my break up with Caroline, thinking it was 'just a reaction' - albeit a delayed one, but others reasoned that the holiday period can be devastating following a break up. I found it patronising, but it covered my tracks for a while so I went along with it. For the first few days after I went back after Christmas, my hands were still severely bruised, so I told a brief story about being mugged and then changed the subject quickly, not wishing to dwell on the lies that I was spinning.

Now I've noticed my reflection in the mirror, I do look grey and haggard, and I have dark circles under my blood shot eyes. I'm not sleeping properly, thanks to Blue's late night horror movies in my head, which are absolutely horrific by the way and I'm becoming short tempered and snappy with everyone I encounter. My work has started to deteriorate in quality; reports and things are never on time - if they are done at all - and yesterday, my boss called me in to her office to discuss my attitude and attendance. That's another thing. I'm either having too much time off or turning up very late.

My boss is called Miranda and I've always got on really well with her. She's very kind and considerate of her staff and is a lot of fun when it's appropriate; I've always enjoyed working with her. She called me in and sat me down with genuine concern for my well-being. She asked how things were going; she knew Caroline and was worried if the break up was taking its toll on me. A normal reaction would be to thank her for her concern, apologise for dropping the ball a few times recently, promising to get my act together from now on, but that was not to be. Blue crawled out from under his rock and started to speak. His influence on me has been growing more and more over the last month or so. So much so, that a lot of the time I don't even realise he's doing it. But this time I did.

"Caroline was a fucking bitch - I'm glad she's gone," I blurted out.

"I'm sorry… What did you say?" gasped a clearly shocked Miranda. As I said, Miranda knew Caroline socially - it turned out that they had mutual friends and had gotten on really well when I'd taken her to work-related events and parties.

"She was a whore. So she's fucking somebody else. Who gives a shit?" I snapped, or rather, Blue did.

"Err, quite, well erm…" Was all Miranda could muster in response, clearly taken aback by my outburst. "But really, Jacob, there's no need for that level of hostility, is there?"

"Cunt!" He snarled.

"Jacob!" Miranda snapped back. "That sort of language is totally inappropriate in the work place! I understand you may be upset, but there's no need for…"

I stood up quickly, cutting her short, suddenly aware of what I'd been saying. Obviously, I'd known what I'd been saying, but everything immediately came clear. It was as if I'd been watching from the other side of a glass wall. I could feel my cheeks burning red with embarrassment, feeling viscerally ashamed of what I'd said to Miranda. She didn't deserve to be spoken to like that, even though none of it was directed at her. I didn't even feel that anger towards Caroline. But I could hear Blue in my head, laughing himself sick. He was literally pulling all my strings like a puppet master.

I apologised profusely, over and over, and Blue mercilessly continued to laugh at my supposed weakness. Miranda looked angry, hurt and let down, but most of all, she looked sympathetic. She truly was a decent human being, who clearly tried to take my recent troubles as the reason for my decline and descent. She'd been sitting on the edge of her desk in front of where I had been sitting, but now she stepped forward and put her hand on my shoulder, looking into my eyes with understanding and genuine care. Her voice was soft and soothing, a balm for my troubled mind. Blue, however, saw the scenario differently and immediately started to scream in my mind about what I should be doing, or, more specifically, what *he* wanted to do to Miranda. I fought the urge to repeat his words, my jaw aching under the pressure as I tried to remain tight lipped. It felt as though he was now actually in my mouth, prising my jaw open.

The look on my face must have been torturous and Miranda asked me if I was alright. If I needed anything, some water? Did I want to sit down? I shook my head furiously, my eyes bulging strangely out of my head and the normally serene Miranda looked very concerned, frightened even. She stepped away and went back to her desk, where she pushed a button on her intercom to her secretary. I assumed she was either going to call for medical assistance or security. Either would've been understandable at that point.

Unfortunately, before she got to speak, Blue took over me. Not just my mind, but for the second time, my body too. The altercation with the poor homeless man was horrendous enough, but this was now a whole new level. I lurched towards her, grabbed her round the waist and pulled her into me. It was all too quick for her to really understand what was going on, so she didn't know what to do in response. My hands reached down behind her and grabbed and groped her bottom, pulling her further into me. As her eyes widened in shock, my penis had clearly become erect and was grinding in to her stomach and groin. Tears welled in her eyes. Disbelief, shock and horror no doubt flooded her senses. Then I spoke, but it was not in my normal voice - it was his voice, or a more 'human' version of it.

"Come on, you little slut." His words, not mine. "Over this desk right now. I'm gonna fuck every last breath out of you."

Again, I felt detached from the whole scene. Yes, it was my body pressed against her. They were my hands groping her, my mouth saying those words, yet I felt as though I was watching a movie from the first person perspective. I desperately needed the remote; I wanted to turn the nightmare off.

Thankfully, I managed to fight back. Fight him back. I released my grip on her rear and pushed myself away from Miranda. I did so with so much force that I flew back and stumbled over the chair that I'd been sitting on. I collapsed to the floor and looked up at the dreadful scene of an open-mouthed, dishevelled Miranda, tears saturating her eyes, leaning back on her desk for support, clearly and uncontrollably shaking with fear.

I turned my eyes away and quickly crawled away like an animal. That pretty much sums up how I saw myself right there and then. I fled into the far corner of her office and just sat there. I curled myself into a ball, hugging my knees and rocking back and forth as I wept my own tears of humiliation, shock and horror at what had just happened.

"I'm so sorry," I said, sniffing back my tears. "Please forgive me... I'm sorry, I'm sorry," I begged, though clearly I had no right to her forgiveness.

I mumbled incoherently and cried for what seemed like forever as I waited for the inevitable security or police intervention. But they didn't come. No one did. I looked up and saw Miranda looking down at me from about ten feet away, understandably wary of getting too close, but she seemed curious as she looked down on this pitiful wretch.

"Who's Blue?" she asked quietly, regaining some composure.

"W-what?" I mumbled.

"You've been sitting there for about ten minutes, yet you just keep saying, 'It was Blue, not me - I'm sorry, it was Blue.' Who is that?" she said softly.

I'd been sitting there for ten minutes, but it felt like a blur of seconds. I looked around, expecting somebody of authority standing over me, ready to take me away, but there was no-one. It was still just the two of us. I was struck with the thought that it was all in my head. Maybe I was having a nervous breakdown. Maybe I was having a delayed reaction to the break up. Maybe I'd imagined all of it. I had to know.

"Did... Did that just really happen?" I said, pointing over to the floor in front of her desk. She looked around and then back at me and sighed.

"Yes, I'm afraid it did." She sounded so cool and relaxed now; surely she couldn't have been through such a thing before. Could she? If she had, it would've been even more traumatic.

Another wave of guilt washed over me, knocking me nauseous at my actions, or, rather, Blue's actions. Still, I should have been, or at least I expected to be, in handcuffs right about now, so why wasn't I?

"Is anyone on their way?" I asked quietly, resigned to what I thought was my inevitable fate. "Security? Police?"

"Well, by rights they should be.....but no. I haven't called anybody."

"Can I ask why?"

"I don't know if I'm honest," she said, smiling gently at me again. "But to say all that was out of character for you is a massive understatement. You didn't seem like yourself - you seemed.......different, someone else entirely. Don't get me wrong, Jacob - I had the phone in my hand and was ready to dial, but then you started to sob and mumble about 'Blue', whoever that is."

"Thank you," I said simply and sincerely.

Sarcastic and sick chuckling floated around my mind. Blue mocked at my 'weakness' again, calling me pathetic and spineless, so I had no choice but to try and block it out, whilst keeping my distance from his victim. She moved closer, no doubt to help me up, but I pulled back and so did she in response. To an outsider, it would seem as though *I* was actually the victim. She picked up the chair and gently slid it over to me, but I stayed on the floor, trying desperately to compose myself a little better as time passed.

"Are you going to tell me about Blue?" she asked softly.

"I... I can't explain... I'm sorry. I know you deserve an explanation... At the very least," I said. "But I just can't. I can't even explain it to myself."

"It's ok," she said, again, softly. "But you need to get some help, Jacob - real help."

"I know," I replied, my head drooping into my hands. I sighed.

"Consider yourself suspended for two months," she said, though now in a very professional manner, as though she was disciplining somebody routinely.

"What? You mean you're not going to fire me either?" I was amazed at her charity, because that's how it felt, like an amazing act of charity.

"No - you need help, Jacob; you've been through a rough time. I should fire you, at the very least, but I've known you for a long time and I know that that wasn't you just then."

21

She had no idea just how right she was.

"Thank you for your understanding," I half smiled.

"Your suspension will depend upon you getting professional help, you know. If you don't, you can't come back. In fact, coming back is a long way down the road just yet. Ok, Jacob?"

"Of course Miranda, I completely understand."

"I'm going to make a report about what just happened, but I won't file it; it'll stay with me until I'm satisfied that everything is ok with you and that you're back on your feet. As I said, if you don't get help, or if there are any even slightly similar incidents, then it goes without saying that your job here will be terminated AND I will forward the file to the authorities. Is all that clear, Jacob?"

"Crystal clear, Miranda thank you again."

She gestured towards the door for me to go. I clambered to my feet and she offered me a tissue to wipe my tear-streaked face, which I gladly accepted and shuffled away. I retrieved my coat without speaking to anyone, and I could sense people watching me as I sheepishly moved towards the nearest elevator. I could feel eyes burning into me, but I just kept my head down low and got out of the building as quickly as I could, then off to my normal journey home on the train with the harrowing sound of laughter in my head coming from him.

So now, here I sit at home, alone at the bottom of a pit it seems. I don't know what to do. People will think I'm going insane and who knows? Maybe I am. But I know he's in there, in here, in my head, in me, bending my will, twisting me to his way. How do I escape my own mind without resorting to escaping this world and ending everything? If I blew my fuckin' brains out, that'd stop him!!

I must find a conclusion, but for now my body aches, my head aches........but that could just be Blue stomping around in there. I need to sleep.

Hello, allow me to introduce myself. I am Blue. Well, that clearly isn't my real name and I don't particularly care for it, but it is how he refers to me, so I thought the moniker would suffice for now. My real name to you is of no concern and besides, you couldn't actually pronounce it in any case.

I have noticed from behind the windows of his eyes that Jacob puts his story down when he can on this little contraption, so I thought to myself, why the fuck not?

He is currently sleeping off his pains and stresses, poor chap, but as he actually fell asleep on his couch after writing to you, this machine was left switched on. Therefore, I thought I might as well take the opportunity again to use his physical body to perform this menial task for me.

So, here I am, in all my dark glory!

This is actually a turn of events for me; I know he wrote earlier about how I was displeased with him for writing about me in this way. And although I do like my anonymity, I have since thought that I could communicate with you in the same manner. Besides, no one is going to believe his tale even if I write this out for you in graphic detail. I'm smiling as I write from his mind; I can see his fingers dashing across those little buttons and MY words coming up on this glowing screen. It's amazing what you people - you humans, I mean - have come up with over the years. I'm impressed.

Of course, I have seen such things before; this isn't the first human I've tormented, you know. I've been playing my games and twisting the minds of you people for generations and, for the record, there is no chance whatsoever of me stopping. Of course at some point I will probably grow bored of little Jakey here and I'll find a more fun host. Then again I might be able to keep this bag of meat and bone going until he dies of old age or more likely kills himself. Either way, then it'll just be on to the next poor fuck who I take my dark, twisted or lustful fancy for. Who knows, maybe next I could pick you. Maybe not, but it could be your wife or husband, or maybe your son or daughter - or maybe just the person you're fucking on the side? Ah, the possibilities are endless and in response to their screams for help all you people do is medicate or try to talk my victim through his possession. It's actually hilarious to me.

Because you have all these new sciences, which again I'm impressed with, as I've seen them all develop over the years; you seem to think that you can explain away everything. Well, I'm here to tell you that you fucking can't!

Over my many years, I've had all sorts of people trying to get me out of someone or other. Village elders, witchdoctors, shamans, priests, rabbis - they've all had a go and some of them, I hate to admit, have done a pretty good job. Of course, sometimes I've just gotten bored and moved on to some other unfortunate cunt and naturally they have taken all the credit, but yes, they have, on occasion, made it too uncomfortable for me to stay. However not a single fucking one of them has actually succeeded in 'casting me out', fuck that, never happened. But in your modern times, you seem to think it's all a science, that it's the victim that has a problem. That it's just a symptom in their minds that can be cured with medication or therapy. Then if you can't find the problem, or more likely myself or one of my kind just doesn't want to go, then you lock the poor bastard up in one of your facilities where your doctors keep going over and over and fucking over everything until the victim wants to kill him or herself!

Either that or they are so drugged up that we just get bored and move on to another because we aren't having any real effect or fun anymore. At what point does my victim become your victim too? They are the ones that get imprisoned in your white rooms, locked away from their loved ones, unable to go out into the world at large, unable to interact with society and all because I've twisted their little minds. It's tragic, well, it's tragic for your victim, not for me or my kind. We find it sickeningly twisted and funny.

Of course, in those good old days, they had asylums and things too. Other people were banished from their settlements, or just plain killed for what they (or rather we) had done, but now you seem to give them drugs and send them on their merry way, and when they (or I) do something horrendous, it's white room time straight away - or that's how it seems.

What I'm trying to say is that you have gone so far down the route of science and understanding of things, you are arrogant of the fact that there are things that you don't understand, or will never understand, because you aren't meant to understand these things. Why are modern humans so obsessed with finding out about things that exist millions of miles away from your own planet that will not affect you in the slightest for maybe thousands of years, if at all?

The planet you live on is fucked. More to the point, you're killing it, yet you're spending vast amounts discovering other places that will not help you. That is more to my point. You don't even understand everything on this fucking planet yet and I am just an example of these things that you don't understand. Now, don't get me wrong, I am not a physical being, so how you destroy your home is not really any of my concern. There will be enough of you around for me to torment and corrupt for a long time to come, I can assure you of that.

It's just that I suppose I miss a good fight with the old religions, which sounds ridiculous I know but still, I do. I used to so enjoy it when a priest of *whichever faith would come to do battle and try to rid me from your realm, fat chance he had of that! I do miss a good exorcism like in the old days.*

Anyway, I'm bored now. I just wanted to introduce myself, and I've just thought of the joy I will get tomorrow when Jacob sees all this in his private journal. But I will go now. Oh, I think I will punish him, too. I did tell him not to write anymore on here, so therefore I believe it is my right to punish him for doing so. Hypocritical, maybe, but I can do as I please - he is my victim after all. I know just how to punish him, too; I'm sure he won't be able to resist telling you when he wakes. Until next time, I bid you a dark farewell.

Friday, 23ʳᵈ January 2015

It's been two days since my last post. I woke up in a pool of blood yesterday morning. I was still lying on the couch, so I must've fallen asleep after my last journal entry. My laptop had fallen to the floor - thankfully undamaged and in sleep mode. I can only think that I had been sleepwalking, but knowing what I know now, no-one actually sleepwalks; it's something (or someone) inside them that make do it. Blue taught me that. It was he who made me get up and go to the kitchen to get a knife.

I woke with a carving knife loosely in my right hand. My grip had faded as I slept. Blood had been seeping slowly from me over night, it seems, because it had dried all over me and the couch. Other thicker areas were still sticky to the touch, and as I looked closer, my frightened eyes took in the sight that I had carved the name 'Blue' into the underside of my left forearm. I would obviously have woken up for such a thing, but he must've stopped me from doing that. He's now forcing me to hurt myself, I fear what will happen next and where this will go. I wonder with horror at just where he will lead me to next?

I was covered in blood and had to shower, the sting in my arm horrendously slicing into me, as the cleansing water and soap washed over my wound. With every wince I made, I heard his sick laughter. I realised he was in complete control of me now and I didn't know what to do or where to turn. I stood under the flowing shower and wept and wept until I had no more tears to shed; maybe ending everything would be the easiest and quickest way out. But would he let me? I doubt it very much. That would be too easy.

I need to learn to control him, or at least be able to stop him taking over. He can hurt me, or at least make me hurt myself. From what happened in the alley with the homeless guy, as well as what almost happened with

Miranda, I know he can make me hurt others. It frightens me to think of just what he is capable of making me do. I can't research mind techniques (or whatever they call it) online, or in books, because he might be watching what I'm doing! I'm writing this now thinking that he's 'asleep', but I can't say for sure - I'm just trying to document my story because I need people to know what's happening to me. Whoever is actually reading this now, I just wish I could scream out to you for help. My life is falling apart, my sanity has long been eroded and I do not know what my fate or future will be. I want to fall on someone's mercy. I want to beg on bended knee, but I have no-one to turn to, no one.

Monday, 26th January 2015

My weekend was hell. I didn't write anything on here because, in short, Blue wouldn't let me. I made a conscious effort that I would not go outside, at least that way I can ensure the safety of others. I may just be his plaything - I'm resigned to that fate - at least for now, but if my withdrawal from society saves another from his wrath then at least I'm doing something good.

It was a time of torment, but as I sat around, I made some progress in learning to keep the beast caged - at least for short periods of time. It isn't really a technique as such; it's more about concentration and willpower. I imagined a cage or room and tried to visualise him being pushed back and down into the space in my mind. At first, he just laughed at me, which was disheartening initially, but I forced myself to continue. I feel my sanity and life are at stake.

Undeterred, I continued on. Each time, he laughed and abused my mind, but each time I felt a little stronger. Then, gradually, it felt as though I was getting a grip on him and having an effect on moving him into his cage. The best way to describe it is as though I could grab him in my outstretched hands and physically drag him to the cage door only for him to slip out of my grasp at the last minute, like a creature covered in oil.

The more I tried, the closer I got, and then gradually I noticed that his spite and laughter seemed to fade from mocking to anger. I knew then that I was winning. All weekend, or as much as I could, I continued the practice. It became very exhaustive, on top of which, when I took a break to recover, he would immediately double his vile taunts and try to make me hurt myself. On one occasion, for example, as I was making some tea, he had been quiet and lulled me into a false sense of security, so I didn't expect him to try to scald me with boiling water from the kettle as I poured it. It was close. A little caught my hand but I ran it under cold water - it was just a minor injury, but it could've been much worse.

The battle of wills raged for the rest of the weekend and I was on my guard constantly. The more I restrained him mentally, the angrier he became. I have lost count of the amount of painkillers I've taken to soothe my aching head - they do seem to have an effect, though. I could describe it as making him drowsy, as opposed to making my pain fade, but either way, they were having the desired effect for me. However, the effect is getting less and I'm therefore having to take more - whether that's because Blue's getting stronger, I cannot say. I hope and pray to God that that isn't the case, because there are only so many drugs that I can take until they start to fuck me up physically.

Tuesday, 27th January 2015

I'm in a happier place than I've been in for weeks! I was able to write yesterday quite freely - if not a lot – and as I was writing, I had put Blue in his cage and it worked!

I didn't want to log it down until I knew I had been successful, but now I feel confident because he's in his cage now - and I literally want to sing and dance at the prospect of being ME again. Basically, yesterday morning, after my horrendous weekend, I woke and decided to try to cage him first thing. He seems to be at rest more or less when I sleep - apart from certain occasions when I'm being punished.

It almost felt like I was creeping around in my own mind, trying not to wake him, mentally shackling him and gently guiding him into his cage, before locking it - and it worked!!!

I refer to it as a cage because that is where I feel a vicious animal (which he seems to me to be) would be locked, but in hindsight, a more appropriate place would be a padded cell. The image now as I write seems more fitting: a wild-haired, crazy-eyed, spitting and snarling creature in a strait-jacket, bouncing off the walls in a padded cell deep within the recesses of my mind. Yes, that's much better. Very comforting.

I write now to let you know that he is still in there. I can hear muffled screams and howls from time to time, but, ultimately, he is under control. I feel so proud of myself because I achieved it through willpower alone. After all I've been through; it's as if the weight of the world has suddenly been shifted from my shoulders.

I know this is not over. I am not going to just carry on as normal; I am going to get some help or advice at least. I've been pondering this since yesterday as well. Who do I speak to? The idea of Blue being in his padded cell made me wonder. If I go to the authorities or a doctor of some kind, is there a possibility that I may end up in the same kind of place that Blue is in my head? I don't know if things have changed in that regard with modern medicine, but ultimately, I think you get my point.

Therefore, I've decided to do something that I never ever thought I would do again for the rest of my life: go to confession. I am a lapsed Catholic. It was my parents' faith (and mine, too, I suppose), but as I grew up, it didn't seem to be of any worth to me. Gradually I stopped going and never really thought about it, until I was reading back my posts on here - and obviously I read what Blue had put down (or forced me to write for him when I was asleep!). Anyway, that got me thinking about the 'old' ways of dealing with such things and I thought, well it can't hurt can it? So, I'm off to church now and I'm comfortable that Blue is locked up nice and secure in his cell, which means I can go outside into the real world without fear.

Even if the priest thinks I'm crazy, it's a confession. It's between me and him (and God of course). I'm not actually sure what I'm going to tell him, or how much, but it might be helpful just to unburden myself. Plus, it gets me out of this place for a couple of hours, with the added benefit of stocking up on painkillers - just in case!

I will document what happens and what he says later on.

Tuesday, 27th January 2015 (continued)

Well, I went to the local church this afternoon and it was a strange experience after all these years. I was struck by the majesty of the place; it truly was a beautiful building with stunning iconography, statues, paintings and windows everywhere I looked. It took my breath away at times.

It felt strange to be there. Not just because I was in a church (I've been to weddings and christenings for friends and family), but because I was there for me. Not just me but a serious reason to be there - like something you see in a movie or something. I was there as a little boy with his parents because that was simply what they did, and to be honest, for the most part, I didn't understand a lot of it as a child. Then as an adult, I didn't believe in it anyway. Now however, this was a genuine 'spiritual' reason to seek out someone of knowledge on a subject that I knew little about and I have to say it was frightening and intimidating.

When I walked through the doors, I could feel my stomach turn with anxiety, but then, worse still, I could feel a similar knot in my mind. Blue was aware of my surroundings. I had to strengthen my resolve to keep him in his place, keep him quiet and keep the bastard shackled.

I found and spoke to a priest who was very nice and kind to me. I had decided on the way to the church that I wouldn't actually go to confession – after all, what was I actually confessing to? The assault on the homeless man? The situation with Miranda? No, the majority of my woes surrounded me; it was my own sanity that I was worried about. Please don't misunderstand… I am devastated about those other things, but one step at a time; besides, if I can resolve some issues or get some clarity regarding my own state of mind, I can then move forward with those things. I have already pondered, once I have sorted everything out, that I will offer my resignation at work and go to the police regarding the poor man in the alley. I will take responsibility but I have to get myself sorted out first.

So, as I was saying, I found and spoke to a priest, who was great. I can't really go into everything word for word here and now, but I explained, very tentatively, about what was happening to me. Even though we didn't go into the confession booths, once I had started to explain myself, he took me into his office for privacy. There were other people in the church and though I kept my voice low and respectful, it was probably for the best that others didn't overhear me.

I told him everything pretty much – although I did edit somewhat from the assault details that I have written here. I did say to him that in hindsight I should've brought my laptop with me, but it seemed more sincere as I poured out my heart to this stranger. Just that experience of being able to unload seemed to lift my spirits. At first, as I told my story, he seemed very relaxed and I thought he was going to jump in or interrupt, but thankfully he let me continue with my flow. As the horror and violence and torment became clear, the priest became visibly shocked and his complexion understandably paled to an almost grey hue.

As you know from my last entries, things are turning now in my favour and I am gaining control of my demon. I finally see a light to head towards. The priest seemed genuinely uplifted by my recent breakthrough though, and he smiled warmly. As I felt myself light up and smile as well, the realisation hit me full on that I was indeed winning this battle for my sanity.

He told me that he didn't think it sounded like anything to be worried about from a spiritual or otherworldly point of view; he felt it was probably something brought on by the stresses of work, coupled with a delayed reaction to my break up with Caroline (as well as the time of year, which can drag people down at times). He felt, although some of the things were very extreme, such as the wounding on my arm (though self-harming is very common), some people can go to extreme lengths when under intense pressure. I have to say that I held back with the story of the man in the alley - I was too ashamed to go into too much detail. My (Blue's) actions still sicken me now.

He did cite a few brief examples from around the world where people have gone 'crazy', for want of a better word. Sometimes these people have genuine political or religious views, but sometimes these people were, themselves, victims of circumstance and they just needed help. He avoided using words like 'demon' or 'possession' but I understood what he was getting at. Were all those other people possessed? Of course not. There was a rational argument for all these things. They just needed to be diagnosed and get the help that they needed.

The priest did ask me to go and see a professional, a psychiatrist, who would diagnose me, as well as help me keep my own demon at bay. I thanked him for his time and walked away feeling even better than when I had decided to go to the church.

I do have to point out, however, that throughout the whole conversation with the priest, I could almost feel Blue screaming out. It was as if I had returned the favour and scalded him. I visualised him howling in torment as I poured boiling oil or something over him, writhing in agony in his padded cell, his skin bubbling and blistering while I laughed at him for a change.

I managed, however, to block it out, or at the very least, suppress it. This felt like another victory for me as I walked home and there was an almost palpable spring in my step as I made my way through the chilly streets, stopping to get my painkillers, of course. Just in case!

Now I'm home, I've tidied up my apartment and feel good about that, too. Blue feels safely under lock and key, although I can still hear his muffled raging in the distance of my mind, and I've been thinking over my conversation with the priest. Man, that was so helpful; it really put things into perspective for me. There are learned people out there who study things like this properly - they can help me. I no longer feel alone because there will be someone who can help get me through this and banish the little bastard for good - and I don't mean a fuckin' exorcist!

Anyway, I'm going to unwind for the first time (in forever, it seems) tonight and maybe even have a couple of glasses of wine, watch some trash TV and sleep well. You never know, I might not need to log anything down for a while if this carries on, so unless anything changes, this is me signing off. Goodnight.

Hello - I'm back! Jacob is asleep in front of his television set and I have escaped my prison cell. He's sitting here now, oblivious that he is writing my words down, the pathetic piece of meat that he is.

So, he thinks he has won his little game, does he? He thinks I am forever locked up in his padded cell, bound and gagged with no way out; he thinks I am now his prisoner in the bowels of his mind.

He needs to think again, because as you see now, I am free. I admit that the motherfucker did well to control me, subdue and imprison me in that place, but all good things come to an end. I am more resourceful than he gives me credit for; I am far more powerful and devious than he thinks as well. He will regret binding me - we could have co-existed together as one. I would have been dominant, of course, but together we could've been a force. Now, however, he's fucked to put it bluntly. I will make the worm wish he had never been born.

Life, as he knows it, is over. This is the calm, but the storm is coming and it will be the blackest storm he has ever witnessed, mark my blood soaked words. He can think for now that he has me under control and he will read this no doubt at some point, but that may be too late.

So, if you are reading this, Jakey boy, buckle up - it's going to get fucking messy!

Friday, 30ᵗʰ January 2015

I haven't been on here since Tuesday. It was a conscious decision on my part because nothing has happened to report (nothing regarding him at least, but I'll get to that shortly).

I've spent the latter stages of the week studying on the internet, using this laptop of course, just not opening this journal file. I've been searching self-help techniques, anything regarding the mind really, studying how to unlock more of the mind and realising how little we actually use. It struck me that my mind is like a huge old mansion, but I'm only living in a cupboard in the kitchen - that's how it seems to me and following that analogy, Blue is either locked in the attic or the cellar. I'm not sure which I'd prefer. The point being that I have so much to unlock and develop, it's no wonder that before I learned to control him, he had so much space to roam around and cause havoc. Furthermore, with that analogy, it was also as if I had left a ground floor window open (my low ebb following the break up I guess), so that he could get in and make himself right at home.

Sorry if that was a bit of a ramble, but it's just the best way I can express my thoughts. Anyway, I came back to this file to log something wonderful, but then I saw his words. I admit it scared the shit out of me; the fact that he'd gotten out of his padded cell and taken control again. But sitting here now and reading his vile message just strengthens my resolve to beat the bastard. He isn't real; it's just a part of me expressing myself in the wrong way - that's the way I have to think about this. I can't give him power over me. I can't let him win, I am the master of my own ship and therefore, I shape my own destiny. I will not let that foul creature from within ruin my life!

Anyway, I am getting away from my original reason for being on here today: the wonderful news I wanted to put on here. It is a journal of sorts, after all. I'm seeing Caroline tonight. Hurray!!!

I went out for a walk yesterday and bumped into her in the park. Initially, when I first saw her I was bitter and racked with anxiety, but she smiled and said hello and she stopped to talk. I have to say, it was incredible. Yes, I have been through all sorts of shit recently - as you know - but that maybe just made me more thankful to see her.

Anyway, we ended up going for a coffee and talking and reminiscing about things and we both laughed so much. It really was amazing. Inevitably, we got talking about the break-up and even that was easier, because we both realised that we were both at fault and it turns out that the other guy that she'd been seeing had been lying to her, he was married. Naturally, she ended that, and apparently had spent all Christmas and New Year wondering about us and missing me. To cut a long story short, we are going to try again. I'm so happy after everything that has happened to me and I've documented here that finally I seem to be coming out of the dark tunnel and into the light again.

I'm meeting Caroline tonight and we're going out for a meal and more conversation. I'm trying not to get too carried away, but suddenly life seems to knock you on your ass, but sometimes in a fantastic way. I know that you are probably wondering about Blue........ Well, I'm way ahead of you. I'm going to take some extra painkillers tonight, which will hopefully keep him subdued, and I'm going to avoid any alcohol - or reduce it at least, which means I can keep my guard up and him in check. I feel as though I'm getting a second chance at life.

Saturday, 31st January 2015 (1am)

Well, the night has gone fantastically well, so I just wanted to document it. Plus the night isn't over yet!

I'll have to be brief. We went for a meal at a little Italian restaurant; it was very quiet, very romantic and hardly anyone else around. I had a little wine, but not too much because of 'you know who'. We talked, we laughed and we connected like never before. It was like we were a couple of teenagers on a first date, but without too much awkwardness. The only slightly awkward moment was when she noticed the slight bulge on my arm under my shirt sleeve and asked about it. It was the bandage covering Blue's wound. I glossed over it by saying I had burned myself in the kitchen when I was cooking and she joked about me actually doing any cooking in the first place. We laughed and moved on very easily.

Anyway, one thing led to another, and now we're both back here at my apartment. I can't believe we are back together - I can't remember being happier in my life. I love her so much. Right now she's in the bathroom. She doesn't know about my work situation, but I intend to get everything sorted out and get back and firing on all cylinders very soon, so I've just told her that I'll be with her soon, as I just had to quickly sort out an email for work. She was impressed with my diligence. It's only a white lie so I can get these feelings down. This genuinely might be my last post, folks.

Fuck. She just came out of the bathroom completely naked. She paused and stood in front of me tantalisingly before turning around and walking to the bedroom. My god, she is SO fuckin' hot, that ass!! I really have to go now!

It's now around 5am I think and I'm writing again. Something happened, something bad, something really bad. It feels strange to be sitting here typing it out, but I have to. You will understand in a moment.

We made love; it was amazing, better than I ever remember it. To watch her move, to kiss her, the way we touched each other intimately, to feel her skin against mine, it was beyond words. Afterwards, we fell asleep and I remember her nestling into me and resolving to never ever lose her again.

I woke up from a dream, which was more like a nightmare, in which I was being torn apart, limb from limb, with blood spraying viciously everywhere. Flesh was strewn against the wall and I could hear screams and anger. Rage, my God, so much rage - it was horrendous. The last thing I remember seeing were teeth – horrific yellowing teeth - long, jagged and sharp. Oh so sharp. I couldn't tell if they were smiling at me or snarling at me - there was so much hatred it was like there was an electrical charge in the air.

I jerked awake screaming and I thought I had pissed the bed. Either that or it was sweat. Sadly, it was neither. I looked over, wondering why my screams hadn't woken my beloved Caroline. She was still, so unbelievably still. I pulled back the sheets and was nearly sick with horror and revulsion. There was blood everywhere. Huge open wounds littered her once beautiful body and she looked as if she had been savaged by wild and ferocious animals, yet a carving knife was sticking out of her chest. It sickens me to even describe this here, but I have to document this for future reference. Blood spattered the walls, flesh had been torn from her and discarded on the floor and bed and then I noticed something. As I brushed her hair from her face, so that I could see her one last time, across her forehead was carved the word 'BLUE'.

I was numb. I cried hysterically, screaming her name, then his name and then I just sat and wept. Now I sit here still, with my trusty laptop, telling you all that has happened. At a time like this, why would I write? Well, this has been a document of my recent times and the hell I have endured. Hell cannot be a place as bad as this. I have no doubt that Caroline screamed and struggled. I screamed her name upon discovering what he, or I, had done. I can hear police sirens in the night. My neighbours must have been alerted by the screams from here. Hopefully the police are on their way to break my door down right now. I hope they are. Maybe that way my nightmare can end.

I'm sitting here with my laptop now covered in her blood as I type. I would take that knife again and slash my wrists and throat, but I know he would not let me do that. He would stop me. My guard was down when I found happiness and contentment again with the woman I love, but that was a mistake, because that was the moment he took to escape his cell. I was right. The cacophony of sirens is getting louder now; they must be outside my building. I can hear a commotion outside my door: yelling officers and my neighbours' nervous chatter. How I wish there was a death penalty to end my suffering. Somewhat ironically I will end my days either in a prison cell or padded cell, someone I know and who knows me all too well will delight in that little detail. My only certainty is that either way what years I may have left, they will I know for sure be tormented forever by that vicious bastard I call Blue.[1]

Footnote: The previous is a transcript of evidence retained from a laptop computer owned by the suspect. This document is not for public knowledge at this time. Suspect currently under review and assessment at the Hoffman Institute while psychiatric tests are carried out, pending his trial for the alleged murder of Caroline Fisher.

CHARLOTTE

Chapter 1

She awoke in a bed that she immediately loved but, through her half shuttered eyes, it was also one she didn't recognise. It was so soft and comfortable that it felt as though she were being cradled like a child. Her head sank into the pillows and her body was supported in luxury while the sheets settled around her, wrapping her in an embrace which smelled of a summer morning. Wherever she was, it was heavenly and she didn't want to move or even open her eyes fully.

Reluctantly she did open her eyes and blinked at the sunlight breaking through the weave of the curtains at the window. It wasn't too harsh, just enough to lull her awake from her slumbers. From her position still curled up in the soft bed she tried to look around the room for signs of recognition but saw none. Her eyes were now fully open and scanning intently but still nothing was familiar to her. She propped herself up on her elbows, with a little alarm, but mainly curiosity, she mumbled

"Where the fuck?"

She looked this way and that for something, anything, but no clues were forthcoming. She sat bolt upright, moving her hands behind her for support as she continued to gaze. It was a beautiful room, painted in soft pastel colours which complimented each other perfectly. The furnishings looked expensive and classic, from the curtains to the couch under the huge window, from the seat at the foot of the bed to the two chests of drawers and enormous wardrobe against the facing wall. Only then did she fully comprehend the size of the room itself and the bed she now lay in. It was massive and to make her smile to herself, it was a canopied four poster too! She had always dreamed of having one of those for herself.

She marvelled at the bed for a few moments before continuing to look around the room. To her right there was what looked like an antique dressing table, much in keeping with the other furniture, it was equally as stunning and it was complete with a suitably large mirror attached to two tall spiral posts at the back. From her position she could see herself in the reflection; she felt quite the Lady of the House in such surroundings and gave a soft smile to herself. As she moved slightly to face the mirror the bedclothes moved too and slipped down from her. Only then did she notice that she was naked. She had been so cocooned in the comfort of the bed that she hadn't even realised. She lifted the sheets and blankets to see that her nudity was complete and self consciously pulled them back up to cover herself. Yes, she was indeed completely naked, except for two bandages wrapped tightly around her wrists. She examined them but no recollections came to mind.

Worries then started to spread over her in much the same way as the bed had embraced her, only this was a far from luxurious feeling. The room was completely alien to her. There were no signs or indications as to whose place this was and the bandages made her wonder if she'd had some kind of accident but this room was unlike any hospital room she had ever seen. She thought and thought, racking her brain as to how she got here, where she had been the previous night or who she had met and came up with nothing.

To have a room this size clearly meant that the house itself would invariably be huge and she had no—one in her circle of friends or family or even acquaintances that lived in such a place that she knew of. She started to panic and gripped the bedclothes tightly, pulling them closer up to her chin for protection. She frantically tried to look everywhere, still from the sanctuary of the bed, before deciding to be a little braver and slowly eased over to the edge of the bed. First of all, she looked in the mirror to reassure herself that no-one was around that she hadn't seen. Then she ever-so-slowly leaned over the bed to look underneath. Her hands trembled as she reached for the valance hanging down to the floor. She gripped it slowly not quite sure what to expect but her heart raced and threatened to burst out of her chest. She counted down in her head from three to one before quickly snatching up the cloth which revealed nothing and, more importantly, no-one.

A wave of relief spread over her as she settled back again at least in the knowledge that she was alone in the room. She suddenly felt the need to explore; it would probably be the only thing that could put her mind at rest and ease her fears. Tentatively she eased her foot and then right leg out of the bed, closely followed by her left. The height of the bed surprised her as it was higher than she thought taking her a little longer than expected for her feet to hit the varnished wooden floor. She moved herself into an upright position and lifted her bottom off the bed to stand though she still held the sheet up to her chest.

She glanced around the room again but this time specifically for her clothes. There was a chair in front of the dressing table which is where she expected her clothes to be and certainly where she would've casually thrown them if it was her room, but they were nowhere to be seen. She craned her head this way and that but still nothing. Eventually and now a little more confident that she was alone she let the sheet go and moved over to the dressing table. There were many items upon it, hairbrush, jewellery boxes, handheld mirror, perfumes and various creams in delicate pots and fine bottles. After reading some of the inscriptions and labels she realised that whoever stayed in this room had expensive tastes and probably a very good lifestyle. She envied her, the rooms' owner, whoever she was.

She opened one of the jewellery boxes; thankfully it didn't play a tune. She hated those. Inside, there were more examples of quality and taste. Pendants, rings and bracelets which all screamed money. She lifted out a tray to find the usual 'secret' compartment which hid a couple of letters tied neatly together with a purple ribbon, she took them out and examined them but felt guilty about opening and reading them so went to put them back. As she was about to, she noticed a lock of hair, again tied neatly with the same purple ribbon. She took it out and put the letters back, upon examining the lock she could see quite clearly even in the dim light through the curtains that there were two possibly three different sets of hair tied together. There were blond, and at least one or two sets of brunette hair. At first she assumed it would be the hair of someone's children tied together as a keepsake but it didn't have the same softness as a child's hair.

She involuntarily shivered, causing her own shoulder length black hair to shake along with her small breasts. She put the keepsake back and due to her shivering and catching sight of her breasts in the mirror, she wanted clothes. She moved over to the chests to look for them but after rummaging she found little other than photo albums, diaries and more bits and pieces from someone's life which she felt strange about opening and violating. Instead, she left them and moved over to the imposing wardrobe, which was locked but, thankfully had a little key in the lock. Her shivering had only been momentary but she still had a touch of self-consciousness about being nude in someone else's bedroom, in her own home she walked around like that all the time but in a stranger's home? No.

She turned the key and pulled open the huge double doors. Immediately she saw someone looking at her! She screamed and jumped back, away from the wardrobe and the door creaked slowly closed. She moved back over and onto the bed with her heart pounding but nobody came out or made any movement. Slowly she regained her self-control and stood up again before returning to the wardrobe. Gingerly and with her hands shaking, she reached out and pulled back the door. She stepped back and out of reach as the door swung open to reveal another mirror, long and thin on the inside of the door. She smiled and laughed to herself, nervously, before approaching the wardrobe again. This time she did find some clothes, hanging neatly, all pressed and seemingly freshly laundered by their scent now filling the room.

There wear summer dresses, jeans, blouses, sweaters and T-shirts. At the bottom there were boots, sneakers, dress shoes and sandals all of which she liked. She couldn't decide what to pick out, for a few moments she forgot where she was (though she didn't actually know where she was) and flicked through the garments as if she were in her own closet. She decided to look out of the window to see what the weather was like in order to make a decision about what she should wear. She went to the window and flung open the curtains briskly. All that stretched out before her was green, fields, trees and more fields. The sky was blue and cloudless but there was an overwhelming feeling of the outdoors and freshness.

Normally she would love that sight, nature, beauty, open fields, peace and tranquillity. A gravel drive led away from the house or building she was in, off into the distance but she didn't know where it went because she still didn't know where she was. There were no clues out there either, just the occasional bird song, not even a passing car or truck; she was in the middle of nowhere, naked and alone. However the thing that froze her to the spot as she gazed at the beautiful morning was the windows themselves and the fact they were barred from the outside.

Chapter 2

Her worries quickly escalated from panic to outright fear. She turned and ran to the door, turning the handle and pulling hard but to no avail. Subconsciously she knew it would be locked. She also couldn't believe that she hadn't tried the door when she got out of the bed but there was something about still being undressed that had stopped her. Suppose the door had been open, would she have gone out exploring her surroundings naked? It seemed logical to her that she would look for her clothes first and then she'd been distracted by the place itself. She pulled frantically at the unyielding door before banging on it and shouting to someone, anyone for help. Her calls descended into screams when no reply was forthcoming.

Tears welled in her eyes and began to spill down her pale cheeks. She tried to block out scenarios that were now building at the back of her mind and fighting over each other to be noticed. The door hadn't even budged slightly; it didn't seem to be the sort of thing that she could break down either. It looked old and in keeping with the house. The sort of phrase that her Dad or someone used to say sprung to mind, "They used to build things to last in those days."

It seemed true enough in this case.

She noticed another door on the other side of the room, a smaller less robust looking door and she walked quickly over to it. Opening it tentatively, her heart sank. It was only a bathroom, beautiful though the room was, decorated with lush towels, drapes and ornaments and oozed a gorgeous fresh scent, it wasn't a way out.

She moved back over to the window and tried her luck there but again the window was locked solidly. She looked around for something that she could break the glass with but nothing seemed heavy enough. Perhaps she could break the window and call for help, the bars were on the outside at least but as she looked out in desperation of any kind of life there was nothing to find.

Her hopelessness crashed in on her and she sank to the floor. On her knees she put her head in her hands and wept.

The sun shone through the bars and brightened the room. At any other time it would be a beautiful morning that she would want to enjoy. The warming of her skin where she now knelt made her aware of her situation and vulnerability. She felt all cried out and, after a while, she resolved to get herself out, as it was clear nobody was coming to her rescue. She dried her eyes and face on the sheet hanging off the bed and got herself to her feet. She took a couple of deep breaths and mumbled to herself to stay strong and focus. Her pep talk seemed to clear her mind and she clenched her fists in resolve as she went back to the wardrobe.

She pulled out a pair of faded blue jeans and a T-shirt and put them on. She didn't look for underwear, no matter what the situation was she wouldn't be wearing another woman's panties or bra! Thankfully the clothes fit her well. They could've been made for her but she didn't think she could go wrong with jeans and a T-shirt really. She pulled out a pair of sneakers that were luckily her size and put them on the bed, she normally walked around bare foot a lot anyway as she always felt more comfortable and less restricted but a little voice in her head kept whispering that she might have to do some running at some point. She would put them on when, or if, she managed to get out of this fucking room.

For an hour or so she wandered around the room trying to figure out an escape. She repeatedly tried the door and window but again to no avail each time. She looked for things on the dressing table to pick the lock. She found a small pair of scissors, tweezers, a metal nail file and a couple of other small thin objects and she tried over and over again to pick the locks on both the door and windows. The problem was that she had no idea what she was doing; she'd seen it done in movies hundreds of times and they always made it look easy. It wasn't.

Each time she tried to be delicate and precise but it was just too difficult to achieve. Once she thought she'd got it but she was wrong and the building frustration burst her banks and she screamed her anger, throwing her picking tools across the room, before curling up in the corner by the door to weep. She drew her knees up towards her chest and buried her head on them. She thought about another thing she'd seen in movies, a credit card? They use those to break into apartments. Pity she had no belongings to even try it. Whether it would work, she didn't know but then again she didn't know exactly what to do anyway.

She thought about who could be looking for her. Surely somebody would be but the more she thought the hazier her mind was. Of course, she remembered little things that her father used to say and she remembered him and her mother but other things seemed to be surrounded in fog. She thought hard about the immediate past; where had she been last night and drew a blank. She tried to recall who she had been with but again nothing. She tried to think about her friends and who would be wondering where she was. A frightening thing dawned on her that she didn't know who her friends were! No matter how hard she tried to concentrate she didn't know her own friends. She could picture faces that she knew, even scenarios and places where they'd been together and good times they'd had but they seemed quite distant. She focused hard for a recent memory, a recent face and any important name but, each time, her thoughts clouded over and faded.

She thought deeper still but couldn't recall whether she had any siblings, or where she lived? Was she single or married? Did she have a job? If so, as what? Then she came close to the edge of sanity. As she thought of her life and names of friends, because she realised that she couldn't even remember her own name!

Her mind started to slide down the spiral of despair. Everything that she tried to think about just crumbled. Who was she? Where was she from? Would anyone miss her or care about her? Did she have any children? Everything that was even close to being a recent memory or something to cling onto just faded as she focused.

She had been sitting in the corner of the room racking her brain for hours. The house was silent though, by now, she thought of it as more of a cell or prison. The only sound was the occasional bird outside, otherwise there was nothingness. She had no more tears to cry then the silence was suddenly but distantly broken.

She heard a first step, then another and another. At first she thought she had misheard but as she listened she definitely heard footsteps downstairs. Somebody was there; somebody else was inside the house. She had absolutely no idea who it was or could be because after deep thoughts she realised that she couldn't recall anyone not even herself. She shouted out loudly. She called out for help. She begged for the person, whoever it was, to come and rescue her and the footsteps became louder. Whoever the person was, they were now not only moving around but they were walking up the stairs. Finally someone was here. Finally somebody was coming to save her, finally the nightmare was over and she would be rescued.

Her tears returned; yet, now they were tears of relief and joy, she smiled to herself and mild hysteria built up within her. A little voice whispered to her to be careful. It was a voice inside her head. Who the hell is it? Is this the same person who's locked you up in here? Why are you here? What are they going to do to you? Suddenly her smile slipped from her face and she moved away from the door. Clambering to her feet she moved over to the bed. Her instinct was to defend herself. Quickly, she grabbed the small scissors that she had tried to pick the lock with and held them tightly as she retreated to the far side of the bed away from the door. Her body shook as the adrenaline took over and she heard whoever it was reach the top of the stairs. The footsteps continued to get louder on what seemed like a wooden floor. The landing of the house sounded much the same as the floor in the bedroom. The footsteps continued to get louder until she could tell they were close and then abruptly, they stopped.

The stranger was right outside the door now. Her heart raced, her hands trembled. As she gripped her makeshift weapon tightly, sweat dripped from her and a shiver slipped down her neck and spine.

"H-h-hello?" she called out timidly. "Who's there?........Please help me"

There was no response, no reassuring voice and no urgency from the other side of the door, just silence for a few seconds. She was about to call out again but the silence was broken by a loud metallic thud which was undoubtedly a bolt being slid back. Her heart raced even quicker, as a second bolt was opened. Her fist gripped tighter on the scissors. Then there was movement, the bottom of the door lifted up and out into the corridor, she couldn't believe that she hadn't noticed that before; not that it was big enough to aid her escape but she cursed herself for not realising and exploring the possibility. The opening didn't last for long as a tray was slid into the room before the base of the door slammed back down and the sound of two bolts slamming shut broke the silence.

"P-p-please......help me" she cried out to no avail as the sound of footsteps turning away and moving into the distance made her heart sink. She rushed back to the door and banged her fist against it as loud as she could but the footsteps continued moving downstairs and away until there was nothing but her tears returning.

She looked down at the tray and hesitated before picking it up and moving it onto the bed where she sat beside it. There was a small metal pot of coffee next to a cup that had already been poured, some milk, a knife and fork and a napkin. She lifted the metal cover to find a plate of food. Instinctively she knew it was her favourite breakfast, eggs Benedict, bacon, toast and mushrooms. She momentarily smiled to herself. It smelled wonderful and she suddenly felt famished but her fears wouldn't leave her side.

Much more curiously than her favourite breakfast was another thing on the tray, a small glass vase containing a single rose! It seemed very out of place and surreal if she were indeed some kind of prisoner. She was certainly being held against her will at the very least. Things then took a turn of confusion as she noticed the vase was standing on top of a small note. She took it out and opened it.

"My Darling Charlotte, forgive me. All will be well soon, when you are feeling yourself again. I love you. Simon"

She frowned to herself, more confusion piled up in her mind. Charlotte, was that her name? She tried to think, think hard but she couldn't recall it, her mind wasn't jogged in the slightest and, more to the point, who the hell was Simon? Clearly there was a serious message there. Darling? I love you? Feeling yourself again? Her now fragile mind was in tatters trying to figure out who she was and what was going on.

She looked at the food and coffee long and hard. She was frightened, anxious, nervous and extremely wary of touching the food but she was also very hungry. It crossed her mind that she didn't know how long she was going to be there or where her next meal was coming from and, despite the note, there had been no light shed upon her situation. Tentatively she sampled the food, it tasted wonderful. She sipped the coffee which was perfect. She pondered the note as she ate and, before she knew it, she had finished her breakfast.

She read the note over and over again, trying to picture or recall somebody, anybody calling her Charlotte but she couldn't. She even tried to convince herself that that was indeed her name but it didn't fit in her mind. She was tired, worn out, in fact, which she put down to her emotions running wild and mental exhaustion. Her eyes became heavy as did her limbs and she moved the tray onto the floor so she could lie down. A wave of relaxation washed over her and she didn't hear the footsteps return up the stairs and along the landing. They stopped again outside the door and a gentle knock upon it caught her attention.

"H-h-hello...i-is someone.....th-theeeere" she slurred, barely able to lift her head from the pillow.

She looked at the door though it had become hazy and blurred and now she heard a key in the lock. It turned and then a heavy bolt slid back. She managed to lift her head but it ached and she became dizzy. The door opened slowly and she tried so hard to focus at the large shadow of what seemed to be a man stood in the open doorway. She tried to make out who it was but couldn't. The ache in her head made her relax back down and she tried to speak but could only slur and mumble. Inwardly she cursed the food which must have been drugged, she cursed herself for eating it but she couldn't curse the man now standing over her, and making his way to the bed, as she slipped into unconsciousness.

Chapter 3

She woke again to daylight penetrating the room through the weave of the curtains, she had no idea how long she had slept and had no idea what time of day it was as there were no clocks in the room. She instinctively looked at her wrist, a clear indication that she would normally wear a wristwatch, not that she could remember what hers looked like but, either way, that had been removed.

In the now, vaguely, familiar room, she felt just as she had done the last time she awoke, not that she knew how long ago that was. It could have been earlier that day, yesterday or the week before. The truth of the matter was that she had been out for just under twenty four hours. She lifted her head but regretted it almost immediately, as a minimal dull throb that she had barely noticed suddenly became an intense screaming pain causing her to yelp and lift her hands to her forehead to rub and soothe her skull.

She slumped back down onto the soft pillows and closed her eyes, tears pricking at them from pain and the realisation creeping back to her of her situation. She moaned to herself a little and sobbed. She was about to scream out for her freedom when she heard a bolt slide on the door. The flap at the bottom of the door lifted again and a small tray was slid in before being closed again and bolted. She had resisted the urge to yell, curse or plead with her captor. She was more shocked and surprised; she hadn't heard him coming up the stairs so did that mean he was waiting for her to wake up? Suddenly she felt a shiver at the creepiness of that scenario.

She gazed over at the tray; it held another pot of coffee by the look of it plus a small glass of water and a little saucer with something on it. She waited a few moments, more in hope than expectation that he had left; after all she hadn't heard him approach. She slid off the bed and crawled over to the tray, avoiding standing as she expected the pain in her head to increase again. Gradually she became aware that she was not naked but wearing a nightdress. It was beautiful, pale white lace and satin, the sort of thing she'd seen in old movies and always said she wanted. She couldn't even remember knowing that the last time she was awake and found some small semblance of solace in the possibility of her returning memory. Yet there was then the thought that somebody, he, had undressed her from the jeans and sweatshirt she had been wearing and put on her the nightdress! She felt more confused and more violated than ever but still could not remember who he was or she was for that matter, let alone where she was or why.

She examined the tray and then held her breath, just in case she could hear anything of her captor on the other side of the door. The coffee smelled good and she somewhat reluctantly and understandably was hesitant before pouring it. The saucers' contents were actually two painkillers. They were still in their foil covered blister packaging but had been neatly cut off from a longer strip of drugs. She could clearly read on the foil what the drugs were but more keenly she examined them just in case they had been tampered with. She knew the food had been drugged. She had faint recollections coming back to hear of a woozy feeling shortly after eating it. Then her heart pounded at the memory of the shadowy figure entering the room and looking at her before the blackness set in.

She noticed another note tucked under the saucer and took it out, unfolded it and read out loud

"Just to help you with your headache. I love you. Simon"

There were two little kisses marked on the note too. She didn't know what to feel: anger at her imprisonment, frustration at her memory loss, hope that someone loved her, resentment that whoever loved her had her locked away and again more frustration that she didn't know who the fuck it was!

The headache grew worse It felt like a small animal trying to burrow its' way out of her skull. Against her better judgement, she took the pills and swallowed them down with the water before climbing back in bed with a cup of coffee. She took a sip of the coffee before setting it down on the bedside cabinet and curling back under the duvet. She knew she should be angrier and trying to escape but the pain in her head became more debilitating with each minute passed; the sensible thing was to wait.

She woke again, still in the room and it was much later. She wasn't sure what had caused her to wake up but she sat up and looked around the room. She noticed her headache had completely gone and, due to that, she felt much better in herself, despite still being someone's prisoner. She glanced over and noticed the tray with the painkillers had gone which reminded her of the coffee. She looked over and saw that that had gone too. Automatically she pulled the duvet up around her neck for protection and shot glances around the room. Someone had obviously been in the room. Him, no doubt.

Her eye was caught by the flickering flame of a single candle, in front of the window, sitting on a small table, which had been dressed elegantly with a lace cloth, napkin in a holder, cutlery and a wine glass. A bottle of red wine stood by the glass, uncorked and breathing. A silver cloche sat on one side of the table, a single chair awaiting her.

She climbed out of the bed and softly padded over to the table. The light was dimming and the candle light haze was soft and seductive. Another small note sat propped against the cloche, more like a place card from a wedding.

"Charlotte," adorned the card on the front. Flipping it open it simply read, "Enjoy the meal, my love. Simon."

She couldn't help but give a brief smile, despite herself, at the sentiment before frowning and tossing the card to the other side of the table. She lifted the cloche to reveal a glorious meal of what looked like a perfectly cooked steak, with rich sauce, onions and mushrooms. The smell rose to meet her nostrils as she stooped forwards and she immediately started to salivate at the deliciousness of the potential meal. Quickly she put the silver covering back over the food and stepped back. What was she thinking? He had drugged her the last time she eaten. Why would this be any different?

She sat on the edge of the bed, contemplating, but then went back to the door, on the off chance that she had been freed. Sadly, not. She screamed her frustration, her head falling back to let her anger flow free as she did. Just at that moment she heard a door slam downstairs and she became silent to listen carefully.

She heard footsteps on gravel and rushed over to the window. Pulling back the curtains she looked down and could see, between the iron bars, a figure in the gathering gloom of the evening. The man, it was definitely a man, stopped and turned. He looked up at the window and she could just about make out the whites of his teeth as he smiled and then waved sheepishly before getting in to the car parked outside on the driveway. She banged on the window in a vain attempt to get his attention, hoping for answers, pleading for help and her freedom, despite him being the one who was holding her. Sadly the car engine roared into life and he pulled away from the building leaving her utterly alone! Was she? She had no idea if there was anyone else in the house. She thought to cry for help again but who was to say if someone else was around who wouldn't have given her painkillers, cooked her divine looking meals, dressed her and left her sentimental notes?

She poured herself a glass of wine which, on sampling, was delicious; she sat at the table to ponder the endless questions spinning through her head. She felt like a prisoner but unlike any other prisoner she could imagine. Her hunger got the better of her and she lifted the cloche again. She picked up a fork and sampled the sauce which was everything she had hoped it was. She cut through the steak and it was rare, so rare, that it bled a beautiful contrasting red against the white of the plate. Instinct took over and she knew that that was just how she liked her steaks. She tucked into the meal and drank the wine. If she was a condemned prisoner and this was to be her last supper, then at least she would enjoy it and she did.

Chapter 4

As she ate the latest wonderful meal, she pondered her situation, initially with fear and trepidation but gradually more with resolution. She tried to come to terms with everything and slowly, ever so slowly her memory became clearer. The wine had a focusing effect on her mind, at least at the beginning. Occasionally she would shed a tear of frustration when things wouldn't slip into place as she wanted them to, like a jigsaw forming a picture but the odd shaped pieces wouldn't all fit into the places that she wanted them to.

She came to the conclusion and then the realisation that, in actual fact, her name was indeed Charlotte. Everything else seemed hazy in her mind but she was pleased with herself that some things were coming back to her. She tried to focus but the wine made her tired and so she crossed over to the bed and lay down for a while. She must have drifted off because she woke to the sound of a car door being slammed shut. She started awake and jumped off the bed and over to the window, throwing back the curtains to see if it was her captor's return. It was. However, before she could bang on the glass again as before she paused, as he went to the back of the car.

He opened the trunk and looked around, furtively it seemed, which was strange behaviour in itself, as there was no-one anywhere in sight, not even another building. In the now darkened night, he reached into the car and lifted something heavy out. He strained a little but lifted it out in both arms before struggling and eventually managing to shut the trunk with a thud. Light cast down from her window as she watched and he walked back to the house in the illumination. From the bundle he carried she saw quite clearly an arm slip out and hang. The arm seemed limp and lifeless. Charlotte suddenly felt cold and her stomach knotted. Was this man some kind of monster? Was it a corpse that he carried? Had he killed someone?

She gasped in horror at the dangling limb of what seemed from her vantage point to be a child. He couldn't have heard her but he looked up as he walked and smiled. Her mouth dropped open. He seemed so pleased with himself but she couldn't understand what on earth was happening. Fear and panic set in. She had to get out of the room and get out of that house as soon as possible.

She heard footsteps moving through the house below her. She heard bolts clearly being drawn back or forth, much like the heavy bolt on her door. She stayed as silent and still as possible as she listened closely to try to recognise any sounds that she could. Suddenly it became familiar to her and she knew that, whoever he was, he was going down into a cellar. It scared her to know this. She was confused as to just how she knew that but knew it she did. She could hear better than she thought she could, it was as if she had been listening to things from under water, or after a flight. Suddenly her hearing had popped back to her and she could hear incredibly well. What's more, she could smell things, simple things like the soaps in the bathroom on the other side of that door. She could smell the remainder of the few morsels left on her plate despite her having replaced the cloche. Somehow, she could smell something pungent; it was sweat, not just sweat, the perspiration of fear. She knew that she could tell the difference between the scent of someone sweating through fear or exhaustion or indeed high temperature.

There was no doubt in her mind that she knew it was the perspiration of someone, one at the very least, who were absolutely terrified, confused and fearing for their lives. Another thing that scared Charlotte even more was the source of the scent. The 'body' he had carried in was unconscious and would therefore not be in a state of fear. In Charlottes' mind now, there was, at the very least, one other potential victim downstairs. The cold she had felt now become almost paralyzing. She didn't know how she could suddenly smell and instinctively know all of this but the information was just there in her head, basic but natural to her and almost animalistic. She didn't know how or why, she just knew it all to be true

Days passed by, slowly, with tedium, and, gradually they became a week. Each day was the same it seemed. She awoke in the mid morning, which had started earlier but she felt she was sleeping later each day. A breakfast tray would arrive and it would be a delicious meal of some kind. After she had finished she would feel tired but that feeling seemed to dispel gradually with each day. If she were being drugged it seemed to either be having less effect as she became tolerant of it or the drug dosage was being reduced. But why?

After a short spell lying down or having a nap, she would pace the room, endlessly exploring cupboards and drawers but after a day or two she had seen everything there was to see. Yet still she would perform the same ritual though what she was looking for exactly she couldn't say. She only briefly and occasionally checked the door now to see if it was still locked; it always was yet the initial despair that would accompany her futile attempts started to dissipate as each day passed. She started to have the horrible feeling that she seemed more comfortable in her dwelling. What had felt like a cell was almost becoming her natural habitat.

Of course, she would have random outbursts of anger and frustration at what was still her confinement if not actual imprisonment. She would scream and shout and look vainly outside through the bars for a random passing stranger but always to no avail. She would punch and kick at the door, sometimes making her knuckles and feet bleed but there would never be a response. She would swear and curse and then throw items from the dressing table or her breakfast tray across the room but when still no response came she would eventually sob to herself as she picked everything up again. Then she would feel guilty if she had broken something possibly precious from the dressing table. Charlotte would sit quietly and ponder her situation after an outburst. In between sniffs and sobs she tried to put her unravelling life back together. Inevitably later, to calm herself, she would go into the bathroom and take a bath or shower, sometimes both separately just to kill time until her evening meal appeared.

She realised that either 'he', Simon, knew her routine or listened for her to go to the bathroom and start showering because, when she came out, her breakfast things had been replaced with a wonderful evening meal. She considered turning on the shower once she had noticed the pattern and then laying in wait for him but, for some reason known only to herself, she decided against it. Her mind was changing and she didn't know why. She was feeling more and more comfortable in her surroundings, almost as if that was the place she should be. The pieces of the broken jigsaw of her life were slowly but surely changing shape in order to slot into place where they should go.

One evening, while lay in the bath thinking about things and trying to find her lost pieces, she came to the realisation that she knew for sure that she didn't have any children. She couldn't be sure how this was such a definite feeling, maybe a lack of a maternal instinct that she had no pull towards a child or two that were missing her. Whatever that feeling was she knew it wasn't there and what's more she started to have thoughts about a man, a man in her life; possibly a husband or a boyfriend but almost surely a significant other, the only thing about that was, was that man Simon?

Since the initial time she saw him come back with a body, it happened again and it no longer seemed to be as frightening an occurrence as it had been. Naturally, the more she thought about this, the more it seemed to trouble her. Not only was she not yet 100% convinced he was actually her husband but she was gradually less horrified that he was either a kidnapper or killer. Why had all these things stopped leaving her petrified in her cell? What did he have planned for her? Was she to be a victim that he played and toyed with? A loving husband would surely not leave her locked in a room for days, let alone over a week, as she had been confined. Yet still she seemed more and more relaxed with everything until her mind began to spin back and forth between different scenarios and questions.

She felt changes within her, nothing physical, just internal.......mental. She was understanding of her situation and started to think to herself that it was all for the best, for her own sake. Her instincts had started to take over and she had known that her food was no longer drugged at all. She was continuing to sleep later into the day but that was the sleep that her body had needed despite not actually doing anything remotely strenuous during her days at all. Also, that led her to understand that Simon knew that as well. Why else was he no longer drugging her food with sedatives?

Most notably to Charlotte was the epiphany to her that soon, soon, she would be free again. Again, she could only put it down to her own instincts but she knew deep down that, in time, she would be free.

Chapter 5

By the middle of the third week of her somewhat pampered incarceration, Charlotte was settled. Not to say that she was enjoying her stay in confinement but she had come to terms with it. It felt as though for some reason it was necessary. Yet, when she did have her outbursts, they were no longer through frustration and fear. Now they were born of a vicious and violent rage, a rage to be free, to run, to be unbound and un-caged. It was primal and it was raw. She punched the bedroom door with such force that it buckled and very nearly gave way. She hadn't quite realised just how much damage she had done and turned away in anger only to smash the less sturdy bathroom door similarly and left a six inch hole in the middle of it.

Blood ran down her forearm and dripped off her fingertips but she scarcely noticed or, if she did, she was hardly concerned. Her breathing was deep and long as adrenalin raced through her veins, causing her heart to race and the blood to flow freely. She looked down and saw the staining on the carpet at her feet which only then made her look to where the blood was coming from. She had almost pulled the bathroom door off its' hinges in her frustration.

Charlotte went into the bathroom to wash the wound. She ran her arm under the cold water and the basin ran red with her blood. Splinters stuck out of her flesh and she picked them out with her fingernails. She noticed how long her nails had become and decided that she would need a manicure sooner rather than later, once she was free.

She had noticed that she was becoming more and more lethargic during the day and, therefore, was sleeping for most of it, apart from the odd bout of extreme violence and anger when she awoke. She looked at herself in the bathroom mirror and suddenly felt dirty, she had forgotten if she had bathed the day before or the day before that and now, due to the bleeding and adrenalin she was becoming frustrated with herself. She decided to take a long soak in the tub; maybe the warmth would soothe her to sleep and she would feel better for it.

She undressed in the bedroom as the tub filled with water and bubbles. Once she was naked she glanced up at herself in the dressing table mirror. In her first week or two of confinement, when she bathed or showered, she would always shave her legs and underarms as well as lightly shaving her most intimate area. But now it seemed as though it had been a long time since she stopped with her natural beauty regime, she didn't recall making a conscious decision not to shave but she must have done given the abundance of downy hair that now seemed to softly grow on her body. She stroked the hair and smiled to herself at the softness of it, it somehow felt to her much more feminine and sensual than shaving so decided to leave it natural. Charlotte went back into the bathroom and turned off the water once it was good and hot. She climbed in with an exclamation of breath at the heat, easing herself into the liquid embrace.

The warmth, as she had hoped, enveloped her and immediately calmed and soothed her aching muscles. She still had done nothing strenuous but her arm, legs and back all ached as if all the sinews had been drawn tight to breaking point. She soaked herself in the wet heat, the scents from the bath oils going to her head and almost overpowering her. She stroked her downy flesh, gently cupping water in her hand and pouring it over her, not wholly submerged body. She washed her breasts which were tender to the touch, nipples erect and aching for the attention of an absent lover. She slipped her hand down her stomach and was suddenly caught by her abdominal muscles, taut, firm and glistening in the lapping water. She was surprised herself and gazed down at her midriff before glancing to notice the gleam from her muscular yet still slender and feminine arms. She saw, for the first time, she had the body of an athlete.

Charlotte was pleased. She was thrilled and she was excited. This coupled with the water lapping at her body and between her legs caused her to feel aroused and she slid her hand between her thighs to probe at her most delicate folds. Her eyes fluttered at her own expert strokes and, due to her new found high level of sensitivity throughout her body, she began to orgasm. In very little time, she became breathless as her body arched out of the water with her head and neck holding her weight on the edge of the bath. Her toes curled and she gasped out loud as she brought herself to an intense climax.

She practically radiated in her orgasm afterglow. Still trembling she eased back down into the warmth of the water with a little smile playing on her lips. Her breathing eased back to normal as her pussy throbbed from her attentions and she gradually slipped into a gentle sleep.

She woke with a start, not initially realising what had happened but she hadn't been asleep for long, just a lazy nap after sex. She listened and heard the bedroom door bolt. She climbed out of the bath quickly and dripped her way into the bedroom. There was no-one there, clearly Simon had been in and left her meal as usual, he must've woken her from her slumbers.

Just a little disappointed that she had missed him, but, after all, she knew in her heart that she would soon be free anyway. Charlotte went back to the bathroom and retrieved a towel to dry herself off. On her return she didn't bother to get dressed. Who would see her after all? Also, she had recently felt constricted by the clothes themselves, not physically, because she wasn't gaining weight; if anything, she was becoming tauter and much more toned. She was feeling constricted and constrained by the normality and formality of wearing clothes. She preferred her natural state. She wanted to feel free. She wanted to feel alive but, most of all, she wanted to feel ....herself.

After she had dried off, she moved over to the table and lifted the cloche. As usual, she found a fabulous looking dish, chicken. It smelt phenomenal and she couldn't wait to tuck in. By the side of her plate there was a little bundle of papers, tied up with purple ribbon. She smiled as she picked them up and glanced at them. She mumbled her captors' name under her breath and smiled again, like a blushing schoolgirl who'd received a love letter from her secret crush.

Her mind had been continuing to assemble the broken puzzle of her life and imprisonment. The picture was becoming clearer. She had an overwhelming feeling now that Simon was indeed her husband. She couldn't quite remember why she was still locked away like a princess in a tower but she still felt that her freedom was close. Each day he had continued to leave a little note or card with her evening meal, sometimes with her breakfast too but, as she had been sleeping later and later, there had been less need for an early meal. She had been more than satisfied by now with a meal a day, especially a good hearty and delicious meal such as that which was before her eyes now.

She was excited by the bundle and she pulled the bow apart to reveal her gift. She sat at the table and spread out the folded papers and cards, most of which were actually photographs. She picked up her fork and started to eat, inhaling the wonderful scents of spices and herbs. As she ate, she gazed at the photos lay out before her. She picked up a folded piece of paper which read.

"My darling Charlotte, it won't be long now. I hope you aren't getting too upset with me and becoming too angry"

She smiled to herself as she read and then looked up at the bathroom door and the hole she had punched through it. She felt a little guilty but only in a playful way. She continued to smile as she read on.

"You will have your explanation soon, as always. I hope that you will understand, as always, and that you know that I only do this because I love you and can't bear to be without you. Always and forever, Simon. xx"

She frowned at that last section as that was the piece of her mentally short-changed jigsaw that she was struggling to fit into place. However, her smile returned with his sentiment and, as she looked over the photographs, she could see so many that were of the two of them together. The overwhelming themes of the pictures were of joy and happiness. They were both smiling and seemed genuinely happy; the two of them both seemed besotted by each other.

There were also a couple of candid, intimate photos that they had obviously taken of each other. Without being lurid they managed to capture the love and intimacy yet still show the primal sexuality of their relationship. Clearly their marriage was passionate and deep. She wondered how much of that was shown in the photographs or how much was her memory returning.

Her favourite picture, however, was one of their wedding day, very traditional, very beautiful, yet quite simple. Just the two of them looking at each other, seemingly not knowing the photo was being taken. Whether they knew it or not, it was a wonderful picture and it brought a tear to her eye and a lump to her throat. She held it to her bosom and swallowed back the tears. Tears of joy then brought the smile back to her lips.

Despite the deliciousness of the food, she spent a long time eating it as she continued to pause throughout the meal, savouring every mouthful as well as savouring every image. Once finished, she moved back over to the bed with a glass of wine which had, as usual, accompanied her meal. She settled down with the pictures, going over and over them, alternating from laughing to smiling and back again. For over an hour she flicked back and forth until she suddenly noticed a smell that she hadn't noticed before or thought she hadn't at least. She put the pictures down on the bed and climbed off to investigate.

She moved in the direction that the scent seemed to be coming from. Sniffing the air like an animal in the wild, she gently padded over towards the bathroom. She looked down as she hunted the smell and noticed the blood stain on the carpet. That caused her to look quickly at her arm. How could she have forgotten about that so easily? She remembered how badly it had bled earlier. There was a mild scar there but little else; she was amazed that such a small injury could've created so much bloodshed. Any kind of wound that she would've expected to see couldn't possibly have healed so quickly, could it?

She examined the blood stain but it didn't seem to be the source of the scent she could detect and so continued to gaze around the same area. Then she noticed another stained area. It looked older and it looked as though someone had tried to clean it up. Simon no doubt. She took a closer look, getting down on all fours to do so. She sniffed at it; she could smell blood, older blood that had been there for quite a long time. She could smell the detergent or some kind of cleaning product that had been used to get rid of the stain. He'd done a good job because she hadn't even noticed it before, during almost a month of confinement in the room. However now that her sense of smell was so heightened she felt she could detect it from a hundred paces. What's more, to her improved eyesight, she felt she could see it easily now she was aware of it.

She stayed on all fours and continued to sniff it out. Then she had an urge to test it to confirm its' source. Charlotte poked out her tongue and gently stroked at it with the tip. She brought her tongue back into her mouth and sat up straight as she pondered the taste, wrinkling her nose in disgust at the detergent before going back in for a second opinion. This time she lapped deeper for a more thorough taste. Sitting up again she nodded to herself, confirming what her first thought had been. That the blood was hers.

Almost like a connoisseur savouring a fine wine, she pondered the blood and the age of it. It was definitely hers but she was curious as to how long it had been there. She mulled it over and came to the conclusion that it was at the very least a year old, maybe two. That revelation also prompted the thought of just how long had she been there and what had happened to her before that would leave such a blood stain?

Chapter 6

A month had now almost passed and Charlotte had began getting very cranky, to put it mildly, in between spells of happiness. The cards and photographs continued to lighten her days. The self-belief that she would soon be free kept her going but when Charlotte had darker days then those days were ebony black.

Since waking in the early afternoon, her temper had slowly but surely built up to almost maddening levels and during the course of what was left of the day she practically destroyed the room. She sat now as the early evening dusk spread across the sky; she watched the sun dip behind the horizon from a seat in front of the barred window. She waited and enjoyed the last rays of the setting sun and waited a little longer as the sky darkened before turning back to the room.

She looked around, feeling a touch of guilt at the realisation that she had done all the damage. She could hardly believe that she was capable of such destruction but it had been all her. It had been a fierce rage coming from deep within her and let loose to cause carnage. The mirror was shattered; everything on the dressing table below had been smashed and thrown across the room. The furniture itself, old & heavy wooden pieces were all gouged and scratched deeply as if by a blade or some kind of wild animal. Surely not by a young woman?

The bedding had been pulled off the bed and practically shredded; a heap of ragged ribbons was all that remained. So too the clothes that had hung in the wardrobe: all dragged out, ripped and torn, some even looked like they had been chewed on! Everything was strewn around the room and mixed into more than one jumbled mess: knocked over and smashed furniture, broken ornaments and shattered glass.

In a moment of tranquillity and calm, as she gazed around feeling sorry for herself and wondering if she should make at least some effort to tidy the room, the bolt on the bottom of the door slid back. The flap lifted and in slid her dinner tray. She smiled and her eyes widened. She dashed over almost before the flap could close again and, without thinking, just picked up the tray and quickly but carefully took it over to the window. She placed it on the chair she had been sitting on and had to pick up the upturned table up and set it straight. One of the legs had been damaged but it would be serviceable for what she hoped would be her last meal in the room.

Uncovering the cloche she got exactly what she hoped for; yet another deliciously prepared and juicy steak meal. It was accompanied by a bottle of red wine and a glass, as well as a single rose in a thin vase. She sniffed the rose and glowed at the scent. She glowed from head to toe. What a difference from the crazed creature that less than an hour earlier was annihilating everything she could lay her hands on.

Charlotte settled down to the meal. It was as delicious as she expected, just like every meal she had been served in the room. The sedatives had stopped being administered to her food some while ago and she had stopped being cautious, which allowed her to enjoy her food as well as the wine which was amazing.

She finished her meal in quick time. She had tried to savour every mouthful but couldn't help herself from devouring it rapidly. She was sitting contentedly back in her chair with a satisfied grin on her face, sipping the wine when, unexpectedly, the bolt to her door slid back. She paused and turned as her heart raced. When the flap opened again and something was slid into the room on a small silver tray.

The flap was closed and re-bolted. Charlotte waited, eager but cautious to see if anything else would happen. Footsteps walked away from her room and back down the stairs. She got up from her seat and went over to the door; there on the tray at her feet was a notebook. She picked it up and took it back over to the table. She knew as soon as she picked it up that it was very important that she read it. It wasn't quite a flashback or déjà vu but she instinctively knew its importance.

Her eyes were starting to hurt with the main bedroom light on in the room and a few days earlier, while routinely exploring the drawers and cupboards, she had found a few purple candles and a box of matches. She poured the last of the wine into her glass, almost filling it and then jammed one of the candles into the bottle firmly before lighting it. She turned the main light off and sat in the now gathering gloom of the night to read the notebook by candlelight, as she sipped her wine.

"My Darling Charlotte," it began, causing her to beam from ear to ear. Her heart began to race; she settled down and read on.

"I know that you are reading this after a long and confusing few weeks and you have been searching for answers to practically everything. I know that you feel this way because you told me how you felt the last time you were in this position. This has been going on for longer than I can remember by the time you read this book. At the time I write, it has been almost two years but I will be continuing this ritual for as long as is necessary. You may be reading this for only the second time, maybe the fortieth or hundredth, I can't be sure at this moment. But know this, my angel, that I will always be here for you no matter what happens. You told me after your last release that it was the not knowing upon release that was frustrating, let alone all the frustrations that came with the loss of memory. I told you that I would write things down for you and give it to you the night before your release.

I could give it to you sooner, of course, but with your mind being fragile and your emotional turmoil, I worry that it may do more harm than good. That is why I deliver it the night before, when your mind is closer to 'normal'.

So, here we are again, my love. Where to begin? At the beginning someone once said is the best place to start so that is where I shall begin.

Your full name is Charlotte Richards. You were born on the 29th May 1978 your original surname was Anscombe but then, thankfully for me, we met and we were married on your 30th birthday in 2008. I could go on endlessly about where you were born, where you grew up and your childhood and schooling etc etc but when I've told you about these things previously you always said such things were irrelevant to you now. That seems harsh and I know they aren't irrelevant details, but, as you have difficulty in retaining too much information and there is little you remember anyway from that long ago, it seemed to you a waste to clog up your mind with things that have little meaning for you at this point in time.

I am your only family left at this point too so it's not as if there are people that you are ignoring. Given our current situation, the less people we have contact with, the better in all reality! I have kept a lot of your family albums and sentimental things from your childhood but I keep them safely stored away, hopefully one day our situation will change and I can get them all out for you. It would be wonderful to sit together and go through everything with you. The idea of watching your beautiful face radiate with pleasure as your earlier memories come flooding back would make me unbelievably happy. Hopefully, you can find some consolation in the knowledge that from our conversations when we were together at the beginning, you said you had a very happy childhood with your wonderful family.

You used to work in a veterinary surgery; you were always a sucker for animals, especially dogs. You loved that job but unfortunately had to give it all up after the attack. I worked as a lawyer but, again, after the attack I had to quit my job in order to take of you. However, as much as I loved my job, I love you far, far more and I always have to reassure you that it isn't a burden to look after you."

Charlotte read on. Details followed of the attack, what actually had happened as far as Simon could recall, coupled with his best guesses of what had happened. He had seen the incident from a distance and had run to her aid, almost, but not quite, too late. As devastated as he had been, he was just glad that she was still alive....though barely. He told her how he had taken her to the nearest hospital where they hadn't held out much hope for her survival. Upon hearing their assessment he had discharged Charlotte from their care, against their advice of course. He hadn't been able to accept the loss of her and dedicated himself to nursing her back to health and successfully too....... but she had continued to suffer severe side effects from the attack.

Over time they had both come to live with their new reality. He wrote about how he still had faith that one day they would be free of this 'curse' but until that day came and however long until it did, he would be there for her. He would be there 'Forever to take care and watch over her, to protect and to love her, as long as they both shall live.'

Charlotte couldn't help but wipe away spent tears as her heart swelled with joy and love. Her heart had sank and her stomach had almost turned when brief memories came back to her of the attack that had completely devastated both their lives, hers most significantly. Now the blanks had been filled to her memory jigsaw, she started to glow at the thought of her imprisonment coming to an end again.

She remembered it wouldn't last for too long and she knew that she had to make the most of her freedom as she had done on each previous occasion. It wasn't much of a life but it was there to be relished, taken by the scruff of the neck and wrung until every last drop was extracted. She was raring to go; she knew she would sleep long and deep that night, her last night in captivity as it were. She knew that she would sleep undisturbed through most of the day. She vaguely remembered Christmas Eve as a child, not being able to sleep through excitement of the following day. She had a similar excitement now but she knew that that was as far as the similarity went because she knew her body these days would make her sleep. She slept in preparation of what was to come.

Chapter 7

Charlotte woke the next day, not as the sun was rising but as it was disappearing into dusk. Her instincts kicked in virtually as soon as she opened her eyes. Tonight was the night, the night she had been waiting for. She smiled a lascivious smile to herself as she stretched her slumbers out of her suddenly aching bones and joints. She felt strange, but now, thanks to Simon's written words she knew what was happening or about to happen.

She climbed off the bed and paced the room, not quite sure what to do next. As the darkness was falling outside, her anticipation was rising, as was her heart beat. She felt like a coiled spring, taut and tight. She caught a glimpse of herself in the dressing table mirror. She paused to admire herself: Athletic, toned, almost muscular in certain parts of her body; her legs arms and abdomen, in particular now, had a striking definition to them. She loved the way she looked, strong and extremely feminine. The downy hair on her body which she had started to notice just a week or so earlier had now thickened slightly to a soft luxurious texture. She felt amazing and looked amazing.

She didn't realise how long she had been admiring her new look but the sun had gone completely by the time she had noticed. She could detect a commotion in the house, more than detect it though, she could hear it. She could hear specific voices, yet those voices weren't being raised. The only one she could be sure to know was that of Simon, her love. The others, at least two, maybe more, she couldn't decipher and she wasn't sure if she'd ever known them.

Simon was talking to them. Initially he had been sympathetic and they had cried and begged him. Gradually his patience had worn thin and he had become colder, distancing himself from them as best as he could. Then the other people had become angry, mainly through fear and panic but their fear became a scent and it gradually permeated up to Charlotte where she paced the room, ever more eager to be free again.

Time passed but it seemed to drag ever more slowly. She alternated between bouts of anger, shouting and snarling, then erupting into violence by way of throwing objects around the room and smashing and punching whatever was closest to hand. It was dark in the room. No lights or candles now as she could see as clearly as if she were wearing night-vision binoculars. In between storms of rage she would talk herself down, calming herself to be rational as it would only be a matter of time. She literally talked to herself as if two warring sisters were arguing in the darkness, even the calming and then the snarling 'sisters' seemed to have different voices.

Eventually she froze on the spot as she heard footsteps coming up the old oak staircase. She already instinctively knew that it was Simon. Her stomach flipped with anticipation and excitement and that lascivious smile played across her lips, the devil within her made her eyes flare in the darkness.

Her heart continued to race as he paused outside her door. Then it almost skipped a beat as she heard him pull back the bolt with a loud thud. It was a magical sound to Charlotte and her heart now almost pounded out of her chest. The door was pushed open halfway and she could see the dimly lit landing and in that dim light she saw his silhouette, his arm withdrawing from the action of pushing open the door. Tentatively she took a step towards the doorway and he leaned forward to push the door further back to give her full access and the invitation to step out.

Charlotte accepted the unspoken invite and took a couple more steps to be on the threshold of the landing. She gazed up at him, still in the half light and standing back. He stepped forward with her eyes on him and he smiled. It seemed to be a smile of relief, coupled as it was with a light gasp, his white teeth standing out in the gloom. He held out his hand to her and slowly, almost sheepishly, she lifted her hand and put it in his. He gripped her hand tightly but lovingly, instantly making her feel safe and relaxed. Simon stepped to the top of the stairs, slowly leading her behind him and she followed. Her turned back to look at her and smiled once again before stopping and leaning forwards, kissing her on the lips tenderly. She couldn't help but throw her arms around him and kiss him more urgently back. He responded in kind and they stood in a deeply passionate embrace of kisses and love, longing and desire.

Their passions were aroused and frantically they pawed at each other, she was still naked and she tried to get Simon into the same state as quickly as possible but he reluctantly held back. As much as he wanted her there and then, there was something else to be done first. He had been through this scenario many times with Charlotte and although her memory had returned, she was still learning how things needed to be done. Thankfully he would guide her to the next stage and then she would be renewed and her primal animal instincts would take over completely.

They both regained their composure as they parted though their hot breath on each other made it intensely difficult. Simon took her hand again and led her down the stairs; everything started to come back to her immediately. It was as if a thick fog had cleared and now she saw everything with a great clarity. She knew that this was indeed their home; she knew that they had lived here together for years; she knew where the living room, dining room and kitchen all were in relation to the bottom of the stairs as they arrived there. Each step gave her more confidence and now she was feeling that loving embrace of being in her own home. So different from a month ago when she awoke in a room she didn't know, surrounded by 'another woman's things'.

Simon continued to lead though she knew exactly where they were and by her rediscovered instincts knew exactly where they were going. She could smell where they were going; she was drawn to her location. As they walked they gazed at each other lovingly and longingly. Anticipation was so thick it could be cut with a knife. They passed the living room door and the dining room door, both of which were closed as was the kitchen door; she knew what was behind each one. The front door had already been passed and a thick blackout curtain was draped and closed behind it, also covering the small glass panels either side of the door to give total privacy. The house was very isolated but Simon had always kept the world outside as far from encroachment as possible. It was impossible to tell from there at that point whether it was day or night but Charlotte tingled with the night as if it were running electrically through her veins.

The final closed door was no mystery to Charlotte. If her heart could have raced more, it would have done so. They both stood at the doorway and turned to each other with a gleeful smile.

"Are you ready darlin?" He asked

"Absofuckinlutely," she grinned

"I love you," he smiled back at her

"I love you too."

Simon leaned forward, turned the door handle and pushed back the basement door. Charlotte gasped as a scent wafted up the stairs from the cellar; it was a scent of fear, terror and most of all tears. She breathed it into her, she let it fill her and, if she could've bottled, it she would have drunk it. It made her tingle like nothing before. The small hairs on her body bristled, her pupils dilated, it aroused her sexually and most of all it made her salivate. She swallowed hard to control herself. Simon watched all of it and drank it in, Charlotte was incredibly beautiful but to him she was never more beautiful than she was at that moment. Initially, this had been hard to deal with but he had learned to live with it. In fact, as hard as their lives had become, he had learned to adore parts of it, this part in particular.

Simon moved forward first and took the first two steps down before looking back to watch her follow him. He reached the foot of the stairs and flicked on a light switch. Two small bulbs dangling from the ceiling sparked into life, one at either end of the long dark cellar. From pitch black there was at least some illumination, though Charlotte needed little and Simon knew the musty old room all too well. Once the lights had been switched on there had come a gasp, or more than one to be precise. Hidden in the darkness there were now murmurs, sniffing and snivelling echoed through the damp and cold.

Charlotte joined him where he waited at the foot of the stairs and he held up his hand to her. She took it and they walked slowly into the darkened void, as if they were walking onto a dance floor to waltz. He stared ahead with anticipation as he thought of what was to come and glanced to his naked feral beauty by his side with a mixture of pride, love and extreme lust.

The cellar itself was a lot bigger than it had originally been. Simon had dug out from under the house so that its footprint was now considerably wider on one side than that of the house. This had enabled him to put a window in, more fittingly a large reinforced skylight for that was all that could be seen through it from below. Anyone above would just see the dark recesses of the cellars' floor and unable to make out what else, or more importantly who else was in there.

He turned to smile at her again and she knew what to do. She left his hand in mid air as she glided over to the skylight. He watched her walk, the rhythmic motion of her ass and the taut muscles in her legs as she moved athletically and gracefully over to her position. As she walked she glanced to her left. Many gasps and whimpers issued forth from the darkness and a few sobs as she looked into the cage. She smiled at them with evil intent, the braver shouted abuse at her, others begged for help but those begs would soon be for mercy. The shouts would soon be turned to screams as she reached her position under the skylight.

Chapter 8

Simon followed dutifully behind her. Slowly he had walked to take in the sight of his wife. He too glanced with disdain at the poor souls he had imprisoned in his cage as he passed. There were seven or eight, he couldn't remember exactly. There were men, women and children, all of them meat for the beast. They were there for the greater good, they were there for her and she needed their sacrifice even if it wasn't freely given. One reason for their horror and dismay was the separate area by the side of their dungeon. There callously, he had placed the leftovers, the remains from the meals of fine steak that she had predominantly been eating for the last month. Carcasses and odd bones in a sizable pile, a reminder of the horrors they would soon be facing. If someone were to take the trouble, they would probably be able to build three or four complete skeletons out of the remains. Now they were just left in a rotting heap of unwanted meat and bone, incomplete human jigsaws.

He reached his wife's side and glanced at her again The two looked into each other's eyes with love and passion, both knowing what was to come. Simultaneously, they lent in to each other and kissed tenderly. As they parted their lips and opened their eyes, they smiled again while Simon reached back behind him to the wall where a rope hung down, tied off at the wall. He undid the rope which was attached to a simple blackout blind he had installed to cover the skylight now directly above Charlottes head. It all seemed very dramatic and they both revelled in the theatre of the moment.

"Ready?" He whispered to her. She simply nodded, with a mischievous grin.

Simon reached back with his free hand to a second light switch. He flicked the switch and for a few moments the room was in utter darkness.

The inhabitants of the caged yelped with fear, not only in the dark now as before, but this time the monsters were in that blackened hole with them. Simon pulled the rope, slowly drawing the blind up, uncovering the large window in the ceiling. The pitch darkness was suddenly filled in that one corner of the cellar with an amazing contrast as the moonlight flooded in, the FULL moonlight. It was almost blinding against the black. Simon had gone to great lengths to position the skylight for the maximum effect, to let the moon have its' way with Charlotte, filling her with all of its' silvered glory.

She stood for a moment, face upturned to the sky, as she drank the beauty in while the moon drank her beauty in also. As the light bathed her in all its' glory, she looked to be made of highly polished chrome against the black of the room, she practically glowed. Then the change began. It was as if the moon had filled every vein within her and the overflow continued and spilled out of her in diabolical form.

She jerked backwards, her spine arching rigidly, her arms reached out and her legs tightened, trying to stay upright against an almighty force within her. Her knees buckled against that unseen force and she fell to the ground. Automatically her hands reached out to stop herself falling face first into the dirt. Now she was on all fours, panting for breath as her heart raced. Her back arched again and her vertebrae ground against each other. Popping noises could clearly be heard, echoing through the black chamber and turned the stomachs of those in the cage. Simon stood stock still, eyes wide through morbid fascination as they always were at this point in proceedings. He smiled gleefully, not at his wife's pain but at what was to come and how close it all was. All eyes, in fact, were focused on Charlotte. Simon though he had seen this scene numerous times before was mesmerised. The prisoners were aghast but out of their own similar morbid fascination and fear not one could turn their vision aside.

A low rumble, seemingly from deep within her, gradually built and built as it worked its' way through Charlotte and became a guttural growl as her internal organs shifted to fill a longer narrower cavity. There came more sounds of crunching and scraping as bone ground against bone as her limbs stretched and reformed. Her fingers dug into the dirt as she tried to stay upright; her hands bled as they gripped at little. Worse was to come, as the bones in her hands and feet now also stretched. Once finely manicured nails on fingers and toes developed and morphed into thick coarse claws, her digits stretching in all directions to accommodate them.

The downy hair that she had grown so fond of recently, thickened greatly; it became darker and heavy across all of her body. Not quite covering every inch like an animal, she managed to retain at least some semblance of humanity in her appearance but not too much.

The gasps with each new change continued to mix with sounds of weeping from the cage. There was a fear of course and outright terror but there was also a sense of awe at the change taking place. Hearts were racing throughout the cellar, from within the cage, from Simon through exhilaration but none more so than that of Charlotte whose metamorphosis was almost complete.

Simon watched transfixed and, as if to give him his own personal finale Charlotte jerked her head up to face him directly. Suddenly her cheek bones cracked, then her lower jaw the same. Her face narrowed slightly before stretching out from her skull, not long enough to be a snout but long enough to be less than human. The hair on her head grow longer and thicker and her brow also thickened above her eyes while her nose flattened slightly, flaring her nostrils. She panted at the exhausting pain her body was undergoing which also gave her a monstrous look as her whole body shook in spasms with the effort. Again, she looked up from where she crouched in the dirt. She looked right into his eyes, just as hers instantly changed to a glowing amber.

That was the signal that it was all over; the change of her eyes, completion. She settled and caught control of her breathing, softly panting to herself as she took in the change. She looked up over her shoulder at the sky and the low growl returned as she gathered her breath before letting out an almighty howl at the moon, a howl that would awaken the dead. A scream gave out from the cage of a young woman crying hysterically at the realisation, if any had been needed, of just what was about to happen.

Simon tentatively walked away from Charlotte. It had been this way for a long time now, yet he was still cautious as he backed away, always facing her for fear her mood might change and her savagery be brought to bear on him. He reached the cage and Charlotte turned to watch him. He took out his keys and she started to move, at first on all fours, towards where he stood at the cage door. Once she was close enough he unlocked the cage. More shouts and screams came from the inhabitants, now begging for their lives. He pulled back the cage door and now far from wanting release his prisoners backed away into the relative sanctuary of their steel prison.

He pulled back the door fully. There was nowhere for them to go. The cage door and Simon were at one side and the only escape route. The open space on the other side was where Charlotte now stood; to make matters worse she lifted herself up to her full height on her back legs. She towered down over them as the small group cowered backwards, holding and hugging each other for some sort of comfort. Simon watched her with awe and reverence as she was almost taunting her prey. She stepped forwards and then again into the cage as they huddled farther and farther against the back wall before she stopped. Almost for effect she opened her jaws wide as she glared down on them, her jaw cracking as if opening for the first time. Her teeth were elongated and razor sharp, bleeding from the gums where the teeth had stretched, torn and pushed through. Saliva dripped from her over long fangs as they glistened in the over spill of moonlight seeping its' way from the skylight. Another scream was heard from an unseen face hidden at the back of the cluster and that seemed to be Charlottes cue, as her body momentarily pulled back to tighten before lurching forward as she pounced on all her victims at once.

It was a massacre, a bloodbath. Simon pushed the cage door forward but no one was ever going to escape, they didn't stand a chance. Blood spilled and soaked into the dirt floor causing thickened red/black mud. Gore and more blood spattered the walls as she devoured her prey. Screams were shrill and last words muttered as the dying prayed to a helpless God to save them. Claws ripped through the air before ripping through throats and flesh. Skin tore like tissue paper, bones snapped as limbs were torn from sockets and crushed. Skulls cracked against the back wall and bars of the cage.

Before too long it was all over. Charlotte stood in a mess of body parts, flesh and blood. Her fur was matted from head to toe, encrusted with drying blood and tissue. Small chunks of meat fell from her claws and teeth as she stood panting with exhaustion and exhilaration. Then she looked at Simon and despite the mess of other people dripping from her jaws, she managed to smile. A bizarre sight of love and lust rippled through them both.

Chapter 9

Simon reached out his hand to her and she took hold of it, in a surprisingly gentle manner considering the monster that she had become. He led her from the cage and back to the stairs. Her breathing slowed and she started to shape shift again, gradually, as she walked. Charlotte wouldn't change back completely in such a short time but she willed herself to at least return partly; that was the best she could do. She felt pain but such was her adrenalin rush after her spree of carnage and death that she didn't feel her body adjusting anywhere near as badly as the initial change at a full moon.

A genuine 100% full moon only lasts a couple of hours and this had been the peak time, the time for her slaughter. Simon had known it. He'd studied the lunar cycle in great detail for the right conditions to maximise her transformation. In his thinking it would be better for her to be pacing the room, undergoing small changes and temper surges as well as emotional turmoil. That way full reign could be given to her undiluted eruption as the beast, rather than gradual change in the lead up to the fullest of moons. He had tried to give her the build up to the full moon previously but that had resulted in mild transformation which had simply upset Charlotte; the full monster within on the other hand was far more exhilarating for them both.

They went upstairs to their bathroom, not the one adjacent to her 'cell' but to their own master suite bedroom and bathroom on the top floor of the house. She was calming more now, part animal, part woman. He switched on the shower and led her in by the hand. As she stood under the falling water he undressed. Watching her as he did so inflamed him. He took a few moments to watch her stand, water gushing down and giving her remaining fur a sleek almost silken look. Her teeth had receded for the most part but remained sharp like sheathed weapons. The reduction in her small snout allowed her lips to return to their usual look. Her claws too had reduced in size but remained to an extent. All in all, she looked more hybrid, feminine yet wild, taller than her normal height, much stronger but crucially her mind was more like her old self if not her complete physical appearance.

Simon stepped into the shower tentatively and she stared at him intently. He was always aware at that stage that she was still part animal and could rip him to pieces at any given time; that had become part of the attraction, the thrill of the danger. He bathed her as she stood still under the shower, softly stroking the water on her body, cleaning the gore from her fur. Slowly and very careful he closed in and kissed her. She responded passionately, thankfully. Their tongues collided and he felt the sharpness of her teeth like little daggers. When first this had happened it had scared him but now it just added to the thrill.

Their hands explored each other thoroughly; their bodies becoming slick and slippery with a combination of water, soap and blood. Simon opened his eyes briefly to see the redness of the shower floor. It looked as if it had been raining blood and it swirled around the drain. Clumps of flesh and gristle gathered, mixed with hair from Charlottes' victims as well as some of her own that had loosened during her partial change back. He would clean all that mess away later.

Once they both felt they were ready, they stepped out of the shower. Simon grabbed two towels and used the first to dry her off at least partially before she stepped to one side and shook herself dry like a wolf caught in the rain. He smiled to himself as he towelled himself dry; clothes were unnecessary now as they then made their way back into the bedroom.

Once in the bedroom they immediately fell into each other and onto the bed. They continued to explore each other with hands, lips and tongues. Every inch was covered by both of them and the penetration was as intense as it could ever have been; the intimacy which comes from a deep longing, lovers that have been parted and yet it wasn't making love. It was far more primal than that. It was basic, it was animalistic, she was the beast but they were both animals in the way that they satisfied each other and themselves. They rutted, they fucked. It was hard and at times it was harsh but it was exhilarating and powerful. It didn't last long, it was too intense for both of them to last too long before they were sated.

Afterwards, they lay in each others' arms in their post coital glow. A scent of the wild permeated the room; the heat from between them gave Simon sweat on his skin and Charlotte damp fur, their own scents mingled to an intoxicating cocktail.

He looked at her and then gazed down at his body, from experience he knew what to expect. The glow was subsiding and the numbness which had enveloped his body now gave way to stinging sensations. He saw cuts and grazes, some minor scratches and some which had drawn blood. Bruises were starting to show as was a general redness all over his skin. He revelled in the pain. It had been inflicted by Charlotte and so it was all worthwhile.

She kissed him and turned. Sliding off the bed, she got to her feet and looked down at him as she gave a brief smile. She looked over the wounds that she had inflicted and a pang of guilt crossed her face. He winked at her and she knew that he understood completely. No-one else would but Simon did and always will. She bent to a wound on his thigh that was bleeding and licked the seeping blood away. She licked her lips as she rose back to her full height and giggled to herself. It was an almost girlish giggle, yet not quite human which would explain her completely.

He stood too and took her hand, leading her out of the room, they both had a touch of sadness about them but they both knew that it was for the best, as always. He led her by the hand back down the stairs. They arrived at the front door and he opened it to the night. They looked at each other, deep into each other's eyes. So much love and longing. They knew it was only temporary but they both knew it was what she had to do. It was her nature now and that could not and should not be denied. They embraced tightly, pulled back and kissed each other passionately; no words were needed as they both understood.

Charlotte stepped out into the night and the moon picked her out. She turned and smiled as her teeth started to elongate. She managed to give him one last smile before she became self conscious about herself.

He returned her smile and mouthed, "I love you."

She turned away and moved off into the silvered darkness. She moved quickly, her silhouette altering as she moved from the house and into the wide open of the night time. He watched her leave before returning to the house alone.

Simon smiled to himself; joy at what they had just experienced together but it was a smile tinged with sadness that she had gone. He knew she would be back. She always came back. It would be three days that the moon was full enough to be classed as a full moon and that would be the time that it would have sway over her, her lunar lover. It was a lover that he could tolerate her having, because, ultimately she would always remain his wife, his Charlotte. Their love was stronger even than that silver pull in the darkness. He had three days alone now. He didn't feel alone when she was in the house normally because, though locked away, she was still there in some way and he would still be preparing food or fixing things for her or even hunting for victims for her and that took real love.

Simon walked back upstairs. He saw the mess in the shower drain, all the blood stains on the towels and bedclothes. He walked into her other room, her 'prison' and looked at the state of it. What a mess: smashed furniture, torn bedding, scratched and gouged surfaces and a shattered bathroom door. He smiled to himself again. He would have three days to get the house ship shape and back together. He would have three days until she returned; she would return he knew. She always did and when she did, he would be ready.

He would wait until she slept after her exhaustions. He would cannulate her (and bandage it to her wrist so she didn't pull at it), to sedate her and put her back to bed. Of course, she would wake with no recollection of what had happened, aided by a side effect of the sedative that would gradually wear off after a few days. Then he would be counting down until they were fully together again. Her memory would slowly return and her confusion would lift. Clearly this had been a particularly bad few weeks for her and he hoped her condition wasn't becoming worse. At some point, he thought, we might have to move. People were going to start looking into all these unsolved disappearances. He couldn't have strangers looking at them or their property, there were enough dead bodies around that he had buried, which reminded him to clean up the cellar before the next inhabitants. Still, he had three days to do that.

Yes, she would be back and then the cycle and ritual would start all over again for the month, and the month after that, and the month after that and.......for as long as they both shall live.

REFLECTIONS IN A
COLD DARK LAKE

Chapter 1

It was early November and his breath plumed out in front of him as Charles stood at the edge of the lake, bubbles of air flowing to the surface, popping gently. He watched the scene until the last of the bubbles dissipated to nothing. The ripples, too, gradually faded away as his act of violence ebbed with them. The weighting of her body would mean she would never be found - certainly not out here on his land and most definitely not in his lifetime. He would make damn sure of that. After he was dead and gone? Well, who cared?

As dawn began to break, birds awoke and started to sing their morning chorus, causing him to look up at the trees on the opposite side of the lake. Though it was a wintery scene, it was going to be a glorious day; bright and clear, yet crisp, fresh and frosty under foot. He smiled to himself at the beauty of sight and sound on his wonderful property as the sun rose in the distance, brightening the sky with a pale, rosy hue. The birds seemed to appreciate it and so did he – it had been a big reason why he had bought this place, and for so much money, although knowing how to make a deal certainly helped with that. For seclusion and privacy, for such a vista and inner peace, he would always say, "Fuck the expense." Of course, that was easy to say when you had as much money as Charles Carlton.

He took in a deep breath through his nose, as if inhaling the whole scene, his smile growing wider. It was such a beautiful sight. It was fresh, yet stark in the current season, though wonderful and luscious in the summer. It was intoxicating and sweet to the senses. The horror and violence which had been committed there only in the last hour or so seemed a million miles away in space and time. No one would ever know the viciousness of his attack or the pain that she had felt. Her eyes had filled with tears of both agony and terror; the sheer disbelief of what was happening had left her unable to defend herself against him. Sadly for her, or maybe mercifully, it was over all too quickly.

Her blood had been cleaned up thoroughly, her body wrapped and weighted diligently. There would be no need for anyone to look for her and, should anyone try, there would be no way for her to be linked to him. She had been his dirty little secret for quite a time. Now she would remain so forever.

He looked back down at the still waters of the lake. The dark pool was like blackened glass now the ripples had ceased. He stared at his own reflection and smiled; his reflection smiled back at him safe in the knowledge that only the two of them had known just what had taken place earlier. Charles couldn't be sure, but he could've sworn that his reflection also winked at him. He laughed to himself at the very notion before turning away and heading back into the cabin - his luxury cabin in the woods. He would go back to bed before his long drive back to the city; he was tired and needed the sleep. He wouldn't give her another moment's thought because she would sleep too, the sleep of the dead as she rotted away at the bottom of his lake.

Once back inside his holiday home, Charles suddenly became aware of what seemed to him the stench of death emanating from him. He wrinkled his nose, frowned and immediately headed to his bathroom to get cleaned up. He dumped his clothes in a hamper and decided to shower thoroughly. He thought of what he had done and smiled to himself, partly at the brazenness of the act, but also of how easy it had felt to him. Once he was happy that he had showered sufficiently, he stepped out and dried himself.

The sun, though still low in the sky, shone through his bathroom window as the day started to dawn more significantly now. This, coupled with the shower he had taken, reinvigorated him; he no longer felt tired and in need of sleep - he'd had a couple of hours anyway after fucking the girl who was now at the bottom of his lake.

Instead, he decided to drive back into the city so he could get an early jump on the business of the day. Besides, it would take him a while to actually get there anyway. Around 8am he called his wife from the car; he had arrived in the city and it had already come alive with commuters and store owners opening up for the day.

"Hey, honey. Just calling to say I love you," he'd said. "Hope you slept ok last night."

He had told her the previous night that he had been stuck in an awful business meeting that was destined to go on until very late. He'd told her that he was too tired to drive the long distance home and would just get a hotel room; he knew how she would worry about such things. She had been disappointed that he wasn't going to be home, but would rather him take the safe option and do the sensible thing, though she did comment about how, recently, he had been staying late or overnight in the city more frequently. He'd brushed that aside by saying how he worked hard and late to give her the best things in life and the dream home that they'd craved, to which she begrudgingly agreed. She told him she loved him, too, and wished him a good day. He responded in kind, before hanging up and swearing at another driver who had cut him up.

Charles immediately stepped on the gas and chased down the "fucking idiot" in question and caught up with 'him'. He turned out to be a 'she'. He accelerated past while giving her the finger and swerved dangerously close to and in front of the woman, causing her to swerve herself. Thankfully, she was a good driver who managed to calmly control the situation and pull in to the side as he sped off.

Satisfied with himself, and his machismo restored, Charles looked back in the rear view mirror as the woman got out to quickly inspect her car for any damage he may have caused. He adjusted the mirror slightly and it briefly reflected down onto his backseat. There, lying on the seat was the girl from the lake. She was bound by ropes, covered in old sacks - as he had done - but her face was exposed, her flesh pale and wet. Bleeding scars oozed across her once pretty cheeks and her eyes blackened. Her hair was soaked and stuck in strands to her face, with the deep gash he had made on her hairline sickeningly exposed. Her mouth was swollen, split and bloody; her teeth were missing due to his brutality, yet she tried to mouth something to him through her tear-filled eyes.

He saw all of this in split seconds. His mouth fell agape, his heart raced and he struggled to stay on the road. He looked back to steer then behind him again, but he could no longer see her. He struggled more with the car, his mind frantic. He looked back again to see where she had gone, but that was one time too many because, when he looked back, he had strayed into oncoming traffic. He wrestled his vehicle off the road, but hit the kerb with force. His wheels at an angle that made the lead wheel buckle viciously on first contact.

He lurched forward, his airbag deploying, saving him from any significant damage. Shaken and dizzy, he clambered free of the bag and car, his jelly legs making him tumble and fall to the ground. Passers-by rushed over to see if he was alright, but he was more eager to check his back seat. He did so; there was no one and nothing there. Sirens filled the air as the emergency services quickly approached the scene. He checked the car again, as well wishers asked after him. His mind cleared and he began to get angry at their encroachment. He was about to tell them all to "fuck off", when he saw the uniforms rushing in and thought better of it.

The police officers quickly checked the scene, making sure there was no fuel leak, and therefore potential for explosion. They pushed everyone back. Charles was ushered to the ambulance that had arrived on scene; he protested at first, but eventually allowed the paramedics to examine him for injury and concussion. He sat on the tail of the ambulance as he was checked over, nervously watching the officers checking out his vehicle. Would they find anything? Was the girl really there? He shook himself mentally. Of course, she wasn't. She was safely at the bottom of his lake. He knew this to be true, but still he gave a sigh of relief when he heard the police saying that everything seemed ok - apart from the front wheel.

He was released by the paramedics and returned to his car. Just as he did so, he heard a car horn beep as it drove by; it was the woman with whom he'd had the earlier altercation. She drove past smirking, shaking her head at him. He seethed inside, before pulling out his phone from his jacket pocket. The police came over and asked him questions to which he gave short sharp answers in order to get out of there as quickly as possible. Once he had dealt with them, he called one of his employees, instructing them to get a tow truck to his location and send a car to pick him up immediately.

After getting off the phone, he looked down at the wheel and grunted his frustration. As he looked up again, he caught his reflection in the wing mirror. The reflection was smiling back at him, but he knew he wasn't smiling himself. He sharply looked around at the officers who were leaving the scene, then back at his image in the glass. Now the reflection's smile slipped. It turned to a frown and then a snarl, the snarl of a wounded beast it seemed to him. He involuntarily put his hand to his face, but the refection of his hand didn't appear in the mirror at all. Charles gasped in shock just as one of the officers turned around and asked if he was ok. He mumbled that he was and hesitantly backed away from his car.

Frantically he grabbed his phone again. He dialled to angrily berate his staff for keeping him waiting. He was told apologetically that the car and truck would be with him imminently and, before he could say another word, the two pulled up. The car arrived across the street and the truck in front of his own car ready to tow. He simply hung up and clenched his fists in anger as he walked around his wrecked car, being careful not to look at it, save he caught another glimpse of himself in the mirror or something in the back seat. He had no idea what or who he would see.

Chapter 2

Charles went to his office, but was distracted for most of the day. Though he had been pronounced physically fine - and indeed he felt fine in himself, his mind was everywhere but on his work. He pondered the accident itself - clearly it wasn't too serious or life threatening, but it could've been worse if another car had have hit him, or he hadn't been able to get the car off the road. He received much needed good news by late morning: the mechanics had phoned him relatively early on to tell him that his car would be fixed by the end of the day. He thought it would've been out of action for a few days at least, but it seemed that the damage wasn't as extensive as they, or he, first thought. Thankfully, being the boss of your own firm, which employed its own mechanics to run a fleet of company cars, had its benefits.

He also thought, not surprisingly, about the girl. His victim. She wasn't his first and he was sure she wouldn't be his last. He just couldn't figure out why he'd had the episode of seeing her in his backseat like that. It wasn't a flashback. When he had covered and tied her up her face was covered, too. He'd dumped her in the lake and hadn't seen her since; yet there she'd been, uncovered and soaked to her poor dead bones.

He tried to push it (and her) to the back of his mind as he had done so successfully with the others. There were also the reflections. "What the fuck was that all about?" he said to himself, rubbing his right temple. He wondered if maybe he had actually got a bang on the head, a possible concussion, or maybe the paramedics didn't know what they were doing. He tried to remember when it happened - it hadn't happened before, to his knowledge - only after, the accident. That was it, the accident. He convinced himself that the crash had caused it.

"But what about up at the lake?" a voice seemed to whisper in his head, mischievously.

That could be rationalised by the light or breeze rippling the lake, though he didn't recall either of those things affecting the scene. He put it all down to that. He decided, now it was clearer in his mind, that there was nothing to worry about and therefore would throw himself into his work for the rest of the day.

He did just that, with enthusiasm. He was horrendous to his employees, ripping into them over any slight mistake that they may or may not have made. Even though, for the most part, little had gone wrong with any of their work at all, he still managed to find fault. He attended one large meeting with a firm that he had intentions of taking over - the terms were poor that he offered, yet he squeezed them down to a rock bottom price. The family firm was practically on its knees, all broken men when they left the meeting, but Charles was delighted with himself.

Just before the day's end, he received a call from his chief mechanic, who informed him that his car was ready. He locked his office and took the elevator to the basement car park. He stopped off at the mechanic's office to pick up his keys and made his way over to his vehicle. His car was in his specific space - the equivalent of three spaces either side of his were cordoned off at all times. No one would ever be allowed to park too close to his car, even if it meant them having to park blocks away in the rain or snow. Suitably his space didn't have his name on it, it simply his title, 'President'. He loved to see that each day.

He smiled as he approached his beloved vehicle, partly reflecting on his day, his great business deal, filling him with a sense of power at how his underlings had cowered before him. He was pleased to have his car back, but with each step that he took towards it, his smile faded a little and his pace slowed until he found himself just two steps away from the driver's door at a complete halt and with a knot in his stomach.

He pressed the button on his key to disable the alarm but, suddenly, he could feel an acidic taste in his mouth, sickly and horrible, like bile rising in his throat. He paused again and took a deep breath, reaching out tentatively to the door handle. He froze on the spot like a mannequin. He withdrew his hand and, instead, cautiously raised himself up to his full height and then on to the tip of his toes to peer in his back seat. There wasn't anybody there - in fact as clean as his car was usually, it seemed that the mechanics had gone the extra yard for him.

Suddenly feeling stupid, he looked around the lot to see if anyone was watching his odd behaviour. Even though that part of the place was empty, he could hear echoing chatter and laughter in other parts of the basement. The noises and then the sounds of car doors and tyres squealing made him realise that there was nothing to fear. He had made sense of it all much earlier. He reached out again and this time opened the door, cautiously peering around and then inside the gleaming car.

"Sir?"

Charles jumped. His heart raced and he spun around with his back pressed to the rear passenger door. A young man, unknown to Charles, was looking over curiously.

"Are you okay, Mr Carlton?"

"Er... Yes... Yes, I'm fine," he blurted. "Why?"

"Well, erm, you seem a little..."

"A little what exactly?" snapped Charles, his embarrassment turning to anger.

"Oh, nothing, Sir. Have a good evening," the young man half smiled, before hurriedly fumbling with his own keys and getting into his car as quickly as possible and out of the car park - all under the red hot stare of Charles Carlton.

Once Charles was alone again, he suddenly wished he wasn't, though he would never admit to that, of course.

He took a deep breath and tried again. This time, he got into the car and sat in his seat. Breathing slowly and deeply, he realised that his hands were shaking; he felt clammy and his palms were slick with sweat. He knew he had to get himself under control. For a split second, he didn't think and he looked up at the rear-view mirror and saw his reflection. The reflection glowed back as he saw his whole head and face screaming and on fire.

Quickly, he dived out of the car, screaming. He desperately patted his hands on his head to put out the flames that weren't there. He lay humiliated on the ground and began to crawl away from his car, weeping quietly to himself.

"What the fuck is going on?" he spluttered under his breath.

He sat there for a few minutes until he collected and composed himself. Once done, he wiped his eyes and looked around in shame at his own sense of weakness, checking that no one had seen him or his little breakdown. He got to his feet, straightened his jacket and tie and brushed any dust off him from the ground. He looked around again and then back at his car. Shaking his head, he lifted his leg and used the toe of his shoe to push its door shut. He set the alarm and backed away from it, keeping his eyes firmly on the backseat as he did so - just in case.

Charles returned to the elevator and pushed the button to go back to his office. The doors closed and still he kept an eye on his car until the last second and the metal box started its ascent up his building. He let out a huge exhalation, not realising that he had been holding his breath for so long, causing him mild surprise and a little dizziness, but now he felt safe - or safer.

He tried to think what to do. He could get a taxi (though he loathed that idea). His underlings used taxis. He didn't. He could ask if there were any of the mechanics still there who could get him a vehicle from the carpool. Time was passing, however, and he wasn't sure if that was possible as he looked at his watch. The doors of the elevator opened at his floor and he was struck by the obvious, the penthouse, of course.

The top floor of his offices had a penthouse suite; he'd had it fitted out a couple of years earlier when he'd had a number of very lucrative deals on the go. He had been able to bring in clients from across the country and overseas' business associates. In the long run, it paid massively for itself - no hotel suites to pay for, plus it added a certain impression that he wanted his peers to be seduced by. Occasionally, he had used it himself for 'entertaining', but having the cabin gave him extra privacy. Tonight, however, it would be the perfect sanctuary while he got his mind together.

Charles entered the penthouse, shrugged off his jacket and stood at the huge windows, looking down and out over the city. In the wintery scene, the sky had already turned to darkness and the street lights were twinkling like a sea of stars. Car headlights beamed and travelled along the streets guiding their owner's home from work or shopping. Apartment lights were coming on as people arrived at their homes, while, in other buildings, lights went off as offices and stores closed. Bars lit up as the day turned to night and a whole other set of people started to come out - some going to dinner, others to either wash away their day, or to celebrate or commiserate. Some just needed a drink......or something stronger. Soon, no doubt, police sirens would punctuate the soundtrack of certain areas of the city as the seedier side of society became more prevalent in various insalubrious proceedings.

He went to the bar in the corner of the living room and poured himself a Scotch over ice - not too much ice, however. He wouldn't want to spoil the quality. It was one of his favourite single malts, one that his clients would appreciate and, indeed, some had commented on. He savoured the drink and moved back to the window to gaze down, his calmness returning, and he felt the tranquillity in the room. The peace and quiet was all encompassing above the ebb and flow developing beneath him. The thought of people going home resonated with him and he sighed under his breath as he realised that he would have to ring his wife to tell her he wouldn't be coming home again tonight.

"Hey, honey," she said, in her usual cheerful tone, knowing full well who was calling from the caller ID.

"Hi darling...," he sighed down the phone in the most sorrowful manner that he could muster.

"Charles? Whatever's the matter?"

"Well, first of all, don't panic. I'm ok, but..." He knew how to lay it on thick.

"Charles? What is it? What has happened?"

He could tell she was panicking already, just as he knew she would.

"I had a car accident this morning."

"Dear Lord, Charles. Are you sure you're ok? Where the hell are you?"

"I'm ok - honestly I am," he said, in a sheepish voice for maximum effect.

"This is just awful! What happened, honey? Are you hurt?" She was getting more and more frantic by the second.

"Someone ran me off the road on my way to work," he lied. "I've been checked out and they say I'm not too banged up, but I just need to take it easy for a day or two."

"Are you at the hospital now?"

"No, they released me, but I'm a little too shaken up to drive home." A partial lie at least, he thought.

"Do you want me to come and get you? Oh, Charles, I'm so sorry...." As she spoke, he could hear her running around the house, probably looking for her car keys.

"Errr, darling, no!" He panicked for a moment before regaining his composure. "I'll be fine. Honestly. I'm going to stay in the penthouse at the office for tonight, ok?"

"But I can be there in a half hour or so," she said, a little suspicion rising unmistakeably in her own voice now.

"Errr, thanks but.....no, my love. After what happened to me earlier, I couldn't bear the thought of you driving on the roads tonight." He already had one eye on how he was going to occupy himself for the evening. "Especially as it could be quite icy out there on the country lanes," he reminded Gloria.

He was very good at thinking on his feet. This was most useful in business and great to cover his extra-curricular activities, too.

"Well, ok."

She hesitated for a moment. He did sound as if he was just being thoughtful after all - and she remembered being shaken up herself after a minor fender bender a few years ago.

"If you're sure you'll be alright…"

"Of course, darling," he said, grinning to himself. "I'll be fine - just a bit down that I won't be with you again tonight."

"I know. I understand, but……"

She was going to offer again to pick him up; maybe he had over played his hand.

"Doctor's orders, an early night and plenty of bed rest they prescribed." He put the final nail in her rescue plan. "I'm just going to crash out here in a few minutes and hopefully that'll help to straighten me out."

"Aw, poor baby," she cooed lovingly. "Well, you get some rest and call me if you need anything at all."

"Will do, darling - don't you worry about me. Love you." He sealed it.

"Alright Charles, love you too." She hung up.

"Dumb fuckin' bitch," he mumbled beneath a smile and threw his phone onto an armchair. He thought for a moment or two, pondering his options, before a broad smile spread across his face and he sighed again as he whispered to himself. "Cheryl."

Chapter 3

When he'd called Cheryl, she'd said she had plans. She was at no man's beck and call, but she had told him that she would be free later on. He didn't argue - he just knew he wanted her and as soon as possible. She said she would get to him around or eleven or so; maybe before, maybe later. He expected her to be later - she liked to make him wait. He smiled after getting off the phone. He had plenty of time to take a nap and relax properly, thus being fully prepared for the kind of night that he had in mind.

Charles shaved (or, rather, manicured) his stubble and then showered; he always took time with his personal grooming, but did so particularly tonight. The time allowed him to calm his mind and the long shower helped his body relax. Under the massaging heat and pressure of the water, he realised just how tight his muscles had become - he was like a coiled spring. As he stepped out of the shower, he heard the buzzer sound, which triggered whenever someone pushed it in the elevator for the penthouse. He came out of the bathroom and answered it.

"I'm here," she said in her usual seductive and breathless voice.

"Well, come on up," he replied deeply, though he couldn't help but grin in the most lascivious manner.

He pushed a button on his intercom, which allowed the elevator up to the penthouse. The only other way to access the place was with a key, his key. He unlocked the door so that she could enter and returned to the bathroom to finish his preparations as she made her way up the building.

Cheryl arrived at the penthouse and closed the door behind her. She had been there a few times before and knew the layout of the place. It was a large living area, with a bar, plush sofas and an armchair, coffee tables, large plasma television on the wall, a hidden sound system and two floor-to-ceiling windows looking down and out onto the city. A bathroom was situated off a small corridor where she could hear Charles brushing his teeth. Just beyond the bathroom was the bedroom. She knew that one very well. In there was a huge bed, large wardrobe and two bedside cabinets, another plush couch and another full-length window. The whole penthouse was decorated in light cream colours, with soft furnishings, cushions and dim lighting. It had cost a lot of money, but it was, without doubt, an extremely comfortable and luxurious place to be.

Charles finished in the bathroom and emerged, wearing a black towelling robe; he was in his early fifties, but had kept himself in good shape. He had once had black hair, but it was now greying at the temples, cut short with rough shadowy stubble on his chin of similar nature - he could easily pass for a man ten years younger. A gym membership and plenty of holidays had allowed him to hold on to his youth far longer than he had hoped for and now he was enjoying the benefits.

He saw her in the living area. She had already poured herself a glass of white wine and now she stood in the same place as he had been earlier, gazing down at the streets and city below. He refilled his glass and made to move over to join her. First, however, he paused for a moment to take in the sight of her.

She was wearing a long dark purple evening gown, so dark in fact, that from a certain angle, it almost seemed black. It looked to be made of silk and clung to every inch of her slender body like a second beautiful skin. She was around five foot six tall, but with the black five-inch stiletto heeled shoes, she was close to Charles' own height of almost six feet. She was a picture in her own right. She had naturally dark brown hair, which was tinted slightly with a dark purple colour, cut straight into a perfect line at her shoulders, with the same just above her eyebrows, framing her face perfectly. Deep blue eyes and soft pale skin, with only a hint of mascara and eye shadow, combined with a very dark berry-red lipstick, gave her a stunning look- almost a Hollywood starlet image from a bygone era.

She heard him sigh and she smiled to herself. She knew the power she had over men and always used it to her advantage. She took a sip of her wine and continued to look down on the city streets. He took a step over to her and could feel himself rise beneath his robe. She turned at his approach and looked him square in the eye stopping him dead in his tracks. She held his gaze for a second, before glancing down at his straining erection, now pushing through and parting his bathrobe. Her look only increased his ardour and she looked back into his eyes before taking another sip from her glass.

They stood there as if frozen in time before she lifted her right hand to her left shoulder and untied the simple bow that was the strap on her dress. The material slipped forward slightly, but not completely. Still maintaining eye contact throughout, she then swapped her glass to the other hand and repeated the action on the right strap. The dress, now totally undone, slipped from her body and straight down around her feet. The material made the garment glide effortlessly from her flesh to the floor, emitting a gentle swishing noise as it did so.

In complete nudity now save for her stilettos, she stood staring at him as if nothing had happened, then elegantly lifted her glass again and sipped. He marvelled at a sight he had seen before, but still left him open-mouthed as it literally did now. She couldn't help but raise a wry smile at this and then she moved.............slowly. She walked the half a dozen paces to him and he lifted his hand to touch her, but she deftly avoided his reach and instead walked past him and towards the bedroom. He pivoted on the spot, not taking his eyes from her, drinking in every inch of her amazing body; she glided as if walking on air. Her hips swayed gently, causing her pert buttocks to softly move in rhythm. Her hair swayed too, at the back, side to side, but only slightly. The muscles in her back and thighs added to the athletic and feminine grace of her movements.

He drained his glass and followed behind like a puppy. She knew he was following as expected, but, just for effect she glanced over her shoulder at him. She reached the bedroom and turned around to face him. He arrived, still dazed and open-mouthed with a look of fascination on his face. Her halting made him stop and stare one last time, before he could take no more. Charles slipped off his robe and faced her, as naked as she was.

Words were clearly unnecessary now and he moved in and took her in his arms. He showered her with deep kisses on her swan like neck, moving carefully to her chin and lips, before releasing her down to the bed. He moved above her and used his lips and tongue to cover her entire body, starting with her arms, breasts, stomach, hips and thighs before moving back to her shaved pussy. He could've stayed there tasting the sweet dew emanating from her, but he wanted desperately to be inside her fully.

He brought himself up to her eye line and slowly eased his cock into her. She gasped as he did so and he held his breath as he slid into her, her warmth encapsulating him. She wrapped her right leg around him, pulling him deeper into her, her black stilettos glinting in the soft lighting. He opened his eyes and looked into her. She returned his gaze like a sinful fallen angel being fucked.

He pulled back and out of her. She had been here before and knew exactly what he wanted. He stood now on the floor at the end of the bed and she slithered down to him, reaching out and taking him in her hand, gazing up at him, before taking his cock in her mouth. Very slowly and gently she worked him back and forth, squeezing tightly with her hand, not wanting him to finish too soon. Then she stopped and stood, before turning her back to him. Bending over to show her perfectly toned ass, she parted her legs and placed her hands on the bed.

It was a sight to bring tears to his eyes; such was her beauty and lasciviousness. He couldn't take it any longer, so he slid back into her, feeling the sensations all over again and, judging from her inflamed reaction, so was she. He pounded more vigorously into her as they both raced to climax. Hard, faster, harder, faster and harder still. He was almost there when he glanced to the side of the room at the full- length mirror hanging there. He watched himself fuck the girl, taking in every glorious image of her body being impaled on his stiffness. The sight, the sound, the scent, but then...........

As he felt he was near to the end, the image in the mirror changed. The girl was still there, still beautiful, still hot and still being fucked. But now, instead of by him, it was a version of him. And it was horrific. He looked scarred, burned, disfigured. He looked as if he was bleeding from open wounds and sores all over his naked body. A tail appeared, thrashing around behind him and horns started to appear, sprouting from his head like hideous shoots encroaching in spring. He slowed to an almost standstill, and as he did so, so did the monster staring back at him, Cheryl, unaware of what he saw, was continuing to push back onto his cock. With unadulterated horror, he noticed that her lower back, ass and thighs that he could see in the mirror were covered in bleeding scars and gouges, with blood oozing out and pouring down her legs - the same blood that now he could see all over his claw-like hands in the glass.

As Charles stared in terror and disbelief, he could sense that not only was he looking at the creature in the mirror, but horrifyingly, it was looking at him too. He threw his head back and thought he heard himself roar like a wounded animal at the sight, but in fact he had screamed in horror. He pulled out of Cheryl and collapsed in a sobbing heap on his plush rug. Cheryl had pulled the other way at the blood curdling scream he had emitted and matched it with one of her own as she clambered onto the bed and pulled the covers over her as if to protect herself from something.

He lay on the floor sobbing as she peered over the bed at him. She had started to cry with fright, fear and confusion and they both wept in appalling unison, but she had no idea what had just happened. Slowly, he crawled over to the mirror on his hands and knees, afraid of what might be there, but needing to know. She watched him in disbelief, sobbing to herself as she tried to gain control. He touched the glass. The coldness of it at first seemed harsh to him, before he looked and saw his reflection - his normal reflection staring back at him. Cheryl watched, a mixture of confusion and revulsion, becoming more and more concerned by the surreal turn of events and she slowly began to manoeuvre herself to the edge of the bed, furthest away from him. He continued to stare into the mirror mumbling to himself, or to the mirror - she couldn't be sure, but she didn't want to hang around to find out. He pawed at the glass unaware or unconcerned that she passed him briskly, picking up her dress on the way out, not waiting to put it on until she got back in the elevator and was safely on her way out of there.

Charles stared with fear and wonderment, like a baby or animal staring at themselves for the first time. The fear rose in him again when the image smiled back at him, as though he was actually talking, then it turned its back on him and walked away. It walked to what would have been the other side of the bedroom behind Charles, but once the reflection got there, it kept moving and getting smaller as if walking until it shrank into the distance. Then there was nothing left at all. Charles sat in disbelief, utterly alone, with not even a reflection in a mirror.

Chapter 4

Charles woke up, naked, in the foetal position like a fresh new born. He shivered with the cold, despite the fact that the penthouse was set at a comfortably warm temperature at all times. He was still curled up in front of the mirror when he awoke from what had seemed like a horrific nightmare. He caught his breath and rolled onto his back, trying to recall the events of the night before. He smiled to himself as he thought of Cheryl, grinning further as he remembered her dropping her dress. He rubbed his eyes as he sat upright before then clambering to his feet.

As he made to go the bathroom, he started to recall parts of his dream, but couldn't put it into any context. He urinated in the toilet then turned, still bleary eyed, to the mirror, blinking rapidly, rubbing his eyes some more. His heart raced and he tried to breathe, as he realised that last night hadn't been just a nightmare. His reflection was gone.

He stared and stared and started to shake uncontrollably. What did this mean? Was this even possible? He ran back into the bedroom to check the mirror there and as he approached, he paused first. It came back to him that that was the mirror that either he had dreamt about or had actually 'caused' this to happen. That was the only way he could rationalise the whole thing.

He tentatively approached from the side, putting his hand out in front of it so that he could see any reflection, but there wasn't one. He slowly moved himself more fully in front of it so that he was standing there, still naked and vulnerable, staring at himself in front of the large mirror - except that he wasn't staring at himself. He was staring at the room behind him and nothing else at all.

Charles sat on the edge of the bed and, not for the first time in that situation, wept openly. He didn't think about anything at all - it was just pure emotion, like a frightened little boy afraid of the dark and what lies within it. That was all he could see, darkness. He stayed there for about an hour until he could cry no more, when an inner voice seemed to tell him to pull himself together. He stood and went back to the bathroom and showered, but not before he hung a towel up in front of the mirror. He didn't know why - it would still be a reminder, even if he managed to get his mind onto something else.

While showering, he tried to make sense of what was happening. He even came to the ridiculous question in his mind of "Am I a vampire now?" He laughed it off to himself; he had watched too many movies. But what the fuck was happening? Why had this come about? Had somebody done this to him? These kinds of questions spun back and forth in his mind with no genuine answers or conclusions. However, it did help him to focus his mind and pull himself together, even if he couldn't rationalise events. Once out of the shower, he dressed and his mind continued to the point that he thought,

"So what if I don't have a reflection? It's not going to change my life."

He wondered how many times a day he actually looked in the mirror. He figured it was only vanity anyway - he could avoid that. He felt stronger and far more resolute. He actually felt *powerful*. He had overcome a mentally traumatic event and had come out of it with renewed vigour. There was one other thing that he still had to overcome, his trauma in his car.

He left the penthouse and went straight down to the parking garage in the basement. Confidently, he exited the elevator and strode over to his vehicle which stood alone on that Saturday morning. There were no other cars in sight. No one was around. He realised it was still quite early and the stores wouldn't be opening for another hour or so. He pressed his alarm on his key to unlock the car without breaking stride, and as soon as he stepped up to the door, he opened it and got in without even thinking about it. As he sat down, he exhaled. As he did the night before, he hadn't even realised that he had been holding his breath the whole time.

He started up the car immediately, then he looked in his mirrors, nothing. It was a surreal and strange sensation, but not painful, and in his mind it wouldn't be detrimental to him. He revved the engine excessively, a feeling coursing through his veins - a feeling like going to the edge of the abyss and returning triumphant.

He slammed his car into gear, reversed out, his tyres squealing, as he roared out and away from the parking lot. He sped up onto the street and headed for home. He no longer thought about the backseat, though as he drove and when he had to stop at a red light, he quickly checked his rear view mirror for his reflection that was still not there. When he pulled up in traffic, he checked any store window at his side to see a reflection of his car, but with no driver - at least not to his eyes. He wasn't yet aware whether other people could see his reflection or not, but at that moment he didn't care. It was strange but suddenly kind of fun.

He arrived home still smiling to himself, exhilarated by the strangeness of his recent events, feeling born again. He pulled up dramatically in his long drive way and stepped out of the car. He paused and looked around the vast, manicured grounds surrounding his home and inhaled deeply, smelling the air, feeling refreshed and soaking up the life that he had built for himself. He turned, even loving the sound of the gravel from the drive way under his feet.

Charles walked up to his front door and was greeted by his wife, Gloria, a beautiful woman in her day, but her pining for children he didn't want had left her feeling unfulfilled and empty and now the years showed in her face. However, to most, she was still a wonderful, giving and attractive woman and she would help anyone out, often assisting numerous charity events in the city. She would've made an amazing mother. Many people had commented on such, yet it was sadly not to be - thanks to Charles and his ambition and drive for the material things in life (and his secret penchant for other, younger women).

Gloria came out to the front porch and threw her arms around him, kissing him and hugging him tightly.

"Jesus, Charles - are you alright?" she sobbed with relief.

"Yes, yes, I'm fine, darling…" he sighed for extra sympathy, whilst also slightly resenting her being all over him. Reality was killing his mood!

"Oh, Charles - I know you said you'd be given the all clear and you were alright, but I was so worried about you. What happened? Come in and tell me all about it, honey."

They walked into the house. She closed the door behind them as he walked to the kitchen and poured himself a cup of fresh coffee. Gloria scurried along behind him, waiting on his every word. He drank the coffee slowly and retold the story while she sat at the kitchen island and he stood there solemnly on the other side. He told, or rather lied, about the lunatic who had run him off the road. He told of how he had feared for his life and how the only thing he could think about was her during the whole time. She gasped and had a little sob with each ridiculous lie and revelation; the more she reacted, the thicker he laid everything on. He explained away his lack of injury to pure good fortune, even going so far as to suggest maybe someone was watching over him, to which she whispered, "Amen to that. Amen."

He told her how he didn't want her to worry and that he just wanted to be alone and rest, which was why he had gone to the penthouse. He said that he'd had a few drinks to calm his nerves and started to do some paperwork, but was too exhausted emotionally by the whole trauma, so he had gone to bed early to recuperate fully. To cover his tracks, he also threw in a few more lies about his car and how he had to have mechanics working all day and night just to get it fixed in order for him to get back into her loving arms. To this, understandably, she gasped a little more and a tear rolled down her cheek. She came around the island and hugged him again out of relief and love; he tolerated it for a minute, before gently easing himself free. He told her that he was still weary and, not surprisingly, she understood and suggested he go and lie down for a while, which he gladly agreed to.

Charles went upstairs and she made to follow until he said he'd be ok and that he wanted to be alone for a while. She looked hurt, but again, she tried to understand the 'huge trauma' that he'd been through and let him go. She stood at the bottom of the stairs as he walked forlornly up to their bedroom, even turning back and looking at her with a sad half-smile, which almost broke her heart. He turned again and went to their master suite, while she turned back to the kitchen to find something to busy herself with. He grinned to himself and mumbled under his breath about how he should've been an actor.

Once in their bedroom, he kicked off his shoes and walked into the en-suite bathroom. They had a beautiful and expensive marble bathroom, with an antique roll-top bath and a huge shower cubicle for two - though it had been a long time since they had been in there together - and a separate steam room. They had dual wash basins for him and her - all very luxurious and pristine throughout, except for one thing that was wrong. The mirror over his basin was missing.

"Gloria?" he yelled down to her. "Gloria?" he yelled again a few seconds later. It was a big house and she hadn't heard him the first time.

"What is it, darling?" she called back from the bottom of the stairs.

"What the fuck happened in the bathroom?" he shouted.

"Oh dear," she muttered to herself, remembering, and made her way upstairs. "I forgot about that." She continued to talk as she walked upstairs.

He stood in the doorway of the bathroom. Her mirror and basin were closest to the door; his was next to it. Above his basin was just a blank wall, apart from the screws still in the wall, with remnant shards of broken glass, but nothing else. From where he stood, he noticed that he should be reflected in her mirror, but still there was nothing there but a reflection of the rest of the bathroom.

He could hear her approaching quickly and he panicked, not knowing if she would notice or how he would explain it, he still didn't know himself yet. He moved sharply into the room and stood on the opposite side, facing her and looking at where his mirror should have been.

"What the hell happened?" he said as she walked in.

"Well, it was the oddest thing, and I don't mind admitting it was scary, too. Not as scary as what you went through I grant you, but..." She started to babble and he held up his hands to stop her.

"Just tell me what happened," he snapped impatiently.

"I'm sorry," she whispered. "The thing is, during the night, once I'd eventually got to sleep after worrying about you all night, I heard this crash."

"Did the mirror just crack?" he asked.

"No," she protested. "If it had cracked, I probably wouldn't have heard it, but it was more like an explosion."

"It just exploded? On its own?"

He looked at where his mirror once was and then at her, almost accusingly.

"Honestly, Charles, I was asleep. I heard it and was terrified. I thought someone had smashed a window and I was all alone." She fought back tears, reliving how frightened she had been at the time. "I got up," she continued. "I came downstairs and checked all the windows and was wondering why the alarms hadn't gone off."

He'd had an expensive security alarm fitted for such things, allowing them to move around the house themselves without triggering it, whilst still protecting any possible access points from potential robbers.

"I came back up and checked all the windows and doors and then I turned on all the lights. I was so scared, but I couldn't find anything wrong. I just thought that I must've dreamed it all, so I went back to bed. It took me a while, but I fell asleep," she finished.

She looked so sad, as if she had done something wrong by the way he looked at her, but his mind was already racing with something else.

"Then, when I got up this morning and came in here, that's when I saw it." She spoke again to break the silence that was developing. "There was glass everywhere, so I cleaned it up. Don't worry; we can get a new one, sweetie. You can just use mine for now. We can share just like the old days!" She tried to placate him. As if he was upset over a fucking mirror. No. He was upset over something else.

"What time?" he asked quietly, almost to himself.

"Erm, about 7:30am I guess," she replied, twisting her face slightly, as she thought back.

"I thought you said it was the middle of the night."

"Oh, sorry - I thought you meant what time did I see it." She smiled at the slight misunderstanding she hoped would break the building tension in him. It didn't. "Errr, just before 1am, I think. Why?"

"No reason." He practically breathed the words out as he stared at the blank wall. He guessed that that was around the same time that his reflection had turned its back on him and walked away. He was right.

Chapter 5

Charles spent the rest of the morning in dazed, quiet contemplation, amid slices of fear. He pondered his situation, moving back and forth alone in the bedroom. Meanwhile, Gloria busied herself around the house, trying to give him as much space as possible. Every now and again, however, she would slip into the bedroom to her clothes and accessories and rummage around as if looking for something and making a decision, before smiling sweetly and disappearing off to somewhere else. He could sense that something was going on, but he wasn't sure what it was.

Charles could hear her making phone calls, or answering calls, all the while trying to keep her voice down and being generally secretive. By mid-afternoon, he'd had enough of the subterfuge and came out of the bedroom and called down to her.

"Gloria?" he bellowed.

"What is it, darling?" she cooed as she scurried out of the kitchen and to the foot of the stairs.

"What's going on?"

"What do you mean?" she asked.

"Your endless running around, the phone calls, what's happening?" he said, bewildered.

"Oh Lord. I didn't want to worry you or bother you, but..."

"But what?"

"We have that benefit tonight - the new hospital wing, remember?" She sounded genuinely apologetic, but his stomach turned at the thought, especially with his mind in flux.

"Fuck," he mumbled under his breath, letting out a deep sigh.

"Oh, darling. If you're still not up to it, I could go alone," she beamed sympathetically up at him. "I'd understand. Your health and well-being are all that matters to me."

He knew how much she loved going to such events, yet he loathed most of them. Sure, it was good for business - a little philanthropy never hurt the image or profits as far as he was concerned. Plus, there was always a healthy supply of new contacts to be made. But the idea of glad-handing lots of snobs and wealthy pricks irritated him at the best of times, let alone when he was tormented inside as he was at that moment. It was ironic that, unbeknown to him, he was seen as a 'prick' by most other people who attended the events. If only he knew how many of their hearts sank when he approached.

"Right," he sighed, slouching on the banister like a teenager who'd been told not to forget his chores, before turning back and sulking off to the bedroom.

Later that afternoon, they were both busy preparing themselves for the social event. Charles avoided shaving; he had only manicured his stubble the night before and he cared less about personal grooming when his companion for the evening was Gloria. He then took a quick shower, whilst Gloria bathed for what seemed like an age.

He stepped out of the shower cubicle and wrapped a towel around his waist, before absent-mindedly looking up. He gazed straight into the mirror above Gloria's wash basin and there was his reflection. He stood open mouthed, but his wife was too busy pampering herself to notice. He stared at himself, long and hard. Something wasn't quite right, but he couldn't put his finger on it. He stared harder and then it became clear, literally. He could see himself, but only just - he was almost transparent! His refection had returned and he was visible, but he could see the tiles of the shower cubicle wall behind him. Fuck. He could even see the shower head dripping down through his body. He couldn't work out what this meant. Was last night a surreal dream? Or, more likely, a nightmare? Had he been drugged? His mind raced until he heard her voice.

"Are you okay there, darling?" asked Gloria.

"Errr, yeah. I mean yes. I'm fine," he muttered, realising that she must've been watching him stare at himself a little too much. He quickly finished up and went off to get dressed whilst his mind raced anew.

It was a little after 7pm and they were both almost ready. The limousine was arranged to pick them up at 7:30 precisely. It would take half an hour to get to the benefit, so they would arrive at 8pm. The V.I.P invite they had received stated a 7pm arrival, but Charles knew he wanted to arrive once everyone else worth knowing was already there. He liked to look as though he was the guest of honour, even though he rarely was. While they waited for the limo, they both had a drink to relax. Neither of them were sitting down, both standing as if they had stalled in the middle of an awkward dance. Gloria had the vacuous fear of creasing her very expensive gown if she sat down once dressed. The fact that she would soon be sitting in a limousine for a half hour was lost on her, as he pointed out.

He'd finished two large scotches as the car glided into the drive way exactly on time and the couple walked out to the waiting driver, who was calmly holding the door open for Gloria, who smiled politely. Charles, as classy as ever, tipped the driver unnecessarily as he entered behind her. They settled into their plush seats and headed for the lavish hospital benefit and finally Charles switched off from his problems. He felt he'd earned a night like this.

The benefit was indeed lavish. It was held at City Hall, a colossal building, dating back two and a half centuries, with marble floors, stone pillars expertly carved, vaulted ceilings, with beautiful paintings adorning the walls like the most opulent jewellery. The great and the good of the city, as well as the surrounding areas, dressed in their finest Chanel and Armani, were all in attendance.

The benefit was clearly going to be a huge success for the new hospital wing - a charity auction had been organised and almost everyone made generous bids on every item that had been donated. It seemed the community had a great many benefactors with pockets deep enough to fund such things when needed. There was even talk of two or three of the philanthropists arguing over whom would get the naming rights for the new wing. Their respective partners had to drag them off each other at one point, allegedly.

Inevitably there was gossip, too. The inside track of this or that business deal, plus, of course, who was having an affair with who and all sorts of other mindless chatter, laced with the usual niceties and pleasantries that came naturally to those people.

There was one piece of mysterious chatter which Charles had heard, regarding one of his great enemies and business rivals, Ian Money, who was conspicuous by his absence. The man never missed one of these functions with a chance to brag, a chance to get one up on his competition - most notably Charles Carlton. They had been at loggerheads for many years over a deal that had gone bad. Once upon a time, they had been best friends, but a dispute over finances and rumours about Charles having a dalliance with Money's wife had led to an enormous fall out, with potential legal battles, which were never resolved, and threats of violence against each other.

Ian Money was apparently missing. He hadn't been since late on Friday night, but nobody knew anything for sure. It was just gossip and rumour and counter rumour, but nothing concrete. Charles would keep his ear to the ground. If his old buddy's business was at death's door, he would just have to open that door for him.

As the evening wore on, cheques were written, dances were danced, hands were shaken and surreptitious deals were agreed. Charles and Gloria were involved with as much as they could handle and, thankfully for him, he managed to relax and get his mind off all the events of the last thirty six hours. That was until he saw Cheryl.

He'd just come out of the bathroom and was walking back along a balcony running all the way around the huge ballroom when he saw her. At the farthest point, the balcony swept into a beautiful and wide staircase, which flowed down to the main ballroom area. As he walked along the balcony back to the stairs, he glanced down at the dancing, chatter and laughter of the attendees. Everyone was having a wonderful time and he saw Gloria in her element, no doubt trying to twist arms to organise another similar event for another similarly worthy cause. He couldn't help but smile to himself at her efforts and then smiled further when he realised how happy she made him. He hadn't thought about her like that for such a long time. It was as he approached the top of the stairs that the smile was wiped off his face.

He stepped aside to allow an elderly lady and her husband to pass on their way up and, as he did so, out from behind them stepped Cheryl. She looked amazing as she always seemed to, wearing another breath-taking evening gown, although this one was a little more conservative than what he was used to seeing her in, with its deep red velvet and very subtle flower design flowing through it. For a very brief moment, he wondered what she was doing there - though he wondered more who she had come with. The truth of it was that she had a lot of influential friends herself; she wasn't an escort or a hooker. She did what she wanted, with whom she wanted, and was very discreet.

He froze on the spot and so did she. All the colour drained from his face and likewise; she thought she'd seen a... A what? A madman? A psychopath? She hadn't hung around long enough to see what was happening to him, but it sure enough scared the hell out of her. So much so that she knew she didn't want to see him again. She turned away and walked right past him at a brisk pace. Charles stood on the top step not really knowing what to do. Could he really just go down to the party and forget her, or more importantly, what she had seen? Though he was curious as to what she actually did see, he knew what he'd seen himself and hoped never to see again. Everything else was still a mystery to him.

He dithered as he watched her go off to the ladies' room. She looked back, but it was more to check that he wasn't following her. He looked down again at Gloria having fun and he took the next step down to join her, before changing his mind and quickly spinning around to go after Cheryl.

Charles stood in the shadows behind a large arrangement of flowers, especially commissioned for the event as decoration, as were the flowers throughout the lavish affair. Now, though, they gave him cover to keep out of sight without drawing too much attention to himself, yet they were still close enough to the powder rooms that he could swoop in when she exited. He just hoped that she came out alone and no one else was around. The bathroom door opened and out wobbled the old lady from earlier. Her companion came over from a seating area that Charles hadn't seen, so he quickly sidled over to make sure no one else was hanging around the foyer. Luckily, with the elderly couple now shuffling away, he was alone. He waited for a minute more when the door opened again and out walked

Cheryl, looking as though she had composed herself, but that would soon change as he walked over and whispered her name loud enough for her to hear.

She stopped, startled and looked this way and that as he walked over to her. He took her by her arm without saying another word and pulled her away from the party and down a corridor. There was a small velvet rope across the corridor at hip height with the words 'No Admittance', but he unhooked it and gently, but forcibly pulled her along after him, putting the sign and rope back so as not to cause any curious members of City Hall staff to come snooping. She quietly protested through fear, as he pulled her out of sight. When he was satisfied that they were out of ear shot of the other guests, he stopped.

They were in another large corridor, equally ornate, with elaborate frames and pictures of the founding fathers of the city from when it was just a basic settlement all those years ago.

"What do you want?" she snapped, as they came to a halt against a wall, shrugging her arm free of him.

"Look," he said, slightly out of breath. "What the fuck happened last night?"

"How the hell should I know? One minute you're fucking me like a man possessed and the next you're on the floor staring at yourself and screaming like a.........man possessed!"

"At myself?" he questioned.

"What do you mean?"

"At myself, you said."

"Yeah, in the mirror." She furrowed her brow at the seemingly stupid question.

"Wait. You definitely saw me... in the mirror I mean?" He was getting desperate and his voice became more erratic as he spoke.

"Who the fuck else would it be?" she snapped again and moved to step away, when he noticed for the first time that behind her, in one of those ornate frames, was actually a mirror.

In his confusion and twisted filled mind, he hadn't actually noticed they were standing in front of a mirror. He stopped and looked at himself. His reflection was coming back. It wasn't whole or solid, but it was definitely more opaque than it had been earlier at home in the bathroom.

She paused at the look on his face and then looked behind her and noticed the mirror. She couldn't quite put her finger on it, but something seemed strange - almost surreal.

She panicked and, in his distraction, she turned away and ran back up the corridor. He didn't go after her – he just stood and stared at himself. He turned to look down the corridor and caught a glimpse of her disappearing into the distance before turning back to the glass. However, his reflection didn't turn back, but continued to look down the way she had gone. Charles took a step to his right then another, but the reflection looked back down the other way and stayed stock still in the centre of the mirror. It then turned to him of its own accord and looked into him deeply before it spoke.

"Well if you don't want her, I'll have her," it whispered as if in his mind. The lips moved and with those words but the sound seemed to be directly in his head. It moved the opposite way from where Charles stood and in the direction of where Cheryl had run to. It moved to the end of the frame before disappearing at the edge and into nothing. Charles was aghast and stood staring into the empty glass, which now just reflected back everything in the corridor............everything except him.

Chapter 6

He broke out into a cold sweat with fear and panic. The thought crossed his mind of just how the hell he was going to get out of there. He hadn't yet realised just what other people saw in his reflection. Was it there or not? Was it transparent? Did it move of its own free will? He had experienced all of this and more, yet he couldn't explain any of it. But how would someone else see it? Or could they even tell at all?

Once Charles had pulled himself together, he went back down to the party. He had a surreptitious glance around for Cheryl before finding Gloria. He told her that he wasn't feeling very well. "Probably an after-effect from the 'crash'," he lied, adding with ease that the doctors had told him to expect that.

They made their heartfelt excuses and left. Charles came across as less heartfelt, however, due to the fact that he didn't look anyone in the eye. He suddenly felt like some kind of sideshow freak; he was convinced that the 'problem' he had was visual to everyone and not just him and that everybody in the building was staring at him, or pointing and whispering, which of course they weren't. As they walked down the corridors on their way out, Gloria was trying to be sympathetic to him, but Charles wasn't listening. Instead, he was trying to avoid the mirrors on the walls, or even highly polished surfaces, in case they gave him away. He was sure that everybody had noticed.

Luckily, there wasn't too much longer of the event to go and the various limo drivers were parked in the lot behind City Hall, ready to leave. As they approached, the valet was ordered to alert their driver, who promptly pulled the car around to the entrance to pick them up. Charles' agitation was growing and only subsided once they were back in the car and headed for home. He calmed himself and Gloria patted his leg while smiling softly, though there was serious concern behind her smile.

They reached home in good time, but not quickly enough for Charles, who practically fell out of the car in his haste. Gloria followed behind to help him but he shrugged her off. She paused and apologised to the driver, giving him another tip, confident in his discretion regarding her husband's behaviour. Once inside the house, Charles made sure every door and window was locked and the alarms were set before ushering his wife upstairs. He thought for a moment about barricading the bedroom door behind them, but thought better of it. Gloria would think him mad - if she didn't already think so.

Once in bed, unsurprisingly sleep didn't come easy to Charles. Gloria had taken a sleeping pill, but he had refused; he had always been fearful of not waking up or missing a business deadline. Eventually, however, with Gloria fast asleep beside him, Charles succumbed to the Sandman and drifted off, though he had struggled and fought him off for hours. Unfortunately, as Charles had no doubt feared, his dreams were far from what he had hoped they would have been.

His nightmares began with images of a girl. That girl. The one from the lake, the one that he had murdered. She was not the first, but the last.......to date. Anna had been her name; she was a beautiful girl from a small village in central Russia. She had been an intern in his office with an intoxicating accent, as well as a look of mystery about her. He had taken a shine to her sense of fun as well as her work ethic and she was just the sort of person that he wanted to employ, especially as he had grown so tired of boring grey people and their boring grey lives. He saw something new and fresh in Anna; she was full of life and vitality – plus, she was actually extremely intelligent and had a strong sense of independence. So much so that she on occasion answered him back when she thought he was wrong. Everyone else stood back and waited for his inevitable eruption, but so surprised by her was he that he had actually listened to what she had said. Lo and behold, more often than not she had been right. He did erupt, but not at her. At the sheep who were too afraid to stand up for themselves.

He had found himself more drawn to her, more captivated by her and gradually an affair started between them. It was by no means a dominant boss and his cliché secretary type relationship; it was very much on equal terms. There was no talk of love or any such thing, but the relationship held strong for a little over five months of intensity.

One night after they had fucked intensely at his penthouse she had become withdrawn and quiet, after much cajoling from Charles she had unburdened herself but unfortunately and sadly for her, she had dropped a bombshell which couldn't be ignored. She was pregnant. She knew she couldn't get rid of the baby because of her own beliefs and also that of her family and strong faith. Charles was livid. Naturally, he blamed her for the situation and she was distraught. She was devastated but told him that she didn't want anything from him; she would raise the child alone.

Charles initially wanted to believe her, but he got it into his mind that there would be trouble further down the line. He didn't have children of his own by choice and he certainly wasn't going to have some bastard offspring coming back to haunt him in the years to come, let alone alimony payments, tuition fees, child support or whatever else she might dream up to bleed him dry. No. This would end there and then. They were in the penthouse when she told him. An enormous argument broke, followed by many tears, until, in his rage, he took an ornament, a large orb of some artistic merit or other, and as she sat head bowed and sobbing, he cracked her over the head with it. She slumped to the floor immediately, thankfully landing on a rug in front of her. That would be easily disposable, unlike the expensive carpeting throughout. Her blood pooled out onto the rug and he gathered it up. Without emotion, he grabbed a couple of blankets from an airing cupboard to help soak up the excess blood and cover her up.

It was late at night and he managed to bundle her up and get her down to his car in the elevator unseen. He slid her into the trunk and pulled out and away from the garage at speed, before heading out of the city. He had decided in the elevator what to do with her. Just like the others, he would dump her in his lake. He hadn't thought it would end this way with Anna, but a line had been crossed; he didn't have an heir and he didn't want one. What was his would remain his.

He arrived at his lake house and opened the trunk. She lay there helpless, still bleeding profusely, when she opened her eyes, to his shock. Her eyes rolled in their sockets and she mouthed something of a plea for help, followed by more tears. He sighed as if this had become an inconvenience and went to a tool shed on the property. He wasn't one for manual labour; he always had other people to do such things, but this he had to do alone. He emerged after much rummaging and cursing with some lengths of rope and a couple of old brown cloth potato sacks.

Charles dragged her out of the car and down to the water's edge where he laid her. He took one of the sacks and put her feet in it, pulling it up to her waist before thinking about weight. He pondered for a moment, before he strode off looking for suitably sized rocks or debris. He returned three times with enough material to keep her down at the bottom of the lake. Throughout all this, she was gradually coming more awake. He took no pity and started to put some of the heavy rocks and stones into the base of the bag around her legs. She moaned and he paused to look at her, admiring the fight within her. Her strength was one of the many things that had attracted him to her in the first place.

She gingerly lifted her aching and broken head to look at him. Tears and blood enveloped her still pretty face and she opened her mouth to speak. He looked at her in her dying moments with a brief feeling of sadness, but she summoned all her strength to unleash a verbal tirade of anger and wrath. She started to speak so that he could understand her cursing him, before slipping into her mother tongue and reciting something that made him chill to the bone. Even though it was already a cold winter's night, still he shivered even more ferociously as the hatred and bile spilled from her mouth, cursing the very earth he may walk and air that he breathed. His ears rang and the air around him seemed to sing as if she were summoning up the very elements around them and all the spirits of the world.

He could take no more. He clenched his fist and screamed at her to "Shut up!" before striking her in the mouth. She fell back under the force, but continued to stare into his eyes as she finished her native curse upon him. In his frantic and panicking state, he punched her in the face but still she glared at him in defiance. Charles frantically grabbed at and picked up one of the rocks in both hands and lifted it above his head as she ended with "Eternally" and stared at him. He brought the rock crashing down and it hit her just above her forehead. Her hairline split, as did her skull, and blood gushed forth and down her face. She was silent and would remain so now, though her eyes remained open, still looking up at him.

He dreamed now of that night. He tossed and turned in bed. Hellish things twisted through his mind and body as if swooping in from all directions to rend him incapable of defence. He pictured her beautiful face, her broken and bloody face. He pictured her naked, he pictured her sloughed of skin. He pictured her in his bed, he pictured her rotting flesh.

He bolted upright, screaming in his bed; Gloria barely came awake by his side thanks to her sedatives. She mumbled in her stupor asking if he was okay and lifted an arm to soothe him. He brushed it away as he shivered and collected his thoughts, while looking all around to check they were alone. He lay in a cold damp and sweaty patch of sheet, his body slick with perspiration and clammy in the cool night air. He climbed out of bed and put on his robe before going downstairs to get a drink. He knew he wouldn't sleep that night now anyway. He would go to his study and work.

Chapter 7

The next morning, Sunday, was a beautiful day, with glorious sunshine from the outset. Despite the winter, it felt like spring was in the air. Gloria had risen relatively early and gotten herself ready to visit her sister along the coast - it had been planned for weeks. Charles had never really gotten along with her sister, or his brother-in-law, and had immediately turned down the original invitation, Gloria had asked if he wanted to come to 'get away' from it all, but still he declined.

With Gloria gone for a couple of days, he could relax; he could try to think things through and get a few things sorted in his mind, trying to make sense of everything that had happened in a short space of time. When he had gotten up during the night, he had gone to his study to work and that had completely taken his mind off his troubles. He decided to continue upon that track and hopefully his other issues would be resolved in his mind. After all, that was where he felt the problem lay, in his head.

He set to work and raced through his business affairs, organising schedules, planning meetings and working out budgets and timelines; he was on fire and he knew it. He stopped for lunch and settled down in his large and expansive gardens to eat when he heard a car pulling up on his property. On a Sunday? That seemed odd, so he went around to the front to see two men standing in his driveway.

"Can I help you, gentlemen?" he said.

"Mr Charles Carlton?" asked one of them.

"Yes. Who are you?"

"Sir, we are police officers. I'm Detective George Riley and this is my colleague, Sergeant Paul Morrow."

"Erm… How can I help you, Detective Riley?" Charles answered, suddenly feeling sheepish. "Oh wait, please. Where are my manners?

Please come in. Can I get you anything?" He gestured for them to follow him around to the back of the house, where he offered them a seat in the garden. "Something to drink perhaps?"

"No thank you, Sir," Riley responded for both of them. "I need to speak to you about two individuals, Mr Carlton. Individuals that we know from our investigations, you are familiar with."

"Of course, Detective, anything I can do to help?"

"First of all, we are looking into a murder investigation," Riley said, as Charles' heart began racing suddenly with thoughts of Anna. That hadn't taken long for them to find him, but just how did they know?

"The murder is of a Mr Ian Money, who was known to you very well, was he not, Sir?"

Charles paused. Shocked. Surprised. Relieved. He was all of those and more. Part of him wanted to smile, grin in fact, that this wasn't about Anna at all; she was still his little gruesome secret, his secret alone.

"Errr, yes......I know, or rather, *knew*, Mr Money very well. We were friends and very close friends. I'm sad, so sad to hear of this. What happened?"

"He was murdered in his home on Friday night, Sir. In the early hours of Saturday morning to be precise," Riley responded almost robotically and without emotion.

"Oh, that's tragic. Whoever would do such a thing?" His shock was genuine, although deep down he thought 'good riddance to the fat fuck'. He actually had no idea about the incident. The gossips at the fund raiser were going into overdrive, but no one suspected murder.

"We are investigating the murder currently, Sir, which is why we are here. Could you tell us your whereabouts on Friday night? Specifically between 11pm and 3am Saturday morning?" The detective's enquiry would bear no fruit because Charles knew he was innocent and he had an alibi. Unfortunately, that alibi was Cheryl and who knows what she would say about that night.

"I was with a friend," he said smugly.

"A 'friend', Sir? Does your friend have a name?" Riley replied.

"Errr, yes, of course" sneered Charles, but Sergeant Morrow stood with his notebook ready, diligently noting everything that was said.

"Well, I hope you can be discreet with my personal information - I am a married man you know and quite an influential..." he started before being abruptly interrupted.

"Sir, we are police officers carrying out a murder inquiry. Your private life is of no concern to us, unless it is relevant to our inquiries," sighed Riley, putting Charles in his place, before he could manage any further misguided sense of authority.

"Well, quite, Detective." he knew he had to explain. "Cheryl. Her name is Cheryl Baring."

"And do you have an address for Miss Baring?" asked Morrow.

"I'm afraid I don't, Sergeant." As Charles spoke, they both observed him carefully. "Erm, I do have her phone number though," he quickly finished, and went to get it from his phone. When he returned, Detective Riley had just finished explaining to his colleague that he knew who Cheryl was and her known contacts, so she would be easy to trace. Charles handed over the number anyway as he heard the tail end of the conversation.

"And Miss Baring can vouch for you and your whereabouts at the time in question, Mr Carlton?" finished Riley.

"Yes, Detective, she can," he replied, a little weight off his shoulders. He relaxed, then remembered there was something else. "Erm, didn't you say there were two individuals or something?"

"Yes, Sir - I was just coming to that. Are you aware of the location of a Miss Anna Levchenko?"

Suddenly, that weight lifted from his shoulders was back with a vengeance and Charles involuntarily slumped in his seat, looking unmistakably wild-eyed at the detectives, having been caught momentarily off guard.

"Are you alright, Sir?" asked Detective Morrow.

"Errr, yes, yes I'm fine. I erm....I'm just recovering from a car accident on Friday morning," he quickly responded on the spot to cover himself. "Must just be the after-effects of that."

Morrow quickly made a note of it and asked where and when exactly it had happened. Charles spoke easily, explaining the details, safe in the knowledge that it could be checked out.

"So, Miss Levchenko?" Asked Riley again.

"Oh yes - Anna. Yes. She worked for me, or rather at my offices. Just an intern you know. Bright girl from what I understand," he bluffed.

"Really, Sir. We were led to believe that you knew her very well indeed."

"My dear Detective, you don't want to believe office gossip," he said, laughing as he spoke, but only to himself - the police officers weren't laughing. "Well, errr, why do you want to know about Anna?" His mind was already racing, wondering just who the hell they'd already spoken to. Whoever it was would be fired one way or another.

"We are trying to locate her, Mr Carlton, because she hasn't been seen since Thursday night and friends and neighbours can't get hold of her. Apparently, this is very out of character for her, so we're looking into the matter with a degree of urgency and your name came up."

"Well, I'm dreadfully sorry, gentlemen, but I can't help you with that one. Now, errr, if you'll excuse me, I do have rather a lot of work to do. So, if there's nothing else?" He stood and gestured to walk them out.

"Nothing else at the moment, Sir," said Riley. "But as I said, our inquiries are at an early stage, but continuing........in both matters. Goodbye for now, Sir."

The officers got into their car and drove away, while Charles scurried back around to the rear of the house and stopped to breathe in relief and fear, trying to get his thumping heart under control.

Once the officers had left, he waited an hour to decide what to do next. He decided that he needed to be sure and got into his car and sped off to his lakeside house. On the way, his skittishness returned about his back seat, yet he had to overcome it, so he ploughed on. Occasionally, he would adjust the rear view mirror to check his absent reflection was indeed just that, absent, and it was. He eventually arrived at the lake and got out carefully, not really knowing what to expect. He walked to his house and unlocked it, then went through the place carefully. It was almost as if he didn't want to leave finger prints on his own house, but it was just a natural over-cautiousness that filtered through him. Satisfied that the house had been undisturbed, and, more importantly, that there was no sign of the police having been sniffing around, he went down to the lake.

He looked around, not really knowing what he was looking for, really just to reassure himself that there weren't tracks leading them to this place, literally and figuratively. He looked at the muddy ground at the lakeside to see if there were any drag marks where he had pulled her lifeless corpse to the edge, before lifting her up and slowly placing her into the water, and then watching her sink. The ground was indeed muddy under foot where the water lapped; the rest of the ground was still hard and frosty. Any marks had been there since before the winter had kicked in and had hardened the soil. He satisfied himself that there had been no outside interference, though he still felt uneasy. He had left his main house on a bright and beautiful day, almost warm for the time of year, yet now at the lake in mid-afternoon, it was cold, dark, dreary and almost foreboding. He could almost smell the air and feel it pull at him, a cloying scent lingering so much so that he could practically taste it.

Charles could take no more and decided to head back. The police were on a fishing trip; they would never tie him to Anna or her to this place, and as for Ian Money, that was absurd and nothing to do with him. He visibly relaxed a little at that thought.

The next morning, he rose early and called his secretary, even though she was still at home getting ready for work. He told her to get into th office early and make sure all the preparations were done for his meeting.

He showered and went to shave, but his reflection had still not returned. He pondered it all with a sigh and then raked his arm across the entire contents of the bathroom counters, taking everything in one fell swoop and smashing it all against the far wall. He screamed at the top of his lungs in frustration, anger and rage.

In the office he was a tyrant. He snapped at everyone. Nothing was right. Nobody looked right. Everyone was lazy and a slob and he told them all so. He overheard people talking at the water cooler; they were questioning the whereabouts of Anna and he went completely berserk. He said she was a slut. He said he thought she'd been stealing office supplies. He even went as far as to suggest that she was a plant from another rival company after his secrets. Industrial espionage he called it.

Thankfully for the staff, Charles had his major business meeting all afternoon in the boardroom and had left strict instructions not to be disturbed under any circumstances. The staff had their relief from him and gossip continued about Anna. Someone brought up Ian Money and how they were both connected to Carlton. Someone else even mentioned the story of the affair with Money's wife. Whispers built and built until they came to a crescendo, when amid the buzz, some visitors arrived.

Charles was deep into delicate negotiations with his clients when the intercom at his side buzzed. He visibly flared his nostrils and snarled at the interruption, which exasperated everyone, but none more so than Charles.

"WHAT?" he bellowed, as he pushed the intercom button.

"I'm sorry, Sir...," his secretary said, hesitating.

"What do you want, girl?" he snapped back at her, trying to regain his composure in front of his clients.

"I..errr...I know you didn't want to be disturbed, but..." she gasped.

"Under *any* circumstance I said."

"Yes, Sir, but..." She sounded like she was going to cry.

"Spit it the fuck out," he snapped finally.

"The Police are here to see you."

The colour drained from Charles' face and his voice became hoarse as he looked up at the enquiring looks of his rivals' faces.

"Oh, ok, Dianne. Errr........I'll be out in a minute," he stammered, before standing and excusing himself, explaining that it was regarding a matter that the police had asked for his expertise in.

Chapter 8

Charles uneasily exited the boardroom, panic sweeping over him as he did so. He was sure there was nothing to worry about. He had checked the lake himself. "Shit. What if the bastards had been following me?" he thought to himself and mumbled it under his breath as he approached the foyer, where the two officers from the previous day were waiting.

"Gentlemen. Hello. What can I do for you?" he said as he approached, his hand outstretched to shake; neither of them offered theirs in return.

"Mr Carlton, we need to speak to you immediately," stated Detective Riley.

"Of course, of course. My office is this way," he said, ushering them through, before turning back to his secretary and sweetly saying, "Dianne, would you be so kind as to inform my guests that I won't be a moment, please?"

Dianne was half standing to go into the boardroom and about to reply when Detective Riley answered for her.

"Actually, Miss, it would be better if you asked Mr Carlton's colleagues if they could reschedule for a later date."

"Erm, excuse me, Detective," blustered Charles. "But *I* will decide when and how my meetings are arranged, not you."

"Be that as it may, Sir, but this will take longer than a few moments - we need you to accompany us to the police station for questioning."

Charles mouth dropped open; he kept thinking about Anna. They know. They *know*. Dianne stood up, wide-eyed, amazed and shocked at what was happening, her hands instinctively covering her open mouth. Through the glass panelling, other staff were starting to notice and small groups of workers began whispering and gossiping amongst themselves.

Charles was led away as subtly as possible, and it was then that he asked if he would need a lawyer, to which he was told he should. He called over his shoulder to Dianne, asking her to call Edward Beaumont. Detective Morrow paused to inform her which police station to send him to and with that they left with Charles to 'help with their enquiries'.

Less than an hour later, Charles was sitting in a police interview room, with his faithful, well-respected and very expensive lawyer, Edward Beaumont, by his side. Detective Riley and Sergeant Morrow sat across from the two men and Riley explained that he was about to start recording their conversation. Once the machine started to record, Charles was asked a number of basic questions to confirm his identity, date of birth, residence and so forth. The purpose of the interview was also outlined to him and the fact that he was not under arrest.

Charles was asked many probing questions about his relationship with the deceased, Ian Money. He was also interrogated about his relationship with Cheryl Baring, as she was meant to be his alibi on the night of Ian's murder. He told them a little, but was quickly told to withhold the information by Beaumont. It was then pointed out to Charles that his alibi hadn't checked out as of yet as the police were finding it difficult to locate Miss Baring. He was concerned for the first time, but tried not to let it show.

He was asked about his marriage, his business dealings, the way he treated his staff and about his renowned temper. To most of these questions, Mr Beaumont would query the validity or relevance to the inquiry. He also pointed out at various intervals that his client was not under arrest and was free to leave at any time, by way of a reminder. On the occasions that Charles did answer for himself, he invariably replied, "No comment," as pre-instructed by Beaumont, who looked very pleased with himself throughout.

Finally, in order to get a reaction out of Charles, Morrow handed his superior a file. The file contained photographs of Ian Money, crime scene photographs, of the dead man. The pictures were taken out of the file by Riley, who explained what he was doing for the benefit of the recording. He spread them out on the table between the men, doing so deliberately to allow Charles to get a very good look.

Beaumont had seen such things before when accompanying his other clients and nothing usually fazed him, but even he winced at the images. Charles, a man who had secretly killed a number a victims, one of them only a couple of days earlier, merely glanced down and then back at the officers. The body in the pictures was barely recognisable as a person, let alone someone whom he had been close to years before. On closer inspection, there was an arm - or rather a hand - at the end of a bloody mass. There was what looked like a flayed torso, but no head and therefore no face to recognise. Blood stains were all over the room in which the atrocity had taken place; it seemed almost ritualistic in nature in the way the gore was strewn around. On a table by the corpse, there was a specific lump of flesh. It was pointed out that that was, indeed, Ian Money's heart.

Beaumont curled up his nose as he heard how it was thought that the man had been butchered. Charles disassociated himself from the whole thing by not connecting that body with his former friend. He came across as cold and callous, but he knew he was completely innocent of the murder - well of that one, at least. He didn't want to get too dragged into such things for fear of letting slip something about Anna.

With his lack of reaction gaining little purchase for the officers, Charles felt he was getting on top of the situation. He knew they had nothing on him and it was only a matter of time before they had to let him go. However, just as he could sense the relief of victory, a television screen was pulled over on a wheeled trolley from the corner of the room by Morrow. It was already plugged in and set up, a DVD already inserted, and all Riley had to do was press 'play' on the remote that his colleague handed him.

"There is one more thing, Mr Carlton, before we wrap this up," he said.

"Errr, yes - what?" asked a bemused Charles.

"What are you playing at, Detective? Are you fishing here?" questioned Beaumont.

"Just a query, gentlemen." He held up the remote and pressed 'play' and the screen flickered into life.

It was a grainy black and white image. It looked like a security tape from a hotel or apartment building. Charles didn't recognise the place and sat there smiling and shaking his head because he knew that he hadn't been there before.

"This was taken at 1:35am at Mr Ian Money's apartment complex," commented Detective Riley. "You will note something very strange and unusual happening now."

Right on cue, an image appeared. The view was outside the building looking up the street, and, walking down the street to the building, was a man. The man seemed very pale and both Charles and Beaumont had to squint their eyes to get a better view. As they leaned in closer, it became clear why the man seemed so pale. He was completely naked!

They both looked at each other in bemusement and then back at the detectives for some form of clarity. Riley simply pointed back at the screen and they turned their eyes back as if ordered to.

"Recognise him?" asked Morrow, to which Charles shook his head.

"How about now?" Riley followed up right on cue, as suddenly the naked man walked right up to where the camera was and pulled himself up to the lens. It was, without a doubt, Charles Carlton.

Charles sat in his seat totally dumbfounded. Beaumont looked at his client and his mouth fell open; neither knew what to say. Charles had known full well that at that time he had been in his penthouse.

"This proves nothing! It's simply a remarkable likeness to my client!" snapped Beaumont, clicking straight back into gear. "What else do you have? Fingerprints? DNA? Any physical evidence whatsoever?"

"But... I... I... WASN'T THERE!" shouted Charles at the top of his voice, his desperation rising.

"Calm down, Mr Carlton" responded Morrow.

"I think this recording proves otherwise, Charlie," sneered Riley.

"Wait! Is there anything showing my client inside the building?" asked Beaumont, to which both detectives sighed their disgruntlement. "I take it that's a 'no', gentlemen?"

The detectives sighed again and looked at Charles with disdain. They knew in the pits of their stomachs that he was the one they wanted, but they had no physical evidence other than a very embarrassing video. They sat in stony silence.

"Well as my client is free to leave, we shall do just that. Charles? We're leaving."

The two men got up and walked out of the room and out of the building, both keeping quiet until they got to Beaumont's car. They were pleased, but still stunned by events - no one more so than Charles.

"What on earth were you thinking, Charles?" snapped Beaumont.

"For fuck's sake, Ed - I'm telling you the same as I told them. That is NOT me!"

"Well who the hell is it then?"

"I don't know," Charles sighed before burying his head in his hands. Was he lying? Did he know who it was really? He couldn't be sure. Was it his reflection? And, if so, would that make it part of him? "Please just take me home, Ed".

"Sure."

"In fact, no, drop me back at the office," he asked.

"The office? Surely you're not going in to work now?"

"No," sighed Charles again. "I'm gonna pick up my car and go for a drive."

"Well, ok, but don't do anything stupid."

Chapter 9

Beaumont dropped Charles in his office complex garage. The journey had been relatively short and they had undertaken it in virtual silence as Charles was in no mood to talk. They said they would be in touch and Charles got into his own car. As Edward drove away, Charles sat alone and wept. He wept with anger. He wept with frustration. He wept as his mind and reality as he knew it, slipped away.

Once he had pulled himself together, he made a decision that he would go to the cabin. He needed to get away and that was as good a place as any. Plus, if he wanted answers, that would be the place to start. As he drove out into the early evening, he called his wife and told her that he needed some time to work and relax away from the stresses that he had been under. He tried to be as gentle as possible and to reassure her that it was in no way connected to her or anything she had done. He simply needed some time to himself and he would be back in a couple of days. After a few tears from Gloria, and even a few from Charles, they told each other, 'I love you,' and then they hung up. For once, he meant it. He switched his phone off, determined not to be disturbed.

When he arrived at the cabin, darkness had fallen completely. He pulled off the mud track and onto the rough driveway leading to the building, before pulling up outside the cabin and switching the engine off. He paused in his seat for a few minutes, waiting, but he didn't really know why. Hesitating, he got out of the car and unlocked the door of the cabin, looking around still nervous at the thought that somebody, maybe the police, had been checking up on him. It was his secret hideaway that only he and his wife knew about, though the girls at the bottom of his lake had known about it... briefly. And those girls were his secret, his secret alone.

Of course the land was registered to him - another crooked deal that he had swindled a rival out of. Ironically, it was formerly owned by Ian Money. Well, he wouldn't be missing it anymore! The authorities could find out about the property, but why would they look? They weren't looking for anything like a body - yet. That would at least give him some time, he thought, time to try to make plans, maybe get rid of Anna's corpse. But then again it was safe where it was, at least, until they can't find her and maybe then they would be looking for a body. Decisions, decisions and all those thoughts passed through his mind and were exactly why he needed to be away from everything and everyone for a while.

He went back outside and into the now cold and frosty night air. The wind was picking up pace and swirling around his ankles, so he wrapped his overcoat around himself tighter and walked down slowly to the lake. The ground alternated between hard and icy and wet and slippery, where the wind had whipped water from the surface of the lake onto the formerly grassy bank. He stood about four or five feet from the water's edge, gazing across the lake to the far side and the bare trees billowing in the increasing wind. The illumination of the moon on such a clear and cloudless night was picturesque, lending a silvery glow to the blackness of the lake before him. Everything looked as it should. The only exception was the now routine absence of his reflection in the water, something which he had become accustomed to all too easily it seemed. The strengthening breeze made swirls across the water and the moonlight gave an unearthly beauty to the image, then he heard something.

He heard a voice. At least he thought he had heard a voice and he quickly turned to see who was there. Of course, there was no one there; there was no one for miles around in his seclusion. That was why he loved the place. If anybody had arrived, he would have heard their car pull up, and would have seen headlights travelling along the deserted road around the lake, before they hit the mud track up to his property. He was alone and he knew it. The sound continued and he realised that it must have been the wind howling away. Still, he pondered on the lake and what he had done, trying to work a way out of it, his mind galloping with thoughts and plans, each one being discarded as quickly as it formed. The sound continued and he continued to ignore it. The movement of the lake from the wind increased and again he continued to ignore that too, to his cost.

About ten feet from where he stood, a shape began to emerge from the lake. Charles paid it no mind as initially it just seemed like a trick of the light caused by the water rippling and the moonlight dancing across the surface, but gradually it formed to something of a shadow. His mind was on other things, but the 'shadow' seemed to take substance and depth. Its silhouette was solid and whole and utterly black and dense. Charles' mind practically stopped as he took notice of it and peered forward to see what it could be. His head moved from side to side, his eyes narrowing as if to peer through the darkness. He edged forward to see.

The thing in front of him kept rising up; up from the water until it was completely free and he saw that it hovered now a foot above the lake, water dripping from it, causing their own ripples of silver and black. Charles stood with mouth agape, before the thing almost stopped his heart. What was a rough covering of some sort slipped from a face to reveal the cold, dead, wet flesh of Anna Levchenko.

Charles yelped with fear and lurched backwards, but the ground beneath his shoes was wet and muddy, and as his weight moved back away from the sight, his legs became like jelly and didn't respond to his sense of flight. The only outcome was his falling down, down in a tangled heap in the mud and frost. He landed heavily and the air was knocked from his lungs. His back ached and his feet that had slipped so spectacularly from under him were now in the shallows of the lake edge. He steadied himself and pushed himself upright and was about to draw his feet out of the icy water, but he didn't get the chance.

Suddenly, hands reached out of the water. At least two pairs grabbed at his feet and Charles let out a chilling scream that echoed around the area, but no one heard. Everything seemed to move in slow motion before his eyes. The hands were slimy and darkened and cold, so cold; he could feel them through the fabric of his trousers. A pungent smell wafted from the disturbance in the lake. The smell of death, lingering and decaying death. The body of Anna still hovered over the lake, now way too close to him it seemed, as she looked down on the scene, unmoved by his overwhelming fear. The hands took a firmer hold, even though he kicked and struggled. Another pair of hands came up out of the water and aided Anna in the task of dragging him into the lake. As they reached forward, the owners of the hands came up out of the water, their arms and shoulders and finally their heads breaking the surface. Charles' nightmare multiplied as he saw their faces snarling at him.

Charles, somehow through the haze of torment and tears that filled his eyes, recognised the harpies in front of him. Their flesh was pale and waxy and glistened with the water in the moonlight. Their hair stuck to their damp faces, straggled and matted with twigs and dead leaves. Their eyes were white and bulbous as they glared at him from their sunken sockets. The flesh was damaged on their faces from violence inflicted by him and the gouges were now filled with slime, silt and debris from the bottom of the lake. Shreds of clothes or binds that had tied them dangled from their bodies and arms. Their mouths were open in silent screams of torment and accusation at their murderer. Their mouths were filled with more debris and yellowed teeth and each with swollen tongues lashed their hatred at him. His victims snarled at him as they tried to drag him down to their watery mausoleum.

Charles struggled and fought for all he was worth. Anna stared down at the scene impassively, as her sisters of the lake tried to take their revenge upon their killer. He kicked at their faces as he tried to grasp for something - anything to hold on to for any slight purchase. With each kick, he managed to pull himself a little further away and dig a heel into the soft wet bank. Gradually, he inched his way to safety, but not before a final effort from the unfortunates to jump out of the lake and drag him back. He gripped hold of the mud in huge handfuls and launched himself back up the bank with every ounce of strength he could muster. Fortunately for him, they couldn't quite reach him and they slithered back into the water.

He lay on the bank, panting and gasping for breath, his eyes wide with fear, not taking them off the lake for a second. Anna stared back at him. Her sisters also stared at him as they slowly slipped back below the surface. Anna gently lowered herself down, barely making a ripple; such was the grace with which she departed back down to the depths. He waited until he was sure they were gone, before clambering back to his feet and away from the lake as quickly as possible.

He stumbled back to the cabin, cold, frozen to the bone and shaking uncontrollably - partly through the extreme chill, but mainly through the fear and horror he had witnessed. He practically fell through the door and bolted it behind him. He made it to the kitchen and poured himself a very large Scotch, taking a huge gulp, before collapsing to his knees in despair.

Chapter 10

Two days passed with Charles holed up in the cabin. He didn't go down to the lake once but stayed behind the bolted doors with furniture barricading him in for good measure. He plugged his phone into his spare charger that he kept at the cabin and switched his it back on; he saw that he had twenty seven missed calls, largely from his wife and his secretary. He had spent the last forty eight hours in a dazed and confused state. He tried to understand what was going on and, more importantly, what it all meant and how he was going to deal with it. Although he didn't know it for sure, he could practically feel the noose tighten around his neck. It would surely be just a matter of time before everything came out.

He even started to doubt himself regarding the murder of Ian Money. He had known for sure that he hadn't been to his home in years, but the camera footage that the police had shown him seemed to prove otherwise. Was he actually losing his mind? He spent the latter part of his time in the cabin trying to figure out how to get out of his nightmare. Would he be able to use his mental situation as a defence should he be charged with the murder? Was that what they meant when he saw news reports about 'diminished responsibility'? The downside of that was that those people usually ended up in a secure psychiatric facility and usually for longer than they would've gone to prison for. He shuddered at the thought.

Then there was the 'Anna problem', which was putting things mildly. Firstly, no one had seen anything; they were alone when he had killed her. Secondly, no one would have seen him dump her body at the lake. Thirdly, she was only a missing person at that point and finally and, more importantly, who else could he blame it on? His first instinct was to blame Ian Money. The guy was dead anyway so it couldn't harm him. There wouldn't be any forensic evidence due to her being in the lake and the longer that went on, surely the better chance of evidence being corrupted or washed away.

He had gotten the cabin from Money in the first place. Who's to say that the man didn't keep a spare set of keys for himself? He could've been having an affair with the girl for a while up there and then things went wrong and he dumped her in the lake. Charles practically convinced himself that it was plausible; all he had to do was point the police in that direction. He knew that that would be easier said than done, but at least he had a shot.

He started to make the journey home and used the time to iron out any wrinkles in his half-baked plan. He figured out what he was going to say and how he was going to come across as a concerned citizen. The only issue, which was a big one, was the footage of 'him' at Ian Money's home. However, it was only of someone who looked like Charles outside, as his lawyer would argue, which meant nothing at all. There were still no fingerprints or physical evidence putting him inside the place. Plus, as the recording showed, he was naked. Surely there would be some evidence of him in there. The longer he drove, the more he convinced himself that he could beat it.

The only thing that concerned him then was what he had witnessed in the lake - Anna and his other victims. He hadn't managed to get it out of his mind and it still haunted his dreams - when he managed to sleep that was. Then again, no one else had witnessed it; it could've just been an actual nightmare. Also, if he could persuade the authorities to look into Ian Money and they dredged the lake, those horrors could also be blamed on his dead former friend, too.

He smiled to himself and decided to call his wife just as he entered the city limits; she would be worried and would be his 'support'. If he could get Gloria on his side, believing the story that he was creating, it would be a very good step towards helping him get out of the situation that had developed. He called her and told her that he was coming home.

Inspector Riley was sitting at his desk, mulling over events regarding the murder of Ian Money. He had the file open and was flicking through the crime scene photographs, when his colleague Detective Morrow came in.

Morrow was flustered, but smiling, as he approached his superior and said, "We've got him, Sir!"

"What do you mean, Paul?"

"We got the fucker, Carlton; he ain't getting out of this!" Morrow said with relish in his voice.

"Slow down and tell me."

"Cheryl Baring. We've found her"

"And...?" replied Riley.

"She's dead, boss."

"Fuck - what happened?"

"A young woman's body was found behind City Hall last night and she's just been identified as Cheryl Baring," smiled Morrow.

"I don't see a reason to be cheerful in this, Sergeant," said Riley, coldly.

"Sorry, Sir, it's not her death that I'm smiling about."

"So what are you smiling about? Spit it out."

"Well, we have security footage here," Morrow said, producing a disc from his pocket.

"And we have the murder being carried out as clear as day."

"Charles Carlton?" Riley gasped as he sat up straight in his chair.

"Bang to rights, boss. Plus we've already checked that he was a guest at City Hall on Saturday night when the footage was recorded. See for yourself." Morrow handed the disc to his superior, who put it into his computer and started to play the recording.

The footage was grainy and in black and white, clearly taken at night, but it was a relatively good picture. However, the actual pictures that were revealed were not good in any way shape or form. The area was a rear entrance, where there was an access door with a sign painted on the wall that read "Deliveries". A number of rubbish bins stood to one side and a large dumpster stood open with the expected black bin bags sticking out. There was an open area, presumably for trucks and vans to back into when delivering food or catering services for large events like the fundraiser that had taken place on the previous Saturday night. The footage was taken late that night, but nobody had seen fit to review the images. Not until the tragedy that had befallen Cheryl Baring.

As the officers watched, a young woman in an evening dress came out of the rear door. Clearly, it was Miss Baring. She seemed flustered and in a hurry, but she paused and turned back before the door closed behind her. Another figure came into view - a man with his back to the monitor, but well-dressed and clearly someone from the same event that she had attended.

A conversation between the two quickly became intimidating to the young woman, judging by the look of fear and panic on her face. Sadly, there was no sound to the film and the police officers could only wonder what was being said. Either way, it was clearly becoming distressing to Cheryl. She started to edge away from the man and he grabbed her arm forcibly and pulled her back to him. She was unmistakeably struggling to free herself when he produced a blade from inside his jacket. Her eyes widened in terror as he taunted her with the weapon, gently gliding it up and down her bare arms and then across her throat, the cold steel making her shiver and tense for fear of it slicing her flesh.

As dark as the atmosphere seemed to be between the two of them, it suddenly took a turn for the worse. The man slid his hand up her arm to the back of her neck and grabbed her by the hair, yanking her head back painfully, her mouth opening, letting out a silent scream. He seemed to be toying with her and, again, he traced the blade across her throat. She started to tremble and cry at his torture.

"Turn around, you fucking bastard," Riley mumbled as he watched intently. "Turn the fuck around."

"Any second now, boss - just wait," replied Morrow. "Here we go."

As if on cue, the man turned around and looked directly at the camera, clearly knowing it was there. Charles Carlton. He smiled as he did so and even winked at his audience. All the while, he continued to graze the weapon across Cheryl's neck. Without looking back at her, he moved the tip of the blade to just below her left ear and pushed gently, but firmly with enough force to puncture the flesh. Blood oozed and trickled down her neck and shoulder, cascading down between her breasts. Her eyes widened with a wince of pain and then further still at the feeling of the liquid pouring down her body. Her head tilted slightly forward and she looked down to see the crimson flood building and streaming from her and, again, she screamed at the realisation of what had happened. Throughout the horror, her assailant retained eye contact with the camera, keeping his sickening smile in place.

"Bastard," Riley said, his heart racing with adrenalin and his fists clenched in anger as he watched helplessly.

The officers had an obligation to watch the whole recording and, as hardened to such things as they were, even they found the events hard to stomach. They endured the video as the poor victim was sliced through her wrists, bleeding slowly at first, his hand over her mouth, her struggles to free herself making her blood pump faster. He seemed to whisper in her ear and she calmed, unconsciousness and death looming, not knowing what else to do. She seemed in a daze of panic and fear. The officers were hushed as they continued to watch, not really being able to comprehend the trauma that must've been going on inside her mind.

As she weakened, he lay her down on the ground, every now and again looking up at the camera to give as good a show as possible. Her head tilted from side to side illustrating that she was still alive, and he cut the dress from her and threw it towards the dumpster. For a gut wrenching horrible moment, Riley thought that Carlton was going to rape the girl, too. Mercifully he didn't, but that was simply a small mercy as he then proceeded to slice and peel the skin from her naked body. They could see her in pain and agony, but shock and blood loss were taking their toll as she lay, almost catatonic now, in torment, while he continued to revel in his sickening work.

"I've seen enough," sighed Riley, as he stopped the film before the end. He shook his head in disgust at what he'd just witnessed, before Morrow handed him a file that had been brought to them as they were watching the video. He opened it to reveal the scene of crime photographs.

The photos were largely of the dumpster, blood caked all around the open door and large sides of meat piled up inside. Sadly, these were the body parts of the tragic Cheryl Baring, a once lovely and vibrant young woman, discarded like pieces of offal by a butcher. Riley only glanced at them quickly. The vibrancy of the colour photos contrasting with the real time video in black and white was startling even to him.

"Sir," came the voice of a junior officer.

"Yes," sighed Riley in dismay.

"We've just received a call from Mrs Gloria Carlton."

"Well?" Morrow called over.

"You left a message asking her to call you when her husband returned?"

"Yes, yes?" Riley sat up eagerly. He had been trying to get hold of Carlton for the last two days to follow up on the Ian Money case, but he had been 'incommunicado" as his wife had put it. Riley had stressed the importance of helping with their enquiries and Gloria had duly agreed to call the moment that Charles returned.

"Well, she said he called her from his car and will be home shortly."

Riley and Morrow clenched their fists in triumph, knowing that now they would have their man. There was no getting away from the evidence. They grabbed their coats and bolted out of the office to their car.

Chapter 11

Charles arrived home and called out, relatively and surprisingly cheerfully "Honey, I'm home!" before heading straight upstairs. His mood had changed dramatically, especially considering the events he had witnessed at the lake. He went straight to the bathroom to urinate after the long drive. Gloria called upstairs. She had heard a voice but was checking to see if he was really home and that he was alright. He shouted back that he would be down in a minute.

After finishing, he went over to wash his hands at his wash basin, noticing that the mirror above had not yet been replaced. It was then he heard a voice.

"So... You think you have it all worked out, do you?"

Startled, Charles looked around the room before noticing something out of the corner of his eye. Gloria's mirror. Tentatively, he stepped over to it and saw himself in the looking glass. This would be normal for anybody else to witness, but this was a strange sight to Charles and unexpected. He paused for a moment, tilting his head from side to side, lifting his hand up and waving at himself and the reflection seemed just that. A reflection of Charles doing exactly the same thing, his confusion returned, until one hand waved one time too many and the reflection just stood there looking at him, unresponsive. Then it spoke.

"Got a plan have we, Charlie boy?" it said.

"Errr...," was all he could muster as a mumbled response.

"Hmm, quite the master plan I see," his reflection mocked him.

Everyone at some stage or other in their lives talks to themselves. Most people would admit to talking to themselves in the mirror, whether it be a casual, "Looking good" when they're ready to go out, or a simple "Fuck" when they see themselves after a heavy night out. Others would have said something along the lines of, "What the fuck is that?" upon seeing something unsightly in the mirror. However, no one would dream that when they spoke alone in the privacy of their own home, their reflection would respond, let alone start a conversation, but that's exactly what Charles was going through.

"I, errr, I thought you had gone," Charles asked, knowing himself that he sounded stupid, but he couldn't think of anything else to say, such was the surreal nature of what was happening.

"I had, but now I'm back," his reflection replied, staring deep into Charles' eyes with a seemingly menacing intent. "Aren't you going to ask the more obvious questions?"

"W-what questions?"

"Who are you? What's going on? Why is this happening? Why are you doing this to me? Is this a nightmare? How can I make it stop?" His reflection actually seemed dismayed, yet slightly amused at the situation.

"Errr, yes," was all Charles could reply. He rested his hands on the counter top for support, his legs suddenly feeling like shaky and unstable, as his heart raced. Fear rose from his stomach, giving him bile in the back of his throat. "All of those."

"Very well, as you're not very talkative today, I'll tell you exactly what's going on," the reflection began as if talking to a child at bedtime. "First of all, who am I? Well, that's easy and also the most difficult thing to explain. Basically, I am you, or more accurately, your reflection. That much you could pretty much work out for yourself. Whether you consider me 'just that' is your choice. You could also say that I am your conscience, but that is a bit Pinocchio and Jiminy fuckin' Cricket for my tastes!" The reflection laughed with a sickening sneer on his lips before continuing. "You might also consider me to be your soul, but again, I don't feel very spiritual. From my actions, I don't seem to be that way inclined. Either way, it's your prerogative. Consider me one of those, all of those, none of those or just a fucked-up part of you."

Charles pulled a stool over to the basin and sat down as the reflection continued to tell him the tale. Swinging between terrified to fascinated, Charles didn't take his eyes off the image for a second.

"That's right, Charlie. You get yourself comfortable." The reflection's sickening smile returned as his audience waited. "What's going on? Why is this happening? Why are you doing this to me? Well, to put it simply, you are cursed, Charlie." The sick smile practically slid from the image's face and he glared with malicious intent as if deep in to Charles' soul. Charles felt a shudder slide like ice all the way down his spine.

"What? Why? What do you mean? Charles was actually surprised and in disbelief, yet there seemed to be more disbelief on the face of his reflection.

"Charlie, I know what you've done. I KNOW," it said.

Charles didn't know how to respond. His secrets were supposed to be just that, secrets. His and his alone. He had been alone when he had committed those vile acts and killings; he had taken great lengths to keep his privacy and hide everything and yet now he was being told that effectively his secrets were no such thing.

"I was there throughout EVERYTHING, Charlie. I saw what you did to those girls and I admit it, I enjoyed it. You are one sick puppy, Chaz!"

The reflection laughed openly in his face, seemingly leaning forward as if he was going to come right out of the mirror itself. Charles simply sat there with his mouth agape in horror.

"Why are you doing this to me?" begged Charles in bewilderment. "Why are you taunting me?"

"Now, don't start getting defensive, Charlie, as though you are the injured party here. As I said, you are cursed for what you did. Remember your last little kill? Anna Levchenko?"

Charles was now feeling guilt and shame, perhaps for the first time in his life, and he simply nodded his response.

"Yeah, you bet your ass you do. Well you see, you've been using your little fuck-nest up at the lake for a while there and indulging your little killing sprees too. Having a ready-made disposal point on your doorstep is very handy and I've been witness to all of your 'activities' too, but at some point you have to pay the piper as they say. Little Anna, well she was the turning point, wasn't she? The one you did wrong that you shouldn't have done."

The reflection tutted and shook his head before continuing.

"She was from an old Russian family, from a little town called Evagrad, in the middle of that huge country. You wouldn't find it on most maps. Well, they have their ways, their traditions and their customs, as most ancient countries do. They also have their stories and their legends and, in such places, I mean the really out of the way places, where they are still living their lives as their ancestors did hundreds of years before, those places still hold fast to their superstitions and, more importantly for you, their curses.

Not only did you do wrong to Anna - I mean, you fucking murdered her! But you murdered her unborn baby, too. *Your* unborn baby. Her dying breaths were devoted to cursing you until your dying day. The power and the hate and the death that you, yourself, had already put into that lake is a seriously potent brew, Anna and her curse were the catalyst. She has found new sisters in those dark, cold waters and they are consumed from beyond death's veils to have their revenge on you. All of them. You saw all of that darkness a few days ago; you witnessed it for yourself. You may be wondering where I come in. Well, no need to ask. I am the manifestation of their power and rage on this plain. I have been set free!"

Charles suddenly jumped back and off the stool, staring wildly at the mirror. The realisation was finally dawning on him. For all the strangeness of recent events, he had tried to rationalise it all. He had tried to make plans to get out of everything and make good his escape. Yet now he was in a whole world of horror and he felt as if he were being dragged down in to the pits by it.

"Hitting you hard now is it, my man?" the reflection taunted again with a sly wink. "Hey, I'm just an extension of you."

"So, so that was really you? At Ian Money's place?" asked Charles, his heart racing.

"That's right. Naked as the day you were born," laughed the image. "In case you were wondering, I was naked because that's how you were and therefore, me, when I left you. I couldn't leave any fingerprints or anything so I had to make it as obvious as possible so the old authorities can nail you down for both of them."

"B-both of them? What do you mean? What else have you done?" gasped Charles.

"Oh that's right. You don't know yet." The image laughed at him again. "Ah, sweet Cheryl - she was a beauty, right?"

"What the fuck? No, no, you haven't... Please tell me you haven't!" Charles started to sob uncontrollably as his life unravelled before him, along with his sanity.

"Oh fuck, yeah! I really wanted to fuck her like you did, but duty called, so I made sure they got a good look at you and I mean a *really* good look and then I let them watch as I butchered the bitch. Man, that was fun," it said, grinning back sadistically.

"You evil fuckin' bastard? wept Charles.

"Hey brother - I'm just an extension of you as I said. I just had to turn things up a few notches to take you down. That is my calling and why I now exist. If you have a problem with me, I suggest you take it up with Anna."

Charles slumped to his knees, unable to stand, before sinking down onto the floor. He felt he was having a heart attack; such was the pain and anguish in his chest. He started to shake and his flesh became clammy. He tried to get his breathing under control as he clambered to his feet. In his mind, he decided to do as his reflection had told him and take it up with Anna. How he was supposed to do that he had no idea, but he felt that the lake was the place to go. She was the key and he had to find out how to stop what was happening.

He paused at his basin and ran the tap, splashing cold water onto his face and cupping a handful to his mouth to ease his parched lips. He heard voices downstairs and wondered who was there with Gloria, but he couldn't make it out. It seemed like a pleasant conversation - no shouting; she wasn't calling upstairs for him, so she obviously knew who it was. Then he heard a sickening scream. Gloria's scream. Immediately, he moved to her mirror and there was no reflection. Where was he? Charles didn't need a second guess and he bolted out of the bathroom and back down stairs screaming her name.

Chapter 12

Charles raced down the stairs and went straight to the kitchen, where Gloria could usually be found, and sadly that is exactly where he found her. She was on her knees facing him, her face bleeding from violent blows, tears of confusion spilling from her eyes and down her trembling cheeks. Behind her and standing over her was the 'other' Charles. He held her by her hair with a carving knife at her throat, as Charles rushed in. The entire colour visibly and quickly drained from her face as he did so. She had been preparing a meal when Charles, or who she thought was Charles, came in and he promptly attacked her, beating her for no apparent reason. She was in unadulterated agony and fear.

As Charles had entered, no one could imagine what was going through her mind. Her 'husband' had her on her knees with a blade at her throat and then her husband walked in to confront her husband.

"No!" yelled Charles. "Please! I'm begging you - don't do it! Don't hurt her!"

"Ch-Charles," sniffed Gloria as she fought back tears unsuccessfully. "Charles, w-what's happening? I don't understand."

Charles was fighting back his own tears, tears of hurt and anger as he watched his wife's torment. He watched her agony, her pain and confusion. Here was a woman who loved him unconditionally, accepted all of his many flaws and yet would blindly follow him wherever he asked her to go or do whatever he asked. His time had come to show his equal love for her and in true Charles Carlton fashion......he turned and bolted for the door.

As he ran he could hear her scream his name in desperation, desperation that her life was undoubtedly about to end in a horrific and violent way. He also heard his own laughter but coming from the 'other' in the kitchen. He paid no attention to either as he made it to the front door, flung it open and raced to his car. He heard the laughter seemingly getting closer behind him which only served to increase his heart rate and make him tremble and shake.

He got in the car and fumbled with his keys. Out of the corner of his eye he saw the 'other' move quickly yet without actually running towards the car, in fact it seemed to glide across the distance. It was a strange sight which someone less terrified would marvel at but Charles knew his life was in danger. He revved the engine and as he screeched away sending debris and small driveway pebbles spinning away in a cloud of dust, the 'other' seemed to unbelievably pass through the closed passenger door! A split second earlier Charles had been making his escape alone and yet now this thing was sitting right by his side, grinning inanely, yet it all seemed to happen in slow motion.

Momentarily, Charles sat open-mouthed, awe struck by everything that was happening but in the distance he heard a police siren that made his foot hit the floor as he accelerated away as quickly as possible. He didn't know whether the police car had got anything to do with him but that noise certainly made his mind up to run, as if on auto-pilot be bulleted away from his home without a backward glance, even with his unwanted passenger.

He drove as fast as he could away from his dream home that had so quickly turned into a nightmare and yet the nightmare was going with him and there didn't seem anything he could do to stop it. He tried to think, think hard. He had been devious enough in business and with his affairs and 'disposals' but every route his mind seemed to take looking for solutions it came up with a dead end. The 'other' sat there smirking to itself, watching him, studying him but saying nothing. Seemingly its work was done, his sanity was truly shattered, madness was taking hold and surely that had been the ultimate goal for it. He glanced over at it and its smug smile seemed to be proof of its victory.

Charles drove hard and fast, he hadn't been aware of where he was going, he just wanted to be away from the horror but he seemed to be heading towards his cabin. It seemed a logical place to go, if indeed as the 'other' had said that Anna Levchenko had cursed him from the lake then surely that would be the place to stop it. He still didn't know how exactly he was going to do it, but at least he knew where to go, he would figure it out on the journey.

Back at his house, the police arrived. The sirens had indeed been for him and the detectives arrived just as Gloria stumbled out of the front door and slumped in a heap on the front steps. They screeched to a halt and jumped out of their car and over to her as she lay sobbing and bleeding. Her face was a mess of cuts and bruises, the 'other' had let her live but that wouldn't help Charles. She cried and mumbled about how her husband had beaten her and threatened her with a carving knife. She was distraught and confused but her story was enough to strengthen the officers resolve to get her bastard of a husband.

Riley held and comforted her; Morrow had already called for assistance and the paramedics as they pulled up in the driveway. They could hear the back-up rushing to their aid and they knew the clock was ticking to find Carlton. Thankfully she explained about his cabin and the area where she thought it was. She hadn't been there herself but she'd seen maps and documentation from when he acquired the place. When Charles had originally got hold of the cabin, she'd thought it would be for the two of them. Sadly Charles then quickly realised the potential of the place for just himself. She had always known about his secret life but had never come to terms with it. She'd always hoped that one day they would go together, now though, that dream, like so many others, was over.

The paramedics arrived and seconds later so too did two other police cars. They handed over Gloria to the medics and told the first officers on scene to check and secure the house. The second pair of officers were told to follow Riley and Morrow as they started their pursuit of Charles Carlton to his cabin hideaway.

Charles drove at high speed, almost on auto-pilot. Luckily the majority of the journey took place on long country roads where there was little traffic, if any. He was taking treacherous corners and hairpin bends perilously fast with no thought for himself or others. Occasionally the odd car would have to swerve out of his way or pull over to let him pass, followed by shouts and abuse aimed at him through an open car window. Charles seemed oblivious to it all as he sped to his destination, his unwanted passenger grinning menacingly by his side.

The 'other' chipped into his mind with thoughts and whispers about his victims and what they went through; the hell that they had suffered and how it would be nothing compared to what Charles would soon experience. Charles tried to block him out but it was impossible to do. The relentless taunting was like a constant whine that made him want to scream.

Despite Charles' speed, the police spotted him up ahead. They gradually started to close the gap between them as they themselves started to power on. The closer they got, the more they noticed how erratically and dangerously he drove and so made a conscious decision to hold off. They kept a safe distance between themselves and their prey with their sirens off but kept him close enough that they could catch him when required, hopefully before anyone else got hurt or worse.

Charles became more and more frantic in his mind, as his world continued to fall apart. He weaved this way and that across the road but then suddenly he found focus, the dirt road leading to his cabin had come in to view. His shoulders which had tensed suddenly slumped back, his grip on the steering wheel loosened and without thinking he started to slow down. It was as if he'd been burning up but had now stepped under a cool shower which soothed him.

He drove off the main road and followed the track as it wound down to the cabin. He had done this many times, often with a girl by his side who, at some point, would become another victim. Now his companion was his own reflection, whose face was a twist of delight and wicked glee at Charles' impending fate. He arrived at the cabin and pulled up slowly, calmly; he seemed resolved and defiant. His mind was a jumbled mess of thoughts, fear and trepidation yet determined to win his freedom from his nightmare, a determination to survive.

He stepped out of his car and walked slowly but purposely past the cabin and towards the lake, unaware that behind him the police had seen him pull off the road and were now headed down the track themselves. His reflection had simply stepped through the closed car down and now appeared by his side, whispering more taunts and abuse as if to make his mind snap and crack under the pressure. Charles stopped still, ten feet from the edge of the lake, just before the bank eased down to the water. The gloom in the air was almost pushing down with a physical weight, the sky turning a sickly green grey as the clouds gathered ominously above, emanating a charged electrical scent. He looked up and then down, staring at the lake as the breeze swirled the water around in a circular motion, forming a whirlpool effect as if in response to his presence. He hadn't decided exactly what to do or say. Should he beg? Demand? Plead? As he stood there at the scene of his crimes, he suddenly realised that he hadn't thought this through.

"Anna?" he whispered, surprising himself with his tameness. His reflection stood by his side, laughing and taunting him further. Charles turned and glared at the 'other' before turning back to the lake. He took a deep breath, filling his lungs before letting loose

"Anna, you fucking bitch!!" he yelled as loud as he could

Instantly the surface of the lake seemed to react. Air bubbles rose and popped, just a few but enough to make Charles take a small step back. The 'other' mockingly applauded the achievement and laughed heartily

"Well done, Chaz, you've certainly got more balls than I gave you credit for."

Charles ignored him but felt as if he had at least made a connection, maybe he could 'summon' her and if that were the case, he could control her, or so he hoped.

"Anna, release me, you whore," he shouted with defiance

More bubbles appeared on the surface and the clouds above darkened further. Rumbles of thunder rolled across the sky. His fight or flight reaction kicked in but while his mind wanted to flee, his body wouldn't or couldn't react as suddenly a huge gush of water erupted from the lake. It was as if a whale was there and blown a jet of water up into the air and as it came down it landed on and around Charles, drenching him through. It took his breath away and as he recovered he looked out to see Anna rise from the water at the point of the eruption. She rose unaided and continued to do so until she hovered a foot above the surface. Water dripped from her and splashed down into the lake. As she rose, she was accompanied by a serenade of howling winds whipping around her as if announcing her arrival.

Her pale features seemed to glow beneath the darkening skies; the atmosphere around her seemed to be of a cloying blackness. Her eyes were now wholly black, shining like polished jewels. Her wet hair stuck to her face, the wound on her forehead which he had inflicted now oozed a putrid black puss. Her milky white flesh was waxy and slick, the light reflecting and highlighting the black of her eyes and wound. She glared at him and he stood stock still, frozen with fear at the image as she floated high, looking down on him with disdain and hatred.

By now the two police cars had arrived and pulled in behind his car. They had been expecting to pull in and arrest him without fuss but they had arrived to see the figure rise from the lake and now all four of the officers stood by their cars, staring in disbelief. They briefly glanced at each other initially but now could not take their eyes off the horrific sight playing out before them. They stood open mouthed and if not outwardly, at least internally, they were all shaking with fear.

Riley tentatively stepped forward. He knew they had to do something and his authority made him take the lead, despite his reservations. He slowly moved forward and his colleagues, against their better judgement moved slowly after him. Gradually they edged closer to Charles who seemed to be shouting at the thing from the lake. They couldn't make out what he was shouting as the gale intensified as if from nowhere. They saw what at first looked like a shape or figure by his side but to their eyes it seemed distorted and flickering in and out of focus. The 'other' had done its' job and delivered Charles to his well earned fate. Now it was no longer needed and was fading back to whence it came. It laughed sickeningly at Charles which distracted him to the point of turning to see it gradually vanish, like Alice's Cheshire Cat. It disappeared save for the tortured grin which seemed to mock him one last time before it too vanished into nothingness.

That distraction, causing Charles to turn, was to be his undoing as, when he looked back at Anna, two blurs of slimy black flesh whip out from her and reached out for him. One grabbed his arm, the other locked on to his leg. They gripped him hard and as they did so he saw more bubbles rise to the waters' surface. The 'tentacles', for that's how they appeared, pulled him slowly towards her. At the same time he saw the heads of his other victims rise from the depths, all of them wide eyed and seemingly with a taste for his blood and death. They rose as Anna had done; they rose up to waist depth before all simultaneously holding out their arms, not to grab him but to receive him.

The officers froze again, a nightmare they could not comprehend was unfolding before them and each one felt that they had to wake up sooner or later, yet the morning didn't come.

Anna opened her mouth as Charles was dragged to her. As she did so, a mass of fluid like thick molasses poured from it. It gushed down her pale chest and dripped off her chin before she let loose an almighty scream. It was a scream to wake the dead, quickly rising in pitch so much that Charles' ears started to bleed and he slumped to the bank while being dragged. The officers all instantly put their hands to their ears to block it out but as they did so, all the windows of the nearby cabin, as well as all the windscreens and windows of the cars, shattered at once causing them to duck for cover on the ground.

Charles screamed back at her in one last act of defiance but he knew it was all over as he was pulled to the brink of the lake. He continued to be pulled forward, off the bank and, for a few seconds in mid air, he was supported by the slimy black flesh of the tentacles as they gripped him harder. Then he was inches from Anna and he stared at her. She sneered back at him before her sisters-in-death reached up and grabbed him. He wept finally, as his undeniable fate was sealed and the women took a firm grip of him. There was to be no escape. They had him now and he would share their eternity at the bottom of the lake. They pulled him down and under the water. The officers clambered to their feet to watch aghast, as Charles sank below the surface. His final scream could just be heard before the water, slime and putrescence filled his mouth and lungs.

Anna looked impassively at the officers before effortlessly descending back to her watery grave. Suddenly the water became still and calm and the sky cleared as if nothing had ever happened. Yet beneath the surface they would torture and torment him ever after in the cold depths. Charles Carlton would get exactly what he deserved.

HARVEST

Chapter 1

Eric woke up flat on his back and with a head that felt like it was about to split open. His immediate thought was just how much he had had to drink the night before. He screwed his eyes tight shut before trying to open them and focus. He yawned and gasped loudly and thought fuck it, he'd have ten more minutes before getting up. He kept his eyes closed and made to roll onto his side but found that he couldn't even do such a simple task. He couldn't move over because, in his clouded mind, he hadn't even realised that he was manacled to the surface on which he lay........and it wasn't his bed.

He opened his eyes to see just what was going on and why he couldn't roll over. Immediately he was startled by the light, it was if he was staring at the sun itself but, in actual fact, it was a very large fluorescent light which looked to be moveable. Regaining his sight fully, he looked around to see that he wasn't in his bedroom, he wasn't in any bedroom that he could remember for that matter. He didn't panic as he had woken up in strange bedrooms before (on numerous occasions) but this didn't even look like any bedroom he'd ever seen. He lifted his head from what suddenly seemed a very hard and uncomfortable pillow and gazed around the room.

The walls were blank, no pictures, no artwork, no wall hangings of any kind. He peered around from his prone position and noticed that there wasn't even any furniture in the place at all. No bedside lamps, not even a bedside table. No chests of drawers or wardrobes, there was absolutely nothing in the room save for the bed that he lay on. Only then did he think to look down at himself and realise the situation that he was in.

He was naked on a table, not a bed, and, furthermore he was strapped to that table. He was restrained by heavy duty black leather belts with buckles that held his wrists and ankles. There was also a very tight strap across his waist and one across his chest. He would normally have pulled and wrestled at his restraints to loosen them and he did try his best to free himself but there was nothing he could do because as hard as he tried, he could not move a muscle. He tried to flex his arms to lift his wrists and hands but absolutely nothing happened, save for a minor twitch. He tried the same with his legs but, again, a mere twinge in his thigh yet nothing of note. His frustration built and built and panic started to set in.

He started to wonder if this was some girl's idea of kinky sex, maybe a chick he'd pulled the night before but he couldn't remember the night before. He didn't mind a bit of bondage and restraint play but this was going too far. His total lack of movement was more than just a worry; he was completely helpless and thought that surely no sane girl would do this to him? Whoever it was, didn't they know who he was, after all?

He struggled again, or at least he tried to, but this time there wasn't a twinge or a twitch or anything at all. He could lift his head but from the neck down there was absolutely nothing of movement whatsoever. Just numbness, the only activity of any kind was only going on inside his head which was rapidly spinning out of control with fear - cold hard and unbridled fear. Fear of what was to come, fear of where he was, fear of who had done this to him and fear most of all of what the hell they, whoever they were, were going to do to him.

"Hello?" Eric called out feebly

There was no reply and he was struck by the faint echo that returned to him. There was nothing but silence and the echo fading to nothing. He called again to no avail. He sniffed but couldn't halt the moisture from pricking at his eyes until a single tear slipped down his check. He coughed to clear his throat in a vain attempt to 'man up' and called out again.

"Who the fuck's there? C'mon, somebody must be here.......HELP!!"

Suddenly there was a sound and it caused him to jump, at least inside his head because his was clearly incapable of any motion whatsoever below the neck. He craned his head to look over to his left where the sound had come from. A door opened in the otherwise completely white walls. In walked a figure in green theatre scrubs, a mask, hat and surgical gloves and the figure was pushing a trolley which housed a computer and screen. The trolley was pushed over to the side of his table and electrical cables unravelled and plugged into socket points across the room.

"H-hello. Who are you.........Please, can you help me?" Eric whimpered

The figure ignored him and continued with their work, switching on the computer and logging in through various sites and programs until they were happy that everything was set up as required. Two webcams were positioned, one attached to the overhead fluorescent light hanging above Eric and the other on top of the computer screen for the side view. These were switched on and adjusted to pick up the best angles and the picture quality was checked on screen. The figure seemed happy and left everything as it no doubt should have been before exiting the room as efficiently as they had arrived. Eric called after the figure again but it was as if he didn't exist or was invisible.

Eric thought and thought; he still couldn't remember what had happened the night before and therefore tried to reason that either it was all a dream or some kind of practical joke. He could tell that this wasn't a dream; it was all way too real for that. He could smell the sterility of cleaning products; he could feel the harsh pillow under his head. Earlier, before the numbness had completely kicked in he could feel the roughness of the bindings around his ankles, wrists and body.

No, to his mind, the only thing this could be was a practical joke, a sick fucking joke yes, but a joke nonetheless. He thought of his friends, he wondered who would pull this sort of gag

"Billy, Jake? C'mon out guys I know it's you......haha....ha" he tried to convince himself, "C'mon boys, ya sick fucks.......this ain't funny anymore......guys?"

Silence fell in on him. He suddenly realised the full weight of the term, the silence being deafening, but it also seemed to have substance because it seemed to be crushing him under that weight. He started to cry to himself, his mind couldn't conjure anything to comfort him in his own personal darkness and the tears flowed freely. A sound came again from his left, as the door opened again and in walked a figure. It may have been the same one as before and Eric assumed it was but it could've been anybody dressed as they were in their theatre costume.

The figure approached, pushing a trolley. As it rolled, a metallic sound rattled through the room and cut through the oppressive silence. It was placed on the opposite side of him and as he craned his neck to see what it contained, the sound of another trolley arrived being pushed by another figure dressed as the previous one. The trolleys stood side by side and Eric craned his neck to see what lay on them but a green surgical cloth covered their contents. Both figures ignored him and were soon joined by a third who pushed another but bigger trolley; this was placed on the other side next to the computer. The three 'surgeons' looked at each other and nodded before making their exit in silence. From their height and build they looked to Eric like women, nothing out of the ordinary he thought, as lots of surgical nurses and indeed surgeons were women but this was clearly not a normal situation and he'd be shocked if this was an actual hospital.

He tried yet again to call for help or to get at least some form of acknowledgement from them but the door closed behind them without even a backward glance to him. He lay alone on the theatre table; the light was too bright for him to look directly up at it. He didn't want to close his eyes because the thoughts in his mind were creating images of what was to come and that was something that scared him even more than the reality, if that were possible. His head instead moved from side to side and just looked at the trolleys that had been assembled. The two on his right no doubt contained surgical equipment; the two to his left housed a computer and what looked like a number of plastic boxes though they were largely covered with a green surgical cloth too.

Eric could do nothing, clearly no help or explanation was to be forthcoming, he could only wait for what was going to happen and, as he closed his eyes, finally he prayed to any God that he could think of that all this was just a stupid joke pulled by his friends. Sadly, for Eric, no God was listening or if they were, they were unable or unwilling to help him.

Chapter 2

The numbness and mental anguish had lulled Eric if not to sleep but into a slight trance. He was woken by the door opening and now four people entering together. They all looked the same, similar heights and builds and all in the same uniforms; he couldn't tell one from the other but the one that walked in last seemed to be in charge because the others moved to positions behind trolleys and checked all their contents. The fourth walked around the table and stood by his side looking directly into his eyes. It was the first time that any of them seemed to acknowledge his existence and for a brief moment he felt as though there may be some kind of end or escape from his torment.

Through the harsh light he squinted and he felt he could definitely make out the eyes of a woman; the harder he focused the more he could see the slight eye make-up and feminine eyes.

"Hello, Eric. Remember me?" She said.

It seemed so long since he'd heard a voice, any voice but his own.

"Please......tell me what's going on? I don't know how I got here but...."

"We brought you here, or rather we had you brought here" she said.

"Oh......and where is here?"

"Does that really matter? Besides, you haven't answered me yet. Remember me?"

"Errr......." Eric drew a blank, not surprising in his current mental state of panic but especially with the theatre garb obstructing her face.

Realising this she lifted her gloved hands to her face and lowered her mask. She was a very attractive woman but his mind couldn't place her. Try as he might he just couldn't picture her or where, or even if, he knew her. She sighed as he frowned with a mental shrug. She looked at her three colleagues who all complied with the unspoken request and removed their masks. Each one then stepped over to the table and peered down at him as he lay there like a curiosity in a Victorian asylum. He looked at each in turn; one of the faces was vaguely familiar but he couldn't picture where he knew her from, if indeed he did know her.

He glanced at each one again before looking back at the first who had spoken and frowned again his lack of knowledge

"I'm sorry. I really don't know who you people are."

"Not to worry, Eric. It's just as we expected.........fucking typical" she sighed before replacing her mask and the others followed suit before returning to their various equipment.

"Please, at least tell me who you are," he shrieked in his frustration. "Please!!"

"Rebekha Faulkner," she said, almost exasperated. "Remember me now?"

"Err.....," he pondered the name. Something was there on the tip of his tongue but it was taking it's time to form into a reality. Rebekha sighed again and mumbled something to her colleagues who took out a bag of blood from a box. They set it up on a drip stand which appeared from the back of the room and he hadn't seen, before connecting it to the tube sticking out of his arm that he hadn't even felt one of them insert.

"Wait.......didn't we.....," he hurriedly spat out

"Fuck?" she responded icily. "Yes, we did."

"So......"

"So why are you here? Well, some of us don't like to be used. Some of us don't like to be mistreated and thrown away like a used toy. Some of us have self respect and in turn deserve to be respected."

She spoke with authority and a calmness in her voice but also with an underlying venom to each sentence.

"Oh, err....." he didn't know whether he should apologise, beg for mercy or pray to a god he didn't believe in. He still felt he hadn't been given any kind of rationale for being there in that situation.

"You really are a piece of work, Eric and, before you ask, yes, at one point or another you slept with all of us."

Eric looked around again at the four masked women and felt awkward and slightly embarrassed, especially as he was now at their mercy. He tried to compute what was happening to him and feelings of guilt slowly built up within him but he didn't feel guilty or feel that he should feel guilty. Anger then rose up within him, which overtook and swallowed up the wave of mild guilt and he became enraged.

"What the fuck? So this is payback because you all had your hearts broken?" he snapped with vitriol.

Immediately he was to find out that that was the wrong thing to say and to the wrong people.

"You arrogant prick!" Rebekha seethed beneath her mask, to the point where she ripped it down from her mouth to vent her spleen fully. "Hearts broken? No Eric, more than that. Each one of us was used by you, yes some feelings got hurt but you used all of us and then tossed us aside. We were all promised something or other. We were all taken in, stupidly, by your charm and your position. We were all fans of yours at some point. You abused that loyalty but, more than that, you physically abused us too. Zoe here was only fifteen when you seduced her!"

She pointed at one of the girls, the one at the computer station who glared at him from above her mask, Rebekha continued to name them in an effort to shame him.

"Julie was given, by you, a cocktail of drink and drugs to make her more pliable to your 'charms'. You sick fuck"

The second woman, stood at his side and inserted another cannula into his arm, ramming it in more harshly as she was named. Unfortunately he couldn't physically feel the sharpness as it dug into his vein.

"And then there's Courtney, here" stood by her side, assisting no doubt in what was to come. "She was a massive fan of yours, she travelled all over the country to watch you and your band. Finally, she got back stage and what did you do? After you'd had your fill you passed her on to the rest of the band to use as they wished, all the while telling her that she was special. Therefore she said nothing in the hope that she could be with you again."

Rebekha shook her head in disgust at him, Courtney looked down with shame and tears in her eyes at the revelations made public

"You're an animal," Rebekha finished.

Eric was suddenly very quiet. He'd always felt that he was just living his rock star dreams but in the cold and harsh light of the revelations and the cold and light of that operating theatre, the guilt soon built back up to overwhelm him.

163

"And you?" he croaked hoarsely.

"Years ago, we dated.............doesn't sound too much to worry about does it. But I stuck with you even when things were getting out of control. The drink and drugs used to take over and you used to beat me, abuse me and humiliate me. But I was 'in love' so just stuck at it. We even got engaged at one point so I thought we were going to last the distance. I was warned. Oh boy, was I warned but did I listen? No. You loved me or so you told me, then you'd have another drink, snort another line, whatever you wanted to do to me you did. And hey, surprise, sur-fuckin-prise you can't even remember me!"

Rebekha wipe a tear away as her voice broke and Eric looked at them all. He was shame faced and tormented but that still didn't bring back the memories or remove his victim's pain.

"I'm.....sorry," he whispered

"You're sorry?" snapped Rebekha "Hey, girls, he's fuckin' sorry"

They all looked at him with disdain in their eyes. Such a feeble apology would do little to stop the plans that had been formed for some considerable time. At least one of them snorted their derision but they all seemed to laugh behind their masks.

"Should we let him go then?" they all, in unison, shook their heads at the suggestion "Sorry, Eric, but we haven't come all this way to give up now"

"W-What the hell are you going to do to me" a tear slowly trickled down his face as realisation of just how deep the shit he was in dawned on him.

Chapter 3

"It's like this, Eric," Rebekha started, as Courtney uncovered a tray of surgical implements by her side. "I am a fully qualified surgeon these days. Julie here is a nurse. That's how we got chatting and realised we had something in common....you. Zoe and Courtney we didn't know but, through the wonders of the internet, we managed to come together and share our war stories, again, all about you. Between the four of us we hatched a little plan. We could have a little cathartic release; we could gain some revenge upon you; we could make a lot of other people very happy and on top of all of that, we could make a shit load of money." All four of them laughed at that last remark.

"And your p-plan is what exactly?" Eric now feared the worst but couldn't do anything about it. He couldn't move a muscle save for his head and even that was starting to numb, just like his body due to a clear liquid being injected into him through a drip by Julie at his side.

"Well, you see, there is something known as the dark web which I'm sure somebody like yourself knows all about." She didn't wait for a reply before continuing, "And there are a lot of people currently logged onto a certain site which carries a live feed from this very room via these cameras." Rebekha pointed them out and Zoe pointed to the live on screen images and in a comical fashion the women all waved at the cameras and laughed.

"And......," Eric tried to firm his voice but failed.

"And, those people, some of whom are your fans by the way, are offering cash for parts of you! Isn't that great?"

"You've got to be joking." He simply couldn't believe what was happening. "That's sick!" Eric managed to spit out the words before his tongue numbed

"Maybe, but they're *your* fans. For instance, we have people wanting to buy your fingers. We started at $2000 each but somebody, a fellow guitar player I'm led to believe, has offered $20,000 for a whole hand! That got us thinking about your potential. Imagine it, $20,000 per hand and that's just the start really. We had fixed prices but when this guy offers that kind of money we decided to let them bid against each other. It's going to get wild to be honest," Rebekha gushed enthusiastically, seemingly revelling in her new thoughts as the twisted auction neared.

Eric was in tears but could do little to stop their flow. Tears of sadness at his inevitable demise and death, combined with tears of rage and frustration at his incapability to do anything to stop his captors. Rebekha was in full flow and was taking gleeful delight in explaining the rest of the harvest.

"There are the obvious things such as your eyes. We have a number of besotted young girls who want those. Your internal organs are attracting more interest than we thought but, as it turns out, there are some of your fans that need transplants and what better organ to have as a replacement than one from the famous and legendary singer and guitarist, Eric Blackman!" she mocked. "Then there are the more creative things such as your vocal chords. They're going well. People seem to think they will have your voice and therefore a short cut to a singing career. Also, the brain. There's a thought that at some point a transplant will help them come up with all your lyrics and future hits. Obviously, some of these ideas are from people who want to cryogenically freeze your bits and pieces for future reference. As a musician your ears are worth a pretty penny as well."

They all stood watching him squirm internally, relishing every second as the madness started to take hold and he screamed in his mind but there was no outlet for the scream to be released, as his mouth was not reacting to his brain. Instead that harrowing and heartfelt scream just bounced around the walls in his mind, echoing and seemingly intensifying as it did so.

"Your blood is doing particularly well, actually; fans can actually and literally have you running through their veins. This table has grooves cut into it which allows the blood to drain down to the bottles on the floor at your feet. There's a lot of it and we can sell it in smaller amounts so that it'll go further. Plus, Julie mentioned that as we want you alive for the most part, we'll be giving you transfusions. That means there'll be a hell of a lot of blood coming out after it's passed through you so technically it'll still be yours. Obviously the first few pints will be the premium content and therefore a higher price but it all adds up doesn't it?" She patted him playfully and sarcastically on the cheek but he couldn't feel anything. "Then there are the special items........"

Eric glanced towards Rebekha, his eyes being the only part of him that was still responding to his brain. She winked back at him as a sickening smile, which he couldn't see beneath her mask, spread across her face.

"Your cock and balls of course. They are prized indeed but there is another speciality about that area." She laughed almost hysterically at his torment "Your semen. It's tripled what we expected in pre-orders; we've had to put a minimum bid of $250,000! The conundrum then becomes do we have just one winner or is there enough juice to split? That actually is where the smart money goes, the sperm" She said, very conspiratorially, in hushed tones.

"The reason for that is, of course, that you will be dead so not only will somebody have the chance of bearing your child, or children, but they will also have the opportunity of a strong claim on your estate. I'm sure you're worth a few bucks even alive. That's also not forgetting the money to be made from books and television appearances that your future offspring can rake in, and so on and so forth."

There was activity then. The computer screen started to flash with new bids from various people out there in the recesses of the dark web. Fans of the more morbid persuasion held back revulsion and tears as they tried to be practical, thinking and commenting in posts that;

"Well he's gonna die anyway so we might as well have a piece of him" or

"This will be a good investment for the kids college fund" or

"If I can get his hand transplanted to replace mine I can play guitar like him?" or

"I just loved him so much, I want him to be a part of me forever" or even

"I can buy a piece now; it'll triple in value once the record labels cash in"

Eric could do nothing obviously but wait for the end, which he hoped would be mercifully quick but he doubted it would be. A large transplant bag was brought out from under one of the trolleys and readied for use.

'Staff' waited on the corridor outside the theatre for the transplant bags in order to run them down to their delivery drivers. Outside a fleet of vans, cars and motorcycles awaited the various organs and body parts. All drivers and riders were working on commission to get their cargo to the delivery point as soon as possible, though not one of them knew exactly what they were transporting. There were even two helicopters standing by for big ticket items which were expected to go to particularly wealthy bidders; delivery, however, was not included in the price.

Elsewhere in the country, for those who wished for an immediate transplant (or for those who couldn't afford cryogenics as well as the organ/body part) there were a number of illegal theatres opened, ready and waiting to go just as soon as their clients won the required piece of meat. Surgeons that had been previously shamed or struck off were scrubbed and ready to go at a moment's notice.

The women all stood waiting for a timer to tick down on the screen which meant that bidding was over for the first item on the agenda (or menu); that item was indeed Eric Blackman's left hand. The clock hit zero, the nursing staff turned to Rebekha.

"$87,000 wow!" Zoe said, a smile stretching her mask and her eyebrows rose at the amount. The girls gasped, they looked at each other sure in the knowledge that this harvest would surpass all expectations.

"Scalpel," called Rebekha, holding out her hand. Courtney briskly and efficiently handed it to her.

She made the first incision around Eric's wrist as he gazed down at the surreal scene. Blood oozed from the slice in his skin and gently started to form a scarlet river in the grooved table, trickling down the slight tilt of the polished steel surface and dripping to collect in bottles below his feet. He felt nothing at all; he didn't feel it was real; he must be dreaming, surely. Sadly he wasn't.

"Well, ladies. I think we're going to be rich," Rebekha smiled at her colleagues. "We should certainly do much better this harvest than the last time!"

WELCOME TO EVAGRAD

Chapter 1

Michael Green was thrilled with the idea of a gap year. Although, having aced all of his exams and at the ripe old age of 21, he wasn't really thinking of it as a gap year. He'd worked hard through school and university and would soon be heading into the real world and working, probably for the rest of his life unless he struck it lucky and retired early. Before hitting the real world he wanted to explore it; he desperately wanted to have adventures. Michael wanted some fun. His parents had been wonderful and they were immensely proud of him but he felt a need to break out of his restraints, the restraints of family. He'd been brought up to value his education and the luck of good parenting that all too many of his peers had not been so fortunate to have. He knew he'd been lucky to have that upbringing but after his years of study he wanted to experience life and 'something different' before the probable drudgery of a career.

He had thought about getting a good job, more of a career actually and making a good living to make his parents proud of him. Though in truth his parents hadn't wanted him to take time out at all, they had been insistent on him going into law or the medical profession. They only wanted what was best for him but many arguments had built up recently over his decision to go abroad and 'find himself'.

His father had told him that he could do all that a few years down the line, once he had set himself up. His mother had wanted him to be 'respectable' - whatever the hell that was supposed to mean; get a nice job, meet a nice girl and buy a nice house, no doubt having lots of nice babies for her to dote over too.

But Michael hadn't wanted to wait, he wanted to do it all while he was young, even 30 was too late and too old to do what he wanted. As for his mothers' wishes, well he wasn't entirely sure that he wanted to do any of those things at any point but he really didn't want to break her heart and shatter the dreams that she had had for him for so long.

As an only child he was all too aware that he was their one shot at being grandparents but he just didn't see himself in the role of a tied down parent with needy kids whining and crying for his attention constantly. That wasn't even bringing in the cost implications; he was very aware of just how much kids cost to bring up these days. Then there was the moral argument. Why would anyone bring a child into the world with the state it was in and the direction it seemed to be heading? He was no fool, he had given all these things much thought, especially for one still young. He had friends who were in the same situation but they were looking to 'settle down' already with steady girlfriends, two were talking about getting engaged in the next couple of years and one was already expecting a child with his girlfriend. Plus he knew of others that were in similar positions. All those things scared the life out of Michael.

He knew he was in a fortunate position financially; he had been given generous pocket money growing up, a perk of being an only child as well as having numerous part time jobs during the summers and weekends. He had saved up most of the money that he had received for recent birthday and Christmas presents and now he had a good amount to go travelling with. It wasn't a fortune but he could be frugal and make it last quite easily should he have to.

Michael had pondered going away with a few of his friends but actually wanted to do it on his own. As much fun as it would be to go away with his buddies, there would still be discussions about where to go, how long to go for, pleasing everybody and then the inevitable bad blood when someone dropped out at the last minute. Then there would be the possibility of someone running out of money and the others having to pay for them or one of the guys getting into trouble and having to be bailed out, quite possibly literally! As much as he loved his mates he didn't want the headache of it all, plus he wanted to go where HE wanted to go and do what HE wanted to do. This wasn't going to be a couple of weeks or a month in the sun getting drunk and stupid, this was to be a life changing experience for a year. He couldn't (and didn't want to) expect anyone else to commit to such an undertaking.

A few months earlier he had thought about asking his girlfriend Amy to go but, thankfully, the idea was short lived because just a couple of weeks later she dropped him. He had been downcast but not quite distraught; they hadn't been together that long, just three months. It had been fun but never really anything serious despite his mum adoring the girl. In fact, his mum seemed more upset than he was. So that had been his final decision, go where he wanted to go and do what he wanted to do. Now he just had to decide what those two small things actually were!!

Michael sat at home, his parent's home, pondering the internet and looking at various destinations. He discounted many for various reasons: Australia, New Zealand, Philippines, Thailand and basically anywhere in that part of the world due to the distance of the flight. He wasn't an especially nervous flier but if he could avoid long flights, a stop-over and another long flight he would. That pretty much ruled out South America and Africa too. He had never really had any desire to visit those places either, despite seeing rave reviews on various travel sites about how wonderful the people and various countries were.

He came to the conclusion that he would either go to North America or mainland Europe. He'd been to the U.S. a couple of times, once on a family trip to Florida, like lots of Brits before and after him. The second time was to see friends he'd met online in Kentucky and visit the 'Scarefest' horror convention, which had been fantastic; the people had been great and so had the place itself. It felt so much better going to somewhere that wasn't 'touristy', as much as he had enjoyed Florida. He started to think about doing a road trip across the States, maybe take in parts of Canada too! That sounded like a great idea.

The alternative to that offering was to go to mainland Europe, of course. Now Michael had always loved being a European and he knew that with everything about to change across the Continent relatively soon he thought now might be a chance to move about without lots of visas and changes to systems and borders. He hoped that wouldn't ever be the case but the days of free movement through the Continent sadly appeared to be numbered. Again, he had been to the mainland many times, in particular, Germany and France, on multiple occasions as well as Bulgaria, Italy, Turkey, Belgium and Spain. He had enjoyed most trips but especially Germany and France, he just simply felt at home there. Not going to tourist traps, just places that he wanted to go to and he absolutely loved it every time.

So that was his dilemma: North America and a road trip or parts of Europe that he hadn't been to? He had decided against European places that he'd visited as he wanted to do something new. He'd said to people many times, when trumpeting Europe, about how he loved the idea of going around from place to place in a relatively short time span. So many different cultures and languages and customs all close enough to travel between in a day. Just the thought of how much he could see and do in a year would be amazing. Especially in the modern world with so many new states that had come out of larger countries to gain their own fierce national identity that they upheld with great pride.

He'd also had a yearning to go to Scandinavia for quite a while, the mountains, the landscapes, the fjords, the language, the people and the legends. It was all very appealing; no wonder he was having a hard time trying to make up his mind. He checked endless websites and travel blogs, so many reviews for this and that, so many stars and 'likes', he soon started to feel jaded and even more confused than when he'd started searching for ideas. He sighed to himself and fell back onto his bed in frustration and confusion. As he laid there, his phone started to ring, he sighed again at the realisation that his phone wasn't in his pocket but on the floor and he would have to get up. He groaned to himself and rolled over the edge, leaned down and picked up the phone.

"Hello?"

He had glanced at the screen to reveal his grandfather's face and number, immediately he worried if something was wrong.

"Michael, it's Gramps," came the old man's voice. "Hello?"

"Yeah, Gramps, I know. Everything ok?"

"Yeah, everything's fine here. You ok?" asked his grandfather

"Sure, what can I do for you?"

"Well, your mum told me that you've got this idea to go off travelling for a while. Is that true?"

"Yeah, that's right, I'm just debating where to go. It's between...."

"Before you decide," interrupted Gramps, "I want you to come over so I can talk to you before you make any plans you might regret."

"Oh, Gramps, I really want to go. I don't want you to start trying to talk me out of it," whined Michael, sure that his mother had tried to get family members to put doubts in his mind. Obviously, she was worried that her baby boy wouldn't be able to handle himself out there in that big, bad scary world.

"Talk you out of it? Don't be stupid! I want you to go. I just want to help you with a number of things that might be very useful to you"

"Such as?"

Michael was curious and his brow furrowed as he spoke

"Not on the phone lad. Come over as soon as you can" Gramps said.

"When?"

"Tomorrow afternoon, there's a lot I need to talk to you about. It's important and could be the making of you, Mikey, my boy," somewhat cryptically Gramps spoke with a certain kind of glee in his voice and almost a longing.

"Alright,"

Michael was at least curious and he did think the world of his grandfather and the feeling was mutual.

"I'll be there around one ok?"

"Perfect, I'll be expecting you. See you tomorrow."

They both hung up. Michael rolled back on his bed still furrowing his brow but shrugged it off. Gramps probably wanted to give him a few quid to spend or something. At the other end of the line, his grandfather sat back in his chair and sighed with a smile on his face. He looked up at a painting above the fireplace in the great room where he sat; it was a portrait of his own great-grandfather. Gramps lifted a glass of brandy from by his side and raised it to the painting in a toast

"Finally, someone to claim what's ours," he grinned then sipped.

Chapter 2

Michael arrived at his grandfather's just after one pm the next day, a Saturday. The day was cold, dark and gloomy especially given that it was meant to be spring. The house was at the end of a long lane on the outskirts of the small town where Michael and his family lived, most of his extended family still lived in or around the town; no one had been much for spreading their wings except for holidays. Maybe Michael could be the black sheep, at least for a year, and do something different. He'd always felt a little different after all.

The house was large, very large and old; it was out of keeping with the chocolate box houses at that end of the town. It had been some sort of coach house many years ago and Gramps had bought it and converted it into a home. Sadly, however, Michaels' grandma died suddenly twelve years ago and the place became neglected as Gramps wallowed in the misery of her loss. Now he lived there alone, still sprightly for his age but not one for gardening or housekeeping and the rambling old place seemed to get on top of him. It was imposing and dark in places but Michael had always loved the house. Gramps said that he would leave it all to him but he couldn't bear to think of a world without Gramps in it.

After ringing the doorbell, Michael stood on the porch waiting for his grandfather to make his way to the front door. It had always taken a while purely because of the size of the house. He looked up at the dark and brooding sky, perfectly in keeping with the old house; he could imagine many an old story being told about the legends of the old coach house and tales of headless horsemen rampaging across the countryside looking for souls to steal. As he watched the blackened clouds rolling across the greying afternoon sky, large spots of rain started to fall from them, soon soaking everything in their path in very short time. Michael edged closer under the porch to avoid getting drenched just as he could hear the front door being unlocked.

The door opened and Gramps stood beaming at his grandson, so delighted to see him. It had been a while.

"Mikey!! Oh, my boy it's so good to see you," gushed Gramps as he threw his arms around his grandson with delight.

"Hey, Gramps, how ya doin?" Michael responded, while returning the hug with mutual pats on the back for good measure.

"I'm great, great but come in out of the rain, lad. I want to hear all about what you're planning. Come on inside."

Gramps stepped aside to allow his grandson entrance and closed the door behind them. Michael paused in the hallway while his grandfather closed up and then ushered him into the main part of the house. He had visited this place many times and it had always filled him with wonder. Not a mansion by any stretch of the imagination but still a large place and filled with history which gave it its grand and imposing presence, especially in such a small and rural town.

They walked into the large open room, known as the Great Room; it was no doubt the most imposing room in the house, hence the name. A very high ceiling with beams stretching along and across it, gave it age and history. Michael had always had that sense of grandeur as a child but even now as an adult it made him feel small and slightly insignificant. He had always day-dreamed about the many people who had passed through those doors and spent the night or lived in the building at various points in its long history. Gramps had often told him stories and 'filled his head with nonsense' as his parents would have it but, to Michael, it was and remained a place of fascination and wonder.

He sat on a favourite plush, if worn and dated, couch at the end next to his grandfathers' favourite armchair where he settled down. A large pot of coffee had already been set down on the table in front of them with two mugs, milk, sugar and biscuits.

"Would you do the honours?" Gramps asked and Michael poured drinks for them both.

As he did so, the old guy reached down by the side of his chair and picked up a large cardboard wallet which seemed stuffed with papers of some kind. Gramps opened it and looked inside, checking carefully. It seemed the contents were to his satisfaction before closing the flap again and stuffing it by his side and crossing his legs. Settling himself more in the direction of Michael so that they could talk, Gramps began.

"So young man, tell me about your travelling plans."

"Well," Michael passed a mug of coffee to his grandfather as he started to talk and they both sipped on their respective drinks. "I'm kinda torn really"

"How so?"

"Well I like the idea of going to the States, doing a road trip really but I want to take a full year out. I can't do a road trip for a year but I could go to Canada too, that'd be cool. Then I thought I could maybe get a place for say three or four months on the East coast, visiting places up and down there. Then the same on the West coast and have another four months or more in between to travel here and there and explore."

"That sounds like a hell of an experience I must say and it's a very big place, so even with all that time there'll be things you can't get to but it'd be amazing," agreed Gramps.

"Yeah, it would be. It'd be awesome"

"So why are you torn? What's the alternative? I'm assuming you have one?"

"The alternative," nodded Michael, "Is mainland Europe, not tourist places. Been there done that, you know?"

"Oh, I know exactly what you mean," Gramps nodded enthusiastically in agreement.

"Yeah," continued Michael after they both took another drink. "Small out of the way places, small countries or big countries, capital cities that don't get many visitors because everyone goes to the same tourist hotspots. Back street bars and restaurants that are amazing, undiscovered gems that are hidden away. Everywhere in Europe has got centuries and centuries of history. The different dialects and languages, the customs, the food and drink, the people...."

"Alright, calm down," laughed Gramps, holding his hands out in submission to his grandsons' obvious enthusiasm. "I understand. I get it. You have quite the conundrum on your hands, lad. There's a strong case for either side. I can see your dilemma."

Michael sat back in a slump and took another drink, sighing as he did so.

Gramps looked at him and smiled, shook his head with a light laugh and said, "So, how are you going to decide?"

"I don't know. I really don't know," Michael flopped his head back onto the couch and sighed again as he looked up at the huge expanse of ceiling and dark beams.

The old man watched his grandson struggle internally and mused over his own thoughts. He hoped that Michael would go for his idea, do something extraordinary, have an adventure, fulfil both their dreams no matter how fantastical and who knows maybe have a future unlike anyone else's. Of course, there was always the possibility that his grandson would laugh at his proposal or maybe not laugh but think it ridiculous. He hoped not, the long standing dream was precious to him and he could think of no one in the world better or more capable of fulfilling it than Michael. What's more, he longed for Michael to reap the rewards of such an undertaking. He pondered and mused for a few more minutes before being unable to hold back any longer.

"Not wishing to throw a spanner in the works and make your decision harder but do you mind if I throw another possibility into the mix?" he said.

Michael rolled his head from its position on the couch and looked at his grandfather with a furrowed brow.

"Is this why you asked me over?" he questioned.

"Well, obviously I wanted to see you but.........yes."

"Go on."

"Now, this might seem a bit strange and not what you were expecting," Gramps grinned and became excited as he began his tale, "but I want you to go to the Urals."

"The Urals?" Michael frowned harder at the prospect, disbelief seeping into his mind almost immediately "As in the Ural Mountains? You mean the ones in Russia?"

"Haha, of course the ones in Russia," laughed Gramps.

"Gramps, I really am not the one for mountaineering you know. I want to enjoy myself too, not spend a year up a bloody mountain!"

"No, no. Hold on and let me explain," Gramps pondered for a moment and tried to think of the best way to explain his story.

"Do you remember the tales I used to tell you when you were little? When I used to tell you about my family and going back all those years to my great-great grandfather and even farther back? Remember all that?"

"Yeah, the old country you used to say. Hahaha," Michael chuckled to himself with fond thoughts of days gone by.

"Exactly, the old country and you'd sit there on that very spot wild eyed with wonder about things you never really understood," Gramps smiled and laughed to himself also at those happy memories

"Of course. Good times, Gramps," Michael beamed back at him.

"Well," momentarily Gramps smile dropped and he became much more serious. "Those weren't tall tales to entertain you, you know. They were all true, as true as I'm sitting here."

"But..." started Michael.

"I swear on my life, it was all true. Obviously, I left out some things because you were only young but not a single lie passed my lips, I promise you."

Michael paused and contemplated as he tried to recall at least in part some of the stories and legends of his family that his grandfather always made sound so amazing. While he was thinking things over, Gramps started to rustled and rifle through his folder, picking things out before discarding them for something else. Settling on certain pieces of paperwork, he set them aside for reference. All the while Michael pondered him and his history.

"Many years ago, Michael, many, many years, one of my ancestors and therefore yours too, of course, went off to explore the world. Which to all intents and purposes back in those days was what we call mainland Europe. Of course, real explorers with ships and the backing of their Kings or Queens went farther afield but for most people exploring or travelling the world meant the mainland. A lot depended on finance but you could travel where you wanted to if you had the heart and stomach for it and as I said a bit of money for food and lodgings.

Well, our ancestor, a chap by the name of Thomas Abraham Eva did all of that. He toured through Europe: all the countries, districts and provinces, small towns and villages and big cities, following rivers just to see where they took him. It was an amazing journey by all accounts. Really, it sounds like the kind of thing that you want to do, doesn't it?"

"Oh, yeah, sounds great," Michael gasped, always rapt by his grandfather's expression and enthusiasm when he talked about such things. Gramps continued to his awe struck and captivated audience of one.

"Well it was during his journey that he had ended up in the Urals. He had been travelling for quite a long time, around two and a half years by then and he had become quite worldly wise. Young Thomas had opened himself up to everything, taken in new experiences and revelled in it all. Much like you he liked to travel alone. He could look after himself, he wasn't an idiot. In fact he was wise beyond his years, some say too wise but that's a point of view I don't subscribe to.

Anyway, he ended up in the Urals, the southern Urals to be more precise. The north is way too cold and icy, treacherous in places. It takes brave people to live and thrive up there but the southern Urals in the west is where he found himself. The other side, in the east is what we know of as Siberia. Again, from talking to people on his travels and studying maps of the time, for what they were, he had decided against travelling over the mountains and into Siberia. Don't get me wrong he thought about it, thought hard and long but the harshness and distances to cover would've been extreme to say the least, especially in those days. We're talking about the 16th Century here, you know?"

He paused as Michael nodded while pouring them both fresh cups of coffee. So much with his ancestors journey, whether tall tale or not, resonated with Michael and he kept quiet but attentive as he prompted his grandfather to continue with his coffee refreshed and steaming. In just a few minutes Gramps had already captivated Michael just as he always did as a child. Now though he would have a much better understanding and realisation of the story and, what was to come, could or would change his entire life forever.

Chapter 3

"So, there was our Thomas, up there in the Ural Mountains," Gramps continued as Michael sat captivated. "Or rather at the south-western tip of the range to be precise. Now people automatically think of that sort of place as a freezing cold and barren wilderness and, yes, there are times of the year that that's exactly what it's like but, the other side of that is when the weather is better. During the summer, for example, it's beautiful: lush forests and miles of green fields, punctuated by hills, streams, rivers and lakes before it gets more unforgiving up in the mountains. On the slopes and in the surrounding countryside it's idyllic. There's wildlife, tons of it, huge elks and brown bears, wolves and foxes and even lynx. There are hares and gophers and grass snakes and lizards as well as glorious fish in the lakes. From what I've seen parts of it look like parts of Canada. You couldn't tell which one was which if you compared photographs."

Michael was practically drooling at the thought of the place. He loved the idea of the contrast. He imagined it all as Gramps explained but he was also imagining the harsh winter and the amazing scenes of the dramatic mountains. Of course, as he had already said, he was no mountaineer but the thought of the place was already stirring his imagination.

"There are mines there too, iron, copper and even gold in certain parts. It's just a relatively undiscovered part of the world. Can you imagine what it was like all those years ago? Hardly any western Europeans would have been there back then. Thankfully he knew a few languages from his school days and because of his yearning to travel he had kept up with as many languages as he could. He wasn't an expert by any means but he always got by and picked things up easily, much like you, lad," Gramps smiled at Michael, who returned the smile bashfully but didn't interrupt, desperate and more intrigued to hear the rest of the story.

"Anyway, his travels took him to the Urals and he loved the place. He loved the countryside and the mountains, the lakes and the rivers. He felt alive most of all, truly alive and he absolutely fell in love with the local people. Don't get me wrong, just like anywhere in the world there were some folk with whom he didn't get along, to put it mildly, hahaha," chuckled Gramps with a wistful smile.

"How do you mean?"

"Well, let's just say that at times he could be a bit of a ladies' man, our Thomas and leave it at that for now," Gramps gave another little smile to himself.

Michael frowned at him, wanting the whole story and not just edited highlights.

"Ok, Ok. The fact is that he was a bit of a scoundrel back home in England. He regularly had affairs with married ladies and a couple of times he was attacked and almost killed by jealous husbands. He could look after himself thankfully and always managed to get out of the sticky situations in one piece but eventually he realised that he'd pushed his luck far enough. He'd had enough and decided to seek pastures new, so to speak. Now some of those married ladies were very generous when bestowing gifts upon him, for erm, services rendered if you know what I mean?" Gramps paused and Michael smiled and laughed to himself as he nodded his understanding.

"Thomas was no fool. He hadn't frittered away his ill-gotten gains, he'd kept it all. So much so that he could bank roll himself for going away. So once he'd arrived on the continent, he not only had a fantastic time of discovery and adventure, he also had some wild times and some life changing times without doubt. The point being that he couldn't help himself but continue with his chosen lifestyle choices in the Urals area too.

As I said, he was there for quite a while. I think almost two years and the thing is he actually fell in love with the place. The people, in the most part, were warm and kind, considerate and helpful. Obviously at first he was seen with suspicion and wariness but as he wasn't considering himself as a tourist and they had had little contact with tourists he slowly managed to gain their trust."

"Sounds awesome, Gramps."

"I'm sure it was, until he started to go back to his wicked ways of sleeping with the wives and daughters of the little town where he was staying!"

"Seriously?" laughed Michael.

"Damn straight he did, and it was no laughing matter. A couple of the locals were out for blood, literally. They wanted him dead. It was a small town in the middle of nowhere but they had a Mayor and a kind of sheriff with deputies. I don't know what they are called but effectively the elders of the town had 'officials' which was lucky for him. If it had've been a less civilized town or village, they would probably have just killed him and left him in the mountains for the scavengers to pick at."

"Fuck!....Oh er sorry, Gramps," cursed Michael, immediately feeling guilty.

"Hahaha, it's fine, Mikey, you're a grown man," laughed the old guy.

"So how did he get out of it? I'm assuming he did get out of it, didn't he?"

"Well now, you can believe this or take this with a pinch of salt but I'm going to tell you exactly what I was told by my Grandfather. I believe it and I can back it up so you should believe it as the truth, but, when the dust settles, only you can know what you really think," Gramps looked at his grandson imploring him to be open minded and dreading that he would dismiss it as other ancestors had apparently dismissed it

"Go on, I'm open to anything," Michael responded with a smile.

"That's the best way to live your life, lad," Gramps returned the smile with pride at the young man before continuing.

"Anyway, as I said they had officials, town elders, a council and a form of law keepers. Also, Thomas had been there for a while and he'd become one of the community. Obviously not so ingrained as to have become one of their own but he wasn't just someone passing through. Therefore, rather than have him killed and dumped as his accusers had wanted, he was instead banished from the town. He was taken by a group of men out into the wilderness and was to be released, pointed in a direction and under no circumstances to return. Well that was the plan at least....."

Gramps paused for effect and poured himself the last from the coffee pot. Clearly teasing his Grandson with the unknown and poking at his natural curiosity.

"Well? Go on, what happened" Michael had shifted literally to the edge of his seat.

"No one knows for sure, not 100% that is," he sighed. "But legend has it that something had come down from the mountains."

"Something? You mean like a bear or wolf?" asked a puzzled Michael.

"No, definitely not as simple as that, something far, far worse," grimaced Gramps.

"What?" Michael gasped.

"As I said, we don't know but whatever it was it laid waste to the party of men. They were hunters and warriors all but this creature, this 'thing', slaughtered it's' way through them. There was blood, so much blood, severed limbs and broken bones. Bodies were strewn everywhere, the bodies of hardened men who could all look after themselves but not against an enemy as powerful and vicious as the one which destroyed them that day."

"Wow. So what happened to Thomas?"

"Miraculously," sighed Gramps again, shaking his head, "he survived. Not only that but he dragged two of the men to safety. Once they were out of danger he struggled but got them back to the town. One carried over his shoulder the other stumbling along supported by Thomas. They were broken and bleeding, all three, but Thomas saved them. Once they had gotten back to the safety of the town a fresh group of hunters went out to search for their fallen comrades. All they found were body parts and blood stains in the snow. It looked clearly that at least three men had been dragged off into the wooded slopes to the mountains. The remains had teeth marks and flesh torn from the bone. It must have been a horrible sight."

"What happened back in the town?" asked Michael, clearly enraptured by the unfolding tale.

"Well, the injured men were made comfortable but little hope was held out for them and sadly before the following night, both succumbed to their injuries; however not before relaying the story to the elders of the town. Thomas, too, had told his story and what the injured men had had to say only backed up his version. What's more, one of the men he had saved had been one of the men wanting him dead for seducing his wife. This all proved to the elders that he was actually a just and honest man, he was brave and loyal and he must've been wronged. They apologised and agreed that he had been misjudged, even though his guilt had been proved, his lover's husband forgave Thomas before he died."

"My God!" exclaimed Michael.

"That's not the end of it," beamed Gramps, "Thomas, in the coming weeks, was hailed a hero and not long after that the Mayor, who was an elderly man, died. Everyone's first choice was Thomas to be the new Mayor of the town which he graciously accepted."

"Very cool," said Michael.

"Ah, but this is where the story changes. Thomas' darker side came to the fore."

"How so?"

"He took on the role and was doing very well but, you know the old saying, power corrupts?" asked Gramps.

"And absolute power corrupts absolutely," finished Michael.

"Exactly! To cut a long story a little shorter. Over time Thomas took control of that town and I mean totally. There was very little contact with the outside world and, in short it became his little dictatorship, like his own country almost. No one did anything without his approval or say so, he received bribes from everyone for everything. It became a sizable town and it was growing but Thomas made sure it didn't get too big. He didn't want interference from the major cities or authority sticking their noses into his affairs. Gradually he started to put the rougher men into positions as his bodyguards; therefore, he became untouchable and all powerful in a relatively short space of time."

"Bloody hell, devious sod!" blurted Michael.

"Hahaha, true, I suppose," laughed Gramps. "Now, for the part that involves you, my boy!"

"Me?" Michael had forgotten about some loose connection and vague reason why Gramps wanted him to go the Urals.

"Yes, the thing about Thomas was that the power went to his head and he started to make laws, some were good and the people liked him for that but it seemed that those laws were just made to keep everyone on his side. Which for the most part, perhaps surprisingly, they were very much on his side. However, one law which he made and it seems ridiculous today, was that Thomas and any and all male heirs he may have would be forever immune to prosecution within that town's limits."

Gramps awaited Michael's response but the young man remained blank, not quite taking in just what he was saying.

"Do you understand? Forever. ALL his male heirs, are exempt from prosecution and that means you, Michael."

Gramps paused and sat back in his chair, allowing the thought to sink in to his grandson. After a few moments Michael looked puzzled and looked quizzically at the old man.

"Yeah, but that wouldn't stand up now though surely?" he said.

"It does, Michael, I've already looked it up in the town charter."

He reached down to his file and pulled out a copy of the charter and various documents for the town plus a photocopy of the translations into English.

"These translations have been done by a friend of mine, a Russian teacher. And in anticipation I've made tentative enquires to an acquaintance in the town itself, a historian of the area. I was tempted to go a number of years ago but with your Grandma's health deteriorating I never managed to pull it off. I'm too old now but this could be a golden ticket for you."

"But," was Michael's only stunned response.

"You'd be like a God, Michael; you'd practically have your own town, all for you. Just think of it. You could go anywhere, do anything. You could never get into trouble. You could literally get away with murder!!"

"Gramps! I couldn't.......... I wouldn't," stumbled Michael, shocked that his grandfather would even suggest such a thing

"I don't mean literally. But just think about it."

Michael did think about it. He got up and paced the room as he thought. He stopped and looked out of the window as the grey sky continued to pour rain down onto the miserable day. He ached for something else, anything else; if nothing else it would be an adventure, an experience that would stay with him.

"There is a house that is still in the family name and, obviously, thanks to Thomas, it always will be. Plus financially you will have nothing to worry about as I will foot the bill to get you there and back, whenever that may be of course, providing you want to come back!" Gramps laughed.

"Of course, I'd want to come back!" snapped Michael

"Yes, yes obviously, but I'm just saying that you might love the place as Thomas did, especially as he's done all the ground work. You just go and reap the rewards."

Michael turned to look at Gramps who was standing now and holding out his file for him.

"No pressure, Michael. Read this now or take it home but at least give it some thought."

Michael took it and said his goodbyes, eager to get home and learn some more.

Chapter 4

Michael poured over the file, this way and that as he looked into every detail and every possible way that the story could be a hoax. There were sketches and paintings that depicted Thomas himself, various accounts of life under his 'dictatorship/leadership' stories about his legendary night of bravery. Mainly 'confirming' that he had fought off the great beast but no actual eye witness account written except from Thomas and the two dead hunters who were no doubt delirious and just glad to be alive.

There were a few other tales of 'something' coming down from the mountains but nothing to confirm or contradict the story of Thomas. The closest Michael could find was during his own research online. There was the story about a place called Kholat Syakhi, higher up in the Northern Urals but these days known as the Dyatlov Pass. It turned out that in 1959 a group of very experienced skiers were in that area and had set up camp one night. They were never heard from again. A search and rescue team went out to look for them and discovered a scene of carnage. Experts examined the site and it was reported that the skiers had fought frantically to get out of their tent, tearing it open. They had fled either in stocking feet or barefoot through the deep snow. One member of the party had been found with severe brain damage but absolutely no skull injuries. Other members were found away from the camp, seemingly running from something, barefoot and barely clothed, had succumbed to hypothermia and frost bite. Perhaps most shockingly of all was that one man was found with a fractured skull and his eyes and tongue completely missing.

There were theories but no explanation. One school of thought was that it was the same 'thing' that had come down to Thomas' town four centuries earlier, or at least one of its' offspring, if not the actual beast or creature. There were other similar stories, sightings, legends and tales but the Dyatlov Pass seemed a viable story as it was relatively recent and therefore had been examined and documented more clearly. For all his early doubts, and there were many, Michael knew he was getting drawn in by the legend of Thomas Eva. Added to that were the ideas of doing something different, a different country, different culture, different customs, different people, different rules........though according to Gramps, NO rules....at least not for Michael!

Over the following days and weeks there many phone calls and visits to Gramps, all very secretive as he knew that his parents wouldn't approve of such an expedition; they certainly wouldn't understand. He clarified as much as he could. Gramps had told him that Thomas had set up an English school and one of his decrees was that all children from that day forward were to be taught English as a second language. Thankfully that had been another law that had stuck with the town, which would make life so much easier for Michael who didn't understand a word of Russian.

Gramps had acted as a go-between to introduce Michael to his friend the historian, a man named Drago Toshev. Michael had managed to 'talk' to him only via his social media messaging service, patchy and intermittent conversations at best. Drago had assured both Michael and Gramps that he would arrange meetings with other well-connected people in the town who would help him trace his ancestors and then see how things went from there. A further month passed for Michael to make his preparations. He had all his paperwork and documentation, passport, birth certificate and family trees. His flights were booked via Gramps. He had his money (in cash), partly his savings that he insisted upon using and partly from Gramps.

He had told his parents that he was going off around Europe. It wasn't strictly a lie but they wouldn't understand his whole truth anyway. He promised his Gramps that he would write a journal for him to read and, if possible, depending on the internet connection, he would e-mail him with his progress. Then, finally, early June came and Michael went to say his goodbyes and thank-you to Gramps who, in turn, handed him an old, a very old, envelope, sealed with purple wax and embellished with an intricate stamp. He was told not to open it himself, it was a letter handed down through the generations and written by Thomas Eva himself, to 'his heirs that may follow him'. Only to be opened by the highest authority in the town to prove Michaels' legitimacy as heir to the town. Michael frowned that it all seemed a little excessive but he took it with him anyway. Then he was off to find his destiny, just as his ancestor, Thomas Abraham Eva, had done almost five hundred years before him.

Michael's journey was hard but bearable; the flight was almost seven hours with a two hour lay- over in Amsterdam. This was followed by another relatively short flight to Kazan. Then he had to get a coach to Orenburg, close to the Kazakhstan border. He found a nice and seemingly quiet hotel and stayed over for the night in the relatively small but beautiful city. Michael treated himself to a good hearty meal and a bottle of wine, purely to help him sleep, of course. Though the journey meant that he only managed to get halfway through the bottle before his eyes began to feel heavy and he had to retire.

While he had been eating, Michael had managed to converse with his waiter in broken English/sign language about the best way to get to his final destination, the town that his ancestor had renamed after himself and still known to that day as Evagrad. At first, the waiter had either not understood or had never heard of the place but, eventually and with the aid of a colleague, he told Michael that he could get another bus to take him close by the town but then he would either have to walk or hitch a lift the rest of the way. There were also barely hidden frowns as to why a tourist would want to go to such a backwater, to which Michael explained that he had family there, not entirely a lie.

The next morning, with his rucksack topped up with food from the breakfast buffet, Michael managed to catch the aforementioned bus and even got off at the right point thanks to his jovial bus driver. The journey had taken almost four hours through winding streets, then long country lanes before hitting rough dirt tracks as he and his fellow passengers were bounced around. Michael had barely noticed the time or discomfort as his mind was wandering while he watched the scenery roll by his window as he munched through the last of his scavenged breakfast items.

It was even more beautiful and dramatic than he had hoped it would be. Sweeping hills giving way to harsh mountains, streams and rivers joining lakes, open fields and woodland. Small villages and settlements dotted the landscape occasionally punctuating, not spoiling, only adding to the scene before him. The bus driver had yelled back to him that his stop was where the bus had just pulled up. Michael disembarked with a smile and nod to the driver who returned the smile but with a chuckle and a shake of the head as the doors closed and the bus trundled off into the distance.

Michael stood alone at the side of the road. It was utterly quiet, not a car, truck, train or anything else seemed to move or even make a sound. He couldn't hear or see any animals or for that matter, any birds. Of course it was a beautiful place but at that moment it was completely unnerving. He had been dropped at the mouth of another dirt track. Heading off into a forest in the distance, there seemed to be a parting between the trees as the track entered. The bus driver had pointed in that direction.

"What the hell" mumbled Michael as he set off in search of his 'destiny'.

He walked for miles and the forest seemed endless. He was thankful that he had set off early. He would have hated to have to walk through such a place in the dark and alone, as it was the high and thick treetops blocked out a large portion of the sunlight leaving the place in perpetual gloom. He continued on his not so merry way, his feet throbbing and his back aching, occasionally stopping to drink from a bottle of water though his buffet pickings had long since been consumed. Eventually, however, and very thankfully, he felt he could hear noises ahead, not just noise but people and the general sound of hustle and bustle of those people going about their daily lives.

Michael smiled to himself with relief as he paused to listen more carefully. Satisfied that civilization lay not too far ahead he found renewed vigour in his stride and on he went. He reached a clearing as the forest came to a gradual end and he stopped. What lay before him was a small winding track going downhill. It led to what could only be described as something out of a period drama he'd seen on TV. The light was growing dim but he could clearly see some people riding horses and other horses and cattle pulling carts. Fires were being lit in some parts of the small town yet also he could see a few electric street lamps lighting up.

An old wooden sign, a few feet in front of Michael and to his left, bore a large word in Russian. He had no idea what it said but (no doubt, thanks to Thomas Eva) underneath in old and flaky paint were the words in English, 'Welcome to Evagrad'.

Chapter 5

The gloom and darkness seemed to be creeping up on Michael. It seemed to be coming up from behind him, from the forest and he had to make a decision. Stay and look at the place, go down and explore or turn back? He was never going to turn back and head through that forest, not a chance. He started to feel as though the forest itself was watching him and slowly the darkness was reaching out to cradle him in its blackened arms. Therefore, he was not going to stand there and watch from a distance. He started to move forward and down the dirt road. He couldn't see the people clearly enough to make out anything other than figures moving around but he had a strong sense that they could see him even as darkness was falling. He felt as though he was expected, as though eyes were following him and his every step along that dusty road into town. He started to have thoughts of Jonathan Harker travelling through Transylvania which made him chuckle to himself, what he was doing wasn't so very different. The thought of what happened to Harker however was enough to make him push the Bram Stoker references as far out of his mind as possible.

Eventually, he reached the edge of town. He could see people now more clearly and the town itself. It didn't seem so bad on first impressions. Yes, it looked a little dated, some would say 'cute' or 'olde worlde'. Well to be fair, it looked lost in time, another era long gone but it had its charm nonetheless. With renewed hope that he hadn't been impaled as a mysterious stranger just yet, he continued on despite still having certain trepidations about what to expect. He had already decided that for tonight he would just find a hotel or hostel or something and bed down for the night. He was getting hungry though so maybe he could get somewhere to crash and then find a restaurant or something. One thing he was not going to do was start shouting his mouth off about who he was and who his ancestor was, no, that could wait......if at all.

Michael tentatively wandered further and further into town. He noticed people looking at him and small groups forming and muttering to themselves and each other. He started to feel extremely self-conscious, understandably so. He had visited many places and been a rare tourist in certain small towns, yet this, somehow felt different. It felt almost surreal. The inhabitants looked modern through their dress yet they mingled with others who seemed from many years ago, not from the times of Thomas Eva but from a bygone age. Cars and vans drove along streets side by side with horses, carts and even a couple of old carriages. Electric street lamps flickered but then further down the road where the street lamps were either not working or unused. There were a few braziers freshly lit and smoking as were a long line of flaming torches bracketed against street walls. It wasn't at all a cold evening so the fires were surely only lit for the light.

Michael looked behind him and noticed that the small groups were joining together to form crowds; they were increasing in numbers and all eyes were on him. Panic started to creep up his spine and he decided he should get off the street as quickly as possible. Up ahead he noticed a sign in the dimming light, a picture of two tankards clashing together, held by gnarly fists, a pub/bar/tavern or inn, he didn't know what it was called in Evagrad but he knew he wanted to get in there and off the street. He quickened his pace and got to the entrance in double quick time.

"I fuckin hope they serve food," he mumbled, as he took a deep breath and stepped through the door without thinking what was on the other side.

To his very great and pleasurable surprise it was indeed some kind of tavern or inn. His heart slowed as relief washed over him. He hadn't realised just how quickly his heart rate had increased on his short journey through the town under such intense scrutiny. Still, as he would've expected, the few patrons that were in the tavern all turned to look at him as he shuffled in and immediately looked for the most secluded table possible. He spotted one in a corner and headed for it. The whole place was dimly lit with candles and oil powered lanterns that hung from above the old bar. The tables and chairs seemed ancient and sturdy, no doubt decades old, at least judging by the smoothness of the wood from years of use, surprisingly comfortable too. He sat and breathed out heavily allowing himself to relax.

The others in the inn peered at him for a minute or two before turning away, they were mostly middle aged or older men and it seemed as though they had weighed him up but thought of him as not a threat so ignored him and went on with their games of cards. Smoke filled the air and he noticed almost everyone one of them either smoked a pipe, cigarettes or a cigar. It seemed so strange coming from a culture now so used to clean air in public spaces. He had been to places like Berlin in recent years where some bars would still allow smoking but as a general rule it was rare these days.

Michael looked around and, taking the place in, he actually liked it. 'Rustic' didn't quite fully encapsulate the tavern, it was rougher than that. It was honest and hard and that seemed to cover the patrons as well. They all looked weather-beaten, with skin as tough as leather, bearded most of them, drinking ale and eating thick bread and some sort of sausage/salami. Then he remembered just how hungry he was and started to glance around for some sort of waiter/bar staff.

Michael noticed that despite the locals seeming indifference to him, he was still being watched from across the room. In a small alcove, a thick candle flickered, illuminating two faces. Shadows danced across the visage of a man who looked around fifty years old. He was big, broad and brawny. He had a thick beard in a goatee style, long dark hair hung down by his face onto his shoulders. He mumbled something to his companion who Michael could not make out. The man listened to whoever he was talking to but all the while he didn't take his eyes off Michael.

As Michael's unease began to resurface, the figure from the shadows got to their feet and emerged into the light, such as it was. He expected another figure much like all the other gnarly bruisers that were gathered before him but he could not be more wrong or more surprised.

Into his eye line she walked. She was plain and simply dressed but all the more beautiful for it. Long black hair cascaded down to her waistline. She wore a long purple skirt and loose cream blouse but with a thick black belt around her waist which just accentuated her figure. She looked plain because she was so natural, but she looked amazing. No western surgery, no designer clothes, no manicure or false nails, barely any make-up at all as far as he could tell in the candle and lantern light. He couldn't imagine this girl posing in front of the mirror for 'selfies' with a pout to put on her social media, he doubted she even had social media!

She walked over to the bar and knocked on it with her knuckles, as if knocking on a door. Suddenly a curtain was pulled aside from between two large shelves filled with bottles of spirits. Out stepped a short squat man, bald head, thick neck and round as a ball. He looked like he was sneering at the girl but clearly it seemed that that was his usual expression. She said something to him and he poured a tankard of ale and placed it in front of her. No money changed hands. She simply took a sniff and nodded her approval before turning to face Michael. She looked him straight in the eye and he began to sweat and fumble, nervously fiddling with his rucksack by his side. She started to make her way over to him, never breaking eye contact. As she walked, her skirt swayed around her legs and her hips moved hypnotically almost rhythmically. She arrived at his table and, continuing to stare into him, she tilted her head to the side as if she were an animal curiously contemplating a new discovery. She put the pewter tankard down in front of him, leaned back and smiled.

"It's alright, it's the good ale," she said, in an incredibly luscious Eastern European accent.

Michael's mouth dropped open slightly, taken aback by the whole scene as it dawned on him suddenly that he was in a small Russian backwater in the middle of nowhere and she spoke English as if she were from his hometown.

"Err.... th-thank you," he stammered his reply, feeling himself blush.

"I am Katarina," she held out her hand in a formal gesture but a small smile played upon her lips.

"Err...M-Michael," he said.

"Really? You don't sound so sure," she said, semi-seriously but with a devilish twinkle in her deep brown eyes.

"Err, yeah.......I mean yes. Sorry, I'm Michael," he smiled nervously, unable to break the eye contact as if she had him under her spell already.

She sat down at his table, on the chair opposite him, all the while unblinkingly intense but somehow playful in her stare.

"I'm sorry......p-please sit down......would you like to join me," he fumbled.

"Thank you," she laughed to herself as the bull of a man from the bar brought over a drink for her. Still without taking her eyes off him, she picked up the tankard and raised it to him. He returned the gesture.

"Cheers, as you say in England,"

"Is it that obvious?" he laughed self-consciously.

"Yes," was her simple dry response.

Tankards were knocked together in a dull metallic twang and they both drank. Still she studied him throughout and her stare, though achingly seductive, was making him uncomfortable. He felt he knew exactly what a fly must go through when it was at the mercy of a spider in a web.

"Err, do you live here?" he said, desperate for something to say.

"Everyone who is here," she said glancing at the patrons and then nodding towards the general population outside the doors "lives here, we don't get tourists........ever."

"Haha, until now you mean," he smiled, pleased with himself that he had a response.

She didn't say anything in reply; she simply raised her eyebrows questioningly and took another long drink from her tankard until it was finished. Her silence simply added to his discomfort and he could only drink in response. All of a sudden, he jumped as she surprised him by banging her now empty pewter tankard on the table twice.

"You like?" she said and nodded to his drink.

"Er, yeah, yeah, it's great thank you," he said, truthful in his reply as he found the ale, whatever it was, delicious.

He continued to take another sip as the bartender returned with two more tankards; evidently her banging on the table was a drinks order. The man picked up her empty and went for Michaels who was only half way through his drink. The man tutted to himself and looked at Katarina who laughed at the man's mumbling under his breath. Words passed between them which were probably about lightweight foreigners or something. Michael wasn't going to rise to it so played dumb.

Gradually, largely no doubt thanks to the ale, Michael started to relax and even began to enjoy his surroundings. Even, to the extent of a few drinks later, he was the one banging his tankard on the table to call for another round. The ale flowed freely for the rest of the night. New customers came and went, each one casting their beady eye over the stranger from a distance. Mumblings between the patrons continued, everyone in turn being brought up to speed on the stranger sat drinking with Katarina. Occasionally she would nod to a newcomer or have a word with someone who came over to their table but she didn't leave once. She always spoke to them briefly before continuing with Michael. She asked about his homeland and what it was like in England. She asked a lot of questions about his family and his background, all very subtle and with a charm that simply oozed out of her, but she was quizzing him none the less.

A teenage girl appeared with a metal plate containing food, thick sausages, cheese and bread, aromatic and mouth-watering. Katarina had somehow ordered the food in between rounds of ale. Michael was extremely grateful and tucked in, practically devouring the food which was delicious. He asked her lots of questions too, mainly about the town and her family but though it seemed a polite back and forth conversation, she was precise in getting information, relevant information. Naturally the more he drank the looser his lips became but he was very careful not to divulge too much about his ancestry, or so he thought.

At one point he needed to go to the bathroom and Katarina pointed out where it was. He stood and looked up in that direction and suddenly realised just how full the tavern had became. A sea of eyes immediately focused on him. Furtive glances had been cast in his direction as each person had entered but now, as if one, they all turned their attention on him. He was unnerved by the attention and dizzy from the ale and seemed to stand like a deer in the headlights as he was the unmistakable centre of attention for what seemed like the whole town!

Katarina spoke something but he didn't know what; it was in Russian and sounded harsh, even commanding but it had the desired effect and all eyes turned away from him and back to their drinks and mumbling to each other. Michael eased his way through the mass slowly and unsteadily but made the bathroom unaided, just. Once done he returned again through the crowd who all sat like naughty children scolded by their teacher. Katarina sat waiting for him, smiling like the seductress she undoubtedly was.

Chapter 6

Michael opened his eyes to the sounds of crashing and the scraping of wood across wood. He found himself on a bed, a thick and lumpy mattress was beneath him and pungent blankets covered him. He blinked rapidly to clear his vision and looked around at the small room. It was rough and basic but had 'character', a chair in the corner had a small pile of clothes, at which point he realised they were his clothes and he was naked. He didn't remember getting undressed. Then he tried to recall where he was and what he had done the night before to leave him with such a bitch of a hangover.

He knew he was in Russia, of course, and Evagrad to be precise but he didn't know this room. He looked around for more clues but none were forthcoming. He heard voices mumbling in the distance on the other side of a curtain that was hanging over a doorway. He climbed out of the bed gingerly and stumbled over to his clothes, thankfully his rucksack was still there. He quickly made a panicked inventory check to make sure everything was still there that he could remember. He sighed with relief at finding his passport, cash and papers and visibly relaxed with a smile. He picked up his clothes and placed them on the bed, sorting them out to get dressed. As he did so, the image of Katarina came to his mind and his fading smile became a huge grin. He couldn't remember for the life of him how the night had ended, especially leaving him in a place like that, but he hoped he would get to see her again.

"Well, good morning, Michael."

Startled, he spun around to see the beautiful Katarina watching him. She stood in the doorway, no door, just the curtain that she had pulled to the side and stood watching him with a sly smile and a raised eyebrow.

"Er....er...morning."

Embarrassment quickly took over and he grabbed his clothes to cover his modesty as he quickly sat back down on the bed.

"No need to be shy, Michael," she laughed to herself. "Did you sleep well?"

"Yes, thank you," he sighed. "But I don't know how I got here...... wherever 'here' is."

"You are in the back room of the inn, you remember from last night?"

"Yeah, I remember drinking a lot......and you, of course," he blushed as he spoke, causing her to smile.

"Well, you couldn't walk very far, you said you wanted a hotel but we don't have tourists so...... no hotels!" she laughed. "We put you in here for safe keeping."

Her eyes seemed to sparkle as she spoke; he remembered that from the night before at least.

"Who's 'we'?" he asked.

"Me and a couple of men, I needed help."

"Did they undress me too? Haha," he laughed nervously.

"No," she smiled back. "That was me.......now, come on. Hurry and get dressed."

Katarina turned away and walked back into the bar while an even more self-conscious Michael hurriedly got ready to catch up with her, not quite sure where he was going.

Dressed and with his rucksack over his shoulder, Michael emerged back out into the bar area. The squat man and the teenage girl were moving chairs and clearing away tankards and plates from the night before, which was obviously what had woken him. He sheepishly made his way to the door, mumbling his thanks as he did so; the landlord looked up but continued his work without commenting. He could see Katarina on the outside of the open door on the street; she seemed to be scolding another young woman who scuttled off into the street as soon as Michael arrived.

"What was all that about?" he asked casually.

"Nothing, she knows her place," spat Katarina before turning and smiling sweetly at Michael which was a new look from the stern seductress.

She started to walk down the street and Michael duly followed like a good puppy. As they walked he wanted to ask questions, largely because he could barely remember what he asked the night before and remembered even less of her answers, but he didn't want to sound foolish so he tried to think and recall. For her part, Katarina seemed happy to walk through the streets quietly, though only she knew where they were going.

He remembered getting confirmation that all children in the town are all taught English from a young age, which was helpful. Good old Thomas! Gradually as they walked, quite a lot of information came to him but when he found himself stuck he started to ask questions and Katarina seemed to have answers for everything. It was worth asking her just to hear her talk in that delicious accent of hers. He recalled that they do not have tourists and also very little contact with any other towns. The nearest one was over fifty miles away and aside from a couple of tiny hamlets the town of Evagrad was practically its own state. There were no direct roads to anywhere else; dirt tracks through the forest were as good as it got regarding transport links.

Once a month a convoy of small vans and cars would make its way up the hill and through the forest to civilization for any supplies and deliveries that were necessary. That would also be the only time people could send letters or parcels or have them picked up from the next town's post office. Trading could be done then. Businesses such as farmers could send off their goods to sell to wholesalers in the next town and thus get money for supplies or stock. Because of this, the people of Evagrad became incredibly self sufficient because it was simply too hard to communicate with the outside world. They had electricity, of sorts at least, but that was intermittent and not very reliable; generators were used but infrequently.

She explained that certain people of standing in the community had access to modern conveniences like telephones, television and internet but again they were barely used. Evagrad was a place on its own and that was just the way the townsfolk liked it apparently. The town had a doctor and a couple of nurses, a police 'force' – which consisted of a family of three brothers (the eldest Vladimir Drazic being the Chief of Police) and their sons and nephews, a total of eleven officers. Those officers also made up the bulk of the volunteer fire department too. There was a Mayor who was also the town magistrate, Nicolae Zoran. Basically, he was the King of the town and the only one who could challenge him for authority was Police Chief Drazic.

Everything was the way it was and always had been for as long as anyone had known and there had been no need for change, no need for reaching out to the wider world or even their distant neighbours, which was the way they had been brought up and always would be.

They walked across and through the town in the beautiful summer morning light. Just as the evening before, practically everyone they passed or approached turned to look at them or, more specifically, Michael. Being guided by Katarina helped to take the edge of anxiety out of the situation. He kidded himself that everyone was looking at the stunning Katarina, although, deep down, he knew it was he that was the centre of attention. Eventually they arrived at a sizable house close to the far edge of town.

"Where are we?" Michael asked.

"My home," she replied.

Immediately Michael smiled to himself. His hopes were suddenly high, what else was he to think when a beautiful young woman takes him to her home alone. She opened the door and turned with that seductive look in her eye as she had previously. He returned the smile though his was more of an idiotic grin. Katarina walked into the house and he followed her, his heart racing as he watched her ass move in front of him. She walked through a hallway and opened another door into a large living room/ library and in he followed, resuming his puppy status.

He was not greeted by the beauty seducing him, nor her disrobing. Instead a man was sitting in a large leather armchair which he filled completely. He had a thick goatee beard, shoulder length hair framing his harsh looking face, open neck shirt with greying hair bristling up from his chest. The man was a brawny looking beast, maybe early fifties, clearly a man of hard work and also a man that Michael vaguely recognised. It was the man staring at him in the inn the previous night before he had met Katarina.

"Papa, this is Michael," she said. "Michael, my father."

Under the gaze of this man, especially realizing it was the father of the object of his desire, Michaels' building libido collapsed on the spot.

He stepped forward to the man in the chair and politely but shakily offered him his hand. The man looked at it tremble and back at him before reaching out and taking it.

"Welcome to Evagrad, Michael Green," he boomed.

Chapter 7

Michael dithered and blushed; he was suddenly and obviously caught off guard and added to that, the man looked absolutely terrifying.

"Err, nice to meet you......., Sir," he replied, trying to figure out when, but assuming he must have told Katarina his last name.

"Please, sit down."

The man gestured to a large couch in the middle of the room facing him and behind where Michael stood nervously. He did as he was told immediately and Katarina and her father shared a look that was either comedic or of derision, it was difficult to gauge.

"How are you finding Evagrad Michael?" asked the man, studying the newcomer.

"Erm, well, I've only been here one day so it's difficult to say but so far I'm glad I came," he looked at Katarina, smiled and blushed. "I mean, Katarina has been very hospitable........, Sir," he finished politely, before looking down at his shoes in embarrassment.

A roar of laughter greeted him as Katarina's father looked at her and then Michael before adding

"I bet she has.............By the way, no need to call me Sir. I am Drago, Drago Toshev"

Michael paused. He knew he'd heard that name before but couldn't quite place where from but then, like someone switching on a light for him, there it was, Drago Toshev the historian and contact of Gramps!

"Yes, that Drago," said Toshev, knowing that the penny had indeed dropped for Michael.

"But......," he looked again at Katarina. "Is this just a coincidence or....," Michael trailed off before saying what he was thinking, some kind of set up.

"It is of course no coincidence, Michael. Your Grandfather has told me all about you and I have, as requested, been looking at your 'situation'. I know of your claims and I know them to be legitimate. The town of Evagrad will be yours, of course."

"B-but.....I haven't come here to take over.....I...I...," stumbled Michael.

"But you are here and it is your birthright. What is the problem?" queried Toshev.

"I, err, I came here to explore and have a holiday really. I can't expect to...."

"Michael, you are the rightful heir to Thomas Eva's town, we are named after him. He was our father of sorts too. This town became his and now.....it will be yours."

"B-but I can't......surely.......the people that live here.....their homes...."

"Michael," Katarina spoke up. "You would be seen here as our leader, treated like a King. The people would love you."

"And those that didn't?" asked Michael.

"Those that didn't...........," Toshev rumbled with a hard look in his eyes, the eyes of a man who would settle for nothing less than obedience from all, ".......would learn to."

"This is all happening too quickly, Mr Toshev."

"Drago, please."

"I'm sorry, Drago. I've only been here less than twenty four hours and you expect me to take over the town, a town I don't know and where no-one knows me?"

"I know you already, Michael," Katarina smiled.

"That's right, Michael; you already have allies. Not that you will need allies as you have the blood on your side," Drago implored. "We are a traditional people here. We have customs and history and we keep ourselves to ourselves. What is decided here stays within the town. We live by our own rules and our own heritage. That heritage comes from your ancestor, Thomas Eva."

"But, as I said, I don't even know this place," Michael protested. "It's incredible that this could happen but it's.......just very overwhelming."

"Hmm.......I understand......I shall tell you how I see it. You stay for a time, as you were going to but think about things differently. Instead of thinking about a holiday, think of if you could live here," Drago offered but then threw in his bargaining chip with a very sly smile. "Katarina here could be your very own and personal tour guide and show you what we have to offer."

He followed that wonderful suggestion with a lascivious laugh unexpected from a man about his daughter. Katarina practically sparkled with a smile and pout that would make any grown man weak at the knees. Was that the clichéd offer that couldn't be refused?

"Well," Michael blushed yet again. "That would be very kind, if you don't mind."

"Haha" Drago laughed heartily. "The English gentleman, eh, Katarina?"

Again Katarina needn't do anything but smile before she made to exit the room for dramatic effect, her skirt brushing past him and causing her scent to waft in her wake, just to inflame Michael a little more.

"You will not be under pressure, Michael; we want you to want to be here. But be assured that you are in no danger here. Even as a stranger, you are free to come and go as you please. You are freer here than anywhere else in the world, I promise you that. No-one will hurt you here because no-one will be allowed to hurt you."

"But people don't know me or who I am."

"Michael, I swear on my daughter's life that almost everyone in the town knows who you are and what you are. The reason why everyone was staring at you was because they wanted to see you for themselves."

Michael pondered on Drago's words as the gruff man stood and left the room, leaving him alone to think. The words sank in deep and joined the words in his mind from Gramps. Michael found himself wondering if it was possible to actually have a life in Evagrad after all. Of course, he hadn't really been there long by any stretch of the imagination but the idea of being a 'King' was obviously alluring. The thoughts of Thomas Eva came back to him: moulding a town, a people, a culture all to his will, it would be amazing. After all, what else did he have at home? A few friends and family of course but no girlfriend and no actual job were waiting for him there. He could actually build a whole new life here; he could be whatever he wanted here.......he could *do* whatever he wanted here.

Michael laughed to himself, getting carried away, it was absurd surely.......wasn't it? But then again, on the other hand........

"Michael?" Katarina stood in the doorway looking at him.

"Errr, yeah, err," Michael mumbled, as he was brought out of his deep thoughts.

"We have food prepared, won't you join us?"

"Oh, yes, of course. Thank you."

He got to his feet and followed after her as she turned and walked into another room, a kitchen/dining area where Drago was already seated. In front of him was a wholesome and delicious looking spread. Nothing fancy, just good old fashioned hearty food: bread, beef, potatoes, various vegetables and jugs containing sauces and gravies.

A jug of ale sat nestled in the middle of the table. Drago sat at the head of the table and poured himself a drink from it. Michael's glass was already filled and waiting for him at his allotted seat opposite Katarina. He didn't ask and they didn't mention anything about Katarina's mother/ Drago's wife or her whereabouts or if she was alive. He didn't want to offend or ruin the delicious meal that he was tucking into so he kept his thoughts to himself.

"To Michael" Drago toasted raising his glass.

Michael blushed a little again before lifting his glass, as did Katarina and all three chinked together as Katarina added to her father's words with a large and sly grin.

"To the heir of Evagrad."

Chapter 8

Michael didn't know what had hit him when he woke up, but felt it must've been something strong and bull-like. He was lay face down; he could feel that he was lying in or on something damp but couldn't decide what it was. It was cold and it smelled bad. The other thing that he could sense was a breeze; he knew he was outside but where? He had no idea.

He became aware of a rumbling noise. It wasn't loud but he could hear it a few feet away from him. He realised that it was voices, the voices of people mumbling to each other. Michael tried to open his eyes. It was difficult for him at first as they seemed to be stuck together. A little effort freed him and he was temporarily blinded by the sunlight burst that hit his sight.

Once his vision became clearer, he noticed that he was indeed lay outside in the sun and there were crowds of townsfolk gathering around him. Some were arguing amongst themselves; others almost coming to blows and being separated from each other. He heard from somewhere within the crowd screams of horror, cries of anguish and loss. Anger, rage, fear and heartbreak were all mixed in as the volume grew on the people's discovery of the scene in which he was at the centre.

He rolled over onto his side and then his back so that he could sit up and see for himself what was going on. Immediately he wished that he hadn't done so. The dampness that he had been lying on or in was sticky to the touch and he soon realised that it was blood, congealing blood and it was everywhere. It was all over the ground on which he was now sitting, as well as all over him. It soaked and covered his clothes which were torn and almost in rags about his person. It was all over his skin, as if he had been swimming in the stuff. More so than the blood which was making him gag was the gore that dripped off his arm and hand as he raised the limb. He started to shake in disbelief as the trauma of his situation kicked into his mind. He gazed about to see body parts lay in the dirt: hands, legs, a couple of heads were all clearly visible, as well as piles of intestines and internal organs discarded like unwanted offal outside a slaughterhouse.

It was impossible for him to register what was going on and what had happened to leave him in this place and in this situation. No horror movie, no book and no experience he could ever endure would've prepared him for this traumatic scene and, as a result, he sat there in the gore and cried to himself in panic. The crowd's noise grew increasingly louder and the waves of nausea within him built too, to the point that he turned to the side and vomited. Cold sweat spread over his skin causing the drying blood to slicken and run again down his arms as if to partially recreate whatever had happened to put him there.

Michael looked up as the crowd parted; the town's police officers came through, or rather fought their way through what was threatening to become a mob. The two burly officers came straight to him and very roughly picked him up by his arms, twisting them behind his back and pushing him in the direction that they wanted him to move. It was painful for him, yet the daze that he was in numbed him somewhat from the harshness of his treatment though some in the crowd would say it was the least he deserved.

He was taken to the local jailhouse and thrown into a cell. Hardly a word was spoken to him but it was clear what the police thought of him simply by the look on their faces. Disgust, anger and fury were all transmitted in waves at him through glares and sneers of contempt.

The jail itself reminded Michael of old Western movies: a small town sheriff sat at a desk and behind him were iron barred cells; a bad guy in a black hat sitting in a cell waiting for his gang to come and break him out. He imagined the cool sheriff calmly loading his rifle while his deputy waits outside for more bad guys riding into town for their captured leader.

Sadly, this wasn't an old movie classic, it was real and although the room and cells looked that way there was no cool and calm sheriff awaiting the bad guys. Instead there were two officers that looked like they wanted to rip him a new asshole and were both more than capable of doing just that.

Michael could do nothing. He tried to ask what had happened but he was ignored by the officers who, in between scowling at him, amused themselves chatting in Russian, not the English that he had been used to hearing since he arrived. Instead, he sat there in his cell, on his dank and stained bunk, pondering what the hell was going on. He thought about his loss of time and memory. He felt that he had only been in the town for three days that he could remember; rather this was his third day. How much had happened in such a short space of time and it was all so overwhelming that his head spun as he tried to make sense of it all.

One thing that he could piece together, albeit tenuously, was that he had woken up at the tavern the morning after the night before when he had been getting to know Katarina. He had been drinking and eating with her and then woke up in a strange place with no knowledge of how he had gotten there. The next day he had been with her again, eventually going to her home to meet her father, who 'coincidentally' turned out to be Drago Toshev, Gramps' contact and town historian, allegedly. Again, he had eaten and drunk with them before waking up in a strange place with no knowledge of how he got there. That was surely no coincidence. Also, he remembered that it seemed as though her father had been in deep conversation with Katarina and sent her over to him in the first place at the tavern upon Michael's arrival.

He swung this way and that in his mind; on the one hand they seemed so welcoming and eager to help him in his quest to claim his birth-right. But that was never really a serious intention of his in coming to Evagrad. It had been partly for Gramps and partly an adventure. They had been insistent and resolved to him taking over the town after he had barely arrived. Why? Also, it seemed too much of a coincidence that after drinking and eating with them, twice, he had woken up alone in a strange place with amnesia. Had he been drugged by them, he wondered?

Another and more pressing question kept screaming in his mind, what happened last night for him to wake up in a back street in a pile of gore and horror? He was still sitting in the clothes, or rags of his clothes, from last night and he stank the place out. Flies were seemingly spreading the word about the blood-fest in the cell, judging by how they were flocking to him in droves. His arms ached due to his constant and futile attempts to bat the little bastards away. His lips were dry but each time he subconsciously licked his lips he could taste the drying blood of others on them, which added to the nausea that he had never stopped feeling since waking.

He sat there in a daze of questions, flies and a sickening stench for what seemed like hours. The officers occasionally stepped outside to stretch their legs; one went out for food for the two of them, whether lunch or breakfast Michael couldn't be sure. They smoked and drank coffee. One of them gave Michael a small cup of water but that was the only connection made between the officers and Michael; the other cop even seemed to mock the water giver for his kindness.

A break in the monotony and anguish came when the door of the jailhouse opened and in walked three men, none of whom were Clint Eastwood coming to save him from the Sheriff and his deputy.

They looked at Michael with curiosity and he sheepishly looked back. He felt like an animal in the zoo behind the bars of his cage. Amongst their number was Drago Toshev. He didn't really know whether to consider him an ally or not. Sure, he talked a big game about getting him his birth-right and looking after him and making him feel welcome, even seemingly dangling his own daughter as bait to snare him! But the more Michael had thought about things in isolation the more he felt he needed to be wary around Drago.

"Mr Green, allow me to introduce myself," said a stout man in his early sixties with receding grey hair and piggy eyes. "I am Nicolae Zoran, the Mayor of Evagrad."

"Err P-pleased to meet you, Sir," stammered Michael, surprised that the Mayor had come to visit him. He held his filthy blood-stained hand out through the bars to shake hands with him before remembering the state he was in and apologetically withdrawing it.

The Mayor looked around at Drago and the other man with disdain. Whether it was for Michael or the condition he had been left in it was difficult to tell. The other as yet unidentified man mumbled something in Russian at the two officers. He had a rumbling power in his voice and the two quickly jumped up from their desks and fetched a bowl of warmish water for Michael to clean himself up a little at least.

They waited for Michael to get himself a little more refreshed. Though he was desperate to shower, at least he managed to get some of the stink off himself. As the three men waited, they talked to each other at the far side of the room, out of his earshot. Mainly they spoke in English, unless words were harsh judging by their tone, when they slipped into Russian.

He couldn't hear what they were saying but obviously they were talking about him. If it wasn't obvious, their constant looks over their shoulders at him emphasised the point.

Once Michael had dried himself on the rough and threadbare towel that he had been given, the men walked back over to him; this time the Mayor held out his hand cordially.

"Once again, I am Nicolae Zoran, the Mayor of Evagrad. It is a pleasure to meet you, Mr Green. Welcome to our town."

"Thank you, Sir. Please, call me Michael," he replied, reaching out and shaking the man's hand.

"As you know already, this is Drago Toshev, our historian and one of our Elders (he hadn't mentioned that to Michael) and this fine and robust fellow is Vladimir Drazic, our Chief of Police."

Michael still had his hand outstretched for the officer to shake but he stayed rooted to the spot looking him up and down, clearly not impressed with the Englishman. Drago stepped forward to avoid any awkwardness, grasping his hand warmly.

"Are you alright Michael? We will have you out of here soon, don't worry."

Michael smiled gently but said nothing. The men all looked at each other and then the Mayor excused them to Michael before retiring back to their little huddle at the back of the room. Michael could do nothing but return to sit on his bunk. Still not knowing what he had actually done but from the scene he had awoken in, he feared the worst. Just a few days earlier he had been finalising his trip and brimming over with excitement of the adventure and the possibilities to come but now..........

His thoughts were interrupted as the three men came back over to him, the Mayor in front, leading the way for Toshev and Drazic, Drago looked pleased with himself, a big smile spreading across his face. By huge contrast, the Chief was far from happy, scowling all the while and almost visibly biting his tongue so as not to blurt out what he was really thinking.

"Tradition, Mr Green. I mean, Michael," began the Mayor with a benevolent smile, "is a very big part of our lives here in Evagrad. Because of this, we always have...," he looked around at Chief Drazic pointedly before continuing, "and always will embrace the past. It is what makes us who we are as a community. Our history, our beliefs, our culture and our traditions are what make us special, as far as we are concerned at least."

His head bowed before looking up at Michael and smiling, almost sweetly. Michael simply nodded at the three of them, still not really sure what the Mayor was getting at but his manner was warm and genuine; he actually seemed a little subservient towards Michael almost as if he were seeking his approval.

"That's understandable, Sir, but........"

"What does this mean for you?" The Mayor finished his thought for him.

"Erm....yes."

"Well, Michael, a lot of our community can trace their family back a long way, a very long way. Some, myself included, can trace their ancestors back to the town that was just a village, not even that, a settlement, barely more than a camp. Everything changed for the better upon the arrival of one man...."

"Thomas Abraham Eva," Michael returned, finishing his sentence for him.

"Yes," smiled Mayor Zoran with another nod (or bow) of his head.

"And......I'm his direct descendant."

"Yes, Michael, you are. More than that though, you are his rightful heir."

As Zoran finished there was an audible growl from Chief Drazic who scowled at the men and their discussion.

"There are some of our people who would discredit your claim, Michael, based on the fact that they say they too can trace their ancestors back to Thomas Eva."

"And I'm guessing the Chief is one of them?" Michael lent forward and whispered so as not to inflame the situation.

"Exactly right, Michael," the Mayor whispered back to him before standing straighter and speaking louder, "However, *bastard* offspring have no claim on the estate of Thomas Eva, our rightful founding father. Only you have that."

At that point The Mayor reached into his jacket pocket and produced an envelope, Michaels's envelope, from his rucksack. It was documentation of his family tree and various photocopies of birth certificates dating and tracing Michael all the way back to Thomas, legally everything was proven. He immediately looked at Drago Toshev, who had clearly been through his bags, either at the tavern as he slept or when he was at Toshev's house with Katarina; unless she had taken it. Either way, he was starting to trust the pair of them less and less, not even taking into account that he was still thinking that they may have drugged him.

As he was thinking all of this to himself, Chief Drazic shouted over to one of his men. An exchange went back and forth, in Russian, no doubt for Michael's benefit, and angry voices were raised before the officer stood and marched over to Michael's cell. He stared at Michael before reluctantly unlocking the cage door. He didn't open it, he simple stormed off, clearly furious.

Instead, Toshev stepped forward and opened the metal door saying, "Michael, you are free my boy."

"Just like that? I'm free?"

"Correct, Michael. You cannot be charged with this crime or any other. You are the heir to Thomas Eva and therefore Evagrad is essentially....... yours," added Mayor Zoran.

Michael stepped out of his cell sheepishly and very much aware of the officers who all stared at him with contempt. He took a couple of steps towards the door and both Drago and Zoran parted for him. Toshev even rushed to the door to open it for him. Zoran smiled and gestured for him to leave freely, with his arms outstretched before him, adding another little cherry to top Michael's cake of bemusement.

"Drago here, will take you to your family home. Once belonging to Thomas, now it is yours, of course."

Chapter 9

Michael stepped outside, closely followed by the eager Drago, keen to share with him what had happened and what was to come. Drago urged Michael to walk on in the direction that they were already facing and then quickened his step to catch up and walk alongside the Englishman.

Michael looked at him suspiciously, shaking his head he turned to the Russian and said, "Would you mind telling me what the fuck just happened back there?

"You are free, Michael. You're free!" He beamed back.

"I was free last night, Drago. What happened last night and why am I covered in blood now?"

Speaking those words out loud seemed to bring another level of realisation to Michael's mind and he stopped dead in his tracks as a cold shiver passed through his body.

"Come with me. I will explain everything back at the house, I promise, but not here on the street," urged Drago, furtively looking around as the towns people seemed to be stopping in their daily activities to gawk at the two of them.

He put his hand on the small of Michael's back to escort him away from the main thorough fare and through side streets, a better and quieter way of getting back to Toshev's house. Michael was still in a daze, confused and bemused and not a little frightened by how his circumstances had changed in little more than a few days. Now he wasn't sure if he was a criminal but, then again, he had just been released. He didn't even know what he was supposed to have done but, judging by the aftermath that he had woken up in, it was far from good.

Eventually they arrived in silence at Drago's house. Michael was obviously in a tortured world of his own inside his head while Toshev was excitedly thinking of the future and trying to hold all his thoughts to himself. Silence suited them both just fine.

Drago opened the front door and held it open with a beaming grin for Michael to enter first, which he did. Drago followed but then dashed in front to open the living room door and bid Michael to take a seat and get comfortable. Drago then rushed off to get his good brandy and came back quickly polishing two glasses, one he gave to Michael while he opened the brandy bottle from under his arm and poured them both a glass.

"Cheers, as you say in England," Drago shouted heartily, still with his huge grin on his face.

"Cheers," Michael replied, but in a much softer and far less celebratory tone, before swallowing the strong brown liquid and wincing.

"What's wrong, Michael. You are a free man, you can do anything you want............Anything!"

"I still want to know what the hell is going on!" he snapped, frustrated.

"Ok, ok, Michael. I will tell you everything," Drago replied with his hands raised in submission. "First, another drink," he smiled, as he filled their glasses.

"No. First, I want to know something. Have you been drugging me?" Michael stared at him, with a hardened steely look of anger and defiance.

Drago sighed and looked down at the floor before looking back at him and simply nodding with seeming embarrassment. Michael's mouth dropped open in dismay as if to ask why but he couldn't find the actual words.

"Michael, it was for the best. We had to make sure we could look after you and keep you close. We didn't want anybody else getting hold of you and bending you to their will. It was for your protection, Michael. Please believe me."

"We? You and Katarina?"

"Yes, we tasked ourselves with your safety here in Evagrad. You will have many enemies here........you saw the Police Chief and his men. They are not happy that you have come to claim your birth-right," implored Drago. "And there will be others."

"I didn't come here for that.........Not really," Michael sighed in exasperation.

"As you say, but you are here now and it has been approved and accepted by Mayor Zoran and the Elders. You are the rightful heir to Thomas Eva and you are the new Lord of this town."

"Lord?" Michael couldn't help but smile and then laugh to himself at the very notion of the idea. Michael, Lord of Evagrad.

"The title can be whatever you want it to be, Michael. It doesn't matter what you call yourself. It is the position that matters."

"And what about last night? What happened then, Drago?"

"We had to test the theory. Prove that you could not be brought down like other men, prove that you are above the law."

"By doing what exactly?" asked Michael.

"By getting you to kill," Drago responded and fell silent.

Michael sat in amazement; he had absolutely no idea what to say. He was sickened and filled with revulsion at the thought. Disbelief made his head spin in every direction as he tried to take in what he was being told, especially as he had absolutely no idea or recollection of anything that had taken place the night before.

"The drugs, as you call them, aren't from the west. They are a combination of herbs and flowers and things that grow in the mountains and countryside in this area, the area we call home and it is now yours to rule." Drago smiled at Michael conspiratorially, not fully accepting or understanding the fragility of his new 'Lord's' state of mind.

"Fucking hell," Michael whispered to no one but himself, as he stared into space.

"Katarina is very skilled in her art," Drago commented with a smile of pride.

"Katarina?" Michael's head snapped to attention as he spoke. "She did this to me?"

"She made the potion, the drug as you call it. In some parts of the world she would be called a witch but here she creates medicines too. She heals people. We have a doctor and nurses but most people come to Katarina when they sicken. She is talented like her mother before her," Drago smiled at the memory of his lost love.

"So.....last night? What happened, Drago. What really happened?"

"After we had eaten and drank to your future?" he smiled again but sighed as Michael remained stern faced.

"First of all, your drink always had some of Katarina's potion mixed in with it. At the tavern she just wanted you to sleep and be safe so that she could return and know that you were alright. But once we had seen your paperwork then we knew that you were the one, the real heir."

"Hang on," interrupted Michael. "You took my papers when I was at the tavern asleep?"

"Yes. Katarina put you to bed and looked for your passport but found all your bloodlines and history. She took them and brought them to me so that I could check them and bring them to the Mayor as proof. Then Katarina put them back in your bag early before you woke up."

"For fucks' sake," exclaimed Michael, in disbelief.

"It was for your protection, Michael. I swear."

"So you keep saying........Go on with the story."

"Well, errr....Oh, yes. We knew in our hearts that you were the one, so Katarina had been feeding you a different potion as we drank and ate. We knew you were who we expected but had to have proof that the law would uphold your claim. Therefore, we set out to look for men who did not believe in you. The three of us went out into the town very late and found a group of men that did not believe. They mocked the idea. They mocked you and you grew angry, as did all three of us. One of the men grabbed at Katarina and you defended her, but more than that you became like an animal, wild and vicious. You tore and ripped at the man and his friends as they tried to help him and fight you off but they were no match for you. Even four of them together."

Drago paused to pour himself another brandy and by the paleness of Michael's cheeks he felt that he needed a refresh too so eased forward and topped up his glass before continuing.

"Katarina told me that the potion was strong and that is what it can do but she had never seen it act so well before. She thinks it is something within you that has never been released until now. We both think that that within you will help make you a strong and powerful leader for our people. We stepped back and allowed you to glut yourself. You were wild and horrific, a true beast, a fearsome warrior, a berserker from the old times."

"Me?" Michael creased his forehead and his chin dropped open upon each revelation.

"You, Michael. You are a man, a leader, a warrior. You were born to it. Like the stories and legends of Thomas Eva fighting off the beast in the woods and rescuing our people all that long time ago."

More brandy was consumed as Drago continued to try to reassure Michael of his freedom and of what had passed.

"Once they had taken you away, I took your letters back to the Mayor and Chief and argued that you cannot be tried for any crime as you are the heir to Evagrad.........And, as you now sit here, it worked," Drago chuckled to himself with a smug grin on his face.

Michael's scepticism remained but he had nothing to add to the conversation. He could only listen and try to make sense of what he was being told. Then he realised something was missing and he couldn't believe that he hadn't said something earlier.

"Where's Katarina?"

The brandy helped to stop his blushing for once when he spoke her name.

"At your house, Michael."

"My house?

"Remember, the Mayor said I would take you to Thomas Eva's home? It is now yours, Michael and I will take you there soon. Katarina is preparing it for you now. But first, a few more drinks, my Lord Michael?"

Chapter 10

After just one more (large) drink, Drago led Michael through the woods. The afternoon had faded but it was still a warm and balmy day as the early evening sun shone through the leaves of the forest and dappled the green floor. It was a beautiful day and another stunning sight lay ahead.

In a clearing where the trees seemed to hold themselves back purposefully, a building lay nestled and protected from the outside world. It looked very old and as if it had been born from the ground to hide surreptitiously amid the foliage. They walked up to the house and a small path which had obviously recently been tended and cleared. At that point Drago stopped and Michael went on a couple of steps, drawn in by the house before realising and stopping himself, turning to look back at Drago.

"Welcome home Michael" he said. "Welcome home." He smiled and turned away with a chuckle to himself. Michael turned back to the house, bewitched by its dark beauty and as if a silent sirens song called him, he continued his walk to 'his' home.

He arrived at the house, looking in complete awe at it on his approach, it was in some parts dilapidated but still held a majesty of its own. Moss and leaves covered parts of the building and lots of the stonework was damaged, trees overhung large sections which just added to the mysterious feel of the archaic house which seemed to have been there for centuries, which of course it had, but still it stood resolutely waiting, for Michael maybe.

He stood at the porch and looked down at something on the front step which immediately made him screw up his face in revulsion.

"What the fuck?" he mumbled, under his breath.

There on the step was 'something' that he hadn't expected and could never have expected to see. It looked like a cluster of twigs and small branches, woven together to make some sort of shield. It was round and woven and strapped into the circle was a kind of star; it wasn't quite a pentacle or a Star of David however. It looked like it had eight points, possibly, as it was difficult to tell having some sort of dead creature strapped to it. He couldn't make out what animal it was but there was clearly fur, or there had been. Partially skinned and disembowelled, it was stretched across the wooden structure. Its head still attached, it hung loosely to one side and its lifeless eyes stared up at him pitifully.

He looked away from it quickly and up to the door where he noticed that blood (hopefully from the same animal and not another one!) was smeared all the way up both sides of the door frame and across the top, above the door. Flies were buzzing around the dead flesh and blood and this just made him realise that he still had blood all over him and had had all day. Having washed his hands, basically, in the jail he hadn't washed since. The brandy and Drago's explanations had taken all day, followed by the walk out here to this beautiful glade, yet the beauty was now being tarnished somewhat.

Michael looked back at the thing on the ground and screwed up his face again and, as he did so, he heard the door handle in front of him turn. The door opened slowly, while he was still staring at the gore on the step, and he was then confronted by a beautiful pair of bare feet. His head slowly made its way up the sight before him, taking it all in. A long black dress covered the legs from the ankles up, loose fitting it hung but it parted as his eye line moved up to just above the waist. Milky white flesh almost shone in contrast to the black material. The curvature of her cleavage was prominent, as were her nipples, as they stood to attention under his gaze through the thin fabric. He continued his visual tour up her neck to her throat, chin and finally her beautiful face. Katarina stood smiling at him, Michael was lost for words and stood on the step, between him and the beauty was just the dead beast.

"Come in Michael, this is your home now," she said in a soft and husky tone which made him weaken. He didn't look down, he simply did as he was told and stepped over the sacrificed road kill and into 'his' home.

Katarina bowed her head as he passed her and closed the door behind them, sliding a bolt to lock the world outside. They stood and gazed at each other in the hall of the house before she beckoned him to follow her as she gave him a tour of the building that he was now expected to call his home. It was old obviously and in places it looked it. Parts of the walls were cracked and masonry had fallen but considering its age it was standing up well. Michael wondered who had lived there, if anyone, since Thomas Eva's day. There may well have been a caretaker of sorts, waiting for the return of the Lord of the manor!

There was a large open living area, a separate drawing room/office area and he could imagine Thomas holding court there as he made plans for the future of his town. Another large room was off to one side, most probably a dining area and then a kitchen off that. Michael was struck by the age and style and vastness of the house in comparison to what must have been around at the time. This would have been the equivalent to having a mansion next to a village, which when he thought of it that way, wasn't too different to how things were back then in England. It just suddenly seemed so ridiculous when people in the village must've been living from hand to mouth.

Michael followed Katarina around, taking in everything but still had difficulty taking his eyes off her. She glided with grace and fluidity around the rooms and then to what, for the time, must've been a very elaborate staircase; it was dusty and broken in places but looked very ornate even now. She looked over her shoulder with a lascivious smile as she ascended the stairs and Michael reverted to his puppy mode and followed behind eagerly.

She walked along the landing, the skirt from her dress swaying around her legs with a soft swish. He noticed then that she wasn't actually wearing a dress as such; it was more of a black robe, complete with hood which hung down her back and was covered by her long free flowing hair. She showed him to each of the four bedrooms, some cluttered with junk and boxes, no doubt any 'caretaker' had been using it to store things relatively recently. Furniture was draped in huge sheets to protect the pieces from dust, the floors had been swept clean and fresh linen had been placed on the bed in one room, the master bedroom of course. Michael noticed that Katarina had clearly been getting everything ready for him and set up and cleaned enough space for him, he would only need one bedroom for now of course. The bed was also incredibly ornate and bulky. A headboard with carved scrolls and cherubs in flight. Four posts lifting a canopy of thin white muslin above, obviously the thing had seen better days but it still carried much of its original grandeur and looked incredibly inviting.

Candles had been lit throughout the upstairs, though the evening was still light, the trees blocked out a lot of the sun to the upstairs. The rooms therefore all carried an unearthly glow throughout of the half-light mixed with candle glow. It gave a magical feel of comfort and decadence, despite the decrepit state of some parts of the house, though lots of it was hidden by the gathering gloom.

Katarina stopped mid tour of the upstairs and turned to look at him; she gazed up and down and then spoke.

"You have not been able to wash the stench of death and blood from yourself." She looked sad that he was still in the state he had been found that morning.

Michael only just realised what she meant, given that he was transfixed by watching her. It dawned on him that she was right and suddenly he felt extremely self-conscious. He felt that she was repulsed by him.

"I'm so sorry, I haven't had time to....," he started to apologise.

"No, no, Michael. It is I who should beg for your forgiveness, you should not have been left in that state and for so long."

"It's fine; honestly, I'll get cleaned up in a minute."

"You are too kind but.........I have arranged for you to bathe."

With that she opened the door in front of which they stood. It was a bathroom, and what a bathroom. It was again, very ornate, huge and wide with a large window which had been flung wide open and looked down onto the back of the property. Michael hadn't seen that view and he marvelled at what was obviously once an extremely well kept and manicured garden. It was utterly private and despite falling into disrepair and neglect, it could clearly be amazing again. Someone, Katarina or Drago maybe, had been trying to keep on top of it or at least tidied it up recently and it looked to be potentially breathtaking.

Back in the room there was an enormous roll top bath with ball & claw feet which stood in the middle of the room. Candles again were lit throughout and below a large carved mirror on a chimney breast, a small fire crackled away in the hearth, it was utterly intoxicating and seductive.

Only then did he notice that the bath had been drawn and it was filled with steaming water, at least he hoped it was water, it was red. Still it looked inviting and soothing but he had misgivings due to the colour and what he had woken up covered in as well as the slaughtered creature on his doorstep! He looked at her questioningly in hope of an explanation.

"Please get in, it has soothing berries and roots from the forest, I picked them myself this morning." She said, as she gestured to beyond the open windows.

He looked again at the water and did indeed notice small berries and fruits of the wild floating around the edges of the bath. His fears eased, for the time being at least, he started to unbutton his shirt. Much to his disappointment she smiled and left the room. Michael sighed and frowned but continued to get undressed and climbed tentatively into the water, it was hot and he gently lowered himself in as the heat temporarily took his breath away.

Once settled, he relaxed and let his head droop back against the porcelain of the bath. She was right, the infusion of the roots, leaves and fruits that she had picked completely disarmed him and seemed to massage away any and all the aches and pains in his body, aches and pains that he hadn't even known were there. He closed his eyes and allowed the bliss to wash over him like a wave.

After a few minutes of relaxation he felt he was being watched and quickly opened his eyes with a start. He looked to his left to the doorway and it was wide open. There, pausing in the doorway, she stood. Katarina with the hood of her robe up on top of her head, she was mumbling words under her breath as she stood, for the most part, stock still. She spoke words of prayer but also words of incantation, the only part of her that moved were her lips and her hands. Her hands weaved through the air making gestures to go along with the almost musical soft sounds she uttered.

She looked fantastic, but also intimidating, and in a world of her own with her eyes closed as she faced him. He was about to speak but was cut short as her eyes opened sharply to stare directly into his. She untied the belt of her black robe and let it fall open; a flash of white flesh suddenly split open the black robe from ankle to chin.

She stepped forward but eased her shoulders back gently which allowed the satin like fabric to slip gently from her body and ripple to the ground as she took another step forward completely naked. Two more steps and she was at the side of the bath with Michael staring up at her his mouth agape as he beheld the beautiful sight before him.

Katarina did not speak one word to him; she looked at him and gave a brief smile before stepping into the bath. One foot either side of where he sat in awe, she looked down at him with an intense stare for what seemed like an eternity, as he immediately started to strain beneath the water line. She bent her knees and lowered herself down to him, her mouth immediately sought out his and their lips locked together as their flesh simultaneously collided in the water, above and below. Her tongue explored his mouth and he returned the action as the intensity built.

She could feel his cock straining against her skin and this only inflamed her more. His hands took hold of her arms on their way to her breasts where her nipples seemed to pulse such was how they ached. She wiggled her ass slightly and before Michael could do anything he was already sliding inside her, and inside as far as he could reach. The water had been hot but it couldn't have prepared him for the scalding heat now gripping his cock. She rode him expertly, he didn't think it would be long before it was all over, he didn't want it to end but that end seemed inevitable.

However, Katarina had other ideas, she stopped and quickly stood. Her standing in front of him with the reddened water flooding off her exquisite body, dripping from her breasts and nipples, was almost too much to take in itself. She watched him again with that lustful gaze before turning around in the bath. Her back now to him he almost drooled at the sight of her ass now above him. Water droplets running down her back to join those settled on her buttocks before collecting and streaming down her cheeks and thighs.

She bent her knees again and eased back into the water, this time his cock was perfectly positioned to slide straight back into her. They both shuddered as the mark was hit and she rose and fell, impaled upon him. Clearly, it couldn't last for too much longer now and she started to mutter something under her breath. Again it seemed to be some sort or prayer, incantation or poem. He couldn't be sure but it wasn't in English and didn't sound like Russian, not that he was really paying attention to that.

As his orgasm came upon him his head fell back against the bath top as before but his eyes were wide, wide open and he noticed for the first time that on the ceiling of the bathroom directly above the bath was a mural of sorts. No mural that he had ever seen, it looked vaguely like the dead thing he had seen on the doorstep of the house. But painted in red, it was basic and raw but quite intricate, runes and symbols were all around what looked to be an eight pointed star. It still looked wet but he assumed that that was due to the steam from the bath.

Michael's vision of the star/graffiti took just a couple of seconds because his focus was on his orgasm and when it came, it threatened to blow his head off. She gripped him inside her and squeezed as they both thrust together and that was it for him. He shook and trembled, his toes curled and his knuckles went white as he grabbed and gripped the side of the bath so tightly while he called out. Katarina likewise tensed and screamed out; the birds in the trees outside must've been startled because they could be heard fleeing from their perches as the animalistic calls from within the bathroom could be heard echoing through the glade.

He hadn't noticed just how much water had spilled out of the bath and onto the floor due to their writhing but his clothes at the side of the bath were soaked through. They both stayed in their positions, panting to get their breaths back. Katarina eased herself off him and turned to look at him. Her hair tossed across her face, sticking in parts to the perspiration and water that slicked her whole body.

She climbed out of the bath and left him there breathless. She went to a cupboard and took out two large bath towels, one she threw onto the floor nearby him the other she used to dry herself off. He watched her from the bath as she patted herself dry, her breasts moved gently as she swayed, her whole body was a symphony of sex and beauty and he could feel himself starting to rise again already.

"Come on" she said as she smiled at him and made her way to the bathroom door.

Michael couldn't get out of the bath quickly enough and grabbed the towel as he did, drying himself off as he followed her out of the room. She walked along the landing and to what Michael had already seen was the master bedroom. She looked over her shoulder at him fumbling to dry himself as he rushed, his rising cock bobbing about in front of him somewhat comically made her giggle playfully.

He arrived in the bedroom and she turned to face him. The candles were already lit and the room glowed as the sun had now almost set to give a softer edge to the atmosphere. She turned to face him as he looked up and immediately noticed another mural/painting on the ceiling above the bed. Again it was red and stood out against the pale walls and ceiling. It also glistened as if it was wet just like the one in the bathroom, yet this wasn't caused by the steam.

Michael was about to question her about it but when he glanced back to her she was already on all fours and crawling towards him, licking her lips and smiling lasciviously. Very quickly he forgot all about what was on the ceiling as she arrived in front of him and gripped his cock. He would forget all about asking questions for the rest of the night and probably for quite a while afterwards as well

Chapter 11

Michael very quickly fell under Katarina's spell, as any young man would, or indeed any heterosexual man at all, regardless of age. She had him exactly where she wanted him and he was powerless to resist or deny her. She, along with her father Drago, moulded him to their will. He was easy to manipulate, a young man enraptured by a beautiful woman, the mysteries of a new country and its people, the amazing sites and of course the freedom. The ultimate freedom that was awarded him, though he was reluctant and sheepish at first, he gradually learned that freedom also meant power.

To the people of Evagrad, quite naturally, the Englishman went through a number of different incarnations to many citizens at many different stages. He was initially seen as a novelty and a curiosity. People wanted to get to know him, the friendlier of folk of course, though others, the ones who held to the feeling of distrusting outsiders wanted little to do with him. Those people kept him at arms' length though still holding a quiet interest in what he was doing.

He was seen as a rare, very rare, tourist and as such not taken seriously when his lineage came to light fully. However, days turned to weeks and soon into months. Over those months it became quite clear that he wasn't going anywhere. He was definitely not a tourist and when word had spread that he wasn't just staying in his ancestors home, he was officially living there, there seemed genuine concern among a growing number of townsfolk. People didn't like change, especially coming from an outsider. Gradually, certain of the more self-aware citizens started to back Michael and his place in the town. Those citizens were becoming aware of their own place in society, albeit a small society. It was all they had and they had to make sure that they, and their families, were as better positioned as possible. No one knew exactly how things would develop and so they started to align with Michael.

Obviously, divides started to appear, but Drago Toshev had anticipated such times and had made provisions. Bribery and blackmail had a great effect in getting certain families and people onto Team Green. Where that had little effect, intimidation and violence never failed. In his endeavours he was aided by the roughest and largest men that he could find in the town. Word had it that he had gone to a not-so-nearby village and persuaded their most intimidating men to move to Evagrad, a small shack on the edge of town proved enough to get them to relocate and become his (or rather Michael's) personal bodyguards.

Michael, or was it Drago(?) introduced taxes on each household and on businesses too. Unless, of course, those businesses paid a kick back to the 'security' staff that collected the money/goods. As much as Evagrad was self-sufficient to all intents and purposes, money still had to be in circulation and on the convoy trips to get supplies and trade, money could be made.

Michael was quickly building his own little empire, it wasn't long since he had arrived and a few short months later he was on the way quite literally to being the Lord of the Manor! Drago and Katarina had pushed him and cajoled him to make decisions; he hadn't wanted to do some of the terrible things such as evicting an elderly couple from their home, forcing them to live with another family. That was in order so that one of Michael's new entourage could have his wife and children move to the town as well. Thus boosting his support through numbers, the old couple had been against Michael from the start so, fuck them. As well as strengthening the loyalty of the man in question who had his family with him.

The town was in thrall to Michael, but Michael was in thrall to Katarina, whatever she wanted, she got. She loved being treated like a Lady and revelled in it to the point that when she wasn't given special treatment or gifts, there would be hell to pay. Usually this would involve a member of 'security' staff paying people a visit. Some townsfolk had gone missing, more often than not they would return, or in some extreme cases they would be found in a field. Quite often they were at least cut and bruised, sometimes maimed for life, unable or unwilling to recollect what had happened to them out in the forest. Word quickly spread that they had been attacked by the beast from the mountains, the very one who Thomas had saved the men from all those years ago, the same beast or creature that had legendarily attacked the skiers camp at the Dyatlov Pass.

Strangely, despite the almost dictatorship style building in the town, Michael remained popular, at least with some. Those were the people that were making money from being with him and supporting him as well as those unfortunates who had nothing but their faith and belief in the old traditions. A rise in talk of the old beast returning, coupled with an heir of the Eva bloodline reclaiming what was rightfully his, seemed too much of a coincidence. Others saw through Drago and Michael and saw it simply as men getting rich and powerful off the backs of the weak. Those people would huddle in secret meetings and try to make plots to bring the tyrant down, for that was how they saw him and the way the situation was going, the rising of a tyrant.

Michael, the small town boy from England thrived and became drunk with power very easily and very quickly. So much so that he perpetuated all the myths and legends and encouraged all his men to do the same. Spreading rumours about sightings of the beast made people very scared, even the ones who didn't believe in such things were cautious about getting on the wrong side of him and his cohorts for fear of being banished to the mountains and forests. That became a punishment that Michael had drafted into the towns charter for 'treason' against him and his new family.

Katarina was delighted; she played that part of the Lady of Evagrad perfectly, as if she were born to it. Her beliefs and traditions were a part of her whole life and had been since she was a little girl, passed onto her by her late mother. When the myths and legends of the beast were gaining hold she was thrilled that the old ways were making their presence felt and not being lost and washed away with the years. In herself, deep down she felt like a medieval Princess with a town full of people who loved her and her new Prince. In reality she became spiteful and looked down on everyone around her, she had a plan and it was purely about Katarina, she became more like a wicked Queen from the fairy tales rather than the sweet Princess.

Drago was the power behind the throne. He was the one who had brought in the men of the town to be the forced labour to rebuild, fix and improve Michael's home which soon became Katarina's too. Not long after it was suggested, by Drago, that he should also live there, in a separate wing of course, to watch over the new couple and be there for advice. Obviously, that would include building a new wing for him, more forced labour was needed. The building materials were paid for by taxes. Drago therefore, being able to rent his house to someone else, which meant that he still owned the place and lived rent free in Michael's. Once the building work was done the rent went straight into his pocket.

Amongst the gossips, questions were raised about just who was in control of the town. Michael was the rightful heir, yet, he was clearly led by his cock and therefore Katarina was in control. More and more was made of her spiritual and darker side, more was made of claims that she was a witch and she had beguiled him, claims that she never actually denied either. Drago however was always by Michael's side, whispering in his ear, approving or disapproving of every choice and decision made. Plus he was Katarina's father, she may have melted his heart when she was young and no doubt could still do so but he was the head of the household, wasn't he? Debates raged and were argued over, Michael was becoming more like a puppet but who pulled his strings?

Inevitably, Katarina became pregnant, she was deliriously happy and so was her father. Michael was also pleased but a small part of him, getting smaller every day, thought about his old life back in England and how becoming a dad at his age would have scared the shit out of him. As time passed though, he warmed to the idea. People were kind, for the most part, because Katarina was happy and therefore kinder to everyone. The townsfolk's pleasure was short lived however once taxes had increased to pay for things for the upcoming arrival.

An unusual turn of events came when Katarina no longer wanted to have sex with Michael. He had heard that sometimes this can happen but it happened to them almost immediately after confirmation of the pregnancy. Michael was perplexed, they had spent almost every day seducing or fucking each other in one way or another. They hadn't been able to get enough of each other and that was perfectly fine with him and her as well, or so he thought. Katarina told him that she wanted to protect the baby and no matter how many times he told her that the baby would be perfectly alright she refused to listen.

Instead, Katarina arranged for a string of local girls to service Michael instead. At first he couldn't do anything with any of them as he felt wrong and guilty, when it became clear that he would not be sleeping with Katarina until after the birth he reluctantly gave in to her plan. Of course once he started to sleep with the locals he started to enjoy it, he never lost sight of his love for Katarina but it had been her idea so he just thought "Why the hell not?"

Eventually the day of joy arrived and Katarina gave birth to a beautiful, bouncing, baby boy. She wept with joy as she looked at the son she had longed for as did Drago, finally a grandchild, he whispered in Russian as he held him up to the sky for his late wife to look down upon and kiss. Michael had been barred from the house the previous night as Katarina was in labour, he had been told it was bad luck and customary for him to be elsewhere.

He paid a visit to one of the local girls; they got drunk together, fucked and passed out together. He had been drinking a lot more over the recent months, the alcohol making his moods turn nasty, occasionally he would complain to a local in a tavern about the life he left behind. It would turn violent but of course he could not be charged with anything and so would test more and more men when drunk, watching them back down because of who he was.

He was awoken at the girl's house and told he had to go home to see his son; that was how he was told, by a messenger when he was drunk and in a stranger's bed. He rushed back to his home to see his son and for a while the three of them; father, mother and son were the perfect family, with Drago watching from the sides of course. They all seemed so happy and Drago decided that they should have a celebration the following day once Katarina was feeling more like herself after she had rested and slept properly.

The following evening a special family celebration was arranged. All the best food and drink had been prepared, no expense (or other people's money) had been spared. Michael sat at the head of the table, as the Lord of Evagrad, by his side sat his Lady and next to her slept their baby, the new heir who they had decided to call Thomas after the man who had made it all possible. They laughed and toasted the baby and the future. Drago, sat at the opposite end of the table, had told them that the people were putting on a huge celebration in honour of the announcement and Michael seemed thrilled and happy. Katarina seemed underwhelmed but later she informed Michael that she had already known about it but was happy.

Michael ate and drank, the food was delicious, the ale, the wine and the spirits fantastic and he tried them all. Katarina excused herself as she was tired but excited about the next day and so went to bed. Michael was allowed back into the marital bed but apologised as he doubted he would make it up the stairs. Instead he sat with Drago and they drank into the small hours, making plans and devising strategies for business, all drunken and ridiculous but it would be the last enjoyable night Michael would have.

Chapter 12

Michael woke up with an extremely sore head, not first the first time recently. However, this was different to his usual hangover. It was more like something that he hadn't experienced for about a year, just after he had arrived in Evagrad.

His head wasn't the only thing that hurt either. His wrists and ankles had been tied and the thin ropes used to bind them were digging into his flesh. Cutting off the blood supply to his hands and feet, the numbness was starting to set in. He struggled considerably once he realised what had happened but that just tightened his restraints. He had to control his emotions and not panic, easier said than done in that situation but he slowly mastered his rapidly growing fears.

Michael had been laid on his side in a room that he didn't recognise. Dust and dirt was all over the floor on which he lay, making his eyes and nose itch. He tried to look around but the room was dim and dark. Chinks of light appeared here and there so at least he knew he wasn't in an internal room. He rolled onto his back to look up and get a different view but still nothing came to him of recognition. He rolled again onto his other side and this time he saw a door, a slit of light, daylight flooded under the door and thinner shafts penetrated the door itself. It was obviously some kind of rough outbuilding, maybe a shed or garage or something similar with a rough door.

Michael heard noises and listened hard, slowing his breath from the panicking gasps of earlier, to hear more clearly. He could hear voices. Men's voices and they were stood outside the building. Michael wasn't stupid, he had been bound like a prisoner and he clearly had guards outside. He resisted his initial thought of calling for help, instead he tried to focus on what they were saying but seemingly they had resorted to speaking in

Russian. He knew things were bad, very bad, he was the Lord of Evagrad and yet he had woken up in a filthy shack of some description, trussed up like a chicken and with guards posted outside.

Drago had admitted that his daughter had drugged his food and drink when he had first arrived in Evagrad, with her potions from the hills, mountains and valleys. But that was supposedly to look after his wellbeing and keep him safe (as well as allow him to slaughter people to prove his lineage). Now he had clearly been drugged for another purpose by his 'loving' girlfriend. But, for what, he had no idea. He tried to work out the events of the previous evening that had led him to this situation but the heavy drinking (and no doubt a potion or two) had left his mind foggy and him unable to focus. Another noise suddenly brought him back to the here and now, the sounds of laughter and the jangle of keys in a padlock on the door.

The padlock was unlocked and a heavy chain was drawn out of the door which then opened and the morning light flooded in to momentarily blind Michael. He squinted and blinked to reclaim his sight. A large silhouette stood in the glare, partially blocking it out but not making it any easier for him to see. His sight was unnecessary however as the unmistakable sound of Drago laughing to himself echoed through the small space.

"Good morning Michael," he bellowed.

Michael sighed and scowled at Drago as the Russian approached and then stood over him, looking down at the prone young Englishman both literally and figuratively. Michael's fury was building up within him but he was in no position to do anything about his situation. However, he had to know what was going on, he had to know his situation better, or, more to the point just how bad his situation was. He remained calm, controlled and patient, he had to. He swallowed hard and answered his captor......... as best he could.

"What the fuck Drago? Am I your prisoner? I thought I was your master?"

"Master? Hahahaha," Drago couldn't contain the hilarious thought that he would be supplicant to Michael. "Are you serious or just that naive Michael?"

That hurt. As much as he had grown up over his time in Evagrad, rising to Lord of the province, he had come to think of Drago as his friend.

At first of course there was confusion, doubt and scepticism but gradually Drago had been as good as his word in helping Michael to rise and claim his birthright. Initially, or, in the early days of his ascension, if things had not worked out in his favour Michael would have understood. But having built his life in Evagrad and been seduced by his new life and his subjects, it was a bitter pill to swallow to find out that his new life was a fraud.

"So, all of your words of help and encouragement to lift me up, were really just ways to get you to the top?" he said through gritted teeth, unable to conceal his hurt, disappointment and anger.

"Not so naive after all then," Drago chuckled to himself in response.

"So, what happens next? Are you going to go down the Thomas Eva route and banish me too?" Michael spat.

"Not quite,"

"You can't take over anyway Drago, you aren't the heir to Thomas, I am," Michael started to rage at the supposed injustice of being usurped.

"No, Michael, that's right I'm not," Drago smiled "But I have something better than that."

"Such as? I am the rightful heir. It's my birthright as you strongly fought for."

"It *was* your birthright, Michael, that's right. But now it is the birthright of your son...............my grandson!"

Michael gasped. Replaced by his own flesh and blood, yet the baby was innocent of everything but being born. Yet the child was born, and, in turn, became his natural successor, the cruelty of ancient lineage for all to see. Michael immediately realised that now he was completely expendable.

"The mayor has just brought me the paperwork and made the whole thing official," grinned Drago, holding out a fistful of documents. "The heir to Evagrad is your son; I am his grandfather and will now act as his protector until he is of age. *You* are nothing Michael."

Before Michael could respond further another silhouette appeared from behind Drago. Katarina stepped forward and smiled down at him. She bore a slight look of pity, but still carried a smile on her face at the events that had unfolded. A new mother and effectively the mother of the new Lord of Evagrad, she clearly had what she wanted, finally.

"So, I was just a means to an end?" Michael spat bitterly at them both.

"I'm sorry, Michael, but this is the way of things," she said with an almost casual air in her voice.

"So what now?"

"There will be a special ceremony, very special, and you will be a part of it of course. The passing of one leader to the next. It will be wonderful and the whole town will be there to witness it and also to pay homage to their new Lord." She said, smiling with pride. "It will be a day of great joy for all."

"Except me?" he winced.

Neither replied, they simply turned away as two guards came from behind them and picked Michael up roughly and bundled him out of the shack. They dragged him to a waiting cart which was attached to two horses. A frame had been constructed on the cart so he could be stood and tied to it. His hands were untied from behind his back and then re-tied in front of him and attached to the wooden frame.

Before he could ask any questions, the cart was led away and off down a dirt track towards the town. Michael looked behind him to see Drago and Katarina in a more ornate open carriage, her baby, his baby, had been handed to her from a waiting maid and was now resting cradled in her lap as she looked on with a motherly grace. Guards walked along the side of the small procession. Two on either side of his cart and two either side of their carriage, a handful of others walked behind the carriage as they proceeded on their journey.

The procession went through the centre of town. The residents that were in the streets booed and jeered him as he passed, throwing rotten fruit and vegetables at him and some stones before quickly turning to cheer the new baby and his mother and grandfather.

Chapter 13

The procession continued to its destination until a call came from Drago's carriage and the cavalcade duly halted. One of the guards that had been escorting Michael went over to Katarina who handed him something, as well as some instructions. The other three men climbed into the back of Michael's cart. The first man returned and joined his comrades. The men spoke to each other before cutting Michael down and forcing him to his knees. The first guard then produced a jar, obviously what had been given to him by Katarina. It was clear and contained some sort of milky green substance.

Two of the guards held Michael tightly while the final one grabbed his head and tilted it backwards while also holding his lower jaw open. Michael struggled and fought as best as he could but he was no match for any of the men on their own, let alone all at once. The first guard then opened the jar, the stink of which made all those present in the cart screw their faces up in disgust at the stench. He then poured it into Michael's mouth, massaging his throat to make him swallow. The contents were vile and lumpy, more slime than liquid. He choked on the lumps and coughed and spluttered while still trying vainly to struggle himself free. Mucus and tears flowed from him at his exertions and seemingly Katarina took some pity as she handed the baby to her father and jumped down from her carriage and ran over to Michael.

"Michael, please just drink it. It will make things so much easier for you; please, Michael, for your own sake." She begged him and yet again those eyes seduced him into doing whatever she asked.

He allowed the men to feed him the pungent slime as if it were his last meal and he wept as he did so. He wept for his lost life and for his Gramps and his parents. He wept because he knew deep down that this indeed was his last meal, the last meal of a condemned man. He was laid flat out in the back of the cart and the edges of his vision started to blur. He saw Katarina looking over the side of the cart at him. He liked to think that she looked at him lovingly but it was probably his imagination as she started to become hazy to him. He closed his eyes as they began to get heavier and heavier. With each blink it seemed more of an effort to open them again until he stopped trying. His jaw became slack and the men rolled him onto his side at Katarina's insistence so he didn't choke should the vile liquid make its way back up his throat, causing him to vomit. He became pale and his skin took on a waxy and clammy look. Michael became unconscious. Drago had been standing on his carriage watching events, happy that everything was in order, he bellowed the caravan onwards to its' final destination.

The procession arrived at the hillside, the same hillside from which Thomas Eva had returned and been proclaimed as a hero. Torches flamed and smoke drifted off and up into the sky. A large crowd gathered, most of whom were wearing their best clothes. Children and women had ribbons in their hair and the whole place had a carnival atmosphere about it. There were even tents with games for the kids and stalls selling candied foods and other treats.

Off to one side and surrounded by guards, was where Michael lay. He had been taken down from the cart, still unconscious and carried over to a place hidden from the rest of the townsfolk for his preparations. Once Katarina and her father were satisfied that he was indeed ready, she stepped forward and produced a bottle. It contained another liquid, one that would bring him out of his unconscious state, a reversal of the drug she had given him earlier. The first had the effect of a sedative, a very strong sedative as well as a powerful painkiller. All made by her own fair hands, and foraged from the ground and hills they now walked upon. In the western world the concoctions would be banned (or taken on, controlled and legalised for profit). However, out there in the wilds around Evagrad, Katarina was all powerful now; she knew what she was doing and who would argue with her?

She stooped over him and gently lifted his seemingly lifeless head. She opened the bottle and gently poured the liquid into his loosely open mouth. Katarina herself administered the medication and massaged his throat to get the liquid down his gullet. Slowly, it started to go down, bit by bit, and gradually he started to awaken. She poured more into his mouth satisfied that he would swallow of his own freewill, which he did, and so, she lay his head back down and stepped back.

Michael opened his eyes to realise quickly that he was bound still but this time his arms and legs were outstretched and tied down. He was tied to something wooden and very rough, that however was the best of it for Michael Green. A cold breeze was drifting across the hillside on that summer's day and the breeze was his first indicator of agony as he came to his senses. It was in fact his senses that raged and screamed with all their might as the breeze drifted across and seemingly set them all alight.

Pain like nothing he had ever felt before in his life covered his body, his whole body. It tingled in as much as fire would tingle on a hand should it be placed in a furnace. That was the level of agony that he was in. As if he were burning from the inside out and back again. He tilted his head forward, which just unleashed more agonies but what he saw would have killed most men through fright. His whole body had been skinned. He was raw in every possible sense of the word; his bloodied limbs raged and howled their own horrors of woe. His torso screamed in his head for help and he could see his heart quite literally pounding through his chest, pounding through his rib cage! Blood was dripping from him in places, congealing in others. His face, his head and his entire body was a mess of veins and pulsing arteries.

His internal organs stayed in place due to his stillness at being tied down but things, if possible, were about to get worse. The guards that he had once employed now surrounded him. They all bent on command and picked up the structure on which he was strapped. They carried him then down towards the community that were all gathered and having fun. Each footstep towards the masses caused pain as he was jolted and shaken. As they made their way through the crowds, children started to run up to them. Far from being shocked, scared or traumatised, they started to through flowers to him. The flowers landed on him as some kind of tribute but even the most delicate of blooms that landed upon him caused more and more agony in his state of utterly skinned rawness.

Finally they arrived at their destination on the hill. A frame had already been erected in preparation and Michael, strapped to his structure, was hauled into place by ropes and man power. It was a sight to behold as he was winched up to his zenith. He was strapped to a large circle of branches and twigs, formed and bent, twisted and broken into shape. At his back was a star spanning the circle, eight pointed and with berries and vines decorating the piece ornately. It was a giant replica of the thing he had found on his doorstep at Thomas Eva's house. However, now Michael himself was effectively the dead or dying thing strapped upon it.

Once he had reached his highest point, it was at that time that his bowels and internal organs could no longer hold their position without their flesh covering. They slid, shifted and slithered and then they dropped. They dropped like offal from a butcher's bucket, and they hung down from him. A new wave of pain and shock hit him like a hammer between the eyes. The only surprise was that he didn't pass out from the agonies inflicted upon him.

He had been greeted by chants from the assembled throng upon on his ascent to his inevitable demise. Prayers of some kind or other, howls of derision, jeers and laughter echoed along the hillside. His tears and disbelief filled Michael; his body was in parts either numb or screaming with tortured pain beyond comprehension. He started to shiver as his body was in shock, his teeth chattered and through half shuttered eyes he saw Katarina on a small podium-like structure. She was mouthing words that he couldn't hear but the mass of townsfolk were following along. She was actually orchestrating their worship and his sacrifice, for that is exactly what it was.

The sound levels rose to a din, they seemed to be directing their chants as calls to someone or something. Some people became hysterical with their religious fervour; arms flailed in the air, fingers were pointed, hate and bile filled words aimed at him and all at the behest of Katarina. Drago scanned the area and smiled with glee at the intensity and no doubt Michael's desolation and demise.

Katarina's potions were being handed out to various people and clearly they had very strong aphrodisiacs contained within because some openly started to rip at their own as well as others clothes in a state of sexual frenzy. The whole hillside quickly became a scene of horror and degradation; men were fighting over women and vice versa. Bonfires had already been lit and their smoke rose from them around the site, drifting off towards the forest beyond. Music was being played and the sounds from bands of musicians were also starting to fill the air along with the smoke to add to the surreal and sickening carnival feel of the twisted sacrifice.

Michael couldn't hold out much longer and he wished that the fires would make their way over to him to end his suffering. The sounds were continuing to build like those of a religious or political rally. Katarina was at the centre of it all, goading the crowd on to ever greater heights of violence and debauchery. Michael hung like a bloodied and tattered rag doll with all the gory stuffing hanging out of his body.

Eventually there was another noise, a very loud noise in the forest. The townsfolk not affected by Katarina's drugs were suddenly shocked into a hush. The music, in part at least, started to die away and most eyes and heads turned to look into the woods. Katrina shouted something in another tongue, and everyone now stopped what or who they were doing and stood staring into the forest. All became silent with anticipation before another sound, one of crunching and crashing echoing down to the people. Michael managed to turn his head to his left gingerly and partially he opened his stinging bleeding eyes.

A shape emerged from the forest; it was huge and lumbering, lumbering towards the mass. Michael tried as best as he could to keep his eyes open and to try to focus on whatever the hell it was in the distance, though that distance was closing greatly. The crowd closest to the black shape started to move back, quicker and quicker they moved as it neared its target.

Katarina shouted something again to the crowd and a great cheer came back in response. However, the biggest response to her words was seemingly from the shape itself which lifted its head and bellowed out something akin to a cross between a scream and a roar. Katarina smiled with pride, she looked straight at the thing and shouted once more as she pointed to the helpless and dying Michael strapped to his twisted circular throne. Like an attack dog under command, the thing, the beast, the creature lurched forward towards him. Michael opened his eyes briefly; he saw it bearing down upon him. He could smell its rotten breath from yards away. He could see its red eyes boring into him, its opening jaws and rows of sharpened yellowing teeth. It was a silhouette of hate and anger; it was a monster from nightmare and fear. It was a creature of myth and it was the beast from the legend of the Dyatlov Pass.

Mercifully, Michael was seconds from his heart giving out, but, sadly, not before he let out one final blood curdling scream.

HEAVEN OR HELL OR......

Chapter 1

The mouldy wallpaper was peeling from the walls and hanging in darkened strips in the corner of the room. The carpet was stained and filthy, balding patches behind the door and at the side of the bed told a story of the amount of wear and tear in those areas of the endless footfall. The smell of damp permeated the whole room, partly from the mould and partly from the sweat that had been exuded in that room. The sheets on the bed were thinning from literally years and years of use (and abuse). They also stank and were covered in stains of various bodily fluids, sweat, sex, blood and sadly, tears, were all present on those Rorschach inspired sheets.

A small bathroom with a leaking shower cubicle, washbasin and toilet lay behind a door with no lock. The ventilation was also broken which didn't help the mould in the adjacent room, the damp and moisture rarely getting a chance to escape as most patrons were only in the room for an hour or two and were highly unlikely to bother about opening a window to allow fresh air into the place. The owner of the building was equally disinterested, as long as the customers kept paying by the hour, why would he be? This was number 22, just one of 37 rooms for rent in the hotel, all much the same; all that was required was a double bed, a shower and (occasionally) changed, if not fresh, sheets. Privacy was easy to keep because people were barely there long enough to be noticed, as long as they paid in cash and didn't break anything (there was very little to break in any case), there would be no problems.

Inside number 22 there were customers; there was a complete apathy between the two of them regarding the room itself. The only thing either was interested in was business; for one it was financial, the other gratification and release.

They had been fucking for nearly two hours, fucking very hard for all that time. Many positions, occasional breathers to recuperate, but the majority of that time was spent with him deep inside her one way or another. She was April, a slender, almost athletically built 23 year old hooker. She had short blonde hair, peroxide blonde with bright purple highlights, all of which she'd done herself. She had piercings in her nose, tongue and lip as well as her nipples and clitoris. She was exhausted and dripped sweat onto the collection of stains on the sheets from her position now on all fours, while her client pounded away at her from behind.

Her client was a mystery. He had become somewhat of a regular of April's, but she still knew little about him, other than she liked him a lot and she definitely liked being fucked by him, at least a lot more than the usual pond life that she had to deal with to make a living. Though she tried to make good decisions, there was always a piece of shit out there who felt he could do what he wanted to her; she had a number of bruises, expertly hidden by make-up, to prove it. Anyone wanting a more thorough explanation would easily be persuaded by her x-rays of past broken bones - a shame for anyone, let alone a girl of her age. This client was easily one she enjoyed being with. She could be herself and not worry about potential trips to the emergency room.

He was tall and muscular. He carried an air of threat and danger, yet she knew she was safe, almost protected with him, even if it was just for a few hours at a time. He was clean shaven, had thick black shoulder length hair; he had an accent which she couldn't place, yet his voice soothed her. The one strange thing she noticed when once he slept after one of their sessions was that his body was completely hairless. Not shaved or waxed, just completely hairless, as if he was never meant to have a single hair on his body from the neck down and April had checked him in intimate detail.

She knew nothing else about him. Not his name, age, origins or anything. Of course that was nothing new in her line of work, but when she had regular clients, more often than not they would open up at least a little, maybe give her their real name or talk about how their wife didn't understand them, or how depressing life was, or something that they could talk about before or maybe after their transaction. With him, she knew nothing; he didn't use a name at all. She couldn't even recall their first meeting. He seemed to have been there for as long as she could remember, just every now and again he would appear. They would spend a few intimate hours of guilt-free intensity and once he had made sure she was alright, he would be gone. She would feel sad, but knew instinctively that he would return one day. Secretly, she hoped he would return and take her away, but she knew not to where. Outwardly she would never express any of that for fear of spooking him, but a girl could hope.

He continued to power into her and she could feel he was ready to explode. Contraception was an unusual situation with him; she obviously protected herself from pregnancy and condoms were something she carried in bulk, the wearing of which was mandatory for all her clients, but with him it was different. Their first encounter was condom free; she had gotten caught up in the sensation of what he did to her and how he made her feel. She had never done that with any other client before or since, apart from him. After that first session she cursed herself and him for being so stupid and naive, but he simply looked at her, and whispered that she was safe, she could catch nothing from him as it was impossible for him to transmit a 'human' disease and even more impossible for her to conceive from him. She perhaps surprisingly didn't even question that statement, she instinctively knew he was telling her the truth and so it continued their intermittent affair of the flesh, unrestrained and intense until this day.

He came inside her. He held her hips as he thrust and lifted her off her knees as he fired deep into her. She felt the almost sting like quality of his ejaculation, again, unlike anything she had felt with any other man. His sting was amazingly pleasurable; her head span as usual with him at this point and in his recovery he gently laid her down onto the bed. Her heart felt as though it was about to pound out of her chest, but as she lay now in the afterglow, her breathing began to settle and the cold lifted goose bumps on her naked sweaty flesh. He grabbed the sheet and pulled it over her. There was something of the gentleman about him in this action, covering her modesty. He had always done this too.

After a minute or two of lying side by side, he stood and dressed. He said nothing as she watched him, but once he was done, he gently trailed his fingertips along her calf as her leg stuck out from beneath the soiled sheet. She smiled at the act of simple intimacy, almost like two actual lovers, before he picked up his long black coat and whirled it dramatically onto him. Finally, he put on his boots and laced them up. Then the saddest part for her, which brought her back to reality, he took out a wad of bills and as subtly as he could he tucked them under the base of the bedside lamp. It seemed he almost felt an embarrassment at the act, but she soothed him

"It's ok," she smiled "Another time?"

"Another time," he mumbled in his deep voice.

He left, and she watched him go; she propped herself on her elbow as he made his exit. She looked at the cash as the door closed behind him. He always paid her at least double the normal rate; this time it looked as though he'd been even more generous. April rolled back and stared at the ceiling: the cracks, the stains; police cars wailed outside in the afternoon sunshine. Kids shouted, mothers called for or screamed at their offspring. She heard people in the corridor outside. She could faintly hear the sounds of what was more than likely another girl making her living in the room next door. Then she heard what were clearly and unmistakably gun shots out in the street and her reality crashed in on her. A tear slipped down her young pale cheek.

Her 'lover' walked briskly and purposefully. He had a meeting of sorts and he did not want to be late. He moved quickly down the stairs of the hotel and past the hotel's owner at the desk who smiled lecherously at him, knowing full well what he had been there for, just like all his patrons. The stranger simply looked at him; he sneered and glared as he moved past. The owner was a low life, making money off unfortunates.

"Cum again soon," he laughed as he emphasised it just so.

The stranger had passed the desk and was half way out of the door when the owner spoke. He stopped dead in his tracks and only half turned his head back. This act in itself was enough for the weasel at reception to become flustered and reach for a baseball bat under his desk. Luckily for him, the man simply turned back to the street and walked outside. Despite the warm and bright afternoon sun, he still pulled up his collar to partially cover his face and took his shades from his inside coat pocket, his long coat seemingly more suited to winter weather. Still he marched at pace to his destination. He did, however, hear the pathetic shouts from the hotel owner.

"Yeah, you better run, mother fucker. I'll fuck you up good next time."

The stranger made a mental note to deal with him properly the next time he visited sweet April; for now, he had a more pressing engagement.

Chapter 2

Across the city, in a particularly seedy and crime-ridden district, an extremely intense poker game was coming to a climax. An old warehouse was the setting; the table set in the middle of the large room currently had three players though six had started proceedings. The other three had lost large sums of money, one of which didn't have the required funds to repay his backers who staked him. He had wept openly to much mirth from his rivals, before being taken away to find any money he may have had - whether that be savings, his home, car, wife or anything else that could be of value to others. Pay he must, or else.

The other two losers licked their wounds and recovered from their financial losses with differing emotions. One, a banker, simply stormed off in fury, getting his chauffeur to get the car immediately as he pondered the downside of playing with his customers' money. Another simply laughed it off, a genuine high-stakes poker player, who knew the pitfalls, but also had the confidence in himself and his ability to win back his losses and more in another game in another town. He stayed to watch the finale as the game reached its inevitable conclusion.

So, three remained: two crooks and a strange and mysterious young woman. The two crooks, Jed Pearson and Tommy Munro, had been rivals for many years, enduring turf wars, disputed earnings and other dick swinging macho shows of bravado. They both had their grubby hands in money laundering, prostitution, protection, illegal gambling and drugs. They had once before joined together when an Eastern European gang had tried to muscle in on their territories; strength in numbers was called for and unity in those combined forces prevailed as they drove out their opposition in a highly bloody battle for their streets. After that, normal local hostilities and war resumed between the two families. Once a year, however, they put all that aside for one big poker game, this big game.

Pearson would have had the upper hand in this game as Munro was bleeding chips badly, but those chips weren't going to Pearson, they were going to this woman. She looked stunning with her long black hair, very untamed; partly her hair was dreaded and plaited, shaved just above her ear on the left displaying a serpent like tattoo. She wore black leather pants, studded all the way down the outer seam, army surplus boots, low cut black tank top showing the very pale skin of her arms, neck and upper chest. She had small pert breasts and a narrow waist giving her an almost teenage girl appearance. She wore dark purple lipstick on her narrow lipped mouth and very little other make-up. This just highlighted that from the cheek bones to her brow, there seemed some kind of scarring around the eyes, almost like healed burn tissue. Her eyes themselves couldn't be made out as they were hidden behind matt black wrap around shades, she didn't take them off. Her competitors had no idea that no living person had seen her without them.

They had both questioned how she had gotten herself into the game in the first place, but a briefcase full of cash will open many doors. They'd asked her name, but she'd ignored the question and simply sat down at the table, her name was actually Mia. The problem for the rest of them was that she was close to leaving with her cash as well as all theirs too - well, unless they could stop her, one way or another.

After many swings of the pendulum of fortune and skilful play, the chips moved around the table between the three of them. Much cursing and many insults were hurled around as frustration grew with any loss of a big pot, but the vocals came from Munro and Pearson. The woman remained, as she had for most of the day, virtually silent. Simply turning over her cards when required and raking in another pot, in defeat, she said nothing or grunted under her breath in anger at herself.

Eventually, however, the inevitable came to pass when Pearson forced Munro to go all in with his remaining chips. Pearson expected the woman to fold, but far from it as she had continued to raise the stakes further, forcing an irritated and angry Pearson to match her with his remaining funds. This was it, the big showdown. The professional poker player, who had stayed, edged closer in to watch, as did Pearson and Munro's single henchmen who had been allowed to stay.

Munro confidently turned over his ace high flush, to a derisive snort from Pearson, which did nothing to alleviate Munro's anger and this was reflected in his man's immediate tensing as he knew things could turn violent very soon.

"Good, but not good enough Tommy." A grin spread across Pearson's face as he turned over his own cards.

"Full house, Jacks full of Queens" he grinned as he spoke and rather prematurely reached towards the huge pot in the centre of the table.

A clearing of the throat to his left halted Pearson in his tracks. Mia barely moved a muscle, just moving her head slightly towards him. She still wore the matt black wrap around shades she'd arrived in, not taking them off for even a second in the dingy light of the warehouse in which they'd played. She'd been impossible to read throughout as she gave not a single facial expression away, the perfect poker face.

She slowly turned over her cards: two queens giving her four in all and clearly to all in attendance, the winning hand.

"Fuck me!" gasped the pro player watching on; this caused her to sharply turn her head towards him and though her lips didn't move, he clearly heard a woman's voice in his head say with icy clarity, "You should leave........Now!"

A shiver ran through his whole body and he duly picked up his jacket and made for the exit as fast as his legs could carry him, calling over his shoulder

"It's been fun boys, good fuckin' luck."

Munro couldn't help himself but give a very small smile; though he had lost all his money, at least it wasn't going to Pearson.

"You cheating fuckin' bitch!" Was Pearson's predictable response as he snarled at her with the realisation of his huge defeat, his bodyguard making a step forward as did Munro's in response. This would not end well.

She didn't react other than to mentally steel herself, though she had been on 'alert' throughout the game. The two henchmen almost simultaneously went to their jacket pockets to retrieve weapons, they were quick and as far as they were concerned she would not be leaving with her winnings, yes they were quick but not nearly quick enough.

Mia had lent back in her chair, looking relaxed and calm, but this also gave her more space and leverage as she, in a split second, lent further back and gave an almighty kick to the underside of the poker table with a massive force. The table went up in the air, causing the cards and chips to fly everywhere. Munro toppled back in his seat and Pearson dived to the ground in confusion and disbelief.

While the table was still on it's upwards trajectory, she was already out of her seat and over to the first thug, Munro's, to punch him viciously straight between the eyes, breaking his nose and disorientating him massively as he fell to the ground. Before he had even hit the concrete, she had already moved off to Pearson's man. En-route, she reached down and retrieved a blade from her boot. Just as she arrived at the enforcer, he had un-holstered his gun and was bringing it to aim at her but again, he was not quick enough.

She thrust her razor-edge blade deep into the man's gut on his left side and spun around behind him. Still with a tight grip on the blade, she dragged it across his stomach all the way to his right hip before withdrawing. She stood up to her full height as he looked around in a daze as to where she'd gone. She put her hand around his shoulder and grasped his chin, fear and sweat spreading across his face. She leaned forward and kissed his cheek before pulling his head back forcefully, causing him to arch his back and the huge smile across his stomach to open wide. His guts and bowel then evacuated the yawning cavity and spilled out all over the floor. She let go of his chin and let him fall to the ground into his own gore.

She had no time to rest and continued on to Munro as he lay there after falling from his chair and was struggling to get back up. Her blade made short work of him as she ran to and past him, almost in a blur, as her arm almost nonchalantly flicked out and sliced straight across his throat, cutting his windpipe and carotid artery in one swift action. He hadn't even realised he'd been cut until his blood was spilling down all over himself and the floor on which he lay.

Pearson had started to recover, but the table had now landed and splintered. She picked up a broken leg from it and moved at great speed to ram it through his chest. Still he tried and failed to stand, he fell back and stared at her, his final thought being something along the lines of "Who or what are you?" She would have watched the bastard die in pain, but a shot rang out and she felt a bullet whistle past her head.

Mia cursed her sloppiness, but turned to Munro's man lying dizzy on the ground. He was trying to recover from her strike and his broken nose, which explains why he missed her, but that was the only chance he would get. She jumped over the broken table and landed astride the man, shocking him further. She grabbed his head between her hands and she squeezed. She squeezed hard and aggressively. He stared at her through his still tearing eyes as the force she used became unbearable and his cheek bones cracked audibly and caved in; his eyes bulged and soon after, his jaw bone cracked too. Amazingly, he still managed to survive to that point despite the massive agonies he endured; that was until her final push which broke his skull and eye sockets, causing the rest of his face to collapse in on itself. Her hands practically came together in a mangle of blood, meat and bone as he eventually expired. She let go of the sodden mess and stood up to survey the scene of death and destruction.

She had barely broken sweat and didn't even breathe heavily; she picked up Munro's jacket from the back of his fallen chair and wiped the gore and mess from her hands. She looked around and remembered where the money had been placed and retrieved it. There were six bags and cases, each with differing, but still huge amounts of cash depending on the individuals' stake in the game. She opened them all and emptied the vast majority into one briefcase and one gym bag for easy removal. What she couldn't carry, she tipped onto the floor with the cards and chips.

What none of them had known was that she had checked out this warehouse the day before and secreted a few cans of lighter fuel in an old packing case. This she now retrieved and liberally sprayed it all over the corpses and table and the whole area received a good dousing before she picked up Munro's discarded lighter. She first grabbed her ragged denim jacket that had been resting on the back of her chair, naturally the only one still standing, and then she ignited the whole scene before her. She watched it all blaze before casually exiting the building, there would be no finger prints to find, simply because she had no finger prints. She just wanted it to look like another violent mob execution; a few less scum in the world wouldn't be such a bad thing.

Chapter 3

Mia walked to her next destination with a spring in her step, a wry smile playing across her lips. She carried the gym bag over shoulder, the briefcase in her hand. It was a beautiful late summer afternoon now and she needed a beer. Thankfully, it wouldn't be long now until she could get one. She walked into the heart of the city and to the bar for her appointment. As she arrived, a voice called out to her.

"About time - you're late."

"Kristoff" She replied, nodding in recognition to him.

Her smile returned and a light laugh as she sat down at a table outside the pub that they'd been to many times over the years. The tables were at the front of the bar, on the wide pavement. Pedestrians milled past with their shopping in the Saturday afternoon sun and she took a seat opposite her old friend. Almost immediately, a waiter came out with two cold beers as if on command; her friend drained the bottle that he had in front of him and passed it to the waiter. Once he'd left, as quickly as he'd arrived, they toasted each other without words. Just a nod was all that was required.

A minute or two passed as they drank. She collected herself and savoured the beer while he watched her; he glanced at the two bags that she had put under the glass table and then looked at her finger nails and the dried blood and stains.

"Been playing games?" Kristoff smiled.

She noticed the blood on her hands and sighed. She put a little beer on them and washed the remainder off before licking them clean and dry. As she did this, he smiled to himself and gestured through the window with two fingers to the bar tender, who promptly sent their waiter out with two more fresh beers for them. Once he'd delivered and left, she laughed lightly again and replied, "Yeah, poker."

"I take it you won......again?" he said, tapping the bags with the toe of his boot.

"Of course; don't I always?"

She leaned over the table towards him and sniffed before leaning back in her seat and taking another gulp of her beer.

"You been fucking your little April again?" She teased, though playfully, to which he didn't respond, aside from tilting his head forward and looking over the top of his own sunglasses at her with a raised eyebrow.

They both smiled to themselves and relaxed back in their chairs. A few moments of quiet passed between them before they started to reminisce about the old times: how long they had known each other and what they had been up to since they last met. Most of what they spoke of was unheard by passing pedestrians and the other people sitting outside of the bar. What they did speak of was horrific, violent, dark and disturbing, but they chatted in such a casual every day tone that no-one gave them much of a passing glance and even that was only due to their slightly unusual appearance. To some they would've appeared beautiful, yet menacing.

Another reason that people paid little attention to them was that a commotion was building in the street right opposite where they sat. At first, it was a scream from someone, then a shout and then more and more until passers-by started to stop and customers from the surrounding stores started to come out into the street to see what was happening. People also from the bar at which they sat, but the two of them remained in their own private world of conversation; occasionally one of them would get the bartender's attention for yet more beers, but otherwise they seemed completely detached from the growing crowd around the area.

Inevitably, police sirens started to wail, as did those of the fire service and the paramedics. Police tried to push the crowds back, cordoning off the area around the building directly opposite the bar; still Kristoff and Mia drank and chatted, laughed and occasionally disagreed, but the warmth and friendship was strong – there was a genuine history between them which went back longer than anyone could possibly comprehend.

The crowd continued to grow. Some became hysterical. More emergency services arrived to assist their colleagues, but not surprisingly, the news crews and other journalists appeared, all trying to get to the front of the police cordon. The officers struggled to keep them all back until their colleagues arrived. Next there came the helicopters, both police and television news, soaring and circling the building in question. The old friends ordered another round and seemed to be the only ones not on their feet watching the scenes unfold. Traffic had come to a complete standstill around that part of town and diversions were put in place. Their beers arrived, this time with a Jack Daniels on the side; the waiter looked at them strangely as he too gawped across the street before Mia intentionally cleared her throat to get his attention. Evidently he was standing over them and casting a shadow. One glance from the two of them and he apologetically moved away and back into the bar so he could watch through the window instead.

The commotion continued to grow, Mia and Kristoff could barely hear themselves over the crowd and the sirens, the hysteria was building in that normally relatively quiet part of the city.

Kristoff for the first time glanced nonchalantly over his shoulder at the chaos, he sighed to himself at what seemed to be a minor annoyance. Noticing this, Mia also looked up at the building in question.

"I suppose it's getting to that time?" She said

"Yeah I suppose so" he replied, with another sigh and slump of the shoulders.

She finished her drink and retrieved her bags of cash from under the table, standing as she did so.

"Shall we?" she said with a brief smile

He didn't speak, simply finished his own drink and tossed a few notes on the table to more than cover the cost of their drinks. As he stood up she watched him glance down at her bags.

"Next time, you're paying" he smiled.

"I promise" she laughed.

They walked together across the street; it was a wide street but without moving vehicles now, as both ends of it had been cordoned off to traffic. The whole area in front of them was filled with hundreds of people all standing and staring at the apartment building in front of them. Kristoff and Mia didn't look, but walked around the crowd towards the side of the building They walked in silence. Mia seemed to be relaxed but something seemed to cloud over in Kristoff's mind.

Police officers had taped off the whole building, front, side, and rear entrances all had police cars outside, tape across the doors and two officers halting admittance. To anyone else that would prove a problem, not to Mia and Kristoff.

They approached the side entrance in an alley way, immediately, the two officers guarding the door stepped forward, one's hand moved to his gun while the other stepped in front and was about to speak before Mia beat him to it.

"You can't see us" she whispered under her breath but looking directly into the first officers eyes while Kristoff caught the eye of the gun holding cop.

They both breezed past the lawmen like smoke drifting on the air, Kristoff pulled the tape from the door and they entered the building. The two officers returned to their posts, one of them seemed confused as to how their tape had fallen down and replaced it with fresh plastic before the two men continued with the conversation they were having moments before, unaware of what had just happened.

Once inside, they went straight to the elevator. The doors slid open with gentle whoosh and they entered. Mia pushed the button for the 12th floor and looked at Kristoff, who all of a sudden didn't seem his usual self.

"Are you ok?" She asked

"Sure, why?"

"You just seem......different"

She furrowed her scarred brow as she looked up at him.

They travelled in near silence, clearly a dark mood or thoughts were passing through his mind and Mia knew better than to question him. They arrived at their destination and another officer stood outside the elevator to check on any arrivals to see if they were genuine residents, journalists or the general public trying to sneak in. Residents were escorted to their doors and told to stay inside until advised otherwise; everyone else was removed from the building.

As the doors to the 12th floor opened, Kristoff immediately held up his hand in front of the young officer who simply stood in silence, motionless, Mia slipped gracefully passed him followed by Kristoff. The doors closed behind them and for a few moments the officer continued to stand like a waxwork until they had disappeared around the corner of the hallway to their location. After they had left he stood at his post, blinking and rubbing his temples, feeling like a headache was coming on.

They arrived at their destination to find two more officers outside the apartment door. Both officers raised their hands and stepped forward as the two strangers approached

"Residents need to.." began one before Mia interrupted

"Unlock the door" she said to which the other man duly and immediately complied. He pushed the door gently open and she finished with "Now, both of you sleep"

The two police officers both slumped to their knees and then the floor in a very deep sleep, one face down on the carpet, the other propped in the corner against the wall. The door was open and Mia and Kristoff stepped inside, closing the door behind them.

Chapter 4

Once inside the apartment they were in a small corridor and the two of them surveyed the area. It was a relatively small apartment with little if any home comforts or defining touches that would personalise a space. A small kitchen led off the short corridor to the left and opposite the kitchen door were two further doors. The first stood open and contained a shower room, Kristoff gently pushed open the second behind which lay the only bedroom.

Three more short steps and they stood in the living area. Two large windows gave lots of much needed light into the place which contained a simple couch and armchair facing the TV, a dining table and two chairs were placed on the other side of the room.

They looked around the room, taking all their surroundings in. They looked at each other and then at the windows, one of which, the one on the right, was wide open. The light breeze blew back the thin film of net curtain shading the room, causing it to billow. Kristoff sighed as Mia gazed around, then he went to the kitchen. He came back with a bottle of vodka from the refrigerator and two glasses, one of which he offered to Mia though she declined with a light smile. It had been a long time since she'd seen him looking so down but just since they left the bar his mood had seem to turn sour and her heart always sank at such moments.

She gestured with a nod of her head towards the open right window and Kristoff sat in the armchair, vodka and glass in hand he poured himself a drink, placing the other glass on an adjacent coffee table. Mia moved over to the window, pulling gently back the billowing curtain. She looked out to see what she knew would be the scene below, hundreds of people and emergency services all looking up at where she now looked down. They could not see her; no one could see her, Mia was invisible to all of them.

She glanced to her left to see the man they had come to see. He stood on the ledge, cowering and shaking, his back arms and palms flat against the wall as the strengthening breeze blew past him, the crowd below calling up to him and an occasional scream still piercing through the chorus. Every now and again another siren or call from a police officer through a loud hailer would break through. A psychologist or therapist or negotiator (or whatever their credentials said they were) tried to talk him down. The only words he had responded with were that he didn't want anybody to come up to him, hence the police outside but no one in his apartment trying to calm him down. Well, that was until now, but Mia and Kristoff weren't there to talk him down either.

"Hello Ronald" she said, startling him and causing him to falter in his stance.

"What the fuck? I said no cops, leave me alone," he wailed as he regained his footing.

"Don't worry darlin', I ain't with them and I certainly ain't a cop!" she smiled.

"W-what do you want?" he mumbled skittishly looking from her to the crowd and back again.

"We need to talk to you"

"We? Who's we?" He gasped, looking increasingly puzzled

"My friend and I have come to see you, it's kind of an honour you know" she managed to give him a cheeky smile and a raise of her eyebrows above her shades.

He peered around where she leaned out of the window beside him but didn't stretch too far from his precarious position before flattening himself back against the wall.

"He's inside," she said, "having a drink."

"Just drag the fucker inside," came a disgruntled male voice, booming.

This startled Ronald and caused him to falter though he still tried to look back through the other window. He couldn't see anything specifically, maybe a dark shape but nothing he could make out through the gauze of the curtain. His brief glimpse simply increased his growing anxiety and confusion.

"Please, leave me alone.......whoever you are," Ronald began to cry.

His reasons for being in his situation were his own but the last thing he wanted now was to talk to strangers.

"We need to talk to you," Mia said, in a more soothing voice to calm him.

"I don't want to talk to you or anyone else, just go......please," his head drooped as he sighed.

Mia looked at Kristoff, whose mood had continued to decline. He looked back at her, raising his eyebrows in a questioning look. She responded by shrugging her shoulders and shaking her head. Clearly, she didn't think Ronald was going to co-operate willingly. Kristoff sighed a weary sigh and his chin dropped to his chest. He lifted his head and drained the glass before getting to his feet and walking over to the window beside Mia. He gazed out and then down at the scene, before glancing along the ledge at Ronald who stood with his eyes closed and his head tilted up towards the sky.

"This is getting us nowhere" he growled under his breath as Mia stepped back to allow him full access to the window.

"You know," Kristoff spoke out to Ronald. "We didn't come all this way to return empty handed"

"I don't care. Just leave me be. Fuck off"

Frustration built in Kristoff. His fists clenched where they rested on the ledge as he leaned out, as invisible to the crowd as Mia was. She, in turn, placed a hand of calm on his shoulder, squeezing gently to soothe the situation before it got out of control. She had seen that happen many times and it was never pretty.

"Well if you won't come to us voluntarily, there is only one other option"

"Don't come out here. I'll jump you know?" yelled Ronald back at them, as he gingerly shuffled a few inches along the ledge in the opposite direction.

"As you wish," commented Kristoff, who disappeared back into the room.

That remark startled Ronald and he questioned what it was supposed to mean. Did they want him to jump? Didn't they care? Did he care that they seemingly didn't care? Did he want to be saved? His confusion grew and his doubts piled upon his confusion. His thoughts were then interrupted by a sentence from inside the room, Kristoff said the words but those words seemed to be inside Ronald's head as opposed to being spoken out loud.

"It's not the physical you we need to speak to.....Just your soul"

Ronald shivered involuntarily on the ledge, not from the chill wind around him nor the fear of his location but the voice in his mind like ice, bleeding ice.

Kristoff stood in the centre of the room, facing the wall between the two windows. Directly on the other side of that wall stood Ronald, flat against the bricks as he had for what seemed like an eternity as the maelstrom continued a long way down beneath his feet. Kristoff opened his arms out wide and closed his eyes as Mia watched on with a knowing smile. He mumbled words of power and ancient wisdom under his breath. Words that no mortal would be able to remember, recite or even pronounce. His hands, arms and then whole body trembled and shook at the surge building within him.

Ronald stood still in his own contemplation. Was he doing the right thing? Would he really be missed? Doubts grew with their presence but he didn't know why. Who were they? Why were they there? That voice in his head had made his mind spin but things were about to take a further twist and he simply wasn't prepared for what was to come.

Kristoff's outstretched arms moved around slowly in front of himself as if to enclose in a dark embrace and, on the ledge, Ronald felt something. It felt as though he was being soothed, the weight of his decisions were being lifted and washed away. The pain he was feeling was being eradicated. Suddenly his body and mind was becoming more at peace than he had ever known.

Kristoff's arms continued to close together slowly, outside, Ronald felt like he was being wrapped up in the biggest, most comfortable blanket in the world. It was almost like being lifted up into the warm hug of his mothers' arms as a child with a skinned knee; she would always wipe away all his tears and sing softly to him. He smiled to himself at the feeling and the memory that he had long since forgotten. Then things changed.

The embrace became tighter. At first it had given him security and comfort but that all too quickly became overwhelming. It was as if he was now being restrained, held down with an enormous force, gripped by unseen arms. The feeling extended to his mind, trapped in a vice-like grip. In his head a voice came to him, a voice he'd heard all too recently and briefly, the girl at the window. She spoke to him and told him to sit down. Her voice was too seductive to resist, yet, at the same time all too powerful for him to even consider refusal; it was a command that was beautifully delivered.

He sat down on the ledge and the crowd below watched the new development with fascination, wondering if he wasn't going to jump after all. Sickeningly there also seemed to be those who seemed disappointed, largely those who were filming the event on their phones. To the unknowing he seemed to sit as if by a pool with his feet dangling in the cool glistening water when in reality his feet hung down from the 12th floor of the building, the increasingly strong wind buffeting them and making them sway freely. If anything, he seemed in a more precarious position than ever as he sat seemingly without a care in the world. What the onlookers couldn't see was that a few moments earlier he smiled at the thoughts of pleasure but now that smile had turned into a twisted grin of horror, the feeling of heart and mind being crushed.

Finally, Kristoff's palms came together; his fingers interlocked and gripped each other tightly. His capture was complete and absolute; he opened his eyes and focused not on the wall he faced but on the man on the other side. Ronald felt a burning sensation in his back which quickly radiated out through his arms legs and then his whole body. He didn't physically move but he did summersaults internally at the pain, while confusion and fear threatened to rip his mind apart. He wanted to vomit, he wanted to scream, he wanted to cry but he just sat on the ledge like a forgotten rag doll sat on the shelf in a child's toy cupboard.

Kristoff was ready and he took one large step back and yanked his arms to his chest simultaneously. Ronald felt himself or at least something of himself pulled backwards with an incredible and unstoppable force. The agony filled his entire being and he could feel his own mind scream out in his skull, "Noooooooo!!!!!"

That pain continued. As if in slow motion, he felt himself being dragged from the ledge, through the wall and into the room. In a second that seemed to last much longer, he felt the cold breeze of the outside and the last rays of the sun, followed by his senses being dragged through the bricks and cement and then the warmth and slightly air conditioned atmosphere of his room. All those sensations were heightened as if felt on painfully tingling raw nerves.

He stood there in the room, completely disorientated by the terrifying experience. He still had the feeling of a Mother-like embrace but mixed with the agony and horror of the torture of being helplessly restrained in the grip of fear. It was indeed a horrendous cocktail.

"Welcome," Mia spoke.

He stood there like a frightened deer in the woods, wide eyed and shaking. She had retrieved a blanket from the bedroom in anticipation which she handed to him. Only at that point did he realise that he was naked. He took it without thinking or embarrassment and placed it around his shoulders. It stung at first. His skin felt as if it was both burning and frozen at the same time; his flesh felt incredibly raw.

"Where.... are my...... clothes?" he mumbled, as he gazed around the room at the two people before him.

Mia simply pointed over to the window by way of explanation. Ronald looked toward where she pointed and tentatively walked over to the open window. However he did keep looking over his shoulder at the two of them particularly the large man who stood with head bowed but tilted towards him, peering back under half closed eyes. Ronald looked out of the window and down, when he saw the crowds looking up he instinctively pulled back but.....

"They can't see you.........well, not this version of you," said Mia.

Ronald stared at her in confusion and disbelief but then he looked out again and then back along the ledge at where he'd been stood. His jaw dropped open to see himself sat there on the ledge, his feet dangling over the edge. He looked back quickly and sharply at the two of them and tried to speak but couldn't. He blinked rapidly, screwed up his eyes and rubbed them repeatedly which hurt incredibly in their raw state. He wasn't dreaming and he wasn't having visions; it wasn't a stunt or trick. He was there on the ledge and he was looking at himself. He was about to call out but Mia put her arm around his shoulder and guided him away from the window. The only thing he could say was, "But?"

He stood in the centre of the room, naked save for the blanket which hung loosely about him. His jaw dropped down and his eyes looked vacant as if he were a Victorian lobotomy patient in an old horror movie set in a mental hospital.

"It was only your soul we wanted," said Kristoff "And now here it is, fresh & raw"

Chapter 5

"W-Who the fuck are you?" he gasped, trembling with fear, cold and extreme sensitivity throughout his whole being. It was difficult to tell whether the trembling was through his physical or mental state but either or both would've had the same effect. "What have you done to me?" he continued, without waiting for a reply though not entirely sure he wanted an answer.

"I am Mia" smiled the girl with a playful yet sinister look on her face. She glanced over at the huge man in the centre of the room. "This is Kristoff."

The huge man simply stared at Ronald with little more than disdain and a sneer on his lips before stepping away as if repulsed by him. Clearly, he didn't want to be there, his attendance was at best under sufferance. Then he spoke but not to Ronald. He was ignored as were his questions. He spoke to Mia.

"Well, we have what we came for, let us take it and leave this fucking place" he grunted, spitting out those last words.

"Really Kristoff? After all this time you know that isn't how this works. Besides, who takes him?" she smiled again, this time at her companion.

Something seemed to pass between them, a longing? It was difficult to comprehend but Ronald stood in utter bewilderment and confusion let alone the pain and rawness that seemed to be increasing by the second in his ultra naked state.

"There are rules, he has to be given the choice," she said, "Who, for instance, is he going to choose?"

Kristoff grunted again and snarled at Ronald who took an involuntary step back out of increasing fear for his life.

"They were given freewill, remember"

"Which is wasted on them all?" Kristoff sneered

Mia sighed and shook her head; clearly she had known his feelings and heard his complaints many times, over many millennia as it happened. She turned to the increasingly petrified and confused Ronald.

"You have to choose one of us, I'm afraid. I know this isn't easy for you but your time here on this plain is about to be over, therefore you are in a position to choose. You are what we call a floating soul you see. You haven't done anything that would send you to damnation, as you would call it. But at the same time, you're about to commit suicide, which kind of messes things up going the other way, if you catch my drift?" She smiled sweetly as if this were all some kind of tedious little problem that just needed clarification.

"What? I'm supposed to choose between Heaven and Hell? Are you s-serious?" Ronald could scarcely believe what he was hearing.

He took a moment, he stepped to one side to look at the ledge where he saw himself still sitting motionless, he heard the muffled cries and shouts from the gathered throng below and still more sirens from the emergency services. He looked down at himself, was this really his soul? He somehow expected it to be a mist or a smoke of some kind, or maybe as invisible as the air, not that he had ever thought about it. He certainly never expected this! He looked up then at the two strangers, the one known as Kristoff glared at him as he refilled his glass and took another large gulp, tired of the whole charade clearly. Mia looked back at Ronald with that sweet smile; she seemed welcoming and looked as if she would take care of him for some reason.

It seemed an obvious choice but then was it a bluff or a twisted game? He had no idea but based on what he thought he knew, clearly from movies and TV, he could tell who the 'good' guys and 'bad' guys were. He stepped towards Mia whose smile widened with a heavy audible sigh and grunt from behind him, coming from Kristoff.

"Surprise sur-fuckin-prise" Kristoff growled.

"Don't mind him Ronald, he's a sore loser. Come on" she beckoned like a mother at the school gates.

Ronald continued to gingerly walk over to her, glancing over his shoulder at Kristoff who stood shaking his head. His being still raw, each step was agony, as was turning to look at the rejected option.

"You do realise that you've picked the wrong option there, boy?" Kristoff called over

"Huh?" Ronald looked again with a frown.

"Don't listen to him Ronald, he never did like to lose did old Kristoff" smiled Mia just as Ronald reached her, her arms outstretched in welcome.

"It's a sex thing you know" Kristoff called again "You assume because she has the form of a beautiful woman and is kind to you that she must be 'good' don't you?"

"E-erm" was Ronald's only reply.

"However, I'm an angry male with an attitude problem so must therefore be a 'bad' man, correct? The thing is Ronald, I couldn't care less about you to be honest, I've been doing this for a long, long, loooooong time now. We both have. Most of you humans don't even deserve an afterlife. Fuck, most of you don't even deserve this life!! I'm tired of you all; I'm tired of coming to this shit-hole plain and fighting over something like you. The only thing in your favour and that could yet save you is that she's right, I really am a bad loser."

Ronald started to shake; there was something in Kristoff's voice, a kind of reverence despite the unconcealed anger and building rage, that made him pause just before he slipped into Mia's embrace. He looked back at her and she had removed her wrap around shades, he looked and saw.........

Mia had no eyes, instead her sockets were black, deep, seemingly endless save for the balls of fire that spun and rolled independently spitting sparks and dripping liquid flame. Her mouth opened, and kept opening, her lower jaw stretching and contorting ever lower almost as if she were about to lurch forward and envelop Ronald, whole, like a snake.

Her teeth elongated and pushed out of her gums, causing blood to gush from between them as her gum line tore with audible splitting sounds. The bones in her cheeks and jaw cracked and popped, a stomach churning sound as Ronald watched in horror at the sickening sight of flesh mutating over the realigning structure.

Her hands came up to his face and her delicately manicured nails had become talons, claws on bony hands, the hands of a withered crone, not those of the beautiful young woman she had appeared to be originally.

Ronald was frozen with terror to the spot, frozen rigid; unable to comprehend what was happening, where he was or anything at all about the grotesque sight before him. His concentration was broken only when a hand, a large brutal and strong hand grabbed him by the scruff of his neck and yanked him out of her immediate clutches.

Kristoff pulled him completely off his feet and over to him. The she-thing demonic Mia screamed at them both, a scream that shattered the windows. Broken glass rained down on the hordes of people outside. Some managed to run but others weren't that lucky as their escape route was blocked by more bystanders staring up or not noticing as the shards fell with sickening, bloody and in some cases lethal results. Police were heard shouting at people to get back while blood spattered the street below.

Back in the apartment Kristoff still held Ronald by the back of his neck, at arm's length and slightly away from Mia but the fight was far from over.

"He hasn't actually stated his desire yet Mia, darling" Kristoff oozed at her.

She lifted her arm above her head and reached back behind her. She seemed to grab something concealed from within the back of her jacket. Then she brought her arm forward revealing in her claw a large dagger which seemed to bleed from within itself. All in one incredibly quick motion she swooped down with the blade. It sung as it fell. Ronald screamed as it headed, as he thought, for him. With unerring accuracy, the dagger sliced completely through Kristoff's right wrist, the hand which held Ronald off the ground.

Ronald dropped to the floor in a heap, the fist still gripping the back of him before the tendons relaxed and it fell down beside him. He yelled again. His confusion and fear building to uncontrollable levels, placing him in near hysterics as the two creatures fought over him. He looked up and saw confirmation that, not surprisingly, Mia wasn't the only non-human in the room.

He saw where the stump of Kristoff's right arm protruded from his coat, blood would've gushed from the horrendous wound but it didn't; instead what can only be described as liquid light poured from it instead. It was surely light but it seemed to move like mercury, pure dripping light spilling out from him and onto the floor, hissing as it splashed, freckling the furniture where it seemed to melt the fabric and that of the floor beneath them.

Kristoff looked down at his ruined arm and lack of hand and then back at Mia who stood watching and laughing at him, a laugh which would curdle blood. In response Kristoff scowled before, without any warning, he sprang at her with speed and height. He landed on her and she buckled to the ground, dropping the dagger, such was the force he caught her with. Ronald scuttled to the corner of the room where he cowered in the foetal position but his eyes stayed on the two monsters.

He then saw Kristoff lift back his head and his jaw mimic Mia's as it elongated to accommodate his teeth, while they fought for space urgently to increase their attacks, surely this would be to the death and Ronald the unwilling prize. With his teeth at full length and his victim struggling furiously beneath him, seemingly helpless, Kristoff jerked his head forward rapidly and violently. His sharpened teeth like razors immediately found their mark, partly in her shoulder partly in her neck and they sank deep, so deep.

Blood, such as it was, gushed from her and onto the floor, far from being the liquid light of Kristoff, this was thick, black like tar and oozed like slime as it dribbled down and spread. Her tongue, now blackened, slithered out of her mouth as she screamed in pain and her own agonies; it lolled from side to side then whipped like the tail of a cobra.

Unfortunately for Kristoff, and Ronald, Mia had managed to coil her legs up between them as they struggled and the soles of her boots now rested against Kristoff's stomach as they fought. Mia summoned all her force and pushed with her thighs and calves and all her inner strength. It was enough, more than enough as it caught Kristoff by surprise. She pushed him up and away from her with such strength that he flew backwards, unable to catch hold of anything to break his trajectory.

The physical power of Mia combined with the size and weight of Kristoff hurtled him against the wall with such force that not only made the wall shake but the building itself. The wall cracked where he had hit it, in between both windows. The window frames split and splintered and parts of them fell from their positions and down to the ground with the glass.

Sadly, the jolt that rocked the building, of course, also rocked the ledge where Ronald's body still sat, but not for long. The huge vibrations caused it to shift to one side and it obviously could not right itself. Instead, it lurched forward with nowhere to go but down, down, down.

Both Mia and Kristoff stopped the violence and stared at each other. Almost as one they went to the window to see the body of Ronald fall; the crowd of people below also saw the body hurtling towards them and tried to move back. Screams echoed at the horror of the inevitable yet, sadly and sickeningly, lots of those below still tried to film everything on their phones.

Ronald's carcass hit the concrete at high speed with a combination of a sickening dull thud and a sound of cracking as every bone in his body shattered on impact. More screams from the masses ensued, some people were visibly in tears and shaking at what they had just witnessed. Ambulance crews tried to calm those who had fainted or fell into hysterics. Some paramedics rushed with police officers to the corpse in the vain hope that he had survived but it was pretty obvious to all those gathered that there would be no miracle escape of death.

Back upstairs in the apartment the two beings, one celestial, one infernal stood and watched the aftermath below. They both turned on hearing the whimpering of Ronald still curled up in the corner. He had a pained looked on his face, a combination of physical pain, confusion and that of a heart-rending bereavement yet he hadn't been privy to what had just happened.

"Fuck!" was all Mia could say, while Kristoff simply shrugged.

They walked over to Ronald and looked down at him, as he tried to hide his face, not really knowing why. Surely there couldn't have been more horrors to see? As they approached their respective faces morphed back to their more human look, the rage of battle fading from them and normality returning.

"I'm sorry Ronald," Mia spoke. "But that's it I'm afraid."

"W-what do you mean?" he sobbed in response, peaking through his hands at a face that he had thought of as a normal, beautiful woman again.

"You didn't commit.......or rather neither of us claimed you for our own" she said.

"I d-don't understand"

"Your body's down there, Ronnie, your soul's up here," Kristoff sighed. "It's over and you're out of our hands."

Mia laughed to herself as she glanced to where Kristoff's right hand should've been. He scowled back at her in mock annoyance.

"You bitch," Kristoff complained.

"Don't be such a baby, it'll grow back soon enough. Look it's already started to heal. That's gonna leave a scar!" She said pointing at her neck, even though her wound, too, had stopped oozing the black tar-like blood and started to close.

Ronald blinked rapidly and looked at them both in amazement. He couldn't believe that this all seemed like some kind of joke to them. He hadn't really understood what was going on throughout the ordeal and now he was told he was out of their hands?

"P-please tell me......what's going on," he stammered and sniffed.

"Like I said," Mia spoke, trying to be gentle "You were a floating soul, a suicide with no real religious beliefs. We had to claim you but sadly neither of us did..... We failed. It happens, unfortunately"

"So what happens to me now?" Ronald asked, feeling numb everywhere but especially in his mind as it spun.

"You are someone else's property, Ronnie," Kristoff sighed to himself, very matter-of-factly. "Sorry man. Hey, don't forget the cash" he called over to Mia, who smiled jokingly back at him before returning for her poker winnings.

The two of them turned and left the room. As they arrived at the door to the apartment there was a knock upon it. Mia opened it and in walked a cloaked figure, the figure walked passed them, into the living area. Ronald looked up at the shape as it towered over him.

"I have come for you," boomed a voice from the figure.

He saw no features, just a shadow in a hood, the shadow that would take him and hold him as his fate was decided in the realms of Purgatory.

Printed in the United States
By Bookmasters